37-233

12.99

Romey's Place

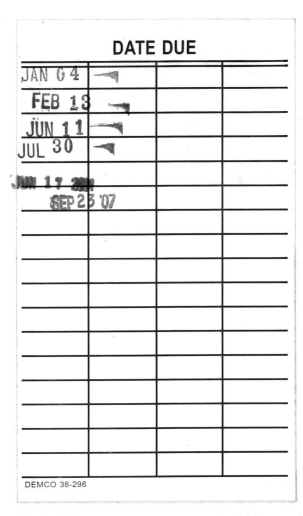

Other Fiction by James Calvin Schaap
Home Fires
The Privacy of Storm (stories)
The Secrets of Barneveld Calvary (stories)
In the Silence There Are Ghosts
Still Life (stories)

Romey's Place

James Calvin Schaap

 Baker Books

A Division of Baker Book House Co
Grand Rapids, Michigan 49516

© 1999 by James Calvin Schaap

Published by Baker Books
a division of Baker Book House Company
P.O. Box 6287, Grand Rapids, MI 49516-6287

Printed in the United States of America

Library of Congress Cataloging-in-Publication Data is on file with the Library of Congress, Washington, D.C.

ISBN 0-8010-6001-X

For current information about all releases from Baker Book House, visit our web site:
http://www.bakerbooks.com

This novel is dedicated
with abiding thanks
to my father,
and
in trustful penitence,
to my son.

―――――――

. . . yearning for the small voice
we all leave bawling
in one lost field or another.

Jim Heynen

Booty

Not long ago, as a freakish October snow-storm—a blizzard really—swept over the lakeshore, my father and I sifted through family treasures we'd taken from the upstairs closets of his house, the house in which I'd grown up. I'd come home to help him. Eighty years old, he was moving, by choice, to Woodland Haven, a managed-care facility. He was alone already then, had been for five or six years, my mother having died after a bout with abdominal cancer that went on so long I thought her leaving might eventually take him too. It was a Saturday, and the two of us sat on hassocks at the top of the stairs, the garage sale pile to his left growing enormous with every square foot we gleaned from the closets on either side of the hallway.

For my father, sorting through the memories stored away in those closets was not particularly painful. It was more difficult for me, I think, because through a series of job changes and difficult professional choices, I've become a museum curator at a small county museum in southwest Minnesota. I deal in artifacts—singletrees, washboards, oak commodes, Depression-era glass.

My father had no interest in what he was unearthing in those closets. I don't remember him saying it to me, but as I sat there watching
him casually discarding his life's baggage, I came to believe that if he
could simply close the door on his whole earthly life a week from now,
when he would leave our family home for the last time, he just might.
I believe I know my father, as well as any human can know any other,
and I'm sure that what he envisioned inevitably coming up the road for
him was more than simply a loving reunion with my mother, a woman
he loved immensely throughout his life.

He knew, as surely as I know anything, that some new and palatial
place was reserved for both of them somewhere among the many rooms
of his Father's mansion. My father does not fear death, even now, when
he is so very close. Perhaps with my mother gone, he fears it even less
than he ever did.

He is not a good subject for a rollicking story. The outline of his entire life has been cut from his deep faith; his life is a testimony. But it's
not even a particularly stirring one of those. His coming to the Lord did
not result from unbridled living, from alcoholism or addiction of any
kind. He didn't find Jesus in the glow of artillery shells or the cannon-
ades of Japanese cruisers in the South Pacific, where he spent most of
World War II. He would be more than happy to tell you that Jesus had
him well in tow long before his war experience.

He was, and is, a gracious man. He never beat his children or was
thrown painfully into a sense of his own depravity after too much wom-
anizing. There were no fits of rage that I remember, and I don't expect
there ever will be, now that he's reached the age where excesses can
hardly abound. For years he chose not to participate in the American
Legion's Fourth of July lottery fund-raiser because he claimed that no
matter how much good it may have done for the community, as a game
of chance, the event taught tawdry lessons about life's basic truths. People
say I was truly blessed to be reared by a saint, and that's what they'll tell
me again when, someday, I go home again to bury my father.

I don't feel any alienation when I return to Easton anymore, not like
I once did. In college, I drove—never walked—up familiar streets because I felt judged. In my own guilty heart I recognized that when I'd
begun to question the deep spirituality of my father, I had become something other than what the town expected—less of a believer, less of a
Christian maybe, less of a saint, certainly, than he was and is.

Why did I feel that way? Who knows? No one is a clone of his or her
father or mother. I once thought it was simply filial regression, a phrase
I'll never forget from Introductory Psych. But part of the explanation

for the differences which exist between myself and my father is attributable to Romey Guttner, which is not to say that Romey haunts me. He's not the wily serpent in the lakeshore garden. Long ago I came to believe that the serpent's real lair is the human heart—Romey's as well as mine. What happened at Romey's place is not something that sears my soul every time I make that last turn east and come up the road toward town, even though the events of that summer before high school will never really leave me, nor should they.

My childhood passed decades ago, and the small town of Easton, Wisconsin, is not at all the same anymore. When I drive up the streets to visit my father, no one knows me—just as, in a way, very few in town remember him, even though my father has stayed in Easton all his years. But he's old, and his time is past. The only people who might remember that he once served the village ably as its mayor are those few as old as he is, none of whom cut much of a swath anywhere in town, except maybe at the senior center.

Romey Guttner is long gone too. I suspect that if I'd bring up his name in the local grocery store, most people would shrug and look at me quizzically. His name is Roman, but no one ever called him that. To me he was just Romey. I can drive past the Guttner house now, but its beige aluminum siding and the bronze glow of the new sun porch make it a completely different place than it was decades ago, all of its sins seemingly washed away by time's able scrub brush. Sometimes I wonder whether those who live in the adjacent houses have even the faintest idea what happened there years ago, what I will never forget.

That afternoon I spent with my father sorting out his past, it was Romey who came back to me, Romey and a long story, most of which I'd never told my father. As we sat there at the top of the stairs, the snow outside raging, we threw out old magazines, sorted through a storehouse of pictures, and unearthed a pair of wooden crutches and a half-dozen old lamps my mother could never bring herself to dump; and all the while, I was growing more and more uncomfortable because I knew one piece of memorabilia wasn't going to be where it should have been. What was missing from that upstairs closet was something of what had been always left unsaid between us.

An old black bayonet should have been there, but I knew it wasn't going to be found.

I sat there and remembered pushing my gloves into stands of long prairie grasses along the river to see if there might be a feed bed there, a place out of the wind where muskrats would chew whatever it was they ate. I remembered poking sticks into mud banks, looking for holes.

Booty

I remembered trapping muskrats, drowning them with a forked stick, pulling their wet bodies up with the trap chain, their fur dark and sodden when we'd lay them on the bank and then perfectly translucent when they'd dry in the autumn sun. All of that came back because of a bayonet that wasn't there.

At the end of the war, my father picked up two pieces of war booty somewhere in the South Pacific—a samurai sword and that small black Japanese bayonet, wooden handled, still greased, as I remember, probably never used. It pulled hard out of its sheath, making a scraping metallic shriek—to me, a boy, the sound of war. Its blade was tarnished, unlike the samurai's chromed brilliance. For all the years of my childhood, both of them were kept in that upstairs closet with what remained of his navy life: an ordinary sailor's hat that looked silly when my sisters wore it upside down to the beach, a duffle bag I used for Bible camp, and some marching leggings I once wrapped around my legs on a rainy afternoon—all of it hidden away upstairs where no one ever saw it.

Except me. The bayonet made a perfect machete. I remember sneaking it along on our trapline for the first time, shoving the long sheath through the belt loop on my side so the hook and hole at the top of the blade caught at my waist, as if I were carrying a sword. I would never have taken the samurai. Its bronze sheath and the engraved flowers made it too ceremonial, but the black bayonet was made to use, not show. Hatchets were sharper and heavier, cleaner in hacking, but a hatchet had no history, not like my father's black Japanese bayonet.

It disappeared one morning at a point where the river flattens and elbows west, at the very spot where I remember catching one day a snapping turtle with the girth of a washbasin, a turtle Romey killed, chopped it into two pieces. The two of us then walked the rest of the trapline, only to find both halves still writhing when we circled back to the bridge. At that very spot, I lost the bayonet, at the spot where we'd killed the ancient turtle.

We trapped both sides of the river, Romey and I, he on the east side, me on the west. In spots, the river was shallow enough to cross in our hip boots; in other spots, not. It happened early in the trapping season. I don't remember why Romey told me to throw that bayonet across the river, but I had done it before, so I heaved it once again. I don't know why I messed up, why it didn't get there like it had every other time I'd thrown it across. But the moment I knew my father's bayonet wasn't going to make it across the river, regret, then guilt, pried me as wide open as that turtle, its insides spilling, as the bayonet spun, then fell without a splash into the flow of the river.

Booty

"Geez," Romey said. He was standing just across the river, and it wasn't like me to screw up like that. I stood perfectly still, my eyes planted on the spot where it had disappeared. But I knew it was gone. Even before it hit the water, I knew it would be lost forever in the roots and clams and rocks.

"You stay there—watch the spot," I yelled, and I stumbled through the wet grass, my hip boots still rolled down and sloshing against each other. "Stay there," I said again, pointing across at Romey, not even looking at him, my eyes still focused on what seemed with each passing second to be an indistinguishable spot of river current.

"You can feel it with your feet," he said. "You'll be able to feel it. It's all muddy on the bottom, and you can feel it."

I unfolded the cuffs of my boots so the edges reached my thighs, and I waded in, my knees stiff against the press of cold water. I had no idea how deep the water would be where it went in, but I kept my eyes on the spot.

The heavy rubber soles of hip boots are not good for feeling something lost on a river bottom. But in the middle, the muck firmed into gravel, and for a moment I thought it could be felt on the gritty stones. I would hear it, I thought, shrieking like something alive when I stepped on it.

"There," Romey yelled, "that's where it went in."

I stamped around, trying to distinguish anything on the bottom, my arms held out from my side to keep my balance in the current.

"Right there," Romey yelled. "You feel it?"

"Right here," I said. I was sure of it. "It's got to be right around here."

"It could go," Romey said. "It could flow along the bottom—you know—the current."

I knew that, but I didn't want to say it. "It's got to be here," I said again. "This is where it went in."

Romey came down off the bank and sat on his haunches at the river's edge, as if it were all he could do. "Don't kick it," he said. "Whatever you do, don't kick it."

I imagined it rolling along beneath the surface, a submarine drifting in slow and awkward motion toward some shallow spot downstream where it could rest up against a rock, a place where you might even spot it from the bank; so I followed the path of the river in my mind, trying to find a rapids or a crossing ahead where the bayonet might come to rest, a spot where we could pick it up after school when we'd come back to look some more.

Booty

I kept walking, feeling over the bottom with my feet, kept searching through the gravel and the mud closer to the edge, but I realized I had lost the exact spot. "Where, Romey?" I yelled. "Where did it go in?"

"Somewhere there," he said, but I knew from the tinny sound of his voice that he'd already given up. It would be impossible to find now, just a stroke of luck, luck which, as my father always said, doesn't exist in a universe where God is in control.

"You keep looking," Romey said. "I'll check the rest of the traps."

I hadn't even thought about time. There were more traps to check, a long bike ride back to town, and then school—we couldn't miss school, couldn't be late.

I kept feeling along the river bottom, alone now and desperate. When I felt anything beneath my boot, I reached in, oblivious to the soaking my jacket took. I remember dipping down to my shoulder, but coming up with only a muddy and leafless stick.

Alone, I could cry. *Why*, I started asking myself, why on earth did I take that bayonet? What was in it for me? The chance of looking cool? We didn't need that bayonet. We'd never really needed it. Hatchets hacked off branches better anyway. Why did I steal it out of the closet the way I did? What did I want to prove? I swore at myself, cussed myself for the lame thing I'd done in the name of looking tough.

"God, please," I said, "help me find it." But right there in the river, I knew my father's God would answer only in stubborn silence. I was sure I'd broken God's trust. What I'd lost in the river's cold flow was something I'd taken from the closet in sin, a sin I knew he wouldn't bless, so I stopped praying.

We must have sung Bible songs that morning before grammar like we always did in the little parochial school we all—even Romey—attended. That day, we must have gone through something or other in American history, in spelling, in math. But nothing of that remains. What's there—and what will be there as long as I live, I suppose—is the emptiness, an almost bottomless aching I felt in my stomach as I tried to feel that bayonet on the bottom of the river.

When that afternoon we returned after school, the autumn sun had dried the grasses along the river. Sweat ran down behind my ears and into my hair by the time we reached the bend where the bayonet had disappeared. This time I went in without pants, barefoot, searching every inch of the muck close to the bank, reaching in for every stick or branch long enough to promise anything. Romey

Booty

stomped through the river with me, but I was the only one who stripped. Even when the sun fell beyond the cottonwoods at the edge of the pasture where the river turned north, Romey never said a word about quitting.

I was the one who had to say what he must have been thinking. "It's gone forever, probably," I told him, stepping out of the muck, my jaw quivering. "There's nothing we can do."

"Tomorrow morning we'll try again," he said. "Tomorrow, Lobo—who knows?"

I knew. I knew very well. God didn't want me to find that bayonet. He wanted me to face the music at home. I didn't deserve to find it—after all, I hadn't asked to use it. I'd simply sneaked it out and taken it along. The night I had taken the bayonet out of the closet for the first time and showed him, we were in Mugsy's back yard, standing around his burning barrel. Our traps, strung on an iron pole, were set over the flame to soak up the scent of burning leaves, a ritual we thought would rid the traps of human smell.

Romey drew the bayonet out of its sheath and held it high above his head, the snapping flames throwing vile shadows over his shoulders and his face. "Your old man say you could use this thing?" he said.

I shrugged my shoulders hard enough to let them know my father wasn't aware of its being out of the closet.

"You just grabbed it?" Romey said.

But the night after the morning I lost that bayonet—and for weeks afterward—I lay in bed and told myself that I had to admit the whole story to my father, if for no other reason than I simply couldn't live with not telling. I was in eighth grade, and the loss of that bayonet colored every moment of sandlot football. Every night, the memory kept me awake. I'd climb out of bed, my hands shaking, and sit perched at the top of the very stairs where my father and I were now sitting, my guilt weighing on me heavily, pushing me downstairs to tell him, to confess.

I was not afraid of some exploding wrath, not cowed by the punishment he might dole out. Punishment would have been welcome. I wasn't afraid of him hurting me. What I feared was my hurting him. Scared to death, I'd sit there at the top of those stairs, right there beside the closet from which I'd grabbed that bayonet. Sometimes from the floor beneath I'd hear hymns coming from the little radio above the refrigerator, my father sitting at the kitchen table, working on a Bible study or a school board proposal, and I'd tell myself that he wouldn't hurt me if I'd tell him, that he'd appreciate the fact that I'd be open with him, that I'd come to him with my sin. But I wouldn't go, because what I feared were his tears.

So I wouldn't tell him. I'd go back to bed and try to sleep, gambling on the fact that war booty meant so little to him, tucked away as it was in the upstairs closet. He'd never know it was gone.

Eighth-grader I was, and I felt the deep stain in me of something I'd never seen in him, something I was capable of identifying as sin. I hid, like Adam, ashamed of who I was before my father's face. I sat upstairs for what seems now to have been hours, staring out of the window where the lights from the park across the street spilled long yellow shafts through the empty branches of the maples.

I never told my father that bayonet was gone, not until decades later, when the two of us sat together on a pair of hassocks at the top of the stairs where I spent too many anguished nights. The samurai still leaned against the wall studs, sheathed and only a little dusty.

"I'd almost forgotten that thing," my father said of the sword when I pulled it out from behind an old aquarium. "We were in the Philippines just a couple of weeks after the war, and they had this whole pile of junk stuff. The CO said we could take what we wanted."

He rubbed his fingers over the flowered handle, and I saw very clearly that the sword meant nothing to him. He handled it as if it were a huge tent stake, then put it down and picked up his own father's high school diploma, dated 1898, unrolled it. "You ever see this?" he said excitedly. "Your grandfather had thirty-six weeks of Cicero. It's listed here, right on the diploma. See that? Thirty-six weeks of Cicero, thirty-eight weeks of rhetoric, thirty-six weeks of Latin grammar—my goodness, what an education."

I waited for him to mention the bayonet.

"You know, that sword is probably worth something today," he told me. "Didn't I read somewhere about a samurai being a collector's item? Maybe we ought to sell it."

I picked it up and laid it across my lap, turning it once or twice.

"You want it, Lowell?" he said. "I don't think your sisters do."

To be honest, I didn't want the sword, not because I didn't value it, but because I did. But I lied. I had to. He wouldn't have believed that I wasn't interested. "Sure," I said. "I'll take it." Right then I knew he would have given me the bayonet too, had it been where it should have been, and that meant the bayonet had always been predestined for me anyway. In taking the samurai, what I'd lost years ago proved always to have been mine. Grabbing that bayonet from the closet hadn't been stealing at all, I figured.

Booty

"You'd better start a pile," he said, pointing. "We have a lot of things to go through here yet. What else we have in there?" he said, nodding back into the closet.

He never said a word about the bayonet. He seemed more interested in whatever was in the old hat boxes in the corner. I honestly believe he'd forgotten that bayonet completely.

"That's it?" I said.

He didn't even look at me. He leaned off the hassock and back into the closet and didn't even acknowledge my question.

"Of the war—" I said, "of what you took back, Dad—that's it? That's all you got here?"

Half in, half out of the closet, he didn't even turn to answer the question, just talked into the emptiness behind the open door. "It's been fifty years since I thought of those things," he said. He pulled out a handful of photos. "Not the war, I mean," he said. "I think of that now and then. Maybe every day something comes back—the way the ship used to rock in the swells—nausea. Smells, I remember—the ocean, oil on everything." He riffled through old pictures and postcards of the Black Hills, Yellowstone. "These are your sister's, aren't they? Janine's? Wasn't she the one who used to collect postcards?"

"I mean, wasn't there more that you took back?" I said.

"I used to have a duffle, remember that? I think you used it, didn't you? It seems I remember you hoisting it up over your back." He looked at me as if he suddenly doubted his own memory. "When you were a kid—don't I remember seeing you with that once? White one. Maybe it's gone now."

The leggings lay in a dusty heap, and a pair of white pants I had forgotten hung from a hanger against the wall.

"You don't remember anything else?" I said.

"You get to be my age and you won't remember things that happened two weeks ago." He flipped the leggings over in his hands, put them on the pile to the left. "Didn't I have the whole business at one time? Seems to me I had my whole dress uniform."

If I hadn't told him about the bayonet, he wouldn't have remembered at all.

"What about a bayonet?" I said. I couldn't let it go—call it some perverse desire to expiate guilt, a confessional. It had happened years before at a place on the river I could have pointed to had we driven out there yet that afternoon in the snow. I couldn't simply let it go like so much auction fare. "You remember a bayonet, Dad? A Japanese bayonet? You had a bayonet too—a little one, a black one with a wood han-

Booty

dle." My father stares when his mind is laboring. His eyes glaze as if the volume of whatever is playing in his head shuts the world out completely around him.

He reached up with his right hand and took hold of his ear, shook it. "A bayonet?" he said. "Japanese—sure—"

"You had a bayonet, a little one," I said, holding my hands apart.

"I remember a bayonet," he said. "Somewhere I have some pictures of the signing of the peace declaration, too. You ever see those? A whole bunch of them. I bought 'em in a set—all pictures of the Japs giving up. You could buy them on Guam, I think. The brass, in their best dress uniforms, chests full of medals. They're all on a ship—Admiral Nimitz, was it? I don't know. I have those somewhere. Maybe Michael wants them."

Michael is my son.

"The bayonet, Dad?" I said.

He was lost in a world of ships and ports and the end of the war.

"You had one," I said, "and I lost it."

He looked up at me, squinting. He had no idea what I was talking about.

"That bayonet." I stretched my hands out again, two feet wide. "You remember? A black one. Japanese—at least you always told me it was Japanese. I lost it. I took it along trapping."

"No kidding?" he said. "You lost it? I remember it, sure—yeah, a little bayonet—this little bayonet." It was all coming back now, replaying. "Sure I remember—I picked up the sword. Everybody wanted swords. And this little bayonet—never used, was it? Never used that I remember. I think it was new, that bayonet—everybody wanted the swords."

And then it was quiet. He was in another world.

"Years ago I took it out of this closet without asking you," I told him. "I stole it, really," I said, "I grabbed it—we used to go trapping, you remember?"

"You and Romey?" he said.

"Me," I said. "Not Romey. It was me that stole it, Dad. I'm the one. I sneaked it out of here—out of this closet—and we used it trapping. I took it," I said again.

He brought a hand up to his face and rubbed his temples with his thumb and fingers, didn't look at me at all. "What for?" he said.

"For trapping, Dad," I told him. "You remember how we used to trap stuff? Along the river."

"You took it?" he said. "You needed it for trapping?"

I shrugged. "I can't say we needed it—not really. I just took it, and I lost it. I threw it in the river—not on purpose. It wasn't on purpose.

Booty

Romey asked for it, see. We had traps on the other side—and I threw it and it went in the river, and I never found it. It's not that we didn't try."

He sat back, brought both arms up on his knees, still shaking his head. His eyes moved quickly from the confines of the closet to the wall in front of him, then to me—like the focus on a camera, even though when he looked at me it wasn't me at all he was seeing. I wish I knew what images were playing there, because I knew he was thinking about Romey and those years when my being at Romey's place must have been torture for him and my mother.

"You lost it way back then? How old were you? Grade school? You used to take your bikes. Sure, grade school." He turned a bit and looked out the window. "The two of you, trapping. Your mother never really understood that," he laughed. "Neither did I, I guess. I should have been more interested in the outdoors, shouldn't I?" he said. "I mean, I didn't really much care about tramping along the river, did I? Still don't." He shook his head. "I should have been a better father. You know there were times when you were out in the woods, and I told myself I wasn't living up to what I should have been. Always too busy with things, you know—with committees and things, village board. I just didn't care much about the outdoors—I didn't care about hunting. I'm sorry—"

"Don't be apologizing, Dad," I told him. "Not right now—all right? It was something I did, that's all. It was a phase."

"But you liked it, didn't you?" he asked. "I remember those carcasses hanging up in the back yard after you'd skin those things—what were they, anyway?"

"Muskrats."

"Yeah, muskrats. Your mother hated 'em, you know." He laughed again. "There they were in our back yard, hanging from her clothesline—purple death hanging there. Whoa, she hated those things—did I ever tell you? Sometimes she'd cry almost—'Do the boys have to do that stuff in the yard?' she'd say." Then, his smile fell. "I'm sorry," he said. "You were telling me you lost that bayonet?"

"It went in the river. I threw it. Not on purpose—I mean I didn't throw it in the river on purpose—"

"I don't imagine you did, but it seems a strange time to tell me now," he said. "What is it—twenty-five years ago?"

"More than that," I said, trying to laugh.

"You lost it, huh?" He shaped his mustache with his fingers and leaned back off his elbows. "You and your buddies heisted it right out of this closet and you lost it in the river—that's what you're saying?" It somehow struck him as funny. He sat back on the hassock. "I guess you got

Booty

away with that one, didn't you?" He giggled. "I suppose it's too late to do any punishing now, isn't it? What are you, forty-what?"

"It's history," I told him.

"Can't very well take you over my knee." He raised his eyebrows and looked out at the snow, and that's when I told him the whole story, how we'd taken it along to check traps, how Romey had yelled at me to throw it across the river, and how it had gone in, how we'd looked all over and never found it.

And once I started, it all came very easily—not the telling, which was still hard, but the story itself. It all came out rushing from my own unforgiven soul, as if I'd been rehearsing the confession for years. He sat there and listened just as I imagined he would, focused on what I was saying. The whole time he stayed with me, silent, through the emptiness at the bottom of the river, school that day, and our return in the afternoon.

I know my father, and I knew that in his mind there were these other currents circulating. He wasn't simply the recipient of the story. What I told him was all being processed. All those years of reading the Bible and interpreting, all those years of laying a moral sensibility over behavior and almost every last action one could take in life—all of that apparatus was processing the facts of the story of the lost bayonet. Even as I told him, what worried me was what his heart was telling him while his mind recorded the images of that bayonet lost deep within the river.

When I got to those moments at the top of the stairs, I told him about real tears wrung from a heart twisted tight as a charley horse. And when I told him, I realized I was angry.

"Some nights I'd sit here at this window when I was a kid," I told him, "and I'd just about die thinking how much I wanted to go down and tell you the whole story. I'd sit here and bawl, Dad—I'm not kidding you." I wanted to hurt him. I honestly did. An old, good man, and I wanted to hurt him. I felt more sin in me right then because even in the telling, I wanted to punish him. It was his fault, after all, that I'd lived with it for so long. "Right here, right here at the top of the steps, and I'd know you were downstairs and you'd want me to tell you. I knew that telling was the right thing. I knew all of that. Confess, you know—confess the whole thing. But I never could—I just couldn't."

He ran his tongue along his lips, and his eyes showed this shadowy kind of questioning. "All of this really happened?" he said. "You're not making any of this up? This is exactly what happened?"

"Lots of nights I sat here and cried," I told him. "But I never told you, not in all these years." I tried to laugh. "Isn't that something?" I tried to

Booty

make it a joke. "I couldn't even pray, Dad," I told him. "I remember sitting right here on the steps and thinking that maybe if I could pray, I could live with it—with having stolen that thing and lost it. But I couldn't because I knew God wouldn't give me a minute's peace until I told you. There wasn't going to be any forgiveness without restitution, I guess. So I couldn't do that—I couldn't pray."

Nothing I could have said could have been more painful. I know that now, and I knew it even as I said it. Maybe that's why I said it.

He pulled his handkerchief up to his face and blew his nose once or twice, then brushed the hanky across his nose, shaking his head.

"You don't even remember that bayonet, do you?" I said.

One eye twitched quickly, nervously. He rubbed at his nose with the back of his hand. "When the war ended I had two daughters I didn't even know," he said, "and I wasn't thinking about a bayonet." He grabbed the leggings away from me. "I don't even know why I saved anything, because all I was thinking about were your mother and your sisters," he said. "You know, your mother worried back then about who I'd hug first when I got off the train—her or the girls." He nodded, smiling, threw the leggings down on the pile meant for the trash. "What did I care about something from that mess in the Pacific? What did I care about some Japanese bayonet off a scrap heap? I wanted home." He turned to look outside at the falling snow, wrapped up in some ideas I wanted badly to hear.

"What gets me," he said, "is why you couldn't tell me." He raised his hands, then folded them in front of his face. "Did you think I'd be so angry?"

"Maybe," I said. "But it wasn't your anger that worried me. I couldn't stand the idea of letting you down. I didn't want to hurt you. That happened once—you remember?"

"Stealing cigarettes," he said, smiling.

"Don't laugh, Dad—please?"

"You're right," he said. "You would have hurt me." He brought his hand up to his lips. "Mom too." He laughed. "It doesn't seem much at all now—a junk bayonet." And then he looked straight at me, full in the face. "Tell me, Lowell—was I always that hard to live with?"

"Of course not," I told him. My fingers began to shake. "You were a perfect father. You were absolutely perfect, the most perfect father anybody could have—"

"Oh, Lowell," he said, "I was far from perfect. I wasn't even close. Don't ever say that—that I was perfect."

Booty

Right then, I would have preferred that he hit me. "Don't say that, Dad," I told him. "That's just like you. Don't say it—it angers me when you say that."

He licked his lips, and I could see the possibility of tears in his eyes. I would have left the house just then had he started. I don't think I could have taken his tears. In so many ways, my father was as strong as an ox—that's what I remember. But in other ways he was unmercifully tender and good, unmercifully good.

"You really thought that, Lowell? You thought I was perfect? Oh," he said, "what did I do?" And he looked at me as if something full and bright yet woefully dark had finally risen to the surface of an old mystery. He reached out for my knee. "I get it, Lowell—why you had so much trouble growing up. It was me, wasn't it?"

"Don't say that, Dad," I told him. "That's the way it always is with you—all your life you took everything on yourself, everything."

"It's like the talk shows—it was really my fault," he said. "It's always the parents—when it comes down to it. And half the time we don't even know—"

"Nothing's your fault," I told him. "I was the one who grabbed that bayonet out of this closet. I took it to the river. I whipped it across. It wasn't your fault. It was me that lost it," I told him. "And I never told you. I couldn't."

"You couldn't talk to me?" he said, quickly. "What kind of father is it you can't talk to—tell me that, Lowell?" He was deadly serious. "What kind of father is that?"

"Don't say that."

That gravely injured look was the very image that had hung before my imagination on so many childhood nights at the top of the stairs. It was full of the very innocence I had always known would slay me, that guilelessness that kept him out of my reach on too many cold winter nights.

"Did you think I wouldn't forgive you?" He took off his glasses and rubbed his eyes. "Did you think I didn't love you, Lowell—is that it?"

I looked away.

"You think I'd punish you so hard?" he said.

"I did wrong," I said, "and I shouldn't have."

"Then I never taught you forgiveness, did I?" he said. His touch—his hand on my knee—felt like a wound. "That's where I failed you—right there," he told me, and he shook me as if I were still his boy. "I never thought you weren't good enough—never thought that, Lowell. Never once." His back straightened. "You remember things about that bayonet that most people would have long ago forgotten," he said. "You remember, even though it's long gone from my head." He pulled his hand away. "Isn't that amazing?" he said. "What you come to understand, Lowell, is how much of life you really don't control. I never would have guessed I came off that way—never." He shook his head. "When you get my age, you start to think how little power you ever had—how little, really, we ever know about what we're up to," he said. "I didn't know any of that whole story." He shook his head. "There are things I missed because I was busy all the time. Sometimes it haunts me, you know? Sometimes I wonder whether—if I'd have done it differently—whether things would have turned out better. Sometimes you wonder whether you did anything right at all."

"Dad," I said.

"I'm serious. Sometimes I say to myself that I should have shelved so much of what I thought was important, you know—I should have gone with you some mornings, walked along that trapline or something—"

"Don't say that—"

"True, isn't it?"

"Not true," I said.

"Don't lie, Lowell—"

"It's not true. I wouldn't have wanted you along—"

"Wouldn't have wanted me?"

"No, I wouldn't have wanted you—not at all. There's a whole lot more you don't know, Dad," I said. "There was a lot I couldn't tell you back then—a ton of stuff I just couldn't have brought myself to say."

"Why?"

I didn't want to answer.

"Why, Lowell—tell me?"

"There was just a ton of things—"

"About Romey?"

"Sure, about Romey—you know what happened."

Of course he remembered Romey. "But why?" he said. "I knew more about what went on at Romey's house than you did. I saw that woman bawl, Lowell. I held her in my arms. You remember? I saw her cry so often I couldn't take it anymore—you hear me? And what was it *you* couldn't tell me?"

"Everything," I said.

"Why?"

"I don't know," I said. "You were who you were, and I couldn't change that even if I wanted to—"

"Did you want to?"

Booty

"Are you kidding?"

"I'm not kidding." And then something that really hurt. "Did you wish you'd had somebody else's father, Lowell?"

"Don't say that," I said. "Don't ever say that."

Sometimes when my father speaks, the words come out as if they are pulled painfully. "If a man would know when he's thirty—" he said, "if he'd really know how little he's ever going to understand life," he told me, "then we'd live a whole lot differently, wouldn't we?" He looked at me. "You remember that parable in the Bible where the rich man begs Lazarus to tell his brothers that there's a Hell?" The bayonet wasn't forgotten, but my father always had a way of losing himself when it came to Scripture. "Christ says that to send somebody back from the dead is foolish—that's what he says—because, he says, he's already given us all the law and the prophets." He nodded. "See, we have the whole truth already, Lowell—we do. But we don't want to hear it—none of us. Not me, either." He reached a hand up to his face, touched his lips with his fingers. "Don't ever think I was perfect. Don't ever believe that."

I couldn't look at him.

"I'm sorry I let you down," he said. "I sure enough did." And then he shuffled through the postcards again and pointed at the closet as if we'd gotten off track.

A little over forty years after that stolen bayonet went into the river without so much as a splash, I'd received exactly the punishment that kept me from telling him the story for all that time.

I went to bed in my childhood room that night, and for an hour or more before I finally closed my eyes, I searched into the darkness, angrily. I felt the old feeling. I thought of going to his room to say something again, to get something from him I still needed.

It was after one when he got me up and into my clothes, because he said the snow had settled too heavily on the branches of the trees. It was October, and the leaves were still on. What got my father up was some premonition that his trees were in danger in the heavy snow.

It was a freakish storm, coming as closely as it did on summer's heels. Lightening occasionally slashed over the peaked corners of our house from a sky made luminous with snow, and thunder rolled and crackled the way it does in May and June, when in the Midwest all eyes look west for the funnels that fall from thick, late-spring skies. The lawn was white and bright, even the sidewalks gone in the kind of heavy snow that seems to fall in clumps.

Booty

"I don't trust it," he told me as we went out the door. "It's too heavy. There's too much weight."

A mountain ash at the southwest corner of the house swept so low to the ground it looked as though it were weeping. The branches of the oriental elms on the south side hung like inverted fish hooks, and the smaller shrubs twisted awkwardly against their shapes. "There's a broom in the garage," he said. "Take the west side."

I ran around the house toward the garage in the eerie light of the storm. Snow covered the garden in the southwest corner of the back yard, though what was left of the cabbage plants jutted up like something eerie emerging from the darkness. Silence reigned as only it can in a snowstorm.

I turned the latch nailed up against the side of the garage, then pulled the door open. I felt along the wall where I thought the broom might be, just as I might have years ago when I was growing up, as if nothing at all had changed. Even in the dark, my hands found the horseshoes I remembered had hung there forever.

The broom wasn't on the wall. The straw bottom showed up in the darkness, where it stood up against the bench. I grabbed it and headed back outside, and right then, all around town, the snow fell too heavily for the elms and maples and cottonwoods that lined the village streets. Still thick with leaves, those trees held far too much wet snow. The temperature was right and the snowfall was heavy enough to make weary branches all over town submit, right then, right at that moment, to the early storm's thick burden; and in the midnight village stillness, the cracking branches rang like gunfire, shot after shot echoing down the empty streets like nothing I'd ever heard before, limb after snapping limb like errant potshots taken in the darkness, one after another, an endless series of vicious cracks followed by the thrashing sound of branches falling in clumps.

I ran toward the side of the house, carrying the broom in both hands as if it were a rifle, then swept and swatted at the bushes. I attacked the oriental elm with the broom over my head. A lower branch had already split, leaving a long blonde slash like an open wound.

And then I saw my father hiked up in a front yard maple, not high off the ground, his booted foot coming down hard, stamping away, shaking loose the burden of snow. Bang, bang, bang—down came his foot, angrily, in a way I'd never seen before, one arm like a grappling hook around the trunk. But beneath his boot, loosened from its burden of snow, the branch rose steadily with every jarring kick and came up free.

Booty

I stood in the thick falling snow, my face already wet, and I felt things come up in me that grabbed the back of my face as if it were a mask of elastic, grabbed and twisted and squeezed tears from my eyes, so much I would have loved to be that branch beneath his feet.

Right then I wanted to piece together a story that will clarify something about who I am, the son of my father, a story I want to tell, a story that includes chapters I would have never dared to tell him, and still don't.

My father needs to hear that story, something I never told him.

Booty

Trash Day Golf

It was the first Thursday in June of the summer after seventh grade, so hot in town that the dew fell thick enough for the two of us to leave footprints in the strips of curbside grass. On the first Thursday of every month, the whole village turned into a garage sale, every last item free, the streets full of treasures in the trash. Enough excitement could spill out of bushel baskets and garbage bins and cardboard boxes to get us up with the sun and on the streets long before the village's big Chevy dump truck picked it all up without paying a whit of attention to the great stuff it was hauling away forever and ever.

That morning, we'd found golf clubs with wooden shafts and unwound black leather grips hanging off the handles like coiled gift ribbons—real golf clubs, ours for the taking; one wood and three irons so ancient they were named in inscriptions on the heels: Mashie Iron, Mashie Niblick, Pitching Niblick. It was the late fifties, in a Midwestern small town, and golf was a dream, at best, to a couple of kids from the lower middle class. Even though those clubs were laid crosswise over the top of an old tan garbage tub across the road from where we'd stopped on our bikes, I figured we had to sneak them away, as if Lewie Tinholt, the man who dumped them, had left them out there just to tantalize boys like us, kids he knew would grab them the moment they saw them, kids he'd then report or chase off himself. Grabbing them seemed too much like stealing—something that good, for nothing. In fact, I told Romey, jokingly, that Lewie was actually holding the two of us in the crosshairs of a .30-30 at the very moment we were standing there picking them up.

"You're crazy," Romey said. We were leaning off our bikes, a foot on the curb.

"I'm making it up," I told him.

"You are not," Romey insisted. "You wouldn't say it if you didn't think it." He had an irritating way of always trying to prove somebody wrong. He loved to argue, to disagree. "Why in the heck would he put 'em out there if he didn't want to get rid of 'em? You think it makes a dime's worth of difference if we pick them up or if it's Rolly VerMulm?"

Rolly was the big-shouldered guy who picked up trash for the village. At that very moment, we could hear the low rumble of the truck taking off from somebody's curb.

"Maybe Rolly wants 'em," I said.

"Sure, dumbhead," Romey said. "Lewie called him and said he'd leave his clubs on the junk barrel—Rolly can pick them up there. Makes sense to me." He rolled his eyes.

My name is Lowell, but Romey never liked that name. Neither have I. He was constantly coming up with alternatives—from Lowie to Leadbottom. Lowell was just too pretty for him. He couldn't get it out.

"You got this thing about getting caught," he said. "You got this thing, like if you get caught you're going to die or something. Where'd you get that?"

"I don't know," I said. "Just the same—"

"Just the same, what?"

I looked down at the cracks in the sidewalk. "Just the same—feels like stealing."

"It's junk, all right? Trash," Romey said.

I hunched my shoulders. "Feels like somebody's going to see us."

"If anybody's up around here, they will," he said. He climbed off the bike, let it fall gently against the curb. His bike never had a kickstand, or if it did, it didn't work. "If it makes you feel any better," he said, "I'll walk up to Lewie's door and ask, okay?" He spit on the sidewalk, a lit-

Trash Day Golf

tle dot of saliva snapped from between his front teeth. "Sometimes you're harder to live with than my old lady."

"It's not that I'm scared," I said.

"Now you're lying on top of it—"

"I'm not either," I said, and I kicked down the stand on my bike, checked for cars, walked across the street, then picked the clubs off the top of the tub, rolled them together in my hands, looked both ways before crossing again, and walked back to the other side.

But I was scared.

I can't say I remember every last moment of that morning. I can't say that the events of that year or more come back to me as if there were a tape recorder playing in my mind during those years Romey and I were friends. But I remember enough to piece things together in a way I never have—in a way I should have. What I know for sure about that morning is that when I walked back across that street, I was petrified by the notion of someone somewhere seeing me and thinking that Pete Prins's boy was grabbing stuff off the street, even if it was from a garbage pile.

But that wasn't enough to stop me. Romey pushed me, but then I'm not saying everything that happened in that time we were best of friends was his fault. He didn't beg me to grab that bayonet, for instance. He didn't even know it existed. Inside, I really knew I wasn't doing anything wrong by picking those clubs out of the junk. They were free pickins, and I wasn't about to let them go into that dump truck. It just felt weird. Grabbing them was so public.

To both of us, the game of golf seemed exotic. I didn't know men who played golf—other than Lewie Tinholt, who never had kids. Romey didn't know anybody either, I'm sure. Neither of us had ever held a golf club, wooden-shafted or steel. All we knew was it was an odd sport, played on huge grass fields where maintenance men actually rode lawn mowers and the men who played always dressed up.

Cyril Guttner never played golf, but neither did my father. To Cyril, Romey said, golf was the sign and seal of the arrogance of the rich, the oppressors of working stiffs such as himself. I don't think Cyril Guttner ever considered himself a communist, but he was likely as close to one as anyone might know in Easton. To him, it didn't matter if the clubs were looted from the trash or bought at some snazzy country club—golf wasn't even a real sport. Hunting was a sport. Bowling. Cards. Golf was for men with soft white hands and fancy pastel sweaters.

We stopped off at my place for a few red-belted range balls we'd picked up somewhere, got back on our bikes, and shouldered those new clubs all the way over to Guttner's, where, in little more than an hour, we had our own golf course set up behind their two-stall garage. The holes were trees and fence posts and the legs of the tar-paper hut where Romey kept a dozen guinea pigs.

Guttner's lawn was a mass of dandelions and creeping jenny cut short enough to make the junk grass look well groomed: weeds and flat stubble that often turned yellow when you cut it in midsummer's heat. If you'd walk barefoot out back, you'd almost certainly slash your toes, a lawn—if you can call it that—not at all like our place, where my father nurtured a carpet as thick and full as a putting green. My dad was always a busy man, but in those hours he wasn't off at some meeting or community project, he took pride in making everything in the yard look picture-book right, perfectly shaped bushes with a splash of the right variety of summer flowers up close to spic-and-span foundations, a half-dozen small flower beds perfectly weeded.

That day was, as I remember, a perfect summer morning on the lakeshore, the air thick with moisture but a breeze from the west holding back the cold swell of Lake Michigan air only a mile to the east. We'd just left seventh grade behind, we had ourselves free golf clubs and our own course—our day was made.

Then Cyril showed up, his hands in the pockets of army-green work pants held up by suspenders over a gray shirt that looked stiff enough to be cardboard, a uniform he wore as proudly as something from the military. That shirt was unbuttoned and spread back over his paunch as if to feature an undershirt festooned with a long spill of something red, like cherry juice, from the point where his slight belly bulged from his chest. No matter how huge Cyril Guttner looms in my memory of those years, he never was a large man. He was short and thin with arms that age had sculpted to look like the long tree branches the lake beached in high water and left to dry in the sun. Romey wasn't big either, but even at twelve, he was already the same size as his father. In a town full of big Dutch men, Cyril even looked a foreigner.

Each of his forearms was decorated with a tattoo the size of a box of chew. But both of them, over time, had blurred into a blend of reds and blues, resembling, more than anything else, a pair of ugly bruises. He had thick hair across the top of his head, as gray and heavy as a fake mustache, even though it was always cut short and straight. He wasn't working then; it seemed he rarely worked during those years Romey and I were buddies. He was part of the big strike at Linear, the huge factory in Brandon just ten miles north, a strike that had opened up like something cancerous and deadly across the face of the whole lakeshore region. Cyril Guttner was at the cutting edge of all of that, full of righ-

Trash Day Golf

teous indignation at the sins of management. "He's union," my father used to say, "insanely so," almost as if it were a curse.

When I remember those days of my boyhood—ours, really, mine and Romey's—I can't remember a moment when simply the thought of Cyril Guttner, my best friend's father, didn't chill my soul. In spite of the fact that his kid was, for a time, my best friend, I don't remember seeing the man in the flesh all that often, because on the streets of the small town in which we lived, he was, during the strike, only rarely around. Even when he was out of town, however, something of him so eternally inhabited that house on Tamarack, right beside the swamp, that I never felt really at home there. The second the weary screen door slapped shut behind me, I was sure Romey's old man would be home the very next moment, even if he hadn't been around for weeks. That day, the day of the new golf clubs, he was there.

"What's going on back here?" he said when he saw the divots we were scraping out of his lawn. "What you think you're doing?" He kicked up a long strap of turf and flipped it over, belly up, then cussed at us some.

"Shooting some golf," Romey told him.

Cyril looked down at his precious weeds and muttered profanities I'd heard before, but only downtown around high school guys. If my father had ever used that language, it would have been sometime in the navy, but he would have been somewhere in the Pacific then, where no one from Easton would have heard a word of it.

"Look here what'cher doing to my lawn," Cyril said. "Beatin' it dead."

"We ain't hurting nothing," Romey said, looking down at the face of his club. "We're just playing is all, just hitting balls around."

"You're wrecking my lawn," Cyril said again. "Look at this here," and he lifted what looked like a scalp with the toe of his boot, then kicked it at Romey.

When I think of those times I was in Cyril Guttner's presence, I remember looking down at my feet, the dirty linoleum of the kitchen floor, or the weeds out back, maybe the little piles of poop Romey's guinea pigs left in funnels beneath the chicken wire. That day, the whole time he spoke, I'm sure I never dared look at him.

"Get outta here if you're going to play that stupid game," Cyril said. "Go somewhere else and beat the crap out of somebody else's lawn."

He meant *my* house. He never looked at me that I remember, didn't gesture or point with his eyes, but I knew he meant we should go beat up my father's precious lawn.

Trash Day Golf

"Shoot," Romey said, loud enough for his father to hear. "Stupid weeds anyway. Who gives a nickel for this lawn?"

Romey could have just as well let well enough alone, shut his mouth, and let Cyril go back to the house. Then we could have picked up the clubs and left. He could have turned the other cheek, but Romey provoked him. He couldn't let it go that morning, couldn't let his old man stumble back to the screen door and make his way into the house. But then, maybe Romey did exactly what his old man wanted him to—take him on.

Cyril covered the ten yards between them quicker than his kid could have raised the niblick and taken a swing, but Romey stood his ground, never backed down an inch. But he didn't swing. He kept his arms against his sides as if he were too proud and stubborn to run from what he knew was coming, and Cyril let him have it across the face with a backhand that started out somewhere around his left shoulder and ended with his arm out above his head, where he held it, like a long and developed follow-through, as if to demonstrate that not only was this a master stroke but there was an arsenal waiting to be called up from reserve.

Romey's knees buckled, but he got a foot behind him and kept himself from lurching backward. He brought his hand up, still holding the club.

"Don't lip off," Cyril said. "How many times have I told you that? Now get out of here if you're going to play that sissy game." Then he stood there as if begging for an excuse to swing again. "Go on," he said. "Get out of here. You drive me ever-lovin' nuts."

That wasn't enough for Romey. "What'd I say, anyway?" he shot back.

"Hey—" Cyril said, and he brought down his open hand, then pointed at Romey's face. "Get lost," he said. "I got more to worry about than having you'se two around here driving me out of my skull," and then he walked away, never turned back to look or say another thing, just excused us like a minor irritation.

My hands were wet and shaky.

"Stupid fool," Romey said to me. "Why don't *he* get lost?"

What he said really wasn't meant for me.

Once more, his old man came at him, growling and fuming in a spill of curses, as if he'd left somewhere far behind whatever bit of fatherhood he had, spitting out anger, arms flung out, anger clenched in his face. But Romey never moved. He curled into a crouch and pulled his elbows up over his ears so all there was for Cyril to swing at were his shoulders and back. He hit Romey a dozen times at least, first with the back of his hand, clubbing him as if his fist were a mallet, then tried to get in a good shot at his face. He kicked where he couldn't reach Romey, and when he knew he couldn't hurt Romey in that position, he kicked harder.

Romey never swung back. He yelled and swore at his old man and screamed that he was getting hurt. Cyril grabbed the golf club out of his hand and used its handle like a nightstick, beat him five or six times on the back and legs, Romey simply taking it all before falling into the grass in a sprawl that was a kind of concession, whipped and silent.

Then Cyril stopped. He didn't say a word, just stood there with the club face in one hand like the handle of a pistol, the leather grip in the other. "Here," Cyril said, and he snapped that wooden shaft over his knee and threw down the pieces. "That's what I think of your fairy game."

This time Romey didn't mutter anything, even when Cyril was out of sight, halfway back to the house. At first, he wouldn't even look at me. He turned away from me in the grass, laid his elbows over his knees, and stared out over the cattails in the swamp just east of his place, as if maybe by looking out there toward the lake he could get himself lost in some other world.

I couldn't very well get on my bike and leave. Besides, I was shaking even more than Romey was. I'd never seen that happen before—even though there were times in the middle of something else—riding bikes, checking traps, hunting crows—that Romey would let slip something about getting nailed by his old man, getting beat on. But then most every kid got beat on back then. It was the late fifties, in a world before Dr. Spock, a world still defined, at least in my mind, by the rod of the book of Proverbs. I don't think Romey ever judged what was happening at his place to be all that much different from what was happening all around. I did.

I picked up the other clubs and held them in my hands, ready to leave. The last thing I wanted to do was cross Cyril again. Romey sat in the grass, getting wet from the dew, just sat there looking over the swamp.

"We can set something up by our place," I told him. "C'mon."

"Someday I'll take him," Romey said. "There'll come a day—and it won't be long, either—and I'll take him. And when I do, they'll cart his carcass away on a stretcher—you hear me?"

He was talking to the swamp. From my point of view, even as a kid, what he was feeling, what he was hiding from me, wasn't so much sadness as pure and simple hate.

I stayed behind him and put the clubs down against the garage wall. "I don't know why you didn't just let him jaw," I said. "Sheesh, now

Trash Day Golf

look at the trouble you're in." I shrugged my shoulders. "It ain't worth getting beat on, is it?"

Then he turned, but didn't speak, just looked at me strangely, in a way that made me think I wasn't getting the whole picture.

One of his little sisters, Annie, wandered back to the garage, oatmeal stuck to her bib. She looked at Romey. "Play," she said, as if she were commanding him. "Play ball."

"We're staying," he said. "You don't know my old man. In a minute, he'll forget everything. It's just the way he does things."

So we did. We didn't leave. We stayed for a while—maybe because Romey wouldn't have left for any money right then. I was scared the whole time. I was always scared at Romey's place.

That was the only time I saw Cyril Guttner beat on Romey, but back then I was innocent enough to think my buddy had it coming, even if it seemed the blood in Cyril's wiry arms flowed pitch black with sin. Romey didn't have to say what he'd said. He shouldn't have talked back. Even a blind man could have seen that Cyril Guttner wouldn't take it, not a word, not in the mood he was in. That's what I thought.

But I didn't tell my parents what I'd seen that day. No way would I have told them. Screaming, yelling, cursing, slapping, kicking—I was sure my parents knew nothing of that world. At our place the degree of sin I'd felt in the combat between Romey and Cyril never existed. My parents sang hymns and songs recreationally, two or three times a day. My mother would play the piano and my father would stand behind her, his hands on her shoulders, and the two of them would sing about Jesus' saving love. If I have an abiding picture of them together, it is that image—the two of them harmonizing at the piano, my mother's hands wandering gracefully up and down the keyboard as if to take advantage of every note the piano offered; and my father behind her, lending her soprano the depth of his love. Before I started hanging around with Romey, I never had a hint of what might have gone on at places like Romey's house, never would have guessed that in some living rooms and dirty kitchens, people lived in fear of what was inside, not out.

"Why don't you boys just go ahead and leave for a while?" Romey's mother said when she came out back a little later, looking for Annie. By that time Romey was standing on the edge of the alfalfa field, right there beside the guinea pig cages, using one of the irons to chop the heads off the dandelions. He still hadn't said much.

Hattie Guttner was not tall, but she was heavy. She had beautiful dark, curly hair that seemed so naturally full it didn't require brushing, hair that had the same reddish glow Romey's did when it caught the

Trash Day Golf

sun. She seemed twice as big as her husband, but she would do anything for us, spoil us in a way my own mother never would have.

She stood there barefoot in the grass that morning, her slippers in one hand to keep them from the dew. "Whyn't you guys leave now? Just go downtown or something," she said, smiling toothlessly. She hated to wear her false teeth. "Here's a couple of quarters—buy yourselves some Coke and peanuts." She was pleading with Romey. "Just get out of his way—you know how he gets sometimes. Just get lost for a while." She jerked her head around as if Cyril might suddenly be standing there. "Sooner or later he'll be gone and you can do what you want."

Romey didn't even look at her when she spoke. He took the quarters and never said a word. He'd talk back to his father when Cyril yelled, but sometimes it seemed that the one he really couldn't take was his mother, even though it seemed to me all she really cared about was holding things together.

She started to walk off when Romey said it, yelled it. "Whyn't you tell *him* to go downtown? We didn't do nothing bad back here."

She turned and took off her glasses, rubbed her fingers over her eyes. "Just you stay out of his way, honey," she told him. "Please now? Doesn't do any good to ask questions—you know how it goes. I told you a thousand times."

She didn't say a word to me, but she looked at me painfully with a face I recognized even then as pitifully human, a face that asked for something I couldn't give her. "Lowell," she said, "he shouldn't say those things, should he?"

"Who?" I said.

She signaled over her shoulder with her thumb. "I'm sorry you had to hear it," she told me, and then she looked around again. "Where'd you steal those things, anyway?" she asked.

"Lewie Tinholt," Romey told her. "They were in his trash."

"He doesn't mind you having them?"

"He threw them away, Ma," Romey said.

"In the trash?"

Romey took one exasperated breath. "We broke into his living room—and stole them right off the fireplace mantle. Got a TV too, and a hi-fi, a big one—and Lobo here killed old Lewie in the process, murdered him."

"You didn't just grab them somewhere?" she said.

"They were in his trash, all right?" he said. "Ask him—he don't lie." He thumbed toward me. "Your kid you can't trust, but Lowell Prins—now that's a Boy Scout."

"In the street?" she said, looking at me. "Tell me the truth—it's not that I don't trust you guys."

"It's like he says," I told her. "We snuck into his house, stole 'em all, murdered his wife too—just like that. It's what we did this morning," I said. "Just don't tell my folks."

She brought her hands up to her hips. "It's trash morning all right," she said. She picked up one of the clubs, rubbed her fingers up the smooth shaft, and scratched a little mud off the club face. She curled the black tape tight around the handle and held it in both hands, like she might have seen on TV, then dropped the club face to the grass and swung, just lightly, at some imaginary ball. "Show me sometime how to do it," she said. Once again, she looked at me.

"I never played it once in my life," I told her. "I don't know how it goes—I mean, with all these different clubs and stuff. My dad doesn't play either." She kept looking at me, looking through me, wanting me to talk. "I mean, you got to get your ball in the hole is all I know."

And at that, Romey crumpled up in laughter, making a bad joke out of something I never meant at all.

"I didn't mean it that way," I told her. "I meant, the object of the game—the thing is to put the ball in the cup—every hole has a cup—" I started using my hands as if I were stroking putts. "Cut it out," I said to Romey. "I'm just trying to explain."

Hattie turned an eye toward her son and raised a hand over her eyes as if some vagrant cloud had just released a bit more sun. And the fact of the matter is—what I'll never forget too—she was laughing herself, her lips tightened over her bare-naked gums, smiling and holding it back until she finally broke into laughter, that hard gritty laugh I'll never forget, the sound of a handsaw being drawn quickly through hardwood. She couldn't have sung a song if she'd wanted to, Romey's mom. Her laugh ran over her vocal cords like a ratchet. She couldn't have sat at the piano, because she couldn't play it, and she couldn't have sung, either, because her voice was worn and fragile—too much yelling and far too many cigarettes.

"I ain't going to tell your mama," she told me, half in a smile. "Don't be scared of nothing now. You just made a little joke. Just Romey's dirty mind makes it bad."

And then she laughed—and smiled.

Things could change in a wink at Romey's place. A minute ago Cyril almost killed his kid, and here they sat, ma and boy, laughing at some dumb little goof they'd read like a dirty joke. Sometimes I couldn't keep pace. I couldn't read them, couldn't get on their wavelength. Sometimes

Trash Day Golf

Romey and his mom would swap dirty jokes and just howl. I don't know that I ever heard my parents laugh like they did, and they certainly never told Guttner jokes—at least not in my presence.

Hattie walked over and put an arm around my shoulder, as if I were her own child. "Do me a favor and don't tell your folks, okay?" Then she looked up at Romey. "I mean about what happened."

I wouldn't have anyway.

"He gets in these moods, and there's nothing you can do until he comes out." The whole time, she was giggling at what I'd said. She kept glancing at Romey. "Isn't that so?" she said to him.

Romey hid behind a yawn.

"Inside, his old man loves him," she said, pointing at Romey. "He does—believe me."

That was the only time I ever saw Cyril Guttner lay a hand on his boy—the only time, even though I knew it was happening more often. Romey never talked much about things at home. All the guys we hung around with moaned about their dads, and so did I, but every kid we ever played ball with, every kid with whom we tromped through fields or swam in the big lake, every kid I knew understood somehow that only Romey had it bad at times, really bad. He never once talked about getting it with a belt or being creamed when he wasn't expecting it—he never mentioned anything like that. But he was the only kid in Easton with Cyril Guttner for an old man, and Cyril Guttner, at least in Easton, was a man many felt didn't share something basic, maybe even the image of God.

Romey stuck that pair of quarters in his pocket, and we went downtown, where he pulled them out and bought a couple of bottles of RC Cola from the cooler in the back of the Wooden Shoe Restaurant. We shared a bag of peanuts in the back booth—counted them out on the Formica, split them up equally, then ate them one at a time. And we never talked much about what had happened between him and his father. By the time we got downtown, we were on to something else—I don't remember what. To Romey, I think it wasn't really that big of a deal at all. Just another day at his place.

He had a fancy decal on the back fender of his bike, a silver decal with the name of an engine on it—Mercury engines. He was proud of the decal, and he should have been—it was great, glowed in the dark and everything. "I got it from my old man," he used to say when somebody would point at it or glance longingly at the back fender.

That's all he'd say. It came from one of the factories where Cyril had worked in the time he spent as Romey's father.

Encounters

It's not hard for me to imagine what I found, at twelve years old, so attractive about Romey Guttner. Even with the specter of Cyril Guttner around, and even though I couldn't have defined it then, I felt a kind of freedom I never felt elsewhere—dangerous, but so exciting.

We hadn't been buddies in the early years of grade school, probably because I lived all the way on the east edge of town. But when bicycles gave us escape from our immediate neighborhoods, we started hanging out together—mutual interest in sports, I suppose, but then everybody was interested in sports. Romey brought me into the woods on the lakeshore. He showed me the way to the river a mile west of town. The two of us left the village for what seemed to me the wilderness, a place far from the looming shadows thrown over town by steeples that seemed then both ancient and imperial.

Cyril chilled me to the bone, but he made life interesting. I don't think he ever disliked me any more than he disliked anyone. I don't believe that who I was, who my parents were, or my grandparents, made much of an impression on him at all. When I was over there, I was just a kid. He knew I was Pete Prins's boy, but I'm not sure that fact affected him as it did his wife.

In town, Cyril had no friends. He looked at the whole burg as a congregation of do-good Christians commissioned somehow to flush the heathen out of the bushes and take scalps for the Lord, then affix them to their lapels like Sunday school pins. Easton people were self-righteous chumps to him, and so was I.

Hattie loved me. I represented aspirations she couldn't help but hold for her own boy, something respectable. I was a solvent that, even if it didn't get out all traces of her husband's character, might at least cover those stains and give her boy a better chance at becoming something worthwhile.

My parents must have worried about my going over to the Guttner place every day, must have secretly hoped, even prayed—my mother, at least—that the Lord would lead me to a worthier friend, someone who would knock on the door before barging into our house, someone who didn't drop dirty words into the conversation without guilt or even the slightest sense that he shouldn't have said what he did. They never told me they didn't like Romey. But my mother was constantly on edge when he was around; I knew that because I was too, for her. My father patronized Romey, tried to be nice. But at first, at least, the two of them never said a word about him or his family, never edged some unease into a conversation with the intent of keeping me at home.

I remember the cold November morning in the eighth grade when we needed a rifle because we'd gotten ourselves trapped by the beast which had wandered into one of our traps. There was nothing we could do with the hatchet we always lugged along, so we had to go back and get one of Cyril's rifles.

That morning Hattie had let us off at the bridge down County Trunk A. Most often, we'd ride our bikes to the river, but when snow or rain made things miserable, Hatttie would take us, leaving the little girls at home. They would sleep until she returned anyway. We'd scrambled down the embankment to the edge of the river, our flashlights shining out in front of us as if in the thick morning darkness we might otherwise stumble on the Loch Ness monster. The east was already flush with dawn, but cottonwoods along the bank kept the bluff grasses shadowed until the sky glowed in muted grays over our heads.

The river's flow was a slow drone, a hum from some distant secret source, the water whispering past half-sunken branches and tall stands of wild oats that fell heavily into the current's edge. Early in the morning, crows would scold and gulls whine, sitting aboard the stippled snowcaps on the plowed fields just off the banks. Occasionally, in the semi-darkness, something would thrash in the water, breaking the peace—a duck maybe, or a muskrat—and I'd jump. No sound I remember ever made Romey twitch. Not that he was stronger or tougher than I was. In physical strength, he may well have been weaker than I was, but Romey was always leather to my thin skin, ever more brave, far less prone to fear.

He held up his arm. "Listen," he said, turning to stone. We stood motionless, scanning the dim outline of the river grass beneath the trees. The only sound was the idle of the Guttner's Ford back at the bridge, a quarter mile south, where Hattie sat and listened to Connie Francis and smoked her Chesterfields, waiting out the hour or so it took us to check the traps.

"I don't hear nothing," I told him, but Romey grabbed my arm, then turned his head just slightly like a dog might.

"Hear that?" he said. "Something big."

He was right. Something was scrambling in the broom grass, kicking up the rustling sound a squirrel makes playing through dead leaves on the floor of a woods, only louder and heavier. It was just up in front of us, where we had a fox trap set in a flattened pan of grass beneath a stand of awkward, leaning maples.

"It's cows," I told him. "You're hearing things."

"Am not," Romey said. "Too early for cows. They're still in the barn." He clicked off his flashlight, and so did I. "We got something big, and it's alive," he told me. "Sheez, you hear that?" He brought up a finger. "Listen." He turned his face back and forth as if aiming his ears. "Stinkin' hippo." He grabbed my arm and pulled me closer. "We got a monster— maybe a coyote or something." I really didn't know whether he was pulling my leg. I had no idea if there were coyotes anywhere within a hundred miles. It was still too dark to see much, but when we inched around the bend in the river, we could just make out movement against the bleached weeds. Something was in the trap, something making lots of noise.

Romey lifted his flashlight, unlit, and nodded to me to lift mine. "Blast him at the same time," he said, holding the flashlight out in front of him like a .45. "You got it? Hit him quick with the light, then slap it off— ready?"

I was thinking it might be a fox, even though I'd come to believe we weren't half as smart as any fox in the township. But that morning I was thinking fox—the mother lode. Beautiful fur, maybe even a bounty,

Encounters

who knows? A tail. I could see it flagging from my bike. I aimed my flashlight.

"Now!" he said, and both of us shot what light we could at the base of the trees, where a single white plume glowed in the net of light. No more than a second and we doused everything, because both of us knew the score. I could almost feel myself soaked to the gills in musk—all my clothes, my jacket and school pants, everything a heap of trash, my mother holding her nose when I'd get home, even though on my way up from the basement I'd be wearing no more than a towel. No school for us that day, and Mom would be furious—the jacket wasn't that old, and she'd never been all that hot on me getting up so early in the morning to trap dirty river animals anyway, because it seemed like such a heathenish thing to do—dirty, not sinful exactly, just dirty.

"Big as a grandpa coon," Romey said. "You see that thing? Monster. Big as a stump." He was looking down at his spread-apart hands. "Big as a stinkin' bull almost, you know? A buffalo or something—skunk as big as a buffalo."

It was all a whisper. We were maybe twenty-five yards away, downwind, still scared to death of getting slain with musk.

"I don't smell him," Romey said. "If he'd already have shot his wad, it'd be raining skunk right now—we'd taste it."

Like a deer, I raised my nose to the wind. He was right. There was nothing there.

He tipped his head away as if to tell me to follow. On our hands and knees we waded through a thin layer of jackfrost on the long grass, trying to get farther out of range.

"Dang," Romey said. "What we going to do with a stinkin' skunk? Stupid thing. What'd he go and get himself caught for?"

"How'd he get there, anyway?" I said.

"Took a train, dumbo."

"Maybe he'll die," I told him.

"Of what? A broken heart?" Romey pulled his hands up as if he were holding a rifle, took aim in the general direction of the beast, and fired off three imaginary shots. "We got no choice, Lobo," he said. "We got to kill him."

"We don't have a gun," I said.

"My old man does." He shook his head. "We got to get his .22," he said. "Ma'll raise Cain, but we got no choice. We can't just waltz out there like we're going to fit him for the glass slipper." He shrugged his shoulders, that smile he loved to wear turning up half his face. "We got to get a rifle and shoot him dead, Lobo. It's the law."

Encounters

"What law?" I said.

"Law of the jungle," he told me.

So often, I never really knew when he was pulling my leg. He'd say something like that and let it sit, as if I knew exactly what he meant. Maybe there *was* a law of the jungle, I thought. If there was, Romey would be the kid to know it.

Once we thought we were out of earshot of the skunk, we ran all the way back to the car, the tops of our hip boots flapping like leather chaps against our thighs. Romey was smaller than I was, and quicker, but I kept up, though about the time I had to fight to get my breath, I started wondering why on earth we were sprinting all the way back to the bridge, as if the palooka skunk were some Brahma bull fast on our tails. Besides, I'd already figured there would be no school—not this morning.

"Ma!" Romey yelled, throwing the door open. Hattie's head was flat back on the top of the seat, her mouth gaping to reveal her bumpy toothless gums. "Ma," Romey said, crawling in and shaking her like a rag doll. "We got a skunk big as a German shepherd," he said. "We got to go home and get a rifle."

Hattie turned her head slowly, as if something in her was tuning in her son's voice.

"We got this ugly skunk," Romey told her and threw his arms wide apart.

"What you going to do?" she said.

"Kill him," he told her.

She looked at me the way she always did, as if she had to apologize.

Romey flicked his head at me to get me in the car, then turned back to his mother. "We got to shoot him or he'll stink us up bad. He's got our trap," he said, as if the whole mess were the skunk's bad idea. "Get us back to town, Ma—hurry it up," he said, pulling himself up next to her. "I got to get the old man's rifle—the little one. All we need is the .22. Nothing big—just the popgun." And then he put his arm around her as if we were all in this together. "I can get him with the .22. I can pick him off and not get shot myself."

"Honey," she said to me, "you got a gun at home?" She really knew better than to ask.

"We'll get one of the old man's," Romey told her, reaching over me to slap the door shut. "Big stinkin' skunk, Ma," he said again. "Huge mother."

Hattie looked at her watch. "We don't have the time—"

"It's not as if we got a choice, Ma," he said. "We can't let him suffer."

"Can't you'se just let him go or something?" she said. "Isn't there something else you can do?"

Romey couldn't take stupidity. "I tried to apologize to him," he said. "Maybe you ought to go out there yourself and tell him you're my ma." He ripped open the clasps of his jacket and held the edges in his fingers. "This is my school jacket, if you want to know," he said. "I'm going to have to bury it, see—and where we going to get the money for another one?"

She looked at me as if I were the one who ought to take control. I remember that woman, tough as nails. I remember moments during those years when she didn't back away from her son's brassy mouth. I remember times when I thought there was something alive and dangerous in her soul. But that morning her eyes were bathed in a sadness and fear I felt deeply, even though I wasn't old enough to know everything. But I knew it had to do with Cyril.

For a time she kept looking at me, maybe hoping I'd tell her to forget it, that Romey and I would just go to school and forget the skunk and the trapline as if the whole enterprise were nothing more than some boyhood game. And the truth is, I could have. But Romey wouldn't have quit until that skunk was dead, and I knew that, even if I didn't understand right then that he wouldn't quit because there was so much of his father in him—so much of his father and the law of the jungle.

"We got to hustle, Ma—we'll be late for school." He couldn't have cared less if he'd be late for school.

Hattie reached down to let out the hand brake, jerked the car into first, and pulled us out of the edge of the ditch, the car leveling as she brought all four tires to the pavement.

"You know as well as I do that I hate this," she said. She was talking to Romey in a voice I wasn't supposed to hear. "You know how he is about his guns," she said. And then she went into a jag that made me feel as if she wasn't fully in charge of what she was saying, started talking and talking and talking, as if there were no one listening but some shadow of herself scared to death inside her. "We got to get a gun," she said, mumbling. "We got to sneak in the house and grab Cyril's rifle. Sure, sneak downstairs. What you askin' for—a miracle? We got to go downstairs and hustle up a gun right from under his nose or ask him, as if he's Santa Claus, I guess. That's what you're saying, right? We ought to just ask the man, right Romey? That's what you're saying. You lucky to come out of this alive and you know it. Rather be the skunk," she said, and more. She glanced at Romey. "Whyn't you ask me to turn water into wine—why not? Whyn't you ask me to put milk back in a carton once it's down on the floor—Romey—you hear what I'm saying?"

"I ain't asking for any miracle—"

"It's going to have to be me that does it," she said. "You hear me?" She just kept talking, all of it coming out in that muffled way she talked when her teeth weren't in. "You listen to me good now," she said. "It's going to have to be me that does it, because your father might just be up already. It's got to be me that gets it, Romey. You hear? It's got to be me that gets it—if there's somebody here going to take all his spit and thunder, Romey, it's me, y'hear? I won't let you in that basement—I won't. You listen to me now for the first time in your life—"

"You know where it is, Ma," he said. "Me and Lobo will stay right in the car. We'll drive the getaway." He leaned over and winked at me. "We're the wheelmen, Lobo," he said. "You and me, right?"

Sometimes Romey would brag about the way he and his dad took out the whole basement arsenal and shot dozens of rounds at beer bottles and paper targets down at the sand dunes. Sometimes he'd be proud of the way his father could sight-in rifles, the way his old man took pride in his guns, the way his old man did things out in the woods, the way my father never did. When he'd talk about those Sunday afternoons shooting, just the two of them out there at the lakeshore, he never compared fathers, really. He wasn't trying to say anything about my father—that wasn't the point. Those times Cyril took Romey out shooting—sighting-in rifles, getting ready for deer hunting, shooting up a whole box of .30-30s, then picking up the shells in the sand when they were still warm—when he'd go on and on about how much fun they'd had, he didn't do it just because he knew I'd be sitting home on Sunday watching the clock, waiting for the Sabbath to pass like a good Christian boy. He didn't say it to mock me. He never did. He said it because those moments with his old man, those few moments, were his joy.

But this time we were in an emergency. The law of the jungle was at stake here: you can't let a creature suffer, not even a worthless skunk. But what I couldn't understand—not really—is why they couldn't simply tell Cyril. Cyril knew a real man couldn't leave that skunk out there dragging that trap through the grass all day long. Cyril would know right away that you couldn't just let it bleed to death or chew off its leg in a dinky little number two trap. If anybody would know that, it would be Cyril. My old man would side with Hattie—just wish the problem away. My mother would have just forgotten the river even existed.

Hattie was pulled up to the wheel as if she were driving in a heavy rain, Romey beside her, his arm still around her, his knees up over the hump in the middle, me beside him on the passenger's side. Nobody said a thing, the radio playing Everly Brothers, something about love, the kind of music Hattie always played on the radio, even at her age. There

Encounters

wasn't another mother in town who fell over backward for me the way Hattie Guttner did. But sometimes when I'd enter that house and hear her listening to what she did on the radio—and then think of my parents with Singspiration playing on the new Magnavox hi-fi in the living room—I couldn't help but think she really should have started to take a few steps toward growing up.

Ten minutes, at most, it took to get back to town, to Romey's place. She pulled up in front of the neighbor's house and turned in their driveway instead of using her own. "Stay put," she said, almost in a whisper, and she got out of the car and nudged the door shut softly with the back of her arm. We watched her as she walked like a child on skates across the ice on the driveway, this hefty rounded figure in the red-hooded sweatshirt she wore over a sweater, and a housecoat, the outfit she wore every dark and cold morning she'd take us out to the river.

"He ain't awake yet anyway," Romey said. "The sun ain't even up. I don't know what she's so scared for."

Dead of night was long gone. The sun threw a pink curtain up behind the thin layers of clouds lying like shallow smoke puddles east over the lakeshore, but it wasn't morning, not yet.

"I don't get it," I said. "What's the big deal, anyway? You shoot that rifle all the time."

Romey turned down the volume on the radio and shrugged. "The thing is," he said, not so much to me, either, "he don't have to know. What he don't know won't hurt him—that's what Ma always says. Shoot," Romey said, the conversation going on in his mind, "it's something that's got to be done."

"We can't let him suffer," I said, meaning the skunk.

It was light enough to see the mottled siding, the rainspout hanging away from the gutter on the southeast corner of the house. Upstairs on the landing just outside Romey's bedroom, two lawn chairs sat where they'd been for as long as I could remember, capsized, flung together, frayed ribbons of nylon hanging away from the frame like unwound bandages. It was November, but the screen door was still on—it never did come off that I remember—and it wasn't latched, maybe a half inch of space melted black between it and the storm door, also left open because Hattie didn't want to make a bit of extra noise.

"What would he say, really?" I asked Romey. "Maybe he'd come along and do it himself."

"Let sleeping dogs lie, Ma always says," he told me, never turning his head. "You ever hear that one?"

"Never," I said.

"Let sleeping dogs lie," he said again. And then, "What's takin' her, anyway? What'd she do, stop for a beer?"

And then there she was—first the rifle, then her arm, then her and that whole sweatshirt squeezing out the doorway slowly, silently. She inched the door shut behind her—ten seconds at least on the latch, all the while holding the rifle by the barrel. Then she turned and started walking again over the ice, tentatively, her left arm out to keep her balance across the driveway.

"Your ma doesn't know how to carry a rifle," I said.

"She don't like guns," he said. "Never has, never will. My dad loves guns. My ma hates 'em."

She walked as if each step might bring on the judgement, then kept her feet parallel, like a skier, down the little slope to the gravel driveway, step by step.

"Sure as heck she forgot shells," Romey said. "You know my ma. She'd forget her head if it wasn't tied on." He reached for the door handle on the driver's side and squirmed out. "You got bullets?" he asked her in a thick whisper.

From the look she gave him, he could have slapped her face and not hurt her as badly.

"I got some hid in the garage," he said. "I'll get 'em."

She poked the uncased rifle in the car at me. I grabbed it by the barrel and stuck it in the back seat—I didn't really want any part of it right then, the Ford's interior light burning bright as neon. I glanced at the windows of the house, which would have been lit had he been up, even though the dawn was coming.

Hattie waited outside for a moment while Romey jogged to the garage, his hip boots turned down beneath his knees. Then, suddenly, she got back in and closed the door beside her. "You sit over here beside me," she told me. "Let him get in over there when he gets back."

Once she shut the door, I couldn't see the icy fear across her face. She rubbed her fingers and her hands. "I don't know why you want to do this," she said. "I don't know why, Lowell." She always called me Lowell, even though Romey never did. "I suppose it's good for Romey, but I don't know what's in it for you—this trapping business and you comin' over here and everything. My lands, what would your folks say about all of this? He's doing it for his old man, maybe," she said, "I don't know. But what's in it for you anyway?"

"I like it," I told her, and I did.

"Come now," she said. "Who'd want to suffer this kind of stupidity anyway? Know what I'm saying?"

"It's just a skunk," I said.

She shook her head back and forth. "It ain't just a skunk," she said, "or I'd be done with it. I don't know what your mother'd say if she knew what you were up to right now," she told me. "What do you think?"

"She wouldn't care," I said.

"You think not?" she said. "Come now."

"She doesn't even know I'm gone. I get back, and she's just awake," I told her. "She doesn't worry."

"Maybe she should," Hattie said.

"What she don't know doesn't hurt her," I said, proudly.

"That's a fairy tale," she said.

The car was still idling. Romey came out of the garage and ran along the frosty grass on the neighbor's lot line, then plowed through the naked hedge between the houses, his hand clasped over the shells I knew had been hidden in an old rainspout above Cyril's workbench for just such a time. He got in my side and pulled the door shut so silently I wasn't sure it was closed. Just like that, Hattie backed us out, gravel popping beneath our tires like gunpowder caps.

Romey turned around quickly. "Oh dang," he said, relieved. "All of a sudden I figured you didn't grab the .22."

"Think I was born in a barn?" Hattie said.

"Never dawned on me you'd know what a .22 was—"

"I'm not as dumb as you think I am," she told him.

I was between them, sitting on the hump. There we sat at the end of the driveway, waiting for a truck that was coming up the street, a carpenter who lived a few doors down. Of all things, the guy stopped, trapping us in the driveway. Hattie glanced back at the house, looking for light, then rolled down the window.

"Any luck?" the guy yelled, loud enough to wake city hall. He probably thought we were duck hunting.

"The boys are checking traps," Hattie told him. "It's getting too cold for them to take their bikes."

"Getting any?" the guy said, looking at us, the stub of his fat cigar stuck in the corner of his mouth.

"Just going out right now," Hattie said.

"Kinda late, isn't it?" he said, pointing at the sky.

"You try to get these kids out of bed," she told him. "You know, it ain't worth their time or mine, as little as they get." She knew very well she had to talk to the guy. "What am I doing getting myself up for them, Slattery—whose trapline is it, anyway? That's what I keep asking myself."

He looked at her in that adult knowing way, as if they both should know that's the way it always is with kids. "Good luck anyway," he said. "Wish I had the time to be out there myself. Great morning, isn't it?" and just like that he was off, the engine backfiring between gears.

Hattie took off slowly, her face up close to the windshield of that old Ford, eyes squinting over the top of the steering wheel. She wasn't tall, but she always seemed slumped to me, always bent over, birdlike, her fingers stout and thick. She always wore men's gloves—Cyril's probably.

"He wasn't even up," Romey said. "He wasn't out of bed, anyway."

"I didn't hear a thing," she told us, although I didn't know if it was meant for us, exactly, as her face never moved from the street in front of her. "I just went down and grabbed the one with the smallest barrel, and I came right back up, quiet as I could." She held a cigarette between her fingers, straight up from the steering wheel. Hattie was the only woman I knew who smoked, and she did it around me only when she absolutely had to or had forgotten who I was in the heat of something else.

"He don't know a thing," Romey said.

"Maybe you're right, but I don't like it," she said. "It ain't over yet— I got the sneaking suspicion. It's his gun we got, you know. He'll smell something. You know how he is."

By the time we got back to the river, the sun had raised a meadow of sparkles on the grass and was working hard at drawing out the damp cold. The parallel tracks we'd beaten down against the bank not a half hour before were the only lines over a perfect sheet of frost.

"For sure don't do nothing crazy," Hattie told us. "It's all I need now is for one of you to get shot in the foot or something—so do it the way he taught you, hear?" She swung her arm up over the seat when we got out. Romey grabbed the rifle. "And don't get sprayed, either. Do it like Cyril would, Romey," she said. "Don't be a cowboy."

When Romey lifted the rifle, reverently, from the back seat, the interior light flashed over the gleaming red wood as if the whole rifle were dipped in liquid glass. He got out of the car and raised the .22 above his head like some Apache before the two of us slid down the embankment.

I remember sniffing the air as we were walking, but smelling nothing. "He might be out of the trap by now," I said. "Maybe we don't need the gun anyway."

"It's a rifle, moron," Romey said, as if he were teaching me catechism. "Anyway, we got to track him down if he left his paw."

I had heard a dozen tales about great hunters tracking wounded deer for miles of lakeshore woods before finally ending the hunt with one merciful shell. "We're going to chase a skunk?" I said.

Romey never said a word, and I trailed along behind him, shamed.

When we came to the bend in the river, he grabbed shells from the box and slapped them into the magazine, just the way I'd seen him practice, time after time, in the basement, when his dad was at work or somewhere out of town.

"You miss and we're cooked," I told him.

He put the rifle up to his shoulder and squinted through the adjustable sights toward some target on the other side of the river. "My old man's got this thing sighted-in perfect," he said.

"He's in bed," I told him. "You're doing the shooting."

"Watch this," he said. "See that branch over there on the other side— see it? Watch." He pointed at a bleached branch jutting out of the current. "One shot," he said.

"You'll scare the beast," I said, but he let off two rounds that snapped right at the base of the branch. One of them connected.

"Give me a shot," I said, but Hattie started honking the horn.

"My ma's having a kid," he said.

We sneaked through the grass until we got close enough to see a ball of black and white fur in front of the tree. Then we dropped to our knees and crept along like marines until Romey held up his hand at the edge of the bank, close enough to the set so that he could eyeball that black and white fur through the notch in the sight.

"Don't you miss, Romey," I said. "Don't even think about missing."

"It's like a bomb anyway," Romey said, not taking his eye off the skunk. "Anybody up close gets it head-on, but way back here all it'll do is stink some on us." He looked at me for a moment. "Like hitting one with a car, you know?" With his thumb he flicked the safety on and off, on and off. "We ain't going to die or nothing, just stink bad."

"Then why don't you just stand up and do it?" I said.

"More fun this way," he said, smiling.

I'd have been scared to death—I know I would have. I had every reason in the world to have more self-confidence than Romey Guttner, but there was no way I would have grabbed that .22 and taken the shot myself, because just as surely as I knew I wouldn't have done it right, I had every confidence in the world that Romey would. In his mind that skunk's chestnut brain was already ripped up by a bullet or two foreordained to get there. Which is not to say that, to him, this moment was not adventure. To Romey, bagging this skunk was a gas—being out there at dawn, sneaking that rifle from the basement, all of that—it was pure adventure. Life was adventure.

He brought the rifle down from his shoulder. "Maybe a little closer," he said, giggling. So we crawled along, both of us, a couple of snakes in the grass, our elbows already soaked, our gloves cold and wet and worthless.

"Now?" Romey said, winking. He was making this glorious moment last as long as an all-day sucker.

He found an old branch in the grass, jerked it in front of him, and stabbed it in the wet ground for a prop. Way up there in front of us, leaves and grass and churned-up earth where the skunk had fought against the chain, turning the whole set into a mess. It was clawing at the trap, a blur, a mass of striped darkness, moving and very much alive, but oblivious to us.

"Lucky they don't fire because they're mad," I told him.

"Smarter than we are," he said, "but most animals are. Hang around 'em long enough and you'll understand that." He steadied the rifle. "Sharpshooter," he said. "Like the Krauts are right down there, you know, and I'm up on a ridge, picking them off one at a time." He glanced up and smiled. "Slow and easy, squeeze it slow and easy, so there's no jerk—that's what my old man says. Watch now."

"You're making a movie out of it," I told him.

"Got to be just right—like Ma says," Romey said, his eye narrowed. "Got to be just perfect. We only got one shot or we're Limburger." Just like that the rifle cracked, and the skunk's tail arched from its back like a fan because the shot was right on the money, just as he'd said it would be, and just like the second one was, and the third, a moment later, just as deft and quick and deadly. The skunk doubled up, its front legs flipping back as it somersaulted and sprawled in the dirt, quivering and quivering some more, then reaching for one last big hunch of the spine, and flattening out, its legs kicking spastically before slowly running down in a ritual of death I'd seen in muskrats and snapping turtles and opossums, but not often enough to keep me from looking away.

"I told you," Romey said. He made the same rifle-shot sound through his teeth again and again and again, replaying those perfect shots. "Nailed him," he said. "You see that?"

"Did he spray?" I said.

"You'd be eating musk if he did." He picked the empty shells off the grass. "That was world-class shooting, Lobo," he said. "You just now saw quality marksmanship." He buried one more shot into the body before pulling himself up from the grass, all the time watching the lifeless mass of fur.

The morning freshness—the slowly melting frost, the grasses, the fresh air—was all there was to smell. No skunk. I tried to wipe some of the wetness off my jacket. "Now what're we going to do with him," I said, "stick him in your ma's trunk?"

"She'd have a fit," he said. "Your old man want a skunk in his peonies? Great fertilizer—"

"You ask him," I said.

We got to our feet and walked through the grass to the set. The sun was just beginning to burn from between clouds thin and flat as open hands to the east. The skunk lay humped on the mess of grass and leaves it had dug up before dying, as if preparing its own grave. I'm not unaware that some people would call everything we did that morning an exercise in barbarism. It may well be, but when I remember the way the two of us walked over to that hapless skunk, the way Romey kicked at the thick round belly protruding into the air, I remember those moments as a triumph bigger than almost anything I'd ever feel again.

"We'll let him lie," Romey said. "After school we'll come out and bury him—I don't know. I don't feel like skinning no skunk." He tossed the rifle lightly in his hands. "We got to get this thing back pronto," he said, rubbing off the water beads beneath his arm. He kicked again at the lifeless body. "Ugly, aren't they?" he said.

I'd never seen a skunk up close before, but I didn't think of that animal as ugly. It looked catlike, its thin and pointing nose beset with whiskers beneath dark and probing eyes. It could have been alive, really. There was little blood. "People have them as pets," I said. "I mean, they get them destinked or something. They actually have them as pets."

"People are stupid," Romey said.

The long fur and the innocence in the animal's face surprised me, because in death it seemed nothing like a muskrat, with its long sharp teeth, and not as ugly as an opossum. "I don't even see a hole," I said.

"Big-time skunk," Romey said. "Hotshot shooting."

"Big-time hunter," I told him, in jest. "Big deal, Romey—poor thing couldn't even move, got his leg in a trap, standing still and everything. Big deal. Some shot. Lots of danger—"

"You couldn't have hit him and you know it," he said. "You'da been so nervous you couldn'ta aimed for a second. You'd been jumping, Lo-man."

"I don't get any practice," I told him.

"We'd both be stinking right now, both of us—smell like the dickens."

I flipped the skunk over with my boot so the trap lay flat on the grass and I could get my foot on the spring. When the tension on the jaws released, that fat leg jumped out as if the skunk were alive.

"A guy could make a coat out of skunk," Romey said. "We can clean this one up, you know. Maybe your ma would wear it to church."

I reached down and grabbed the skunk's leg, then picked it up from its thick drumstick, the way Romey always carried whatever it was we'd caught. I held it up shoulder high, blood dripping slowly now from the end of its nose. "Fifteen pounds, I bet," I said. "*Big* skunk."

"They get big as cows. They got no enemies. Nobody touches them. They got nothing to do all day but get fat—like my ma." He pointed the rifle toward the bank of the river. "Throw him in the grass," he said. "We'll come back tonight," and I swung it back to get some force, then flung it into a yellow patch of grass farther off the riverbank.

"What if somebody comes along—"

"Nobody going to eat skunk, Lobo—except maybe a crow," he said as he pulled the rifle to his shoulder. "The old man would have loved it," he said. "Hotshot shooting like that—just one shot's all we had. Had to flatten that sucker—boom! Stupid thing never had a chance. One after another—bang, bang, bang—you see that?" He squeezed off three more rounds slowly at the twig shaking in the river. The slugs slapped against the flow of water.

"You ought to tell him," I said. "You ought to tell him—one shot, that's it. Whyn't you tell him?"

"You nuts?" He dropped the rifle to his waist, grabbed another couple of rounds out of his jacket pocket and loaded up. "If he'da planned it, maybe," he said. "If my old man had staked it all out—but then, of course, he would have done it himself. No way I would have done it. He mighta hauled me along, maybe. But no way he'da let me have that shot. No way." He snapped off a couple more rounds at a stump on the other side of the river. "All he cares about is guns."

"He don't even hunt that much," I said.

"He's weird," Romey said. "My old man's weird about some things— you know what I mean? It's not so much about hunting, his guns. It's not that, really. He's not that interested in hunting. It's just the guns or something, you know?" Then he looked up at me and asked me a question I won't forget. "What's it like having an old man who's a saint?" he said.

"Whatta'ya mean?" I said.

He looked at me, distanced, as if I'd suddenly turned into someone other than his friend. "Never mind," he said. "We better get moving." He let it be.

The trapline included about a half-dozen or more traps, so we hustled along until we'd checked them all, picking up a muskrat, already drowned, in a trap we'd laid in the water at the base of a slick run down from a cornfield. Then we headed back to the car, where Hattie was waiting, this time not sleeping.

It was late by then, much later than we usually got back. I was worried about school. I was worried about what my mother would say when I'd come in probably ten minutes before school started, still dressed in hunting clothes. I knew what she'd say. I knew her tone of voice. I knew what she wouldn't say.

"It's lucky we got an automatic," Romey told his mother. "If we'd had a single-shot, we might have got nailed, but I pumped him full before he could even get that fat tail up."

"He did good," I told her. "You ought to have seen him. One shot— that was it."

"Big mother. But we left him out there—threw him away in some weeds," Romey said.

I swung the burlap bag with the muskrat to the floor of the back seat. "We'll bury him tomorrow or something," I said, as if I had a handle on the whole business.

"You're going to have to clean that rifle, you know," she said. "If he sees it's been shot, he'll skin you. Sometime today—"

"After school—when he's gone," Romey told her.

"Just don't you forget," she said, looking at her watch. "You's'll be lucky if you're not late for school, I bet."

Romey piled into the front seat, and this time I got in the back. Hattie let out the clutch slowly, and even though we barely had enough speed to climb the lip of pavement, the old Ford roared out of the grass at the side of the road. The sun, at least a half hour into the sky, lay bright stripes on the frost-edged furrows through the fields on both sides of the road. All the way home Romey chatted about how well he'd done, retold the whole story, making himself sound like a war hero—how perfect a shot it was, how that skunk went down dead as a mackerel, went over the details for Hattie, who never said a word. "Work of art, Ma," he said. "He couldn't have done any better himself—I swear it."

Hattie drove home just like she always did, her face up close to the dash as if she'd forgotten her glasses. Maybe Romey knew she was listening, but I never would have guessed. When I think about that time now, I wonder why she did it—trucked us out there on those mornings when it was especially cold or rainy, and even some mornings when it wasn't. She could have simply demanded we take our bikes, as we usually did; but often as not in those cold fall mornings we trapped the river west of town, I'd pull up to Romey's place on my bike and there in the driveway the Ford would be idling, getting warm. My mother wouldn't have thought of hauling us out there at five A.M. She would have said simply not to go if it was rainy or if sleet lay like glass over County Trunk A.

Romey's chatter ended abruptly at the village sign west of town, stopped as if the story was now officially tucked away in some history book. A voice on the radio was making long-term forecasts for the winter. Romey sat by the door wiping a runny nose with the back of his glove, and once more, as I remember, everything got tense. We were coming back to his place, and the two of them—Romey and his mom—suddenly seemed oblivious to my presence, their eyes focused on the empty street running east into town. I held the rifle.

"I could sneak it down there really fast," Romey said. "Just like that, I could have it back where it came from, Ma. Take ten seconds—no more."

Hattie looked as if driving took every bit of her energy.

"He won't be up yet," Romey said. "Shoot, when he ain't working now? He won't be up, Ma."

She took a hand off the wheel to pull her hair back beneath the hood of her sweatshirt.

And then he reached over to his mother and grabbed her arm. "How about Lowell here sneaks it down and the two of us go upstairs and get in his way?" he said. "How about that? He won't gripe so much at Lobo. You know he won't. And besides, he'll never know. He's dead asleep, Ma—you know it."

Hattie didn't move an inch. Both her hands were up on the wheel of that old Ford.

"We need a diversion, Ma," he said. "We can make all this noise coming up the steps, and he'll never know what happened once Lobo gets back upstairs." Romey leaned over and slipped his arm around his mother's shoulders. "It's a cinch," he said. "It's the best chance we got."

Hattie stared so intently at the street in front of her, you could have sworn that country road was a freeway.

"We don't have much time," he told her. "Shoot, we're almost late for school already. That's the fastest way I know, and Lowell won't mind, will you, Lobo?" He looked back at me. "He's not going to get all mad at you anyway."

"I'll do it," I said. "I know right where it goes, Hattie," I said. "I know exactly where it goes—no kidding. I can slip it in there in a minute." And the fact is, the whole thing seemed safe enough. We didn't even have to wake up the old man. It wasn't our fault a stupid skunk had walked into our number two trap. We didn't intend to catch it. We didn't try. And we'd done everything right, too, according to the laws of the Medes and Persians or whatever. We could have let the thing suffer, but we'd sneaked that rifle out in order to do what had to be done.

It couldn't have been done in any more of a righteous way—at least that's the way I saw it. And his own son had done it—Romey pulled it off like some crack marine. The old man ought to be proud. That's what I figured. With them running interference, and the whole thing done so right, I figured the least I could do was slip that thing downstairs where it was supposed to be.

"You don't mind?" Hattie asked.

"I know where it goes," I told her.

"Carry it behind your back—slip it along your leg," Romey said. "He won't be looking out of the window, but even if he is, he won't be looking at you." He turned around as if to wake me or something. "I mean, just to make sure, you know? Slip it into your pants or something. Hide it. This don't amount to nothing."

We took a left at the bank corner and headed past the mill toward Romey's place, the radio off now, as if all our wits had to center on the operation. The Ford's tappets made a swishing sound, even though we were doing little more than a crawl.

I figured they were right. After all, I didn't have a long history of talking back at him like Romey did, and, after all, I was Pete Prins's son and not Cyril Guttner's. Besides, I thought Cyril wasn't about to tangle with my father, since my dad was the chairman of the village board and all that, not to mention just about everything worth being in the church. Besides, it was a good plan—the two of them running interference while I went down the steps and stuck that rifle back on the rack.

This time Hattie drove right up the driveway and came to a stop as close as she could to the back door of the house. Romey jumped out and waited for me. I opened the door and got out myself, keeping the car between me and the kitchen window, just in case. Hattie stood at the front fender and waited.

I held the rifle along my leg like a long splint. I glanced up but didn't see anyone at the window, where the little light above the kitchen sink would have illuminated a face had there been one there.

"He ain't going to say anything to you anyway," Romey whispered. "You ain't his kid."

Hattie walked up the lawn to the cement, then opened the screen door, the spring yawning a little. She used her shoulder to nudge open the storm, turning the knob as she leaned into it.

Romey pulled me up in front of him. "Act dopey," he said. "Act like you don't know any better and you're just walking funny."

I kept the rifle along my leg and walked stiffly up to the back door and through, Hattie holding it open like a gentleman. Romey went in first, banged his boots on the step to make noise. Then he nodded for me to get downstairs. "You see him, Lobo," Romey whispered, giggling, "let him have it!"

It was perfectly quiet in the house. I heard nothing more than the rustling we were making in the back. Coats and scarves and boots littered the back hall, but I waited for Hattie, even though Romey tried to shoo me silently down the back stairs. I wanted both of them in front of me. I wanted both of them going upstairs and blocking out the old man. The back hall door closed, and Hattie marched up the back steps toward the kitchen. That's when I went down the basement stairs.

For some reason, I suddenly had this fear that the rifle was still loaded. I tried to count the shells I saw Romey stick in the magazine, then remember how many rounds he'd squeezed off at the river. But all the while, I was taking that rifle downstairs, a step at a time, scared to death of falling down the rickety steps or making some kind of rumpus, sure that if I did, with my luck the .22 would go off and fire through the ceiling or something and hit Romey's old lady, something tragic like that—because things like that happened, I told myself. Once, right in town, a kid came back from hunting and shot his little brother through the basement wall.

The edges of the old wooden stairs were worn away, and my boots hadn't dried completely. I could just see myself slipping and sliding down. Upstairs, I heard voices, the sound of the hall door slapping shut. Cyril wasn't out of bed, I thought. Romey had it right. Almost always Romey had it right.

I kept my balance over the rumpled rug at the bottom of the steps, the rifle in both hands now, close to my chest, and got my feet beneath me before getting quickly to the other side of the basement, where Cyril kept his rack, the room with the dehumidifier. Voices and the footsteps over the kitchen floor made what was happening upstairs sound like a polka. Heavy shafts of sunlight in perfect squares sat up against the north wall from two cobwebbed windows up on the south wall. I walked past the washer and tub and a downstairs workbench and opened the door to the gunroom, then lifted the rifle onto the wall and made sure I had both pegs firmly beneath the stock. The jumble of noise upstairs had to be Hattie and Romey dancing with the old man, trying to keep him up there for an extra minute, and I had to giggle to think of the two of them doing downfield blocking.

Ten seconds at best, from the base of the stairs to the back room with the guns. Just to be sure, I nudged the rifle once more with my hands to see if it would fall, then turned toward what little light there was in the basement, the light from those messy windows, and walked back through the open door, turned to close it in perfect silence, then headed for the stairs.

"You never as't if you could use that rifle," he said.

It wasn't me who'd done the shooting. It wasn't me who'd nailed that skunk perfectly. It wasn't me who'd engineered the whole dangerous morning. But I should have guessed that when something went awry, it would be me who would be in the middle of it. Cyril Guttner was in the south corner of the basement, opposite the steps.

"Least, I don't remember anybody asking," Cyril said. "You kids are too dang young to be responsible with guns. You can't just go off with firearms like you're grown men—we got laws in this state." He took a drag on a cigarette I told myself I should have smelled. "Bet it was Romey's idea too, wasn't it? Sure it was, the stupid kid."

The darkness brightened quickly, enough for me to see Cyril had a long screwdriver in his hand. He was pointing it up against the white background of his undershirt, scratching his chest, and that's when I realized Romey wasn't wrong—I'd been caught red-handed, but I wasn't really in danger. I could see it in the man's face. Nothing was going to boil over in him. Cyril Guttner wasn't about to pound me up. In his left hand he held the flat top of a white paint can. He stood there in the semidarkness, mad but not insane, perturbed maybe, even angry. But not at me. I could tell it. Say what you want about Cyril Guttner, he understood something here—that I wasn't the one he was going to go after. And then he said something I didn't expect, not at all.

"Don't you got nothing to say?" he asked. "I thought all you people had something to say all the time—Prinses, big Christian people."

Encounters

"I'm sorry," I told him. It's exactly what my parents would have wanted me to say. I had no idea what I was sorry about at that moment, but it was the one thing I thought might take off the edge.

"Man's got a right to what's his." Cyril took a step out closer to the light from the basement windows, then sniffed something up so hard that he twisted his whole face to get it. "Somebody wants to use what's his, a man's got a right to be as't." He stuck his tongue over his lower teeth as if to retrieve some speck of tobacco. "Ain't your old man taught you that? This is America, and what's mine is mine, right?"

I wanted to scream for Romey, to get him down here to take me out of the play. I didn't dare—not for a minute—just walk right past him, because I could feel the way he would make me buckle when he slammed me or kicked me or whatever. My instinct was to lay back, stay out of his way. But where he stood, he blocked the stairs.

"There's people that like to die for doing a whole lot less than you just did—you know that?"

How long could it take for the two of them to discover that he wasn't upstairs? Cyril kept flicking his tongue all around his open mouth. He hadn't shaved. And I knew he was liking this. He had me trapped in his basement, his gun just now in my hands, everything on the scales weighing against me.

"Look at me when I talk to you," he said.

He was wielding the screwdriver like a pointer, but he was smiling—I could see he was smiling behind all that poison. He walked to the middle of the room, leaving the base of the stairs. I didn't make a move. He reached for the string hung from a lightbulb, then stood in the shower of light, shadows forming like a mask over his eyes. Behind him stood an open gallon of paint.

I kept thinking it ought to be no more than a minute before both of them would be down to rescue me—it couldn't be long. I had this vision of them sitting upstairs drinking orange juice. They had to know. I had no reason to stay down in the basement. I had no reason.

"What you got to say?" he said.

"We got this skunk," I told him, the words catching on a raspiness in my throat. "We got this big stinkin' skunk and it was in the trap and it was still alive." Once the words came, they kept coming, kept flowing. "Romey says he figures the only way to get him—he says the way you'd have told him to get it is to shoot him, you know? That's exactly what he said." Maybe I had to brag Romey up. I could do that. "You wouldn't believe what Romey did—he shot that skunk dead—bang!—just like that." I raised both arms as Romey had a half hour before. "Three shots,

56

Encounters

one after another right in that thing—bang! bang! bang! Geez, what a great shot. Dead as anything. Never had a chance to get us, either. Dead right away. You taught him good."

Cyril sniffed some more.

"We thought you were sleeping," I said. "We didn't want to wake you because we knew how to do it ourselves—Romey did. Besides, your wife was along too, you know? I mean it wasn't as if we were out there goofing around or nothing like that."

"You didn't ask," Cyril said. There was a stripe of paint on his shirt.

"You were sleeping."

"Bull," he said, coming closer. "How'd you like it if I come into your old man's castle some morning and just start rooting around and tell you I didn't want to wake nobody up? What'd you feel like if that happened?"

"We looked," Romey said. "There wasn't a light on in the house. You were sleeping. We figured you'd tell us to do it just like we did." Finally, he came down the stairs. He stepped out in front of me. "I even came in the house and looked too. You weren't even up. I didn't want to wake you 'cause it wasn't nothing but a stupid skunk." He laughed, tried to. "And I could do it, Dad. I could—and I did. He tell you?" Romey asked, pointing at me. "He tell you how it went?"

"It's time to go to school, boys," Hattie said, in all innocence. I looked up and saw her thick legs at the top of the stairs. "You're already late because of that skunk. Now get on out of here before I got to go apologize to the principal again. Cyril?" she said. "Cyril—you down there? You send those boys up now, you hear? They don't have time to talk. They can tell you later about the whole story. Go on. Get a move on."

The furnace blower kicked in and Cyril turned away, batting the handle of the screwdriver against his wrist.

"It's way past 8:30," Hattie yelled. "You boys are going to be late again and the principal's going to be hot as snot and I ain't going to lie no more—I had it with you two."

"We better get ourselves off," Romey said to me. "We'll clean up that rifle right after school, okay? We'll do it, y'hear? Don't you be doing it for us—we can do that."

"Ought to be cleaned right now," Cyril said. "Take a rifle out and shoot it, you shouldn't really wait to clean it—not if you love guns—not if they're yours."

I'd have settled for an angry principal. I'd have looked into my mother's wrath and done nothing more than spit. If that man wanted us to clean that rifle, I didn't care what punishment awaited us at school or me at home.

Encounters

"We got to go," Romey said. "You heard Ma."

"All day that rifle's going to be dirty," he said.

"We're late, Dad—already we're late."

"All day."

"Romey!" Hattie yelled from the top of the stairs. "Cyril, you send those boys up now before we get in trouble with the whole town. Good night, I don't know why I let 'em have that trapline. It's the biggest headache—"

"They're cleaning the rifle," Cyril said, and just like that Romey went over to the cupboard and got out the kit. He pulled out the rod and started screwing the parts together. I didn't know what to do. I stepped away and stood beside him as if he needed help.

"You didn't ask," Cyril said again. "You can't just be taking my rifles here without asking, Romey."

"I told you I didn't want to wake you—"

"I know that—you said that already. But it's the principle, see. It's the principle here that gets me. You got to ask. That's the idea. I'm your old man, and this is my stuff down here and you don't just go and sneak off with it without asking."

"How'd you like to be waked up this morning before it was light?"

"How'd you like me to whip you?"

"Cyril," Hattie said again. "Send those boys up now."

"You go," Romey said to me. "This is my job. You never took a shot anyway. Principal ain't no friend of mine—all it'll do is give him a good reason to gripe."

Cyril was still too close to the stairs.

"Go on," Romey said.

So I did. I walked to the base of the stairs, walked past him, and I'll never forget the field of hate or darkness or fear—whatever it was—that surrounded him. The man never laid a hand on me, not that morning, never even reached for me when I walked by; but I'll never forget the aura of his palpable darkness as I walked past him, the chill that would have made me cry if that simple pass would have taken a moment or two longer.

That was it—that was what I saw that morning, the morning I made it to school on time, the morning I got there just in time for morning devotions, the morning Romey didn't show up at all. My teacher looked at me when he noticed Romey's empty desk, and I shrugged. I knew why he wasn't there, but I don't know why he didn't show up all day, and I wouldn't have asked. There were long silences in the life of Romey Guttner, silences I didn't see so much as mysteries as horrors. Sometimes—just sometimes—he'd talk about them, but not often, so I just assumed the worst.

Romey called our house after school, told me to come over so the two of us could go pick up the carcass on our bikes. I didn't ask him how it was it took all day to clean a .22. I didn't bring up what might have happened.

When I got there, Romey was plain old Romey. It never dawned on him to excuse himself. He never was that regular in attendance anyway. "We got to get that sucker," he said when I rolled up on my bike. "You remembered, didn't you?"

He was talking about the skunk.

We peddled down to the river and cut a sapling from a clump at the base of the bridge, slipped a rope around the skunk's back foot, and carried that fat body strung from the pole hung between our shoulders, a couple of safari hunters, like the picture of the Israelite spies returning from the Land of Canaan, all the goods hung between us.

Romey said he'd never skinned a skunk, and even though the pelt wasn't worth a dime, it would be an experience. Globby layers of fat came off the knife like thick oil, I remember, and the beast skinned out almost like an opossum. We did it under the bridge, only the sound of an occasional car or truck passing over us in a rush breaking the silence. Romey had stuffed his jacket pockets full of twine, so we hung the carcass from a brace. I told him to be careful where he'd poke that skunk when he split the crotch to make the first cuts. He laughed, as if I should be the one to tell him anything at all.

He lifted flaps of fur he'd created by slicing up toward the skunk's paw, then peeled the pelt away, slicing through pink gobs of fat and membrane as the fur fell away from the carcass. "Here," he said, "you want to do it? I got the hard stuff done."

Skinning pelts wasn't my favorite thing to do, but I wasn't about to say no. I took the knife from his hand and kept pulling the pelt down a carcass that surprised me, so much smaller it was than what I'd expected.

"It was just like I said, wasn't it?" he said. He wiped his hands off on the long grass. "Wasn't so bad, really. I mean, he didn't go off or anything—and I didn't think he would. My ma—sometimes she exaggerates."

"He was mad," I told him.

"Naaahhh—"

59

"How do you know?" I said. "You and your old lady were upstairs sipping hot chocolate—"

"He wasn't *mad* mad."

"Then I don't want to see him *mad* mad," I said.

"Just pull it," he said. "You don't even have to use that knife now—just grab and pull it down till you get to his front paws."

I tried to do it, but it didn't work.

"Pull," he said. "Just jerk it, wimp."

Once more, I tried it. I grabbed the whole bloody pelt in my fist and pulled again, but nothing happened.

"I mean pull," he said, and he grabbed it himself and jerked the fur off that animal as if there was nothing at all holding it to the carcass.

I made a mess of the skunk's upper body, slicing the pelt time and time again when I tried to get it from around the face and front paws. But it really didn't matter to Romey—the whole operation was only for experience, and neither of us cared whether it was done perfectly. We weren't about to keep the limp pelt. When it was finally off the animal, the two of us sat on the bank, just beside the river, and held it out in front of us, warming our hands in the long coarse fur inside—skunk fur.

"Nothing gets inside fur like this," he said.

"Bullets did," I told him.

"I mean, nothing like cold or anything." He held that pelt up in front of him like a fat sloppy glove. "Wouldn't you love to have fur like this?"

The skunk was hardly beautiful. Muskrat pelts used to shine in the sun when we'd pick them off the bank from the sets where we'd caught them. Once they'd dried out, they wore a gloss like nothing else I knew, bright and shiny. The sun was gone that afternoon, hidden behind clouds that came up from the lakeshore and put the whole day behind a curtain of gray.

We buried it before we left. The carcass we left hanging like some kind of tribute, but the pelt we buried. Not deep. Romey grabbed a stick and kicked and scratched his way into the light sandbank where we'd been sitting until he got down almost two feet and dropped it in.

We pedaled back east, into the face of a lake wind that by late afternoon was cold and clammy, wet as the skin we'd buried. All the way home Romey talked about that shot he'd made, how perfect it was, how it had taken down that skunk without it even knowing what hit it. "Almost merciful," he said.

The law of the jungle.

When we got back to Romey's place, Cyril was gone. Hattie was in front of the TV doing a crossword puzzle. It was getting dark already, time for me to leave. But she cut some fresh banana bread, which maybe I shouldn't have eaten—just a half hour at most until supper time. But Hattie's sweet breads always were good, especially when they were warm. In the middle of all of that mess at Romey's place, she could make the best sweet bread.

Red-Handed

We found our first pack of cigarettes, wet with dew, at some nondescript spot along the road to the lake, a long way out of town and a quarter mile into the woods that belted the lakeshore, and still do. We spotted it from our bikes one day in the spring of our eighth grade year, then pulled it out of the weedy ditch, from whose maw we'd also thrilled to find a whole range of sinful mementos, from empty fifths and hosts of beer cans, to thumbed-over girlie magazines, cheap novels, and used condoms. My mother often worried about my crossing the busy highway when we'd take our bikes a good mile east to the lake, as if cars were the real danger; but even a first-grader can dodge traffic. I don't know that she ever began to understand what splendid dangers the lake and the woods offered.

That first pack of cigarettes was a stained, red and white pack of L & Ms so heavy with dew it felt like a wet bar of homemade soap when Monty, a mouthy kid who often tagged along with us, spotted it and picked it up. We took the pack to Romey's place and surgically removed the wet silver paper, then laid each weed out carefully on a stack of wainscoting, where the sun could pour through the garage windows and roast the cigarettes light and dry.

The next day, we smoked them—all of them. Romey was by far the most accomplished smoker, having done it before. Monty was there too—he found the pack, after all. He would play a starring role in what was to come, a snippy kid with a personality very much like his snippy mother's.

We tolerated him only reluctantly, Romey a good deal less than the rest of us, for reasons I would discover only later. Mugsy was there too, an angular kid with extraordinarily wide shoulders for such a thin frame. The four of us smoked those L & Ms without inhaling and grew to like the grown-up sense of holding a cigarette between our fingers and flicking ashes away casually. Romey's garage was our favorite place to light up, but sooner or later we were smoking wherever we could find a secret place.

We started stealing cigarettes because we couldn't find them in the ditch whenever we wanted them. Romey bought a couple of packs of Chesterfields three or four times, claiming they were for his old man, but the clerks in the grocery stores knew us well enough not to fall for the same excuse too often. In an emergency, sure; and maybe even more often than that to Romey—after all, everybody knew his father. But not three times a week. It didn't take long and we were out.

The Red Owl store had only one checkout aisle, a broad, Formica-topped counter the width and breadth of a town flag, with a cash register at the close end, where the checker stood making polite conversation while punching in the prices and jerking back the lever to register the sale.

"Nice tomatoes today, Evelyn."

"Aren't they, though?"

Tick, tick—shick—shick.

Just behind the counter stood the candy rack, a buffet of Three Musketeers bars and red licorice, baseball cards, long nickel tubes of Bazooka bubblegum, an artist's palette of Life Savers, and a bottom shelf of penny candy—jawbreakers and sour grape bubblegum cinched in cellophane. Above, a wire dispenser advertising Kools held a couple dozen brands of cigarettes in separate chutes that emptied, one pack at a time, when the clerk grabbed the one from the bottom.

The checker didn't mind kids poking around in the candy, making long and deliberative choices, so stealing cigarettes wasn't tough at all. As long as some customer stood before her checking out her sugar and milk and Wheaties, we could pocket weeds almost at will. Hocking, we called it.

My own children are long past the age I was when we lifted packs of Chesterfields, Lucky Strikes, and Kents in flip-top boxes or soft packs from the grocery store racks, but when I think back on it now, I find it strange that I have no specific recollection of standing there behind the storekeeper and wondering, even for a moment, whether Jesus wanted me to hock a pack. I don't even remember second thoughts. I know it was wrong to steal; I knew it then. But I did it, we all did—again and again and again; and what I remember best is the thrill, the high drama and sheer joy of success in pulling that little red cellophane band off the lip of a freshly heisted flip-top pack of Marlboros.

It was Mugsy's sister Sally who got caught smoking early that June, and when she did, she decided the best course of action would be to spread the stench of her crime over the whole neighborhood and thereby lessen the impact on herself. She claimed she had hardly ever touched a cigarette—which was true—and that if her father wanted to know who smoked a whole lot, he should talk to her brother Mugsy and his friends, who were always out there behind Romey's place smoking. What was worse, she said, was that they were stealing! How else do you think they could get all them cigarettes? Stealing. Going right into the store and lifting them from behind the counter.

I knew I was in trouble the day I found out Mugsy was grounded, or so his mother told me, leaning out of her own back door, her eyes blanched with a firm white disgust that seemed to look a whole lot less like grief than anger. "You should know why, too, Lowell," she said as she shut the door in my face.

So that night, not long after my sister Janine left for her job carhopping at Hurley's, I went to bed early, anxiously, knowing that sometime later Mugsy's old man would cross the alley in the back yard, bearing bad tidings. I lay up in bed that night waiting for the judgment while only half-listening to the Braves game, Warren Spahn pitching in St. Louis. In the darkness, the strip of wallpaper cowboy hats my mother had put up along the ceiling line took on an odd luminous shine from the yellow glow of the radio dial behind my head. I was only a kid, but at that moment I felt a full-blown sense of doom. The guilt I hadn't felt in the store, I felt then, even before my parents knew. I was thirteen years old, and I laid in bed that night wanting to die.

When I heard the doorbell, I sat up and crept on hands and knees to the window above the back door, where the news was being told. What I'd heard through the window screen was hurried and blurred, but when

Red-Handed

the door shut I knew very well what was about to happen, so I went back to bed, shut off the radio, then turned over on my side as if I were sleeping.

Soon enough, the upstairs light snapped on, and my mother and father started up the stairs. Still on my side, I stared at the proud head of the eagle in the middle of the black pennant my aunt had given me years before from an old army boyfriend—101st Airborne. Then I shut my eyes.

"Lowell," my father said, not in a scream.

I didn't move.

"Lowell," he said again, "wake up." Still not yelling, but deeply pitched with authority. Convicted.

"Lowell John," my mother said, louder, angrier.

I raised my arm as if to shield my eyes from the unkindness of light in the hallway behind them, moaned as if it weren't possible for me to talk, inundated as I was with sleep.

My father walked into my bedroom and sat on the hall side of the bed. Even though I didn't try to find her, I could feel my mother behind him and hear her crying. Her hands, I knew, were full of clumped Kleenex.

"You aren't sleeping," my father said. "Don't fake it."

I stretched slowly, half turned.

"Mugsy's father was just here," he said.

I felt obliged to look at him, even though I'd have given anything not to. My father's face, his eyes, seemed indistinguishable, outlined as he was by the hall light behind him, his shoulders square and firm. He was not physically imposing at all, but I knew he could crush me.

"Your mother and I are upset," he said, "deeply upset."

I raised a hand like a visor to my eyes, but stayed down. "What's going on?" I said.

"You know," my mother said. "Don't lie now—not on top of everything else."

My father turned to her, as he always did, then raised a hand between them as if to tell her firmly that this was going to be his job and to remind her not to let herself become more upset. "We want to know everything about this smoking business," he said, turning back to me, "everything, you hear? We want you to tell us. We want the whole story, and we want it now." Then he came up off the bed and stood once more. "Sit up and tell us everything. We want the truth."

I pulled myself up on my forearms, and he grabbed my leg.

"Sit up, I said!"

I pulled my legs beneath me, spread the sheet over my knees.

"Everything," he said, "every last thing you know, exactly as you did it. We want the whole truth," he said. "Not something made up, either. We don't want a story here—not another lie. We want it all, you hear?"

My mother grabbed her breath in quick jerks. I couldn't see her clearly, standing behind my father, backlit, as he was, from the hallway light behind them at the top of the stairs.

My very first impulse was to save my own skin—that's what I remember best. My first urge was to try as rationally as I could to calculate what the two of them must have known, and then say only what I guessed was already well established in their minds. I knew I was dead— we all were—but without even considering alternatives, I knew I couldn't tell them the whole truth. I had to get by as painlessly as I could.

"We found 'em in the ditch," I said. "Mainly nobody likes them or nothing, but we just smoke 'em—just being stupid, I don't know. Everybody does it, Dad. I mean all the guys. I'm not the only one or nothin'."

"Where do you get them?" he said.

I kept my eyes down. I figured he already knew we stole them, but I couldn't say the word *steal*. We'd never used the word ourselves. When we needed more butts, we *hocked* them. But the only way out for me was to work the whole thing over an inch at a time—feel my way along the dark outlines of what they knew, what Mugsy and his sister had already spilled, and then stop there on a dime.

"We found some in the ditch first," I said, "like I told you. You just find them, you know? Every once in a while you find a pack or two— along the road to the lake—"

"You stole them, didn't you?" my mother said. "You actually went into the Red Owl and stole them right out of there, didn't you, Lowell John?"

Immediately, I calculated that they already assumed that the Red Owl was our only source. I was just a kid—almost less than that, a child— but for years that bedroom moment has taught me all I need to know about the tenacity of human will, the instinct to protect oneself at all costs, even if it means lying some more. Even with them accusing me of something for which I was unremittingly guilty, even though right then I could have cried, could have bawled my eyes out, my first priority, it seemed, was to keep them, at all costs, from the whole sordid truth. My first impulse was to lie.

"Lowell John Prins, you stole them right out of the store, didn't you?" she said.

Red-Handed

My throat felt torched. One store—okay. They probably had a line on a few packs, but they had no idea how many. I had the other guys to worry about too—what they'd say or already said, whether our stories would match up, but I knew it wasn't going to be me who told the whole truth and sent the other guys up in flames.

My mother created a litany from questions she answered herself. "Why did you smoke in the first place? You knew it was wrong. What did you think, we wouldn't mind your stealing cigarettes like that? Stealing! Did you ever think they wouldn't care? Of course *you* didn't care or you wouldn't have done it. How could you do it to us? You must think nothing of us whatever. What for? It was all a matter of being something, of looking tough—is that it? When you were at Romey's place puffing away, did you ever ask yourself whether this was something Jesus wanted you to do? And when you stole them? Did you ever think about how really bad it was? You couldn't have."

"We know everything," my father said.

They didn't. I couldn't believe they knew everything.

"I'm not saying another word, Lowell," my father said. "We're not going to say anything until you do—you hear me?" With that he quieted her and forced me to talk.

When I remember that night now, years and years later, I can identify three courses of action I could have taken. First, silence. Some of my friends may have tried that—just take the heat and go on. Or I could have struck back, lashed out, even though I had no defense—admitted it but tried to make them see that what we were up to wasn't burglary in the first degree. Romey might have done that. But neither of those alternatives was possible for me because family was a different thing in our house, way different. I knew I had to talk to them, and I had to be reasonable and penitent. At the same time I had to try to save what skin I could.

"We took some—" I said.

"You *stole* them," my mother said. "Say it, Lowell, you *stole* them—"

"We all did—not just me," I told them. "I wasn't the only one. We all did."

My father took hold of my mother's arm without turning away. "Let him talk," he told her. "I want to hear what he has to say—I want to hear him explain it, Mother."

I started my defense with something of the truth. "It wasn't something I wanted to do," I said. And it wasn't. I didn't even like cigarettes. Not really.

"How many times, Lowell?" my father said. "How many did you steal from Alf Franken's store?"

Twenty maybe, I thought—I didn't know. We didn't put notches down on the two-by-fours in Romey's garage. "Not so many," I said. "We just started smoking—it got to be like a habit or something—"

"How many?" my father said again.

"I don't know," I told him. It felt great to tell the truth.

"You've been lying for months now by not telling us anything, by living in this house and not letting on what you were up to. Tell us the truth now, Lowell," he said. "We won't tolerate any more lies."

"Go on," my mother said through her tears. She turned to my father. "I can't ever trust him again," she said. "I'm sorry. He's destroyed everything. He has, you know—what can we believe? You tell me, what on earth can we believe from our son, anyway? From now on, nothing's believable."

Fear and anger seared every last word rising from her hurt.

"How can I ever look into his face and see the truth?" She brought her hands up to her face, then dropped them quickly. She had more to say. "Something's over," she said. "Something's ended, completely."

It was my mother who broke me, who tore down my ability to stay as quiet as I could. When it came down to it, she was the one who made me talk. "I don't know what got into me," I said. "I knew it, you know— I mean I knew it wasn't right to lift stuff—but I didn't say nothing." At that point I felt tears welling up in me because I felt terrible—I did. I felt awful for my parents. I'd never seen them broken, and here I was calculating what I could tell them, trying to stem my losses. I'd let them down big time, but when I cried—and I did—those tears were more than half real. My mother was right—I knew it. Something was broken between us, something would never be the same. I'd never again be their little boy.

My father changed directions. Something quelled and he found a lower register in which to speak, a tone I recognized immediately as something more focused. "I need to know exactly how many you stole," he said, as if without passion. "I need to know that, Lowell. You have to tell me the truth."

Twenty, thirty, forty? I had no idea. "Ten," I said. "I don't know."

"In all?" he said.

I wondered what Mugsy had said—and Monty. "Maybe twelve, I don't know," I said, shrugging my shoulders. "Maybe fifteen."

"Maybe a hundred," my mother said.

"No—" I said, angrily.

Red-Handed

"Fifteen," my father said, as if a deal had been settled. And I knew it had been. He was looking for a way out here—and I know why, even though I didn't then. He was protecting my mother. He wanted out for her sake. There were two crimes here—both mine: I'd stolen cigarettes and I'd hurt the woman he loved. It took me years to understand that, my own share of problems with our kids, but when I remember how quickly we settled up, how he ushered her out of that room, I recognize his impulse to stanch her hurt, even for his own sake. He needed to get her through this.

"Fifteen—okay," he said. "You're going to write down every one of them," he told me. "Every last one, you hear me?"

We settled on fifteen, my breath coming with an ease I hadn't felt since the light was slapped on just minutes before. Fifteen packs. It probably wasn't accurate, a low estimate, but then I didn't really know the number myself. I couldn't do what my father demanded even if I wanted to—list them by day and hour and brand. I remember thinking at that moment something I'd never realized before: my father didn't understand. He didn't know how bad his boy really was. He really couldn't plumb the depth of his son's sin, because that depth wasn't in him. No single moment of my childhood so deeply affected my own self-perception as that one, the moment I realized—and I know this is strange language, but it's the language I would have used when I was a kid—the moment I realized my father was a far better Christian than I would ever be.

Both of them were ready to end it—they were ready to go on, even though the whole truth wasn't anywhere near to being out. I knew it, and I felt a weight in me such as I'd not felt before—this odd feeling that just now, with the success of the lie, I'd done something even more horrible than stealing, something so dark and secretive, so deceptive that even my father—by all accounts a saint—was incapable of seeing and understanding. In effect, that lost bayonet finally disappeared altogether.

My mother couldn't stop crying. Quietly and lovingly, my father told her to leave. What had to be done yet, he said, could better be done between himself and me.

"You talk to him, Peter," she said before she left. I heard her move away through the open doorway. Her steps moved toward the top of the stairway. "I can't be in this room anymore." The handrail stuttered as she made her way down.

My father let the silence go on for quite a while. He sat on the corner of the bed, his elbows on his knees, his face in his hands.

"I'm sorry," I told him.

He didn't look at me. He didn't cry. I'm not sure exactly what he felt—it wasn't anger, I don't think. I found out later that Romey's dad wasn't angry. He thought the whole thing hardly worth the bother. Monty's dad was incensed. He got beat, he said. But in my life I don't remember my father hitting me more than once or twice. Most of my buddies got belted that night, I'm sure. I didn't. My father laid his disappointment on me, the worst punishment I could have suffered, exactly what I'd tried to avoid by not going downstairs in late fall the year before to tell him the story of the lost bayonet.

He rose from the bed and walked to the other side of the room, away from the hallway and toward the circular window he'd set like a porthole in the south wall when he'd built the house with his own hands. He took hold of the little knob at the bottom and turned it as if it were a ship's wheel, back and forth, open and shut. The glow from the hallway light stretched up over his shirt and the back of his head as he stood, hands up on the wall, in silence, leaning down to stare through the window.

"Dad?" I said, and he turned and for the first time looked at me from that side of the bed, the light from the hallway thrown over a face as pallid and gray as anything I'd ever seen. He looked to me as if the life had gone out of him. "It hurts me here," he said, "in my soul."

I wanted to cry. I wanted to.

"Not in my heart, because in my heart I can forgive you—I have to, and I can." He brought his lips up tight under his nose. "You're just a kid," he said. "There are a dozen or more chapters to your life, and I know in my mind that this whole thing doesn't mean all that much—if you want to change—"

"I do," I said. "I don't ever want to see a cigarette—"

"Don't be foolish," he said. "You've got years ahead of you." He nodded. "What you did put a hole in my soul." He brought up his hands in front of him, palm to palm. "You know so much better. You know what's right and wrong. You know it. You can't excuse yourself—"

"I can't," I said.

"Do you understand what sin is?" he said.

I was thirteen years old, and I knew.

"It's much bigger than you are—much bigger," he said. "When you even want to do right," he told me, "you can't." And then he looked straight at me. "When you grabbed those packs of cigarettes," he said, "didn't it hurt just a little bit?"

"Sure," I said.

"Did you feel anything at all?"

Red-Handed

"Course," I said. "It's just—" and then tears came, for real the first time, because I couldn't talk to him without lying. There was nothing I could say that would come out the truth. And I don't think—to this day I don't think—he ever understood that.

"Tell me what you felt," he said.

"Rotten," I told him, "just like I do now. Just rotten. I'm so sorry." That wasn't a lie, of course. I was sorry. I honestly believed, that night, at that time, that I'd never do it again—that I'd never do a thing wrong again. I was just a kid.

"I'm sorry," I told him again. But I knew even then that it was about the easiest thing to say.

"Are you?" he said. "Really, are you?"

"Yes," I said, and it came with a lot of tears.

"You ask the Lord to forgive you," he said, very clearly. "You hear me, Lowell? I'm going to sit here with you and listen to your prayer like I used to when you were a little boy, see—and you're going to ask the Lord right now to forgive you."

I was raised in a house of prayer. I understood what penitence was necessary, but it was in me, too. I knew how to pray—the words; and the emotion was there. I was sitting on the bed, my legs crossed, and I leaned over onto my arms, and for the first time, my father touched me. He wiped my tears with the back of his hand. "Now pray," he said, "and remember you're talking to God Almighty and not just your father."

"Dear Jesus," I said, and when I remember that prayer now, even though the words aren't perfectly situated in my mind, I know that never before in my life did I talk to God with as firm a conviction that there was no ceiling in that room, no doused light above my bed, no strip of cowboy hats. This time the Jesus I'd seen a million times on Sunday school posters, his hands folded, a white radiance beaming behind his head, was actually there, and I was talking to him.

"Please forgive me for all the stuff I did," I said. "I'm sorry for smoking and everything, and stealing. Please forgive me for everything. I shouldn't have done it—none of it," I said. "I know I shouldn't have done it, but I couldn't help myself, and I need you to keep me from sinning some more like that."

The words didn't come out right, exactly.

"I been doing things wrong," I said, "way wrong, and I know it. Please forgive me, Jesus—please."

My father pulled his hand away and stood beside my bed, then backed up to the wall, crossed his arms over his chest, and stood there for a moment watching me. He was not a tall man, and his shoulders were not particularly broad. Already at forty, his hair was thin. His hands were soft and white from keeping books at a company that made ice cream. But when I remember him standing there, the face I saw through my own tears was as strong as granite, as strong as anything I'd ever known.

"You let me down—you let both of us down," he said. "You let everyone down. You let your grandparents down, Lowell—you let everybody who believes in you down, you understand that? You let the Lord down."

"I know it," I said.

"It's like Humpty Dumpty—you can't just put it back together again," he said. He seemed miles away. "It's never going to be the same—your mother's right." He put a hand up to his face, removed his glasses, then rubbed his eyes. "You knew it was wrong—my goodness, Lowell, it's stealing."

"I'm sorry," I said.

"There are things God can do that I can't, you know—and your mother, either." All of it came slowly now. Hours seemed to pass between words. "God can forgive, just like that," he said, snapping his fingers. "I wish I could."

He walked around the bed and stood once more with the light from the hall behind him. "I can't make the hurt go away," he said. "You're going to have to live with what you did—you better know that. It's like you slashed us with a sword, you know—that's what your mother and I feel like. And now you're going to have to live with it yourself. I'm sorry too, Lowell." He took a huge breath. "You're the one who ought to be sorriest here, and you say you are, but I'm really the one who's sorry—I'm so sorry all this happened. I really am." And then he walked away.

I didn't want him to leave, but I didn't want him to stay, either. I wanted him to love me, and I wished I'd never stolen a pack of cigarettes in my life. I wished Monty'd never found that pack along the road. When he picked up that first one, half brown with stains from being wet, I wished I'd told him I didn't care for a smoke because it didn't seem like much of a good thing to do anyway, even if it wasn't wrong. It tasted bad and kept your mouth dry and rotten for most of the afternoon. I wished I'd done so much better.

When he got to the bottom of the stairs, the light went out and my room turned dark as night, only the pale shafts of a half-moon coming through the circular window and lying over the sheets in long ivory bars.

At that very moment, the moment he left the room, I was most like the boy my father thought I should be, most committed never to sin again, never to stray. I was at that moment more of a child of his righteousness than I would ever be in my life.

Today I am the husband of one wife, the father of three grown children, all of them doing reasonably well, all of them believers. I've never robbed a bank or had a torrid affair or killed a man over a thousand acres of good farmland. In that way, I suppose, I'm no better subject for a story than my father is.

It's possible I may be more my father's child than I think. At the moment he left my bedroom that night, I felt a sense of righteousness that I hadn't felt since I was a little boy. But when that awful night comes back to me now, so many years later, it's not my righteousness that I remember. What I can't forget is looking at him and knowing almost the opposite about myself—knowing full well I would never be what he is. It was terrifying in a way, but exhilarating, too.

He never hit me that night. He didn't have to. He'd done what he'd wanted to do, done it so well that the two of us never spoke of that night again. Never.

Confession

I spread white paint over one four-inch slat after another on the picket fence that ran along the alley behind the house, dabbing it thickly into the corners of the two-by-four crosspieces, all the while listening to baseballs cracking off bats on the schoolyard diamond a block east, where kids played all day long, kids I would have been with if I hadn't been sentenced to a thick old brush. All the while, the sun shone perfectly.

Painting the picket fence was well chosen as a punishment, painfully boring, but a test. Every night, my father would come out and look over my work, bending over to make sure every last slat was covered and there were no drips. If he said nothing, I figured I'd done well. My performance was proof of the depth of my contrition and a measure of the state of my soul.

It was mid-June, and on the nights my father was at home, the three of us would listen to ball games on the radio, rarely talking, my mom mending socks or doing something from the bag in the bottom of the closet in the vestibule to keep her hands busy while keeping an eye on me and an ear to the Braves game. I'd keep score on nine-inning grids my father drew up on his factory's business stationery with one of a dozen mechanical pencils from the junk drawer, pencils that said Dairyland Ice Cream. I'd scratch in the pop-ups and the hits and the groundouts in a method I learned much later was my father's own.

For those two weeks, I fell back into the soft arms of a childhood I'd already left, even though the three of us rarely spoke to each other—things were simply too brittle. Janine worked most nights. Even today I'm not sure how much of this she knows. For two weeks, painting the picket fence was my daytime punishment; two weeks together in the living room was the sentence they exacted for my nights. I was grounded, the whole of the punishment intended to rehabilitate me and repair what had been broken. In a childish way—in a fashion that brought them some peace—it worked. Thank the Lord for Milwaukee Braves baseball.

My own son would not understand what happened next, because the world I lived in seems altogether different than the world today, a world in which the church we belonged to had far more authority than it has today. But my father knows; what's more, he remembers a church far more authoritative and vigorous than the one I remember as a child.

Because the church ran more like a government than a crusade back then, the preacher of our little congregation had to find out what happened, had to be told. The whole affair was something less than grand larceny, of course, but dozens of packs had been lifted; and if the truth were known, it wasn't only cigarettes, either. Here and there a lighter, a spool of fishing line, .22 shells, even a fishing reel, I remember. That time when Mugsy grabbed the spinning reel was one of the few moments when I honestly wondered where this might all end. Had the loot ever been fully assembled, we might have been thrown into the hands of the law and declared delinquents. But as I was to discover one night at church, much of the whole story never got out.

We weren't old enough to be fully professing members of the church, and each of us, when confronted by our parents, had confessed. But the church stood in the middle of a small, closely knit village that rather quickly discovered what had happened. We missed a couple of weeks of Pony League baseball, for instance—our absence made our sin public. What we'd done was only a childhood sin, but it was a public sin; and in Easton in the late fifties, public sin meant the involvement of the church.

The three of us who went to our church, and our fathers, met with the preacher on a Friday night two weeks after we'd been caught. I remember absolutely nothing about how that meeting was called—whether it was my father who asked the preacher to be involved or the preacher who wanted to do his job. All I know is that my father never questioned our participating. I know Cyril did, but Cyril had more questions, bigger questions—but then he never lacked for answers, either.

It was my father and I, Romey and Cyril, and Monty and his dad, a man nicknamed Zoot, who, like his son, was thin but muscular and always nervous, constantly squinting as if caught in the glare of the sun. His real name was Baastian, or something Dutch.

It would be interesting to know whether my father was afraid the moment he saw Cyril Guttner. I wasn't old enough to think through the unlikely presence of Romey's father, who rarely came to church at all. It seemed to me then that since the other fathers were involved, Cyril had to be—it was a father and son thing. Someone told Cyril his attendance was required—Reverend Kosters maybe, maybe Hattie. But no one ever forced Cyril to do anything that I remember, and when that night comes back to me now, I can't help but think my father must have felt shaky when he heard Guttner's old pickup come up the street. He must have been there willingly; he wasn't a man who suffered reproof easily. He had to have his own agenda.

And what about Reverend Kosters, who was young, just out of seminary? I can't imagine that any seminary class ever prepared him fully for the likes of Cyril Guttner. That night he must have been stupified to see the man come up the walk.

Kosters was a sweet man who had a way of tightening his lips as if to savor what he'd said when he thought it profound. He wore his thick blonde hair in a crew cut that peaked perfectly at the center of his forehead, over steel-rimmed glasses with lenses so thick they distorted the sides of his face. He was likeable for a preacher, someone almost always looking out for your welfare, and therefore always patronizing, a man whose constant smile was meant to show the world that he was particularly sure God loved him and just about everyone else.

We were even somewhat proud of him. The church down the block had a little mustachioed guy who swung his arms so high on his daily walk to the post office that we were sure Adolf Hitler had made it out of the bunker alive following the fall of Berlin and had surreptitiously made his way to Easton. He had his eyes so firmly on the Lord that he would never even see us up on Mugsy's front porch. Kids from his church said that when he preached he'd yell so loud they'd sometimes have to cover their ears.

Confession

Kosters never yelled that I remember. I have no idea if he was profound from the pulpit; back then, I simply figured sermons were for old
people. But he seemed to care about kids, and he seemed closer to our
age than to our parents'. In many ways he was a boy himself, and when
I think about it now, that fact must have been something of a problem
for my father, who likely didn't appreciate looking to a preacher that
youthful and inexperienced, even if he was ordained.

"Well," Kosters said, once we'd all found seats in the council room,
"I guess we've got something of a problem here, don't we?" He pulled
his lips up tight into a short smile meant to give the impression that what
he'd said was perfectly fitting.

We sat around the long, glass-covered table: the preacher at the head,
my father and I and Monty and his dad on one side, Romey and Cyril
across from us, three empty chairs between them and the preacher.

I don't think Kosters thought of what had happened as being as bad
as my father considered it, certainly not as grave as my mother did.
Whenever he spoke, he joked around, trying to make us feel less in-
timidated maybe, less guilty. He wore a habitual smile, as if to suggest
that whatever words came from someone who confessed the name of
Christ had to be tied up sweetly with happy ribbons. Romey never liked
the guy—never trusted him, he used to say.

I hadn't seen Romey since the whole mess broke. When he'd walked
in the room a little earlier, he glanced at me and shrugged his shoulders
as if to say the whole mess was no big deal. When he took a chair, he
slumped, put his leg up against the edge of the table. But he didn't look
belligerent, either. I don't think my father or the preacher would have
read his look as being hostile, but then as long as I knew him Romey
was never really hostile to anyone, except his father. His slouch and his
half smile made it obvious to me that he hadn't felt the ceiling disap-
pear as I had when I prayed that night in my bedroom.

"So," the preacher said, "who is it wants to start here? Which one of
you guys is going to tell the story?"

The minute my father told me we were going to church, I had guessed
it would be another confession time, but I didn't want to start talking or
even look up at the preacher, because I had to negotiate my way through
a new dilemma; I needed a different voice now because Romey was
across the table. I was not afraid of Romey, but the chemistry was different with him around. Kosters was the preacher, but I wasn't worried
about him all that much. I knew that what I was going to say would be
judged by two important people simultaneously—my father and Romey
Guttner—and that made talking about what had happened much more

Confession

of a problem. In a simple shrug of the shoulders, Romey had already indicated he thought the whole mess was overblown: a couple of packs of smokes? Big deal. I knew, in church, I wasn't about to cry again.

Kosters waited for someone to tell the story.

"Those guys found some cigarettes," Monty said. "They're the ones who started to smoke." He was already on the brink of tears.

We weren't off to a great start. I wasn't surprised that Monty was the first kid to talk, nor was I shocked that he'd blame Romey and me—I could have guessed that before we'd even come in.

"You see it all the time, don't you?" Kosters said. "It's hard to find a dad around who doesn't smoke, right? But what about the stealing?" I didn't watch his face, but I'm sure he looked at Romey and me. "Whose idea was it to start stealing?"

Neither did it surprise me that Romey would speak up. "It wasn't nobody's idea," he said. "I mean, it wasn't one of us guys who just said, 'Let's go hock some butts,' you know? Nothing like that ever happened." Romey put a hand up to his mouth and actually yawned. "It wasn't like some big-time gangsters planned it out. Nobody made nobody else do it—not like we had a gun on 'em or something—we just needed butts."

"How long?" Kosters said. "Has this been going on for years already?" He looked at Monty.

"Them guys were smoking last summer already," Monty said, almost crying.

"Is that true, Lowell?" Kosters said.

I didn't want to talk. Oddly enough, at least at first, Cyril Guttner didn't figure into the energy field I felt glowing around that table. My father was beside me, Romey across the table. "Not until a couple months ago, and that's what happened—what Romey says."

Kosters drew a breath like an old man. "I want you all to look at me now because I want to see your eyes," he said. "The eyes are the mirror of the soul, the Bible says." He waited. "Lowell," he said. I was the only one who found it tough.

He twisted his lips into a gentle smile as he thumbed absentmindedly through the gold-leaf edges of the Bible in front of him. "I don't need to know so much about who and when and how many because I'm sure your dads have been all through that. What I think we should talk about is what you think about all of it now, now that it's all behind you. Anybody have something to say?"

"Monty's been bawling his eyes out," Zoot said, rubbing his fingers constantly. "We've forgiven him already, and we're a long way healed up. It's behind us," he said. "It's all over already." Monty was crying loud

Confession

enough to make me wonder whether some tears were going to be required here again.

"I want to hear the boys, Baas," the preacher said, and he looked back at Romey. "What do you think about what happened?"

Pressed beneath the glass of that table was a church bulletin cover that showed my father's name atop the list of elders.

"I know you think it was wrong—but what's going on in your mind, Romey?" Kosters said.

I had no idea what Romey would say, absolutely no idea. Pictures of three missionary families stared up at me from beside that bulletin cover.

"I'm not doing it again—never," Monty said. "Me and my dad talked about it for a long time, and I'm not."

"Good," Kosters said. "Lowell?"

I kept my eyes down.

"Please, look at me," Kosters said.

So I did. "I'm not going to do it again," I said, straight on, almost more specifically to Romey than to anybody else in that room. But I meant it.

"Good," the preacher said. "Romey?"

For the first time that night I looked at Cyril, who sat across the table looking as if this whole thing were a circus. He was chewing gum, maybe tobacco, a glint in his eyes, a pack of Chesterfields shining through his shirt pocket.

"I ain't doing it again either," Romey said, matter of factly.

Kosters nodded, waited, then said, "I'm happy to hear you say that— and I believe you."

And then, for no good reason at all, Monty simply lost it. His eyes zigzagged and his cheeks trembled through pounding breaths that barely made it through a series of deep swallows that started up from way inside. I thought he was going to be sick. Romey looked at me and rolled his eyes; we both had this awful sense that it was a performance.

"He's been so sorry," Zoot said, one finger hoisting his glasses up on his nose. "I know he won't do it again—I know that for sure, Reverend. Stealing's something he's been taught is flat wrong." He hauled his red handkerchief out of his pocket and stuck it in his son's hand. "We talked about it for hours already. He's got it straight. He's got it all straight."

Kosters put both arms out on the table in front of him and told Monty he didn't have to be so sad if it was all behind him. "All of you," he said, "it sounds like all of you have been through this already—"

That's when Cyril spoke for the first time. "Me and the boy got it straight," he said. "I told him he couldn't just haul off and take other people's junk that wasn't his—it's stealing and he ain't no common thief.

He may be other things," he said, it was an attempt at humor, "but a thief he ain't."

"It's a good thing—" Kosters said.

"I told him if he wants to smoke so bad to let me buy 'em, for cripes sake," Cyril said. "I was smoking at his age—long before."

Kosters looked at my father, as if the two of them shared something. "Honesty certainly is a virtue," he said, nodding. Then, quickly, he looked away. "Somebody else have something to say?" At that moment I was old enough to understand that Kosters, not surprisingly, and despite his office and the vested authority of the church, was afraid of Cyril Guttner.

My father leaned over the table and folded his hands out in front of him. "It's been a long couple of weeks at our place," he said. "This has all been a trial for us, and a lesson, I suppose." His eyes were squarely on Kosters when he spoke. "I wouldn't want to go through it again—I know that much."

"I take it you wouldn't either, Lowell," the preacher said.

I shook my head.

And then Kosters let everything sit for a moment, as if he'd come to the idea that maybe if he'd fish the deep water he'd hook something he hadn't expected to. I'm not sure what he was waiting for. Nobody said anything at all. Monty's sniffling was enough to make me nauseous. Kosters just sat there, one finger up to his nose. I wasn't about to say anything, and I was sure Romey had said just about everything he had on his mind. But still, the preacher waited, nodding his head as if he were hearing some secret message nobody else was. I was looking up at the wall where a picture of my grandfather hung. He used to preach at the church my family had always attended.

"I got things to do," Cyril said finally. "How much longer we got to sit here?"

Kosters kept smiling, as if his own righteousness wouldn't be thwarted. "We all have things to do, Cyril," he said, and he dropped the Bible open and turned the thin pages with the tips of his wetted fingers. "I want to read a passage or two—it's going to take just a minute or so more." He looked up at Cyril as if to get his permission.

"I got more to say," Zoot said. "Our Monty's been forgiven and all that, and we're sorry for what he's done too, believe me. Me and Dorothy—we cried our eyes out about this whole mess. I never seen the wife carry on the way she did." He shook his head. "We're so sorry because we never thought our boy was capable of that kind of thing. Not the way he was raised—"

Confession

"He's not the first in the world—" Kosters said.

"Maybe not," Zoot said. He was building steam. "It's stealing, Reverend," he said. "It's stealing all the same, and we all know the sixth commandment."

"Eighth," Romey said.

"Eighth, then," Zoot said, angrily. He pulled his chair up closer to the table, as if he were about to feast. Then he ducked his shoulders, gestured clumsily Cyril's way, and looked up, almost from a crouch, at the preacher at the head of the table. "We were wondering—Dorothy and I. We thought we'd ask what you think of this idea, see. I mean, it seems clear to us that these boys together are adding up to trouble—I mean, here they are, not even in high school, and we're talking stealing. It's like basic math—put these kids together and you know how it's going to come out—that's what I'm saying."

Kosters seemed puzzled.

"I'm not saying anything about anybody here except that maybe part of what we're up against is in the chemistry, see—it's in the three of 'em or four or whatever. It's the combination. It's the mix." Zoot pulled his fingers nervously, as if to crack his knuckles, then raised his hand like a traffic cop. "I'm not making judgments here. Don't get me wrong. Monty's as much to blame as anybody—he took that pack of cigarettes too, just like any of 'em did. But we're wondering about the gang, you know, the *gang*."

"I don't know that you can really choose—"

"Well, you can, Reverend. Me and Dorothy, we got it thought out a little. We got a proposal." Zoot was armed and dangerous. I was more afraid of Cyril Guttner than any human being on the face of the earth, but when Zoot kept at it, kept spilling stuff in a tone that was dedicated and angry, I got scared.

"He don't want his kid playing with mine," Cyril said and sat back almost casually. "It's plain he don't want his precious little boy with Romey here."

"Now hold on," Zoot said. "I'm not saying—"

"I know you're not saying that," Cyril said, "that's not the words, but it's what you mean." And then he looked straight at the preacher, as if he was about to talk truth for the first time all night. "Ever since I moved to this place I had to learn to translate what people say because they never say what they think." He pointed directly at Zoot. "I know what he's saying, padre—he's saying he and his missus think Romey's to fault for everything. They think Romey's poison. That's what he's saying, and if it wouldn't'a been for him, their kid'd been home sniffin' his ma's skirt."

"Don't put words in my mouth," Zoot said.

"I ain't putting nothing in your mouth that wasn't in your head," he said, "and I dare you to say it wasn't." Cyril put both elbows up on the clear glass, as if he were ready for this, happy it finally emerged. "I'm saying that what you're talking about here is bull. Romey ain't totally to blame."

I was stunned by Cyril Guttner's cussing in church, right in front of my father, right there beneath the Christian flag, the Bible still opened in front of the preacher to a scramble of notes scribbled in the text.

"What's your problem, Mr. Guttner?" Kosters said. "What do you have on your mind here?"

"My mind's full of goodies," he said, laughing. He leaned back and put his hands behind his head, and right then I understood why Cyril showed up that night, even though he had likely never been in the council room of that church before in his life and he probably didn't give a rip about his son's stealing cigarettes. "There's nothing behind what I'm saying here but what I said in the first place, and what I know—and that is this: that guy," he pointed at Zoot, "don't want his sweetie hanging around with my boy because he's scared Romey's handing out germs that come from his old man—ain't it so, Zoot? Ain't that exactly what you're getting at here? Tell me it ain't true," he said, still pointing. "There's more to what's in him, preacher," he said. "You don't know the half of it. None of you Christians ever know the half of anything."

Monty's sobbing rose like a tide.

Zoot kept his eyes on Kosters as if to keep himself in line.

"Is that what you want?" the preacher asked Zoot. "Is he right? You think maybe your Monty ought to stay away from Romey?"

Romey sat there with his leg up, his knee locked in front of him against the council table, all the time shoving his cuticles back with a dime he'd pulled from his pocket. What I remember seeing every time I dared look up to check his face is how much he looked like his father—same bland boredom on his face, as if all of this was the next thing to a joke. Zoot's face was red like cinnamon, his eyes tight in vehemence, his son bawling like the child he so often was.

"Okay," Zoot said. "Okay, me and Dorothy were wondering if maybe the boys shouldn't be kept apart a while—it might be better for all of them."

Kosters sat back in his chair, then slid the Bible off the table in front of him and into his lap. He tried to stay as tough as Cyril while holding that gracious Christian smile.

"I'm saying we shouldn't be playing with fire," Zoot said. "If the woods are burning when they're together, then we best keep 'em apart—that's the whole of it."

Confession

"You're the one playing with fire—scab!" Cyril yelled.

That's when everything blew up.

"He said it, Reverend," Zoot said. "You heard him. I didn't say a word about the strike—not one thing. He's the one brought it up. This don't have diddly to do with what happens at the plant." He brought his fist down on the glass. "We're telling Monty to stay the heck away from your kid, Cyril—"

"Good riddance," Cyril said.

My father was afraid—I could see it on his face. What Cyril had brought up was much more explosive than our stealing, and it was something, back then, I understood so little of—the world of work and plants and unions and management. I was a kid—we all were—and I don't think at that time and in that place I was even aware of the fact that two of the guys I hung around with had fathers who stood in direct opposition to each other. I know Romey had said it, time and time again, how much he hated strikebreakers, but I don't think I knew that Zoot, Monty's father, was one of them.

"That kid's out of control," Zoot said, pointing at Romey, who shrugged. "His old man is gone all the time because he's making life miserable for people who need jobs—"

"*You* should talk," Cyril snapped. Then he looked at my father. "Tell the scab to shut up before I do it myself."

"Listen," the preacher said, "before this goes any further, we ought to send the boys outside."

Cyril folded his arms over his chest. "I say what I want in front of my kid," he said, as if on a dare. "I don't hide nothing from him—that's the way I was raised."

My father signaled with his eyes and a tip of the head. I knew he wanted me out, and I had no desire to stay. I pushed my chair back from the table.

"I think we're all better off if the fathers talk something out here," Kosters said.

"Stay here," Cyril told him when Romey got up.

"I got my own problems," Romey said, and we left, the two of us, Monty following along, still rubbing at his eyes and cheeks.

I was glad to get away, afraid of what we'd left behind.

Outside, the evening air was thick with lake humidity and the sharp smell of cut grass. The sun had already set, the sky above the trees west of church still glowing in a cloudless afterburn.

Monty came out behind us and sat on the front steps, all in a shambles, sat there with his head in his arms without a thing to say. Romey wandered over to the parking lot and picked up stones, and I stood there for a moment between them, Monty still lurching around for breath after all that crying, Romey chucking stones as if what we'd just sat through was business as usual.

That was my choice, and it was no choice. Monty's brokenness or Romey's strength. I headed for the parking lot.

"My old man says Monty is just like his dad anyway," Romey said. "My old man says he's a twink—Zoot is." He was winging stones over the empty parking lot, throwing them up one after another to try to get four in the air at a time, a game we played on the beach. "Think I give a hang about that baby?" he said, pointing at the lump on the front steps.

I picked up a handful myself and took aim at the charred burning barrel near the spot where Romey's stones fell. There wasn't a thing to say about what had gone on or what was still going on inside the church. I just wanted it all over. "Won't be long and we'll be bean-picking," I told Romey. "We're gettin' out of town."

Romey reached down for another handful of stones, then picked up a flat one out of the bunch, thin and round as a half-dollar, and wrapped his finger around it to make it spin. "What I could use is a cigarette," he said. "I'm having a nicotine fit," he told me, cutting loose with a laugh.

Once in a while we'd score on the barrel, but neither of us said much. All I knew was that it was a whole lot better standing in the gravel parking lot chucking stones here and there and everywhere than it would have been half dead on the steps of the north door of the church, all bleary-eyed and choked up with tears.

I had no idea what Romey thought of his old man just then, but I still couldn't believe what Cyril had said right there in front of the preacher and my father. "You hear what your old man said?" I asked.

Romey kept on throwing. "About scab?" he said.

"That word, right to the preacher?" I asked.

Then he laughed. "I can't wait to tell my ma," he said. "She won't believe it either—then again, maybe she will."

You could never guess what he'd say—when he'd laugh and when he wouldn't. Life with Romey was always an adventure.

The Reverend Kosters' voice came up from behind us, and when we turned to the back door of the church, all the fathers were standing there, Monty still on the step. Kosters circled all six of us up for a final prayer beneath the yellow insect light above the back door. He put his hand on Monty's head, ruffled through his crew cut. I stood beside my father,

Confession

and Cyril pulled out a cigarette, facing the street, and smoked right through the prayer.

"Braves are playing in Philadelphia, aren't they?" Kosters said when he finished. He said it loud enough for Cyril to nod when he heard it. "When we get home, we can still pick up the last couple of innings."

We had walked to church that night, my father and I—we lived a few blocks away. But Cyril had taken the truck, as had Zoot and Monty, even though they too lived close to church. They had parked on opposite sides of the street behind the church, but before Zoot drove off, Cyril pulled up next to him and yelled something my father and I understood, even though we couldn't hear the words clearly, covered as they were by the banging of his old tailpipe. Then Cyril pounded the gas to the floor like a kid, the old Chevy blowing a cloud of smoke.

Our walk home wasn't all that long, but I don't remember my father saying a thing to me, even though we'd both heard and seen more than either of us had guessed we would. I don't think it was my sin—my stealing cigarettes—that prompted his silence on that walk home. In a way, that was already behind us. He knew very well bigger things were coming, events he feared much more than his son's iniquities.

He was trying to protect me, I believe, from what he feared; by his moral estimate that was the right thing to do because to him I was a child and he was anxious to allow me to live a bit longer in the innocence childhood affords. What he didn't know was that what pushed him into silence that night was what I was learning on my own.

And thus, prudent silence passed from one generation to the next in our Christian family, my father protective of my innocence, and his son shielding his guilt.

But there was much more to come that summer, much of it pushed along by the inevitability of a clash between two men—Zoot, a man who seemed a jumble of nerves, fidgety as a blue jay, protective of and even paranoid about his darling Monty; and Cyril, a head shorter than Zoot, wiry but fearless as broken glass. And there was the strike, about which I knew very little at the time. I was about to learn much more.

Home Visit

My parents never questioned my going back to Romey's place. Once my picket-fence penance was over, they never said a word to me about Romey or Cyril, never bad-mouthed them or even mentioned a warning; but on those final evenings of June, when the lake breeze had come up from the east and pushed the summer heat farther inland, I can't help but believe that the moment the screen door slapped shut behind me, they fell into silent and individual prayer.

Why did I go back? I suppose someone more deeply affected by what had happened would have simply decided never again to return to Romey's place. After all, there was some logic to what Zoot had said in church—things would have been different for all of us if the combination of kids wasn't what it was.

It is difficult with the passing of so many years to judge my own state of mind at the time—I was only a boy. At church it was Zoot who had proposed the breakup of our little gang, an end to bad chemistry. The gang was the chief sinner according to him, but my father understood that building a wall around his son would not fence out iniquity. Their restricting me from going back to Romey was anti-thetical to their character, even if they believed Romey was the vital cause of their son's smoking and stealing and lying—all of my problems. I believe—I really do, despite what happened—that they did the right thing in giving me my freedom.

Romey's place stood a half-dozen houses from the south edge of town, maybe a quarter of a mile from the road we'd bike to the lake. One afternoon after swimming, we stopped over there to change, to fly up the stairs to his room and peel back suits that had, on the short bike ride home, already dried.

The girls were out back in the sandbox. I remember seeing no truck in the driveway. I had likely determined that Cyril wasn't home and it was safe for me to enter. I don't remember seeing Hattie when we came in. When we hurtled back down the stairs fully dressed, she was holding herself up, both hands down on the dining room table.

It was late afternoon, but she was wearing something like a bedroom smock. That wasn't unusual. Her thick hair was tousled; she looked a mess, but she often did. She pointed at the floor as if to take our eyes off of her. "Pick up those wet towels there," she growled. "Hang them downstairs by the washer."

"You got a problem?" Romey said, but she never heard him. Even I knew that whatever silent ordeal she was going through had something to do with Cyril. "What'd he do now?" he said. He was blocking my path through the house, or I would have run off.

Then the phone rang. Hattie walked to the kitchen, where the phone was parked up on the counter by the toaster. Romey walked into the dining room behind her.

I didn't want to be there, but I had this sense that I'd be a coward if I took off—and I had no great excuses. We were planning on getting a Coke downtown.

She picked the phone up quickly and barely said hello. "I know," she said, five times at least, in a very soft voice. "I know . . . I know . . . I know . . . I know . . . I know." That was all, not even good-bye. Behind her the radio news blared from the Zenith beside the sink.

"Ma," Romey said, "will you open your mouth, for Pete's sake?"

She slumped into a kitchen chair, her eyes darting back and forth.

"What's he done?" he said, but this time it was soft, even endearing, more caring than he usually was. Neither of them seemed conscious of my presence. "Ma," he said again, "tell me what he's up to."

"Everybody's calling," she said.

"Who's everybody? Talk sense, Ma—geez!"

She sat at the table, her forearms on the top, her hands shaking as if she'd just come in from the cold. "Sometimes they don't even say their names," she said. "Sometimes they just cuss." There were tears.

"Who?" Romey said.

"Maybe I ought to take it off the hook," she said. "I don't feel like anybody and everybody telling me anymore, because I know the whole thing—it's only been maybe six calls. Good night, don't they think I know already—"

"Who, Ma?"

"At Zoot's," she told him. "It's a home visit."

"He's there?" Romey said.

"I don't know," she told him. "I haven't seen him since Saturday. I'm only married to the guy—what do I know?"

"People see him?" Romey said. "Did people say he was there, Ma?" She shrugged her shoulders.

He sat down on a chair beside her and tugged his socks on. "I'm going," he said. "We got to get him, Ma," he told her. "You know as well as I do—we got to get him."

"I don't even know if he's there," she said.

"Doesn't make any difference," Romey said, turning back to the dining room. "Get your shoes on," he told his mother.

That's when I took off. I went out the back door, and I don't think either of them ever saw me leave. I picked my bike out of the grass, pedaled off as fast as I could, my wet towel in a roll under my arm. Zoot's place was next door to our house.

We'd seen two county cops fly up the road past us on our bikes on the way into town, and I knew very well what a home visit was, even though I'd never seen one. A hundred strikers would show up around the house of a scab, filling his sidewalks, waiting for him to come home from the factory. When he did, the strikers would do every last thing to provoke him to swing—cuss, spit, anything. Home visits were in the papers all the time because the strike was big news, and Zoot, as Cyril had said in church, was a scab. Even Romey had worse words for Monty's old man. I could only imagine what Cyril would call him when he wasn't in church.

What I knew of the strike was its violence. It was reported in the papers almost every night, even though I'd heard my father complain often enough that the paper was very much pro-union. Some nights that summer, our family would drive past scab houses scarred by paint bombs, my father's silence in those moments—seeing those red-scarred walls and awnings and doors—rising from his deep horror. To him what was

Home Visit

happening was chaos, the darkest corners of the human soul turned inside out by a hatred so deep it was incapable of restraining itself.

I have him in me yet—my father. When I remember those frame bungalows out in the country, scarred with bright red and black, I still feel the fear I saw in my father's eyes and felt in his silence, because I know that he was recognizing something unredeemable, beyond grace. I really believe my father was incapable of understanding what men like Cyril felt in losing their jobs, their livelihoods, because everything Pete Prins believed in told him that men and women were destined to accept their places, their roles, their lots in life. As committed as he was theologically to a doctrine of original sin, he believed management always looked out for their workers' best interests, had the concerns of their workers first and foremost in their minds. The well-being of the help, after all, was crucial to the success of the business.

I remember a story Romey told me about his father and the guys in the foundry. He said some man had come around to watch them work, some man wearing a hard hat and carrying a notepad. Romey said his dad had told him that the guy stood there in the middle of the place for most of an hour, taking notes while they did whatever job it was Cyril and his buddies did in that foundry. Romey said the whole time he was there, watching them work and taking notes, the anger of those workers got hotter than the fire they were tending until finally they just stopped working—all of them. No signal, no talking between them, nothing prearranged. The whole mess of men simply reached the boiling point at the same moment, and they all threw down their gloves and glared at the guy in the hard hat. It just happened, Romey said, because all those guys were enraged at his presence. The whole lot of them just shut down, stood there and stared at this guy taking notes. Never threatened, never said a word—not one of them. Never even spoke to the guy. Ten, twelve of them maybe. They just stood there until the man realized it was in his best interests to get the heck out. So he did. Not a word was passed, not a word, Romey said, proudly. Once the guy was gone, the whole bunch went back to work. To Romey, that was righteousness.

I remember that story because I remember how proud Romey was telling it. And I remember it too because what had happened was right out of TV—a whole crowd of toughs dropping their gloves and standing there in silence, a half inch away from violence. "I'da loved to been there, Lobo," Romey said. "I'da had trouble keeping my hands off the guy, wouldn't you?"

Cars lined the streets from our place to halfway downtown. My chain guard rattled like it always did, but above the clatter from far down the street, I could still hear yells in a slow cadence like a drumroll through the cavern of parked cars.

Zoot's yard was full of people, strikers and onlookers and everybody else in town, so I swung into the driveway at our place and ran up to the dining room window. The house looked empty. If my father was home from work, I knew he'd be next door.

I ran around the corner of the house toward Monty's, the street in front of our place full of cars I didn't recognize. Fifty or sixty people, maybe more, stood massed around Zoot's front porch, many of them laughing and joking as if the whole thing were a picnic, some of them chanting—union guys, I figured. I saw a guy actually eating a sandwich. There was beer too—lots of it.

A mob is a frightful thing, and just to be there shook me deeply. There were big men, huge men. Rough guys. That many men in one small space, that many tough men, that many men who weren't at all like my father—not at all—scared the dickens out of me.

I walked up to the edge of the crowd, where I saw a bunch of others who were only spectators. Dozens of strange faces were milling around Zoot's front door, people my father used to talk about as outsiders and agitators. Some people called them thugs. I didn't know any of them. Not one of them was from Easton. None of them looked to me like a Christian.

But I didn't see Cyril or my father. I hadn't checked the time, so I hoped maybe my dad hadn't come back from work. I hoped he wasn't there.

Lots of people standing around weren't doing a thing. Another fifty, or sixty, maybe more, stood on the grass behind the sidewalk and watched in huddled silence, close enough to hear what was going on, far enough to be out of the line of fire. Up front in the middle there were women too—fat women, some of them smoking, some of them using language I'd never heard before on the street where I lived, certainly not out of adult mouths and certainly not from women. I had the un-mistakable feeling that any wrong move could lead to something unimaginable. I'd never liked Zoot all that much, wasn't that hot about Monty, for that matter. But the whole place seemed poised for some-thing that would never be easily forgotten.

I came up behind Mugsy, who didn't see me until I stood beside him. He was with his parents.

"Prins," he said, "you should have been here." To be heard over the noise, he had to talk so loud it seemed embarrassing. He looked at his

Home Visit

parents, then pulled me back outside the circle. "Sheesh," he said, "you hear those people cuss?"

There was nothing illegal about standing on the sidewalk in front of someone's house, nothing one bit illegal.

"Zoot comes home, see," Mugsy said, "and he gets out of the car—I don't know the people he rides with, but he gets out and these guys start hammering on the car, see—I mean, with their fists. Sheesh!" he said. "The minute they seen him riding up, they get out to the street and hammer—boom! boom!—with their fists, you know? Car's probably dented—I'm not kidding."

"Where is he?"

"He's ticked," he said. "Who wouldn't be?" Mugsy's eyes were flashing—everything was flashing. "Zoot didn't do nothing, Lobo—I mean, it wasn't like he was going to pick a fight, you know? But it wasn't like he was backing away, either. He was trying to keep his cool. Geez, it was something." Then he laughed. "He goes right up the walk, and all around him these guys are screaming—you can guess what they were saying." He glanced up at his father, then decided not to repeat the language. "They're crowding him, see—making it hard for him to walk, trying to get in his face, you know? That's the point of it." He came up close to me. "Like this, see—they're looking down at him and trying to get him to swing."

"Zoot scared?" I said.

"Goes right in the house and locks the door."

"How long ago?"

"Ten minutes—you just missed it." Mugsy shook his head, awed. "Your old man is in there too," he said, and then he pointed to the house.

I tried to look through the front window.

"He walked in the house right behind Zoot—your dad did. It wasn't that long ago—and they're yelling at your old man too, really. Pointing their fingers like he's in with him, you know? Shoot, your dad ain't no scab. He doesn't even work at Linear. He's not part of it."

"He's in there?" I said.

"With Zoot—and the preacher. He's in there too."

"Seen Monty?"

Mugsy cocked his head. "Stuck his ugly face out of the front window a while ago," he said, "but he wasn't outside. I wouldn't be either. If I was him, I'd be in the bomb shelter."

"You know these people?" I said.

He pulled his hand up to his mouth. "Union trash," he said, shaking his head. Mugsy's dad didn't work at Linear either.

Home Visit

"What about Cyril?" I said.

Mugsy shook his head.

"Can Zoot come out and play?" the crowd chanted. "Can Zoot come out and play?" None of them wore jackets; none of them wore union caps, either. But none of them were from Easton. Their hostility, rising as it did in cutting sarcasm, turned our whole neighborhood into a place I'd never known before. And they loved it, every minute. It was like a picnic, their idea of fun.

My hands shook. I stuck them in my pockets.

"Can Zoot come out and play?" It was a chant they kept up, louder and louder, because it was fun. It was a bad, wonderful joke. "Can Zoot come out and play?"

There were cops down the street, but what was happening at Zoot's didn't approach real violence right then. It wasn't as if the whole rout were going to burn down the house—not at all. They were taunting, screaming, bullying, taking joy in Zoot's misery.

"My dad says they hire guys to do this," Mugsy said. "He said they go to some bar and get the meanest buggers they can get. Pay 'em a ten spot or something and tell them to go rough somebody up—that's the way it works—that's what my old man says." And then he pulled his hand up to his face, as if no one was supposed to hear. "You can bet Cyril's got something to do with this, Prins. Everybody knows that."

Then Reverend Kosters stepped out the front door and stood on the porch, raising his hands like he might have in church. But the crowd didn't give a hang. Every time Kosters motioned as if he wanted them to shut up, they'd only yell louder. They couldn't have known he was a preacher, but even if they had, I don't think it would have made any difference. They had a mission, and it wasn't Kosters they were after.

"Please?" he said. "You aren't going to accomplish anything this way—"

The crowd swarmed to the front and cranked up the volume. I wondered why the police didn't come up. It had to be against some law for people to waltz over other people's property, after all. They were making a mess of Zoot's blessed lawn. There had to be some kind of law against it.

"His kid is crying," Kosters said. "You got his wife petrified. He knows why you're here—you made your point, all right?"

"My kids are crying too," some woman yelled.

"Please—" Kosters said again, but he could have been John the Baptist, he could have been Jesus, and the strikers marching over Zoot's precious lawn wouldn't have backed off one inch. I remembered the men

Home Visit

in the foundry dropping their gloves and the smiles that must have come over their faces when the hard hat man finally walked out.

I saw the man who chucked the tomato. He wore a faded gray shirt, had dark hair, and his sleeves were rolled up. He looked like he'd just come from the foundry himself, but he couldn't have. I will never forget that man, even though I never saw him again and never will. Today he's likely long dead. He was heavyset, he hadn't shaved, and he was wearing a flat gray cap. He wasn't all that far away from me when he threw it, and I remember wondering where he could have hidden it, because I would have thought a tomato would make a big lump in your pocket, like a baseball.

It hit Reverend Kosters like a punch, hit him so hard he fell back against the door. Then he stooped to pick it up, because it stayed whole and didn't squash. For a moment he sat there on his haunches, that whole tomato in his hand, and he looked back at the people as if he'd come to understand that who he was and what he was saying were going absolutely nowhere. Before that moment, Kosters likely believed that an ordained preacher stands in a tradition which includes Jeremiah, Isaiah, and a whole herd of minor prophets. Something more than fear was in the preacher's eyes at that moment, something of despair. But he was just a kid himself.

"Can Zoot come out and play?" They started back in on the chant. "Can Zoot come out and play?" Da-dah, da-dah, da-dah—over and over.

"Why don't the cops do something?" I said to Mugsy.

"They don't care." He pointed down the block to two county cop cars standing together blocking the street. "They're union too."

Kosters held that tomato and got to his feet. He was humiliated, but what was written on his face was a pale sense of his own powerlessness. "For *Christ's* sake, I'm asking you to go home." He didn't say it as if it was swearing. Nobody could have read it that way. "You made your point," he said. "He knows you're angry. He doesn't want to take anybody's job, but he doesn't have one himself—can't you see that? He's got mouths to feed—"

"I got mouths to feed," somebody said.

"He knows why you're here," the preacher said. "What's left to tell him?"

"We got stuff we'd like to whisper in his ear," somebody said. "Bring the scab out so we can tell him ourselves."

He was frightened—that was obvious; but he stayed up there. He stood on that porch as if he were wearing the full armor of God, and all the time they were cussing and swearing and laughing.

93

Home Visit

"Bring out the scab!" they yelled. "Bring out the scab. Can Zoot come out and play?"

Kosters' eyes never rested on any of the violence in front of him. He stood there for a time as if he wasn't afraid of them so much as he was afraid of what wasn't going to happen, of the Lord's apparent unwillingness to let justice roll down. He stood there for maybe a minute or two in awed silence, then went into the house.

I remember feeling close to tears myself, so deeply I feared what I felt all around me. I shut my eyes and prayed that it would go away, that something would happen to end it all, because I could feel the trajectory of all of this. But the only voice was the chanting of the mob.

And then, suddenly, silence. Zoot came out and slammed the door behind him as if he were ready to take on all of them.

For a moment they seemed stunned. He stood on the concrete porch like a cartoon figure and started in, the pitch in his voice in perfect tune with his anger—high and shrill. "You made your point," he said, "now get off of my property."

People started yelling all kinds of things, and for a few minutes, the whole yard seemed to settle because they'd lost their unity; they were all screaming something themselves.

"I got my rights," Zoot said. "This is my house, my lawn."

"And you got my job," a woman yelled. "You took my rights."

"Scab, scab, scab," they chanted, picking it up again all together.

I looked back down the street and saw the county cops who'd been in the car get out and stand beside the others.

"This is a free country," he said, "and I got my family—" and he went on and on in that high voice, screeching away in words that became, the longer he stayed with it, less and less audible.

I wondered where my father was. Kosters came back out and stood behind Zoot, tried to say something to him, but Zoot had to lean toward him just to hear. He was a bird in a circle of cats, and he kept yelling, as if somehow he could beat them all back, shut them down completely with nothing but words. He was shot, really. I'm not sure he knew what he was doing. He kept shouting things back, as if every last word and phrase demanded rebuttal. He ranged over the porch, one side to another, yelling a hundred different things, as if an argument would end everything. He really seemed to believe he could win.

"Scabs die, scabs die, scabs die," some yelled.

His eyes were glazed and unfocused, and his messed hair made him look insane. "You can't boss me around," he screamed. "This is a free country. I ain't taking any job that you guys didn't walk away from."

Home Visit

I saw Monty's face at the front window, and his mother. She was crying too. And then my father came out, stood there beside Kosters, the three of them setting themselves up for a shoot-out that I thought would end with all of them dead. The moment I saw my father up there, I felt regret, not simply because he was going to lose anything he staked on protecting Zoot, but because he was so infinitely powerless.

An egg missed Zoot and splashed in a glob on the screen door. People loved it. "Serve him breakfast, serve him breakfast," they yelled, and when Zoot turned to check the door behind him, another one caught him square in the back of the head. It didn't hurt him, but right then it wouldn't have taken much to turn Zoot into what he could become all too easily anyway. Maybe if the egg hadn't been thrown or hadn't caught him the way it did, the whole thing would have died some other death—I don't know. There would likely have been more screaming, more taunting, but if it hadn't hit him where it did—square in the back of the head—Zoot might not have lost control.

But he did. He turned to the crowd and came off that porch as if he were drunk, his arms flailing, lips tightened in rage, fists out front. "Who did it?" he screamed, over and over, not even waiting for an answer. He looked directly at whoever would give him eyes, that raw egg falling in globs over the back of his collar.

He did exactly what they wanted him to do. The people moved in so close to the front door that Zoot was lost in the swirl of anger and fists that swallowed him. They got exactly what they were waiting for—an excuse, because it was likely Zoot who took the first swing. Someone might have shoved him, who knows? People stood so close they must have seemed to him to be in his pockets. They spit, cussed, someone may have even shoved, but then somebody swung, and in a few seconds Zoot was down in the middle, and he was about to get his.

That's when the county cops started coming up—six of them—and my father came off the porch and ran in after Zoot, Kosters right behind him. It was something of a martyrdom, maybe—greater love hath no man and all of that—but right then, just a kid, I didn't think of what he did as heroic, but stupid.

I didn't want to look, and yet I had to, so I stood on the bumper of a car to try to see what was going on in the middle of that mess of people. The crowd surged so thickly around the action, the union guys getting in their swings and keeping the others away, that there wasn't anything to see but the outlines of a melee. Men from town tried to help Zoot, but it wasn't much of a fight. All I could hear was the hooting. Fists were

Home Visit

flying. The cops—but they were walking—still half a block away. Zoot was getting stuck but good.

I jumped off the car and tried to get closer, but a big union guy grabbed my shoulder—didn't say a thing, just grabbed me and held me. He was a man with thick shoulders, wearing a pin on his chest, a man with wart-like growths on his face—that's what I remember. "Stay clear, kid," the man said. "No business of yours. It'll be over in a minute now—they got families too."

The man with the warts was right. The damage was done quickly, and the crowd backed off enough for me to see my father and the preacher each slung between four guys who held their arms and legs and swung them as if they were nothing but feed sacks. They weren't hurting them; that wasn't the point. The point was utter humiliation. My father tried to twist himself out of their grasp, but he was no match for the brute strength of the men holding his limbs. He jerked around, flipped himself as far as he could while the four of them swung him around in a circle as if he were a rag dummy. "I'n't this fun?" they yelled, my father struggling helplessly in their hands.

Had they beaten him to a pulp, I might have considered my father a Stephen, a martyr. I might have even run in there myself. But what they were up to was degradation. I understood the pain on my father's face as he was swung like a child, back and forth and up and around in a circle, people hooting and screaming at him as if he were a child. The man with the warts held both of my shoulders and kept me from breaking away, but there was nothing I could do but feel my father's shame. No one saw it, I'm sure. I'm not even sure there were tears, but I cried.

When I looked back for the cops, I saw Romey. He wasn't interested in what was happening to my father—he only wanted to get inside the circle. His face was set like a steel trap as he pushed past people, shoved his way into the middle, looking over every face, yelling for his old man. He pulled on people's arms and pushed aside some, who recognized him and moved out of his way. He kept yelling, looking around, and then he saw me back on the edge.

"Lobo," he yelled.

I knew what he wanted. "I didn't see him," I said, and the big guy took his hands off me, left me standing there, numb.

"Was he here?" Romey said.

I shook my head.

"What you crying about?" he said, and then he turned and saw, like I did, my father's pants halfway off his legs.

Romey was no bigger than I was back then—smaller in fact. But he was fierce, always was. He ran at the guy holding my father's wrists, pointed his shoulder, and buried it into the striker's knees from behind. The man buckled immediately, and my father's wrists broke free.

Then he lunged for the other guy, tore into him, and when he did, the guy let go of my father and grabbed him. Maybe they knew Romey—whose boy he was. Maybe they just decided to quit because some kid with the guts of a brass monkey fought so fiercely. Whatever the reason, it ended soon after that; the cops finally came in and broke everything up, swinging nightsticks at people's backs and behinds. All of that took little more than five minutes—from the time my father and the preacher had followed Zoot into the crowd to the moment the melee ended. There were no arrests. I know I didn't move an inch forward from the moment I'd come over the lawn from our place.

Twenty minutes later, I watched from the kitchen as Hattie sat in our dining room to talk about what had happened. It was light outside, still wasn't six o'clock; but it seemed the end of a long, long night. I stayed out of everything, my mind fixed on my father's shame, my own tears, and the fact that I'd been nothing more than a spectator, while Romey had slammed recklessly into the middle of everything.

Hattie Guttner was sitting beside my mother, in our house, my mother covering Hattie's hands with her own out in front of them both on the table. I didn't see the girls anywhere. She must have left them at home.

Cars streamed past, some of them still leaving, some of them passing the place as if to catch a last glimpse of the madness—some of them showing up for the first time, having heard about it too late. The strikers were long gone.

There was, really, no place to hide for me right then, nowhere to go. I didn't know who knew what I'd done or not done, but to hear my parents talk it through, to see Hattie broken, to have to listen to everything replayed once more made me almost sick. No one looked at me or even thought of me.

Everything I had felt when the whole mess started had been felt by all of them as well, anybody who'd watched. There were tears in the retelling, sometimes broken by laughs—nobody was badly hurt, after all. But more than anything there was hate, muted right then with Hattie there in our home. I didn't know where Romey was, but I didn't want to talk to him either, because I knew Romey knew what I hadn't done.

When I left the kitchen, I walked through the back door. I don't think anyone noticed. I stood on the sidewalk, at home plate of a wiffle-ball park where I'd played a thousand games—the maple to the right, first base; the newly painted picket fence, the right field wall. Voices still carried across the lawn between the houses; people still milled around on the street in front of Zoot's place, as if a glimpse of the broken eggs could bring back something of the mess that had happened right there on our street.

Three small pines stood in a triangle in front of the burning barrel out back, barely six feet high, but just about the only place I thought I could hide as long as the sun was still up halfway to Heaven. I wished it were night. I wished I were a thousand miles away somewhere, because all of the buzzing in my head—this brawling and swearing—all of it messed everything up; not that life was so good before, I thought. I knew very well that it was Cyril who'd picked Monty's dad out for what had gone on next door. Everybody knew that. Who needed proof? After what had happened at church, it had to be Cyril, even if he wasn't there.

"Lowell, is that you?" It was Mugsy's dad. He was walking home in the alley behind the trees, and I hadn't even seen him, so I picked up a wiffle ball from beneath a pine tree and came out showing it off, as if I'd been searching for something I'd lost. He came over to the fence and put his hands down on what still seemed to me to be wet paint. "You okay?" he said.

I nodded.

"That was a mob, is what it was," he said, looking over his shoulder. "They don't even know Zoot. Even money says they never even saw him before." He looked at me. "You know any of those people?"

"Never saw 'em before," I said.

"They're not from town—that's for sure. That crazy Romey," he said. "You see him?"

I didn't want to admit it, so I shook my head.

"Gutsy and nuts," he said, shaking his head. "Must be nuts. He went flying right in there, right in the middle. Amazing."

"Missed that, I guess," I said.

"You should have seen him," Mugsy's dad said. "The way he lit in there, that was something—guts in that kid is something else." He pointed at the house. "They had your dad too," he said. "Romey took one of them on—you didn't see that?"

"I didn't see much at all."

He looked back at Zoot's house on the corner of the block, where the whole thing had happened. "It's over, I guess. But maybe they'll come back. I don't think Zoot's going to walk off the job—not after what they just pulled." He pointed a finger at me, as if to say good-bye. "Yeah,

Home Visit

well," he said, "got to feel sorry for them too, I guess," and he kept on going down the alley toward his place.

I came around from behind the pines and threw the ball up on the garage.

I'd failed my father when Romey hadn't. I'd stood there bawling, really, when Romey had just flown in and ended it more surely than the cops had. It had never dawned on me to risk my hide the way he had—or the way my father had. I had sat there feeling anger, all right, at my father's humiliation, but not enough anger to make me do a thing about it. I didn't feel like going back into the house. I hadn't earned anything, no part of the conversation. But it was stupid of me to sit outside all by myself, so I told myself that maybe in the house I could be a kid—barely seen, barely heard—the adults so busy talking everything over.

I envied Romey so much I started to hate him. I started to believe that maybe Zoot wasn't wrong about what he said back in the church. Maybe the smoking and the stealing were Romey's fault—maybe their precious Monty wouldn't have gotten his little hands dirty one bit if it hadn't been for Cyril Guttner's kid, because wherever Romey was, there was trouble, even if Romey himself wasn't all that much worse than any other kid we hung around with.

It was Cyril really. He was the reason Hattie was sitting in our house right now. He was the reason Romey had come over, that's why she had—because of him. Wherever Cyril was, there was some kind of damage—and some of that rubbed off on Romey too. Cyril blew up everything, Cyril was hated by just about everyone, Cyril no one could trust—and the man cussed like a sailor, right in church. It was Cyril who scared everybody half to death.

Maybe Romey was the ringleader of every last bad thing because he was Cyril's kid and there wasn't a thing he could do about it. Maybe that was it, I thought. Life would be so much easier without Romey, too. If I weren't Romey's friend, life would sail on smoothly—maybe not because of Romey so much as his old man—that's what I was thinking.

I wished I could run the whole lot of people out of our house and turn on the Braves game and listen in, taking score, writing down the markings on a brand new sheet of Dairyland paper, put my legs up in a chair in the living room with my parents there, shoo everybody else out of the house and have a tin roof sundae and hear the soft clicks of Mom's knitting needles as she mended some socks or made a scarf or whatever she did when those things spun through her fingers, my father reading or something across the room or at the dining room table, one ear on the game.

The back window off the dining room was dark because there was still too much sun outside. I couldn't see in—but they could see me. Maybe if I'd head upstairs for my room or something, maybe I could get away from the whole mess, hide a while up there.

"He wasn't there." Those were the first words I heard as I came in the back door, and they belonged to my mother. She'd been saying that already before I'd left, and she was still trying to make the point. "Right from the start, I never saw him—nobody did."

They were sitting at the table, my dad across from my mom, agreeing that Cyril hadn't ever made an appearance. "I didn't see him," my mother said again. She looked as if what she'd seen had turned her into someone who wasn't about to look back, her face straight and plated, eyes trained on the cup she held in both hands. She was trying to be strong.

"It doesn't make a whit of difference," Hattie said. "It doesn't matter at all because we all know, don't we?"

"You oughtn't say that," my mom told her.

"It doesn't," she said. "Really it doesn't. Because *he* did it. Even if he wasn't there, I know he's the one who did it."

I stood at the sink and took a glass of water. I was afraid of making any noise, or saying anything, or saying nothing. I just wanted to get upstairs without drawing attention to myself.

Hattie didn't appear angry. You couldn't see anything like anger on her face. What she'd said about her husband—how he was to blame—came out as if it was an obvious fact, something everyone understood. "You all know it, too," she said. "You're all thinking it anyway, and you're right."

My mother held tightly to compassion rather than truth. "We don't know," she said. "Nobody knows that for sure."

But Hattie was right. My father knew it too, perhaps better than Hattie herself because he'd been at church not that many nights before when Cyril had exploded. I had no idea what Hattie knew of what had gone on that night, but then, Hattie didn't need to know, since she understood her husband far better than I did. She was as sure as I was that he was the one who'd called out the forces. Of course Cyril had done it, planned it, sent in the toughs. Cyril didn't even have to be there to be the cause of it. He was behind the whole thing. I remembered him coming out of the darkness that morning after we'd trapped the skunk. I remembered my fear that morning I sneaked the rifle downstairs.

Home Visit

"At least wait until you know for sure," Mom said. "He probably didn't have anything to do with it." That was a Christian lie no one believed. It was simply the nicest thing my mother could say.

I stood there outside of the conversation, still reluctant to simply walk away and head for the stairs. If I stood there long enough, I thought, maybe they'd forget me completely, and that's when I'd make my break.

"I haven't even seen him since Saturday," Hattie said. "I haven't seen him for all that time." She raised her chin like someone with real class. "I don't care if he never comes home again."

I took a drink of water and looked over the back yard from the window above the sink. I didn't want her to say that, exactly. As much as I hated Cyril, I didn't want her to say something like that, not in front of my parents. She was talking about the end of her family, about something awful for Romey.

"You don't mean that," my mother said. "You don't mean that at all."

My father was sitting back in his chair, his hands behind his head. "I can't say I recognized any of them—"

"They're all his buddies," she said. "I'm sure of it." Her hair fell in a tangle over her face, seemed frayed where she'd brushed it quickly into clumps at her neck. When we had come back from the lake, she'd been broken, almost unable to talk. Now she was cold and steely. Her fear had hardened into hate.

My father looked up at me grimly, as if he thought I should go, and I would have happily run upstairs as I had planned if Zoot and Dorothy—and Monty—hadn't come in the front door just then without knocking. Blood from Zoot's face still ran in a trickle from a partially bandaged flap of open skin beneath his eye. His lips were puffed and purple, and his breath still came in thrusts. They couldn't have known Hattie was there. Instead of knocking on the door on the far left side of the front porch, the door into the living room, the door guests use, they had come right in the door on the far right side, walked in through the piano room and into the kitchen, where I stood, then turned and stopped when they saw her sitting with my parents at the table.

I was right in the middle of things.

"It's over," my father said quickly. He rose from the table like a sheriff, stood between them, conscious of the fact that Hattie was behind him. "There's no sense carrying anything on here." He pointed in opposite directions with both his hands. "We've got to settle things now—more anger won't do anybody any good. It's time to shut it out, Zoot," he said. "You hear me?"

Zoot had so much hate in him he couldn't even talk, couldn't look at her. I ached not to be in the room.

Dorothy walked past her husband and put a hand on Hattie's shoulder, hugged her as if a little touch weren't really enough. Then Hattie cried, only then.

For a long time it was quiet, even with Hattie's crying and Zoot's anger still threatening. My father kept his hands down on the table and then tipped his head toward the chairs. "Why don't you both come on in," he said. "Nothing better probably than for us to talk this out."

Monty was a carbon copy of his father. While his mom was already sitting beside Hattie, Monty and Zoot stood in the kitchen with me, huffing and puffing, electric with anger. Zoot's stare had broken. I was sure Monty would follow me if I went up to my bedroom, even though he tailed along with his parents.

"Sit down, Zoot," my father said, authority in his voice. It wasn't meant as a plea, but a command. "There's a place here."

Zoot turned his head. Hattie was at the south edge of the table, so he kept his eyes focused north at the window.

"If you think anger is the best medicine here," my father said, "then you're denying everything you claim to believe—every bit of your faith. Now sit down."

Zoot glared at my father.

"Forgive," my father said. "Forgiveness."

Zoot still wouldn't look at Hattie, but he walked into the dining room slowly, kept both hands down around the bar that separates the rooms, not as if he were blind, but as if to say that without holding himself back deliberately, he would lose whatever direction my father had urged within him.

"She had nothing to do with it," my father said. "You know that."

Zoot breathed heavily, as if the fighting weren't over.

"You too, Monty," my father said.

But Monty stayed in the kitchen with me, standing at the stove.

Once Zoot was in the dining room, my father prayed. He didn't say another word. He just shoved out a chair from the table with his foot, signaled Zoot to sit, and started into a prayer. I don't remember the words exactly, but I know my father well enough to be able to outline the intent—and it was peace. He prayed for Cyril—because there was every reason to. More than one person sitting in that dining room with hands folded and eyes closed hated Cyril Guttner right then. Zoot couldn't even talk. I'd watched his wife console Hattie, but I knew what Dorothy likely had to say about him. And Hattie'd just admitted she hoped she'd never

Home Visit

see him again. So my father prayed for him, not because he needed prayers any more than the others, but because Cyril was likely laughing about the whole business right then, about all of their pain.

The prayer was my signal to leave. I still sensed he'd be happier if I weren't around right then. I was still a kid, and I felt uncomfortable being there with so much iciness in the air. Right then, our hocking cigarettes seemed almost incidental.

Rather than go upstairs, I left quietly through the back door again, walked out on the same path I'd just taken in.

Once outside, I walked around the east side of the house in the shadows from the tallest maples in town, all the way around the house, over the lawn, and up toward our front door, and as I did I kept looking at Monty's place. A few cars were still driving by, gawking at the splash of grease staining the siding where the eggs had broken. The red skins of a few tomatoes were scattered over the front porch. Hattie's old Ford, the trapping car, was parked in our driveway, where she must have left it when she drove over from her place.

I heard the music before I saw Romey, but I put two and two together and walked across the front lawn toward the Ford, then opened the door to find him lying on the front seat where nobody could see him, the horse blanket they always used up there in crumples beneath his head.

"See him?" he said. "You see him, Lobo? He just walked into your place. I can't stand the sight of him." And then he swore. I wasn't sure whether he meant Monty or Monty's old man. He had his hands up over his forehead, his arms bent as if he were shading his eyes. "My old man ain't a scab anyways. He says a scab ain't even human because he ain't got a heart at all because all he thinks about is himself—that's it. Human beings have hearts—that's what he says. Scabs are animals, he says." And then he laughed. "I don't know that I'd go that far, because I never saw an animal I didn't like. That's way too kind."

Then he looked up. "Get in," he said.

I jumped in the back seat and pulled the door half latched behind me.

"It's all his old man's fault anyway," he said. "Everything's his fault—don't ever forget it, either. Zoot walks through that line at Linear and every last one of them strikers knows their kids don't eat—it's just that simple. Shoot, my old man is one of the only guys in town that's got guts."

The seat stood between us, so Romey pulled himself up, laid his arm over the front, and pointed. "Nobody sees it his way, either—I know that. Everybody thinks my old man is at fault for all of it, thinks he's nothing but trash or something. I know that much. I ain't dumb, Lobo."

Home Visit

His face carried more anger than I'd ever seen. Those thick eyebrows poised sharply over his stare. "You know what? I'm telling you the truth here—all of this wouldn't have happened if Zoot didn't cross that picket line—that's the bottom line."

I nodded. He was my friend. I was his.

"In my book he's as much a thief as anybody whatever broke into a store or a house or anything like that—and I don't care if he's big buddies with your old man, either. You and me, we get hung for a couple packs of butts. But Zoot? He goes and steals an honest man's job and nobody says nothing. You call that fair?" He looked at me. "That guy some friend of yours or what?"

"He's not," I said. "He's just our neighbor."

"Then why does your old man always take his side, anyway?"

I let out a long breath and tried to stall for time. I kicked at the half-latched door, bounced it against its own play.

"How come?" Romey said again.

"What do you mean take his side?" I said.

"You saw him—inside the house with that scab. You saw him, Lobo—he's out there with the preacher and everything, protecting Zoot like some mother hen."

"I don't know if he's on Zoot's side," I said. "It's more than that."

"How can it be more than that? I don't get it. You explain that. Sure looked to me like he was on Zoot's side."

I'd just seen my father pray in order to keep one Hell-bent angry man from lighting into Romey's mom. I'd just seen my mother try to bring some hope back into Hattie's heart by a Christian lie. "He was trying to keep peace," I said. "He was trying to stop the whole business from getting to what it did."

"He just made it worse, is all—just made the whole business a whole lot worse—that's what he did." Romey had his legs out in front of him on the seat, his arm up over the back. His face was rigid, yet moving, his lips twitching. "Why didn't he just mind his own business and keep his butt at home?"

"He didn't want it to happen," I said. "He didn't want any of it to happen."

"There ain't no middle place in this, Lobo—you hear me? When something like this is going on, people's lives on the line, there ain't no halfway at all."

"You don't understand."

"I sure enough do. When he's over there, it's a clear picture of what's going on."

"No it isn't," I said.

"How can you say that?"

"Because you don't know my old man," I said. "He ain't interested in trying to get your dad's job or—"

"Then why's he over there?" He shook his head. "He's always poking around in other people's business. Is that it, Lobo? Being a big-time Christian means you got a license to go banging around in other peoples' lives? Who appointed him pope?"

My father didn't have to go next door to try to rescue Zoot—that wasn't his job. Zoot wasn't his brother or anything, only a neighbor. My father did it because he thought it was the right thing to do.

"I hate your old man," he said, "all saintly and everything. Mr. Perfect Christian. He ain't even human either." And then he looked at me, waited, as if he were begging another fight. "You hear me?" he said. "Say something. Don't just sit there like a bump on a log—"

"It's the way he is, I guess," I said.

"Tell him to turn down the volume," Romey said. "He thinks he's God or something—"

"He doesn't either," I told him. "He doesn't think that at all."

"Ain't nobody who's God around here—not him and not Zoot for sure. Ain't nobody God in Easton, even if they all think they're his right-hand soldier or something." He reached up to the visor and pulled out a pack of his mother's Chesterfields, slapped the pack against the back of his hand, and pushed in the lighter with his elbow. "You know the truth, Lo-man—you know I'm right."

"You mean about my old man?"

He laughed. Typically. Right in the middle of everything, he breaks out in a laugh. "No," he said, "I'm talking about Godzilla, all right?" He stared at me, then winked, a cigarette dangling from the corner of his lips. One quick lift of those heavy eyebrows, a thin tear in the anger that had crossed his lips, the tug of a giggle, and I knew it was over.

The lighter popped, and a plume of smoke rose in the dead air.

"You want one?" he said.

There we sat in Hattie's car in the front yard of our house—the whole grizzly episode of smoking and stealing not that long behind me, the memory of the night at church not even set in my mind, my father's humiliation still radiating from the lot next door, but I couldn't turn him down.

"Just let me bum a couple drags," I said. I had no desire to smoke. It wouldn't even taste good. But I wanted this thing with Romey.

"Some guy belted me but good in the gut," he said "Some guy slammed me, but it didn't do much—knocked me around a little. Shoot, my old man hits me worse than that." He took a huge drag, the first one from that cigarette, then shoved it toward me over the seat.

He never asked me why I didn't come busting in like he did—why I didn't fight the way he had. He never mentioned where I'd been while he'd been taking hits himself. He never asked, and never really thought about it much, if I know Romey. He didn't think about other people all that much at all—about what they thought or what they were doing. He'd seen me in the crowd before he'd waded into the action. He knew I was there. Without thinking about getting hurt in the least bit, he'd barreled into the action, done what he thought was right, but I honestly don't think he ever tried to second-guess my own inaction, the inaction of someone he obviously considered his friend. It never dawned on him to ask why I hadn't gone into battle myself. Romey never judged me that way at all, never seemed to want to.

It's almost impossible for me now to believe that that night, after everything I'd already been through that summer, I could have been sitting in Hattie's old Ford, parked in our own driveway, smoking a cigarette. But there we were, me and the kid who'd flown into action while I hadn't. I suppose it was the least I could do.

He reached for the radio, and when the Everly Brothers came on, the two of us sat there without talking, Romey's head bobbing with the slow beat of a love song.

Home Visit

The Beanfields

Bean-picking started at six in the morning, when a ton of kids from town would meet in the village park, each of us lugging jars of icy lemonade packed in insulated ice cream bags and, in my case, at least a half-dozen bologna sandwiches with ketchup, or on good days, boiled ham. Romey usually toted along tons of cookies, plus Twinkies or some kind of sweets that wouldn't mush in the heat. We'd hoist all of that in a knapsack or stuff it in a grocery bag or, if you were a girl, some flowered beach bag with a long strap like a purse. The truck to the fields left from the village park at six. If you weren't there when it departed, that day you didn't go.

A tough old guy named Nick Van Dam planted whole sections of sandy soil in green beans that, by midsummer, hung thick from the stalks in perfect rows that ran from the edge of the hill above the lakeshore, straight west for just about as far as you could see—close to a mile—all the way to the state highway. Green beans grew heavily in the thick sandy soil and the humidity that almost always gloved the lakeshore. For at least two weeks in July, sometimes longer, a rowdy crew of forty kids, on hands and knees, could keep busy at a rotten job. But for us, the pay was monstrously good.

Today, some child-labor law would likely keep kids from working that hard, but back then parents loved bean-picking because it was a primer in a work ethic most parents considered the best education of all. For kids, picking beans was a measure of adulthood, a rite of passage. It was hard work but good money, and the nearest we'd come, in the late fifties, to a youth culture. All day long out in the sun, there was nothing but kids around us.

Van Dam had a reputation for investing diligently in his crop but not giving a hoot about his help, an ethic that likely grew out of an old-fashioned mode of parenting that was, right then, taking its last breaths, slowly dying to Dr. Spock's new permissiveness. But that pattern was all around us; some of Linear's own workers would have said Van Dam's disinterest in his help was the right way to teach kids how to work, because that attitude typified life in the workplace. We lived in a different era.

But the fact is, many parents appreciated deeply what Nick Van Dam provided—an opportunity for their kids to make quick money—even if they didn't respect him. And we were afraid of him, not only because he was the boss, but more so because he wasn't an adult who patronized. To him, we were the help, not kids on some rough pilgrimage toward maturity. I wouldn't call him evil, and I never saw him beat a kid or go out of his way to hurt someone, but in the continuum between justice and mercy, it never dawned on Nick Van Dam to believe there was any difference. You live by the rules or you're out. Didn't matter who or why or when. That's the way life was. I'm not sure he would have known how to show love to anyone; if asked to try, he would likely have thought it a strange request, since one might expect being nice from a woman, but not a boss, and certainly not a man—but then, all bosses were men.

He mouthed fat black cigars of various lengths, almost always pinched and soaked between his lips, often unlit. He was bald and he wore a limp old army cap with sweat lines crawling like a blight around his temples. If some kid on the job did something wrong and got caught, he went home—walked back to town, sometimes four or five miles. Very simple.

The rules were scratched down on some unwritten contract all of us were simply expected to know, and the number one rule was clear to all of us: mess around and you go home. Even before we were of age

The Beanfields

to get on the field truck and ride out to the lakeshore acres where he grew his green beans, every kid knew that law, and I don't remember any parents ever complaining when their kid walked back from bean-picking.

I don't believe my own parents ever second-guessed my bean-picking, even though they knew it would be hard work under a tough boss in the hot sun. Besides, my two older sisters had been baptized before me—girl or boy made no difference here. The basic skills of the job required nothing more than quick fingers and limber joints, both of which came in two genders.

Monday morning, the week after the union's home visit at Monty's house, Romey and I were out in Nick's fields just after dawn, the dew so thick the plants hung like willows. The cool lake air was brisk with humidity, the sun still no more than a ruler's length above the pines at the edge of the woods leading to the beach.

We wore jeans and T-shirts like everybody else, and we squatted in the rows old man Van Dam charged us with the moment we left the back of the field truck that hauled us all out there. Day in, day out, nothing particularly exciting awaited us, just long hours of picking beans off stalks, then dropping them into five-gallon pails we all brought along ourselves, part of the work arrangement. Once our pails were full, we'd jam the beans into wrinkled burlap bags Ernie, Nick's top field hand, distributed before we stepped into the rows.

Almost everybody in Easton had a nickname. Ernie was called the Toad because somehow he looked like one. His arms were sinewy, his muscles well defined, but he had an unnatural stoop, a pointed thin face, and an odd nasal tone to his speech that made him easy to mimic. He wasn't heavy, wasn't even really pudgy, but he lumbered when he walked, Igor-like. The day he turned sixteen he had quit high school to work for Nick, and it was obvious to all of us that, come July especially, he loved his job—playing field boss to the hilt, flashing his handheld scale like a weapon whenever some kid yelled for him to weigh-in a full bag. He went at his job magisterially. He'd pick up a full gunnysack of beans in one hand, his skinny arm popping veins, bounce it once or twice to settle the beans, hook it with the scale, lift, then wait for the needle to sweep across the scale's metal face. Once he had a reading, he'd take the card each of us were given, and he'd mark it with the silver punch he carried in his back pocket—first bag, forty pounds; next bag, up to eighty-three; third, 127, and so on.

We were paid by the pound. At two cents per, sometimes the oldest and fastest pickers could get 350 to 400 pounds and earn eight bucks for

The Beanfields

a long day's labor. One summer my sister Janine bought a flute with the money she made bean-picking.

The Toad came by already that first morning with a pack of Kools hanging out of the pocket of his flannel shirt. He was, at best, four years older than we were, but he must have been standing in the wings of Heaven's great stage when the brains were handed out. He never was too bright, and he was only a bit bigger than we were. As scared as we were of Nick Van Dam, we never really shook at all at his field boss. It was early. Romey was faster than I was, but neither of us had probably picked more than a half-pail.

"Guys got caught stealing weeds, I hear," he said, smirking. "I can sell 'em, you know—if you need 'em."

The Toad may not have had the smarts for high school, but he knew how to skewer boys who were hot for smokes. He bought cigarettes by the carton, stuck them under the dash of the field truck, and sold them, turning a quick profit.

"What do you got?" Romey said.

"Kools," he said, pointing at his pocket.

"Menthol," Romey said as if they were for girls. "Filters?"

"Yep."

"I don't have no money yet." Romey got to his knees between the rows. "That's why I'm out here."

Even though the cool lakeshore air on the trip out required a flannel shirt, it didn't take long for extra clothes to get too hot in the fields. Toad grabbed the pack in his pocket, then slipped his arms out of his shirt, holding the Kools in his teeth. "You're going to have to go without," he said, tying the arms of the shirt in a knot around his waist. "I don't work on credit." Then he pulled out a cigarette himself, flipped back the cap of his prized silver Zippo, a speckled trout breaking water etched on the front. "How about you?" he said, looking at me while lighting up. "Or you quit once your old man slapped your little patty?"

I looked up but didn't say a thing.

"Old man was ticked, I bet," he said. "Big church man like that—kid stealing weeds—balls of fire," he said, "I bet you caught it royal." The whole thing was funny to him. Pinholes dotted the gray T-shirt he rarely changed, as if someone had spit battery acid down the front. "You know, when I was a kid, I never got caught," he said, spitting between the rows. "Been inhaling since I was ten." He curled his tongue and flicked out a smoke ring.

We were on our haunches, feeling around for beans in the heavy plants. It wouldn't be long at all and he'd play a larger role in the events I've never

The Beanfields

forgotten, but when he stood there in the rows and talked down to us, I disliked him. Maybe it was prejudice—he simply wasn't somebody I wanted to be. But Romey disliked him too, and Romey was no upstanding citizen himself. I think it was smarts, or lack of them. Romey had them, in his own streetwise way. The Toad never did. I just wished the guy'd go away—that morning and every morning we were out in the fields.

"What your old man say, Romey?" Toad said. "I bet *he* didn't raise no stink."

Romey leaned forward and crawled down the row a foot or two. "I can't repeat the words out loud," he said, making a joke. "There's girls around here too close."

"Come on," Toad said.

"Just think 'em, Toad," Romey told him. "Just think of the worst ones old Nick there ever says—and then add a few of your own favorites."

"Aw, go ahead," Toad said.

"Can't," Romey told him, his fingers back in the beans. "I'd get myself struck dead." He pointed at me with his shoulder. "Besides, got the saint here next to me. He's got angels waiting to strike guys like you and me—they're all holding howitzers, too."

I didn't mind him saying things like that.

"Then how is it your old man is still around?" Toad reached up beneath his shirt and scratched his chest, giggling at his own joke. "How come he didn't get his long ago—answer me that?"

Romey was stringing him. "My old man's the devil," he said. "And you know how it is—the Lord can't get the devil. They're in cahoots. You ever read the book of Job, Toad?"

"C'mon—"

"They're in cahoots. If they aren't, then why didn't the Lord just shut him down when the devil said he wanted to bug Job—you know that story, Toad?"

"Ain't no story like that."

"You pagan," Romey said. "It's in the Bible."

"Job's there, sure," he said, "but there isn't no league or something between God and Satan."

"You go read it," Romey said. Then he looked at me. "Ask him—ain't it true, Lo-man—God and Satan aren't exactly buddies, but they got things worked out, kind of."

"That's right," I said.

He had Toad off balance and he knew it. "You saying that if God wanted to blow us all away," Toad said, "he'd have to check with Satan first?"

The Beanfields

"Exactly what I'm saying. They got a deal worked out. God can't take out my old man—"

"Can too," Toad said.

"No, he can't—I don't care what you think. He needs him."

"God needs your old man? God can do anything he wants on his own," Toad said.

"Sure he can—"

Suddenly he had an inspiration. "No, I know, I know, I know—maybe the devil does God's dirty work," Toad said. "Ain't it so, Lowell? God needs the devil to do what he don't want to." He giggled again. "Who's going to make life miserable if there's no Satan around—isn't that so?"

"You saying God's got dirty work to do?" I asked him.

"Sure he does. Of course he does." He looked around the field, but it was far too early for people to have their bags filled. "He's got dirty work or else what's he got to save us from—answer me that."

Romey crept along his row and stayed at it, his fingers busy in the wet plants.

"You saying the devil's like God's hired man—like you, Toad?" Romey said. "Is that what you're saying? It's like Nick is God, and you're the devil." He looked at me. "That sounds right, doesn't it, Lobo?"

"Sure," I said.

"That's why he keeps your old man around," Toad said. "Gives people something to get mad about, you know?" He was dead serious.

"Toad, maybe you ought to think about canning all of this—dump the beanfields and be a preacher," Romey said. He leaned back on his haunches. "Chuck that scale and go back to summer school and start learning something good and smart and then come back here and start preaching—a man like you."

"I don't know nothing," Toad said.

Romey looked at me. "Lobo, tell him—let him know how smart he is."

There was something pathetic about Toad—was then and probably still is today.

"I don't know if he'd make a preacher," I said. "He'd have to give up smokes—"

"I could do that," he said.

"And no more fooling with women. You just got to marry a fat one and then never once look again at another girl," I said.

That shut him up.

"And you'd have to give up working for Van Dam," I told him.

Toad looked around as if Nick might be sneaking up behind him. "I could do that—you know, he don't pay me dirt." He leaned his gaunt body over as if it were some treacherous secret. "He don't pay me enough to get by at all—I can't hardly afford my car."

"What you think preaching pays, Toad?" I said.

"Mor'n this," he said, laughing.

"But you got to go back to school," Romey said. "You got to go to school forever, and then you get out and you can't smoke and you can't swear and you can't," he waited, looking around as if jittery himself, "you can't chase women—it's like Prins says."

"Once the strike's over, I can maybe get on at Linear," he said.

"They don't pay crap either," Romey told him. "Just ask my old man."

That's when Van Dam yelled from somewhere west. Just like that, the Toad was gone. He was gawky and pimply, and when he walked down the rows, especially in front of the girls, he swaggered, his thumbs curled in his front belt loops. He amused us. He broke the tedium.

Romey sat there with his hands on his thighs. "No matter what, Lobo, I can't do anything better today than I already did—my good deed for the day is in the bag, scout's honor."

"What do you mean?" I said.

"I just kept Toad from being a preacher."

Romey was quick and deft with his hands, a champion picker when he wanted to be. He had figured that what he ought to make was five or six bucks a day, so most days he'd work like a madman, then pretty much quit while I tracked up the row behind him, trying to catch up. By late afternoon he'd loll along beside me or sit on his duff between the rows, chewing beans and flicking the ends at me. I wouldn't call him lazy. He didn't have a lazy bone in his body, but he was calculating. Often enough, he knew what he wanted to do.

Nobody wore shorts, and most everybody wore T-shirts. The only way you could tell girls from boys, once the sun got hot, was bare backs and babushkas. Great pickers came in both genders, but the bean-picking girls were always slightly older than the boys, because older guys got better jobs once their shoulders were big enough to bale hay for some farmer or lug cement for their fathers, jobs where they made more money. Girls stayed in the fields if they couldn't carhop or babysit, many of them until they were sixteen years old, sometimes older. Back then, to us as well as most boys on the crew, any of the girls with any kind of looks seemed fantasies, big-time high school girls who were, from our standpoint, real women.

Ginny Meinders was one of the best pickers, tall and willowy, but terribly strong. Unlike some of the older girls, she paid attention to the eighth-grade boys, largely because she loved a good time. She wore loose old shirts or tank tops, and her long arms could sweep easily through the rows. Sometimes whatever she wore was loose enough to gape so sweetly when she'd hunch over the rows that no boy within fifty yards could pick a handful.

It took only a day or two before we started to plan our whole day around Ginny Meinders. At dawn's early light we'd wait for her to get down from the field truck, then follow along close enough behind her to get assigned rows somewhere near to where she'd be picking. Being beside her was a mixed blessing. While being close was enough to offer a fantasy from the drudgery, she was super quick with her hands, so quick that if you looked too much she'd be half a field ahead in a half hour—and that didn't look good at all. Not only was she out of our immediate view, she'd be showing us up as if we were a couple of third-graders—and she was a woman at that. It was tough for me to hang in there. I wasn't that quick. But good day or bad, Romey could usually keep up with her if he wanted, and he wanted. Sometimes when he'd be up close, he'd simply sit on his haunches in a trance or try to chuck beans down her shirt.

"Romey," she'd say, almost schoolmarmish, standing up to shake a bean out, "I don't know what to do with you."

What happened in the beanfields one day that summer has to do with Ginny Meinders, even though she likely knew very little about the Linear strike and probably didn't even know Cyril Guttner at all. About a month had passed since my parents had learned of the whole smoking business, not quite two weeks since Zoot's terror. Time had coaxed healing back into our daily lives, even though what had happened made my conscience feel a bit more jagged when I'd take a cigarette from the packs Romey eventually started buying from the Toad. Out on the beanfields, we were three miles, maybe four, from Easton, the steeples of those churches not even visible from the lakeshore, and all around us were kids. Nick Van Dam couldn't care less what we smoked, and he was happy enough that his right-hand man was making a few extra bucks on the side.

One afternoon it was as hot and sultry as only the lakeshore can get mid-July. Romey had left to answer the call of nature. He'd stood and stretched like an old man who'd spent all day thrashing, when most of the morning he'd been picking slowly, mostly watching Ginny's every last move. He had walked down the row toward the trees—back then, nobody had ever heard of porta-potties.

He came back with a chunk of ice from his lemonade, crept over a row, then lobbed it so perfectly at Ginny, who really never saw him, that

114

The Beanfields

it slid right down her shirt. She yelped, and he stood and pumped his arm like an umpire calling a perfect third strike.

Ginny was not in the least overweight, but she had the kind of strength farm girls almost always had back then, her father a milker. She knew the source of that ice, so without even thinking, she hurdled the row between them and stood there over Romey, a lump in the dirt where he'd fallen in hysterics. She took that ice cube and stuck it under his shirt, rubbed it all over his chest, as if that were punishment. She sat on him with her knees so he couldn't pull away, but then Romey was hardly fighting—he bucked around, screamed and hollered as if it were a brutal assault, and everything stopped around us.

"Will you cut it out?" she said, all the time laughing herself. "Will you stop for once, Romey Guttner? I'm just plain sick of it." The plain truth was she wasn't as sick of it as she claimed.

But the Toad could tell when something was going on somewhere between the rows, because kids would suddenly stand to free up their thighs from the bending. It was as if a whole segment of workers would suddenly strike—everybody on their feet. And that's what happened. Ginny sat there on top of Romey like a rodeo rider, trying to melt that ice cube against his bare chest, Romey sprawled between the rows, both of them laughing. They drew a crowd—maybe a dozen kids all around us, giggling. Nobody saw the Toad come up.

"Get up," he yelled at Romey. "You think we pay you for horsing around?"

Romey didn't stop. He was loving every minute.

But Ginny got off him and back to her feet. "I'm teaching this little turd a lesson," she said. "He's always throwing stuff at me—down my shirt." She kicked him in the ribs.

Romey loved it. He pulled himself up to his elbows, then got his legs beneath him but stayed on the ground. "She's lying, Toad," he told him, still on his butt. "She loves me," he said. "She really does. She attacked me." He pointed at her. "I'm just trying to do my job here, right? And she comes over and she starts attacking me because I'm so good-looking—"

Everybody was screaming.

But Toad didn't like it at all. You could see anger in his face, but it was not anger as much as an emotion that grows from something a kissing-cousin to jealousy, because everybody in the beanfields loved Ginny.

"So what'd he do?" Toad said.

Ginny straightened the old white shirt over her, threw her shoulders back, shook her hair out of her eyes, and politely told the Toad it was none of his own stupid business. "Go weigh somebody's bag," she said. "Don't you have anything else to do?"

That jerked his jealousy a notch higher and spiked the wrath that grew from his humiliation. But he wasn't about to take her on. Ginny was far too formidable an opponent. There was a crowd gathered. This was a public event. He squirmed and steamed and then simply fell like a marble in a pinball machine to the bottom rack, the only place he could score. He couldn't take on Ginny, but Romey was another story—even though Romey was smarter. Romey was someone he could handle.

"I been watching you," he said, but I knew he was staging this for Ginny and everybody else. "All week long, I been keeping an eye on you, Guttner, and you spend a ton of time goofing off, you know that?" He had a hand raised like some teacher he'd left behind in high school. "Some of you think this is vacation or something—free trip to the lake to get away from Mama." He looked around at fifteen, maybe twenty kids standing there watching. "Well, it ain't." In his hands, he was swinging a twist of twine. "Especially not for the likes of you, Guttner."

Romey's eyes came down hard on the sound of his last name.

"Get lost," Ginny told him. She was rubbing the dirt off her hands on her jeans. "You're such a mole. It wasn't nothing. Don't act so big-time. You make everybody sick when you act that way." She picked up her foot and stepped back toward her row.

With Ginny already taking Romey's side, he didn't dare to take on Romey either, right then. Ginny Meinders was in control of the whole event, and Toad was powerless. He may not have been blessed with great smarts, but he knew that much. So he stood there huffing and puffing, smart enough to know he couldn't do anything, but too dumb to realize that all his silly posturing—flexing his shoulders and rolling his hips, sneering the way he was—was so much comic opera.

"Get back to work before I gotta call Nick," he said to the whole crew. "G'wan now," he said. "Go on. Think this is break time here? What you think, anyway?" Then he stood there for a minute, boldly, as if his was the last word. He looked around for somebody to say something, and when no one did, he walked back up the row toward the highway.

It was Romey who croaked like a frog, but Toad never looked back. Maybe he didn't hear it. Maybe he did.

The Beanfields

"Ginny," Romey said, "how about you and me at the Stardust tonight?" He pulled a huge smile, puckered his lips, and winked both eyes, one after another.

"In your dreams," she said, and turned like a goddess back to her row. We were all in love with Ginny Meinders.

At the lakeshore the air is always cooler than it is in town, a mile west, but in July, even spitting distance from the beach, the midsummer heat pushes down hard enough to draw sweat from anyone hunched over long rows of heavy beans. Eighty degrees, thickened by humid lake air, makes the beach the only real relief. At noon hour, work would shut down and the whole crew would run to the nearest shade, back east in the trees, where, hours before, we'd stowed our lunches out of the sun. The rule was you had to stay around the fields during lunch, even though Van Dam gave the whole crew a full hour. He made it very clear the first morning—no trips to the beach; but when the temperature reached the low 80s, even Van Dam turned his back and called off Toad from standing guard along the road down the hill to the lakeshore. Even so, tons of kids would stick around, munching their sandwiches under the pines and birches at the edge of the hill. Not Romey—and not me either.

That summer it was especially hot at the lakeshore, so we'd hit the beach whenever we dared, leaving socks and shoes and shirts behind. We'd go out in the water in jeans that slipped off easily once we got out deep enough. We were boys, but we were cocky and confident we'd already come a long way down the road to manhood. The cold Lake Michigan water, Van Dam's opening-day warning, and a decade of Sunday school lessons weren't enough to make us keep our jeans on, and once we were out far enough from shore, we'd turn into freshwater dolphins, flashing moons as if a row of cheerleaders stood on the beach waving pom-poms and singing the school fight song.

I remember wondering whether my parents had any idea what their insistence on my picking beans meant, in addition to my making money. The work was hard, the humidity high, the sun's glare seemingly omnipresent, with only rare interruptions, it seemed, from fleecy clouds that wandered our way from the west, where the temperature was even hotter. We didn't earn that much money, but what little we did take home seemed like a fortune. I'll never forget that check that first week— almost forty dollars. I felt as if I could buy anything.

But there was so much more to learn at work than an ethic of diligence. Often enough, Van Dam wasn't around at all, off in town having coffee or a beer somewhere, or doing business at the bank. He was there often enough to make himself a presence even in his absence, tough enough that even when he wasn't there, his face was set permanently in our consciences—in my conscience, anyway. I'm not so sure about Romey's. I was afraid of Van Dam. I'm not sure Romey was afraid of anything.

Bean-picking meant our entrance into a high school world where language was much looser than anything I'd ever heard, an opportunity for kids raised in a steeply religious community to loosen adolescent fantasies otherwise tightly bound. I knew Romey loved Ginny, even though she thought of him as little more than a pesky younger brother. While she was only a few years beyond being "just a girl," she was undeniably female, and what Romey loved about her was what we all loved—she wasn't just a snooty high school girl who, three years older than we were, thought eighth-grade guys were all vermin. At sixteen, she was the first real woman we'd ever squared off against, and she was irresistible.

We were coming back through the woods during lunch hour a little over a week into picking, when a kid named Jerry Vanders met us, his fingers up at his lips. "Shut up," he said, as if we'd been making far too much noise. "It's the Toad," he said, "and he's with Ginny. Ya gotta see this."

"Bull," Romey said, right away.

"No lie—I'm not kidding—come on." Jerry motioned us forward through the woods separating the fields from the beach. My pants—both of ours—were tight and wet from swimming, but we followed him like a couple of Iroquois, trying to avoid freshly snapped branches and tiptoe our way on a soaked carpet of black soil and a dozen species of thick green vegetation huddled near the earth.

On a bed of needles, in a grove of pine on the edge of a meadow of swamp grass, just below the big hill that rose sharply to the beanfields, we saw them—Ginny and the Toad, both of them smoking, but Ernie hovering over her with his left hand, trying to make a move on her. Ginny was on her side, not quite giving in, pulling away while not entirely disengaging. I couldn't believe it. I really couldn't. I wouldn't have if I hadn't seen it for myself. She had so much class, after all, and the Toad had nothing. But there was action there. It was something of a contest they were waging, Toad as sure of his offense as Ginny was of holding her ground. It seemed they couldn't decide whether they were after each other or their cigarettes, however, because every once in a while, as if it were required by law, Ernie would let up and they'd take a drag.

The Beanfields

We were far enough away not to be heard. "I don't believe it," Romey said, too loud for Jerry, who shook his head. "Nobody wants smokes that bad."

Ernie pushed his cigarette into the sand to free up his hand and started fiddling with her bra strap.

Jerry just about lost it. "Take it off her," he said. "Go on and take it off—"

"Shut up," Romey said.

I had had grade school girlfriends, but I'd never kissed anyone, and even though I knew it had to happen eventually, it seemed incredibly scary. I don't know that I'd ever seen two kids engaging in what Ginny and the Toad were up to, but something in me knew that this operation wasn't at all standard. The only more obvious gesture Ginny could have given him to register her unease would be simply to get up and walk away—which she didn't. That was the mystery. Whatever was happening between them, it wasn't love. That was perfectly clear. Long and gangly, he was all over her, even though she wasn't enjoying it.

Ginny tightened her elbows against her chest to keep her shirt down, but Ernie wouldn't quit, and when it finally stretched up over her chest, she kicked sideways, like a wrestler, and tore away, pulling everything back down—but not angrily. Even though the Toad didn't stop, neither did she give up the cigarette, so it was his two hands against her one, not much of a contest. She tried to throw him, then pushed him hard, the back of her arms against his shoulders, but he jumped on top as if he were wrestling.

I looked over at Romey because I half expected him to fly into the tangle and do what he could to flip Ernie off. "You going to let this go?" I said.

He didn't seem to hear me.

Toad was sitting on her. She was pinned beneath him, but she wasn't out of tricks. I suppose I underestimated her. Maybe Romey didn't. As soon as the Toad took his hands off her arms, she reached around him with her right hand and held that cigarette behind his back for what seemed to be a very long time. There was a pause in the action. They were saying something to each other. It wasn't as if all of this was really intense or even particularly violent, and all the while, you could hear them talking, Ginny telling him to cool off. That was it—she seemed so unpanicked to us that I couldn't understand what was going on.

The Beanfields

Something happened—I don't remember what, exactly. But he must have finally taken one step beyond the line she'd drawn in her mind, because all at once she took that lit cigarette and ground it into the Toad's back as if his spine were an ashtray. Ernie sprang off her like the Toad he was, screaming and swearing and reaching around frantically with both his hands to try to swat the burn.

Ginny pulled herself up and right then and there pinned her hair up behind her head, as if the Toad wasn't much more than a distraction from some grander purpose. Ernie swore and cussed, but she just watched him squirm, then got to her feet, walked over the sharp grass, and disappeared in the pines back up the hill, every moment of her exit accomplished effortlessly, as if what had happened were simply another chapter in a book she'd been reading over and over for years. Ernie kept cussing and moaning, his legs splayed beneath him as he tried to stanch the burn square in the middle of his back. He didn't go after her. He kept reaching around for a spot he simply couldn't reach with either arm. Then he flicked off his shirt and slapped at his back, tried to twist around and look for spots of blood. We were fifty yards away maybe, and we could see the welt. He kept cussing, but Ginny was long gone.

Romey never moved from behind the tree, but he just couldn't pass it up. "Smooth move, bowels," he yelled, loud enough to be heard on the top of the hill.

I don't know if the Toad ever saw us clearly enough to identify us. All three of us were hidden behind the birch, but I saw the bloodless look on his face when he finally stood, his arms still flailing at the flame imbedded in his back, and tried to locate the source of the jibe. If he did see us, it's unlikely he could have identified any one of us, because we took off running, straight north toward the road to the lake, over dead leaves and weedy saplings, through black and smelly muck—Romey leading, zigzagging through trees. Jerry hightailed it up the hill, but Romey and I threw ourselves down behind an upturned stump, as if the Toad's cussing were machine gun fire picking up little tongues of earth right at our heels. Romey could barely get his breath from all the laughing.

"He's not coming, is he?" I said, looking back, peeking around the roots, my hands in the hard dirt.

"What you sweating, anyway?" Romey said. "He don't know anything. So what if he sees us—so what?" He shook his head. "You think you and me can't handle him?" He stretched above the upturned stump. "He ain't going to chase anybody who saw him get burned the way he did—you can count on that."

"Look at these shoes," I said. "My ma'll kill me."

Romey shook his head. "That was great, wasn't it? You see what she did—" and with a wide arc he mimicked the way Ginny had brought that cigarette down into Ernie's back. "He won't be looking to get no suntan this afternoon," he said. "He already got burned."

"That was something," I said.

"Only problem is, there's gotta be a hole there now. There's got to be—poor boy's got a hole in his shirt. Think what his momma's going to say."

"Going to hurt, I bet," I said.

"Stung him good, she did."

But the whole business was still a problem for me. It was unbelievable—how Ginny would give in to someone as low down on the totem pole as the Toad. Romey didn't seem as mystified as I was. "How come?" I said.

"What do you mean how come?"

"How come she let him do that?"

"Do what?"

"Mess around like that. What'd she let him go and kiss her for in the first place?"

Romey shrugged his shoulders as if the answer was obvious. "Smokes."

"Ginny?"

"Trouble with you is, Lo-man, you got this odd idea that the whole world is full of people as nice as you are."

"No, I don't," I said, shaking my head.

He looked at me as if I were a baby.

"I didn't know Ginny smoked," I said.

"That's 'cause you always think the best. You think Ginny's thinking about catechism or something, don't you?"

"Course not," I said.

"I know better," he said.

I hated to admit it, of course. "Okay, then," I said, "if she smokes, why doesn't she just pay like everybody else?"

"She likes money," he said. "So do I."

"So she puts up with that?"

"What?" he said.

"What?" I mimicked. "Put up with him all over her like that. Wouldn't you rather pay? Good night, he's a worm."

Romey shrugged his shoulders. "You think people all got reasons for what they do?" he said. "She's got hers probably, sense or no sense." He wasn't going to waste much time thinking about it. What he loved was the Toad in pain. "He got himself burned but good." Then he looked at me. "Now he's going to be mean," he said, "you watch." He tucked in his shirt where it was soaked from his wet jeans. "Ern got burned," he said, "and I'm a poet and didn't know it." He slid a hand into his pocket and pulled out his watch. His thick eyebrows jumped, and he shrugged his shoulders. "Ain't as late as I thought it was. Time flies when you're having fun." He jabbed his thumb into my back. "That hurts, I bet," he said. "Can you imagine what that feels like—glowing butt like that?" He looked at me strangely. "What's the matter with you?" he said.

"I don't get it," I told him.

"What you talking about?"

"How come Ginny'd go back in the woods with him? She's so great."

He looked at me in that oddly perplexed way he sometimes did. "The thing with you, Lobo," he said, "is you got something wrong with you, in here," he pointed to his head. "Something got screwed up, because you think the whole world is just like what you got at home or something." He wiped sweat out of his eyes with the back of his sleeve.

"I just want to know why," I said. "It's looney for her—"

"Just let her be," he said. He shook his head at me, then nodded. "Come on. We're going to be late and Ernie's going to burn us all afternoon—you can bet on that." We started moving through the trees. "You got so much to learn and I got so little time," he said, laughing. "That's what my old man always tells me."

"He does?"

"If he's in a good mood."

Midafternoon, your legs feel gimpy from being in a crouch all day long. The air is sticky and thick, and your hands feel shredded from a thousand little skirmishes with the sharp edges of the leaves. Your fingers get numb, and everybody gets lazy. Even the shenanigans go flat. If we'd have been slaves, it would have been time, I suppose, for a song to resurrect the spirit—a song or a whip.

Ginny stood up later that afternoon and emptied her full pail into the burlap bag, bounced it once or twice, gathered the opening in her hand, and pulled it tight. Romey and I were no more than three or four rows away. We'd said nothing to her about what we'd seen. I think Romey understood that to bring it up would have been in poor taste.

She stood and waited for the Toad to come to weigh her in. She was known for her shrill whistling when she wanted him, both sets of fingers in her mouth, but this time, she simply stood and waited. I saw what was going on, and so did Romey. Neither of us could take our eyes

The Beanfields

off her very long. When she didn't whistle, Romey did—Romey the gentleman.

Ernie turned around maybe fifty yards up the field and looked for someone standing. He hated to be whistled at, even though it happened all the time. We watched him spot her, then drop his eyes. He started walking, talking with pickers wherever he crossed rows, trying to be cute. I don't remember where Jerry was by that time, but I don't think another soul on that whole crew had any idea what had happened that noon hour—no one but us.

I was tired and weak and worn, and it wasn't hard for me to just shut down operations, because I knew that a spark was about to light something bigger right here, a few rows away. Romey never looked at me, but he sat down on his butt, his legs out in front of him in the row, because he wasn't about to miss a thing.

Not even after Romey whistled did Ginny make a motion with her hands, but Ernie knew she had a full bag. He hadn't been near her since we'd started picking after lunch, even though he'd been all over the field weighing bags and punching tickets. As he came up the last few yards, he moved more quickly, the last inch or so of one of his Kools stuck between his lips, like a Van Dam cigar.

Ginny pushed the bag toward him; he lifted it in one of his skinny arms as if the weight was nothing at all, and then dropped it once or twice to settle the beans. She pulled out her card. Ernie twisted and tied a swatch of twine around the open end of the bag, then lifted it once more after catching the knot in the hook of the scale. He had his back to us. The burn she'd stuck there looked like a bullet hole. There was no blood.

He held the bag up with one arm, read the total loud enough for us to hear a row over. "Fifty-one pounds," he said and reached for her card when he dropped the bag with a heavy thud to the ground. That's all he said. She didn't say a thing herself. From his back pocket, he retrieved his punch and did his job. Ginny looked at him, put her hands on her hips, but said nothing.

"What'sa matter with you?" he said, cocking his eyebrows.

She glanced down at her card, then rolled her eyes, tipping back her head with disgust. And then she said something neither of us caught, but both of us understood.

"You got a problem?" he snapped back, and just like that he left, toting her bag after pulling another empty one from the bunch at his belt and dropping that one at her feet.

For the first time, Ginny looked angry. She looked down at her card, then back at him. But Ernie was already several rows south, not looking back.

"He spiked her," Romey said.

I had no idea what was going on.

"He gave her more weight than she deserved—I bet you any money, Lo-man. I bet you anything. He gave her ten pounds, maybe—who knows how much?"

"He did?"

"Because he wants to lean on her—that's why," he said. He crawled back toward me, stared into my face. "You get it, blind man? He's not finished with her yet."

I didn't.

He laid down between the rows because he didn't want to be heard, then he talked as if he were speaking to a deaf man, his lips exaggerating every word. "He gave her more weight," he said. "He's paying her."

It still angered me—the whole thing. "What's she take it for?"

"It's money in the bank, dodo," he said. "She needs it. They ain't full of money, Lo-bo—Ginny's folks. Maybe she can't afford to be so righteous."

"But what's she got to give him?"

"She don't know exactly. I think she wishes it was over—that's why she's mad." He got to his haunches.

"Why doesn't she say something?" I said.

"To who, stupid?" he said. "He's management, you know—what's she got going for her?" He looked at Ginny. "Hey, Tootsie," he said.

She looked up.

"Bean brain give you a hard time, did he?"

She shook her head. She wouldn't say a thing.

"How about we get him for you?" he said.

She smiled. "Just what I need is a couple of hit men," she said.

He snarled like a gangster. "Me and Lobo—we do contracts," he said. "Want him taken out?"

She laughed again. She was seated on her rear end, still fuming, her legs sprawled out in front of her as if she didn't want to pick another bean.

"You tell him, Toots—if he plays with fire, he's going to get himself burned," Romey said.

She seemed startled. "How'd you know that?" she said.

"You're a munchkin," he said. "I'm the Wizard of Oz."

Romey whistled the Toad over an hour later, when both of us had our bags full. It happened at a time Nick Van Dam was around, strutting between the rows in the kingly silence he always maintained. Everybody winced when he was around, the whole crew taking everything more seriously, backs lowered in the rows, no talking, no joshing. The boss was not so much heartless and cruel as he was simply emotionless. More often than I care to remember, I watched him send kids hiking home, not a trace of anger, remorse, or even a dime's worth of pity. I did worry about what we'd seen at noon, because I wasn't altogether sure that the Toad didn't recognize Romey's sneering at him— even someone as pressed for brains as Ernie would have figured there weren't many kids in the field brassy enough to risk what Romey did with that bowels comment. Besides, Romey often got blamed for things, but then Romey was guilty, often as not. This time, when the Toad came over to weigh us up, he had other worries on his mind than who might have seen what during the noon hour. Nick was standing there watching his every move.

"You guys full?" the Toad said, all business—no wisecracks, no smiles.

Romey would have had some smart answer if Nick hadn't been around, but we simply nodded our heads.

He grabbed my bag and tied it up quickly like a cowboy champ tying a calf, two or three twists and a hitch. He bounced the bag once or twice, hooked the scale into the twine, and picked it up in one hand, Nick gnawing a cigar maybe three rows away and ten yards back toward the lake.

"Forty-three, looks like," the Toad said, after waiting for the needle to stop jumping on the rusty scale. He dropped it, punched my card, and stepped over the row to pick up Romey's.

"Forty-nine," he said, after going through the motions. Then he looked closely at the bag, kicked it once or twice with his foot, and stared. "You two been picking close together, right? You usually do, don't you?"

Romey nodded.

Nick took a couple of steps closer, then slipped his hand inside his shirt and scratched at his chest. The Toad pulled out his jackknife and cut the twine he'd just tied around Romey's bag. Then he fished around inside with both hands, looking for mud clods, the whole time very conscious of the boss right there watching him, watching the whole thing. "I don't trust it," he said.

"It's all beans," Romey said.

Ernie scooped some out, dropped them in handfuls in the sand to get deeper inside, his eyes on Romey the whole time, glancing up as if he could beat out some truth with his authority. He wouldn't have done that if Nick hadn't been there. He was all steel now, big-time enforcer.

"What's the big test?" Romey said. "You don't trust me or what?"

It wouldn't have been like Romey to put clods in the bag. Not that Romey didn't pull some smarmy deals here and there during that summer we were best buddies, but I was sure then and I'm sure today that upping his weight wasn't something he was guilty of. He didn't have to cheat. He knew what he wanted to pick every day he was out there, and he got it. That kind of cheating, Romey would have thought, was in poor taste. Any mongrel half-brain could shove clods in a bag.

Ernie was smiling because now it had become a contest.

"Go on," Nick said.

Ernie stood there over the nearly full bag, and I saw—I remember it well—some reluctance in him just then. I don't think the Toad believed Romey would have loaded down the bag, but what he had in mind was a show, something to impress the boss—"watch me make these guys wither," that kind of thing.

"I ain't got all day," Nick said. "You think he's loading up, then dump it."

The Toad didn't have a choice, so he dumped every last bean in a pile, then foraged through the clumps.

"You're wasting your time," Romey told them. "You're wasting all kinds of time—including mine. Nothing in there but beans. Go ahead—ask Lowell Prins. Ask him!"

Ernie got down in a crouch to sift through, and he picked up one single clod, just one, the size of a child's fist. I don't know where he got it. Maybe he kicked it up from the ground. Maybe he figured he had to find something if he was going to make the accusation. Maybe he thought he was really wasting the boss's time if he didn't come up with anything. One single clod—he held it up for Nick.

"Piddly," Nick said. "Keep 'em clean, boys. Piece of mud like that costs me."

The Toad held that measly chunk of dirt out, and Romey, in his typical style, cocked his head and sneered at the Toad, twisted his face just enough to spite Ernie, to let him know he thought the Toad was a zero. Not a word was said, only a twist of an eyebrow, one little gesture that became a flame when it hadn't even appeared to carry any heat at all. I'm sure Nick never saw it. But I did, and so did Toad, who read it as if it were a slap across the chops.

"He stuck it in there on purpose," Ernie said to Nick. "Something this big doesn't just climb in the bag."

The Beanfields

But Nick didn't want to make as big a deal out of it. He shook his head and sneered. "Let him be," he said, and then he looked at Romey, pointing at the mess. "Just clean up the row there. This time we'll look the other way."

Another whistle came up from across the field.

"He give you trouble before?" Nick said.

"He's a Guttner," Ernie said. "Can't trust him farther than you can throw him," he told the boss. "I got to check through every last bag."

I couldn't remember that ever happening.

"Some of them you just got to watch close," Toad said. "They'll take ya for everything you're worth if you don't watch every last move they make—some of 'em like this one."

For the first time in the year or so we'd hung out together, I felt something mighty and fisted take hold of my lungs and heart and then squeeze, something that ripped the breath out of me. It wasn't fair and it wasn't right, and the guy had said it as if Romey weren't even there, as if Romey weren't capable of hearing what he could have heard if Toad had been six or seven rows away at the raw end of a stiff lake breeze. He'd said it as if it were a fact nobody in the whole county would have ever questioned—not Nick certainly; and he'd said it proudly, all around us a dozen kids who'd heard it just as clearly as I had. I don't remember a time I wasn't afraid of Cyril Guttner. I can't remember a time I was at Romey's place when I didn't wonder what I'd do, which door I'd take, if Cyril were to come home suddenly. I wasn't blind. There were nights I couldn't miss the anxiety on my parents' face as I'd leave the house, in silence, not telling them where I was going because I didn't want to tell them the name, to say it aloud, even though they knew very well where I'd be. And not for a minute did I wonder what they thought of Cyril Guttner. There would be more trouble that summer, much, much more, but I'll never forget the moment I heard the Toad, who was himself being judged right then, indict the Guttners in a fashion he simply assumed Romey himself would blithely accept, as if some facts were so self-evident that anyone, anytime could announce them to the world like moral absolutes. Romey was a Guttner, and what could you do about that? He was simply going to be trouble. I stood there beside him.

"I ain't got the wherewithal to get mad right now," Nick said. "Doesn't amount to much anyway. Dock 'im five pounds." He looked down at the hump of beans. "Hurry up and stick 'em back in," he said. "There's plenty of time. You're lucky we're letting you off so clean."

We held out our cards and the Toad punched them both, but Romey didn't even look down. Some kid yelled from somewhere across the

The Beanfields

field, but the two of them stood there to make sure Romey filled up the bag. They stayed there and hovered over him, Romey slowly getting down to his knees. Nothing was said.

So Romey filled that burlap bag up once more from the pile the Toad had left between the rows. I kept on picking, pretended I didn't hear any of it—nothing at all. I kept slaving away at the plants, head down, fingers flying faster than they had since early morning, filling my hands with five-inch beans. Romey worked like a nailer, beans flying from the pile on the ground into the burlap until the whole forty-some pounds were back inside, all the time muttering cuss words I didn't want to hear in a tone just soft enough not to be heard explicitly.

When it was over, he picked himself up, tightened the top of the bag into a handle, tied it just like the Toad would have, very methodically, then handed it to him, his flashing eyes the only sign of hate.

Maybe ten minutes later, Ernie came back with new bags for both of us, Nick long gone in his pickup. "Hey," he said, "sorry about dumping you like that, but the boss says I got to do it more often—know what I mean? He says the beans are way too dirty." He dropped the empty bag over Romey's shoulder. "He wants me to get tough." He shrugged his shoulders. "Sorry, eh?"

Romey never looked up.

"I got nothing against you," Toad said from my row. "He was right there, looking over my shoulder, all right? You saw him. He about told me to check you out. He did. He told me before we even got here. He said it had to be done. You get to know him about those things."

"So how come you didn't you dump *his?*" Romey said, pointing at me. "How come I'm the sucker?"

"No difference," Ernie said, bobbing his head.

"You're lying," Romey told him. "You ain't got the guts to tell the truth, either."

"Listen," Ernie said, "I got better things to do than take your mouth," he said, and he started walking slowly toward the woods at the end of the field. He looked back. "Check out your card," he said. "I didn't dock you a thing."

Romey never took his card out of his pocket. For a long time he didn't say a word, nor did he pick. I let him alone for a while, kept going up my row, confident he could catch me whenever he felt like it.

A couple of minutes passed, and I finally tried to start in on something about the Braves, the game coming up that night, maybe—who would be pitching—but Romey wouldn't hear of it. He picked up a hand-

The Beanfields

ful of beans and winged them down the row, just threw them away. "You know *why* he did it," he said, "you know darned well." He was sitting on his knees, as if what had happened had turned his mind around completely about bean-picking. "That's the whole mess here, Lowell Boy," he said, and he picked up a bean, broke it in two pieces, and whipped them at me, one after another, hitting me square in the back. "You know how come he went after me, don't you?"

I didn't say a thing.

And then he simply walked away. He took off down the row toward the highway, away from the lake and toward town. He left everything behind, his bucket and his bag, a candy bar or some Twinkies somewhere in the nest of trees at the east edge of the field, even a half pack of L & Ms, and he just walked home.

I never said a thing. I didn't try to stop him because I knew very well I couldn't say a word.

At that moment, I don't know who was more the enemy—the Toad or me, his friend. Because Romey was right. There wasn't a thing he could do about his being a Guttner; and there wasn't a thing I could do about it either—about being the son of my father. It wasn't a choice either of us had ever made—which family we were going to be born into. Neither of us got to pull some switch or choose from a bunch of slides scattered over a table lit from a bulb beneath. I was thinking right then, all alone between the rows for the rest of the day, that there was nothing either of us had a choice about, because if there had been a way we could have, I believed Romey would never have picked his old man, and maybe, right then, I wouldn't have chosen mine either.

The Toad was over on the other side of the field. At first, I thought Romey just might go after him, try to even the score. But he didn't. He walked straight up the row, his shirt dancing across his butt where he'd tied it. He followed the straightest line between the spot in the row where everything had happened and the highway a half mile west of the field. He just walked away, and he never went back to the beanfields.

"I don't blame him," Ginny said, sitting in her row, her shoulders slumped as if she were tired too. "Not one bit, I don't blame him. I wish I had the guts myself."

For another week or so I got up at 5:30, had breakfast, gathered my lunch, and took off on my bike for the village park, where I climbed up into the back of the truck with the rest of the kids and rode out to the fields in the silence of dawn.

But I never told my folks I was going alone. I never said that Romey, who was a much better picker than I was and whose family was undeniably poorer, had simply walked off the job that day. I never told them, and for that reason I never had to explain why he'd left.

The rest of the season, I hated every last day of bean-picking.

I honestly and truly felt sorry that day for Romey Guttner. I suppose I should have sat there in my row and prayed for him—he was, after all, my friend. But I didn't, maybe because I didn't think of him as powerless. There was, after all, something grand about the way he walked off the job. I knew his old man would have been proud—and he'd have had every right to be.

I didn't pray much for Romey Guttner because I didn't think he needed it. Everybody else did. Everybody else thought he needed something only the Lord could give him, and maybe he did. But I never imagined Romey to be on the level of the poor and widowed, the lame and palsied. And I certainly didn't think of him as one of the fatherless.

When I remember the way he looked at me that day in the beanfields, I really believe he pitied me for what I didn't know. I don't think my father would have understood all of that back then, and I really don't know if he'd understand it today.

The Beanfields

History

When Romey left his five-gallon pail beside a handful or two of beans, walked west up the row to the highway, and then, quite righteously, marched all the way back to town, he left me behind as well. I didn't see him much at all in the next week or so because he never came back to the beanfields, and I did. He was out of town, Hattie said when I dropped over there one night. He was gone with his father somewhere—I didn't know where exactly, but I do remember that when he came back he was wearing a bright blue Chicago Cubs cap.

A little over a week after Romey left the beanfields, twenty boys or more along with a half-dozen fathers showed up at church at the appointed time to leave for swimming in the brand new swimming pool, the first indoor pool in the whole county. It was built in Brandon, at the high school, but in a way, it was a gift to the whole region from Linear Industries, which had long ago made Brandon a showplace town. Kids from all over the county went in groups that first summer and had a ball in a place so huge it had a double-tiered gallery that held as many people as Easton Junior High's old Quonset gymnasium.

I had the night marked on the calendar weeks ahead of time and wouldn't have missed it for anything. I'd called over to Romey's place in the late afternoon, and Hattie said he'd be there at church. She said she expected him back soon. I could tell she was having a cigarette, because the pitch of her voice would hollow and rise when she blew out smoke. She sounded gravelly, but happy.

That night, when the whole group assembled, Romey didn't show. We waited ten painful minutes, at least, at the church, our towels rolled up under our arms, all of us watching precious seconds tick off the clock in the fellowship room. The dads talked furtively, the way men always talked about Guttners. They told us that waiting was good for us, in the tone of voice that suggested martyrdom—patience in the Lord—but it was partially a joke. I'm sure they were anxious to go themselves, but neither did they want to risk Cyril's wrath if they'd be leaving the moment Romey's old man drove up.

But that wasn't all of it, either. In any sort of church stuff back then, Romey—like his little sisters—always merited a measure or two of special grace. Almost always, Romey got the benefit of the doubt from church people; for him they'd go the extra mile. Those fathers waited and waited that night, and the whole lot of us got cranky and didn't go on-time because it was Romey who hadn't showed. Had it been someone from a good home, the dads would have chalked up the absence to sheer negligence, left at 6:30 sharp, and figured the kid needed a lesson. Not so Romey. He was a black sheep, one of a kind in the church we both attended, Romey not nearly so frequently as I did, but most people understood very well that Romey Guttner didn't have the advantages of Lowell Prins. Most people felt he required special treatment, and most people gave it to him, out of love.

Fifteen long minutes we waited. Finally, simply with the nod of a head from one of the men, we left—without him.

It was a Thursday night, the only available night, because the new place was busy with reservations. We had a ball. A backboard and rim were set up on one end, where a bunch of us played swimming pool basketball for most of the night, getting up gracefully in the water to slam home rugged dunk shots. We dove for junk we'd throw to the bottom, did headstands, had a few races, jumped dozens of times off the low diving board in a series of cannonballs, can openers, jackknives, and belly flops that left our chests pink and sore. When we left, the only thing I regretted was chickening out from a soaring vault off the high dive, but then very few kids actually took the huge plunge. I jumped, but I didn't dive—that was too scary. I would have, of course, if Romey'd been there; he would have, that's certain. And I would have too—I couldn't have taken the kidding if I'd chickened out. Next time, I told myself when I walked home from church later that night. We had a ball in the brand new Brandon pool.

That night, there seemed to be more peace than life had offered so far that summer; maybe it was the fact that Romey hadn't been around for a while. I remember feeling a return of innocence. An hour or more after leaving the pool, I could still feel the water in my face, my pores open and breathing with life. I'd been in Lake Michigan's icy cold waters dozens of times but had never felt the prickly scouredness I felt that night in back-seat darkness as we drove home from the brand new Brandon pool, a whole car full of exhausted kids.

The world seemed full of promise: the pool was a huge delight, the edge had gone out of the air at home, my long hours in the beanfields themselves a penance for the sins I'd committed early in the summer. What had happened at Zoot's didn't erase the whole business of stealing cigarettes, but it was a bigger story for the rest of the town, and some of the anxiety dissipated. Both Mom and Dad knew what kind of work bean-picking was, so when I'd get home there would always be something special on the bar in the kitchen, some cookies or cake.

I came in the back door that night after hanging my wet towel and suit over the line in the darkness of the back yard. When I came up the steps from the back hall, my mother asked me how it had gone, and I described the place, from the huge windows on the side and above, to the gallery, to the basketball rim, to the spacious shower rooms. She was sitting in the dining room, the newspaper opened before her, the windows open to a lake breeze that even on the hottest summer days made air-conditioning unnecessary on the lakeshore. I told her how I wished I could go every night, and how I thought we ought to live in Brandon and not Easton. She laughed because that was just so much talk. Like any other Easton kid, I'd soaked in a ton of loyalty to the town whose uniform I'd already worn through four years of Little League. "Besides," she said, "we'd be right in the middle of everything then," meaning the strike. "I wouldn't care to be any closer to that mess than we are."

I'd forgotten about the strike. "Why don't we get a pool like that?" I said. "How come this town doesn't have anything great like that for kids?"

She looked up from the paper and adjusted her glasses. "They have Linear—that's why," she told me. "Easton doesn't even have a factory—"

"Millers—" I said.

"Not everybody needs a cement mixer," she told me, and then she smiled. "Absolutely everybody needs a toilet—these days more than one, in fact. These days three or four."

"There wouldn't be a Linear if everybody still had outdoor plumbing," I said.

"Thank goodness for Linear," she said, looking back down at her paper.

I poured myself a glass of milk from the refrigerator. "I'd never do any schoolwork if we had a place like that, Mom," I said. "I'd be there every night."

"All the guys were there?"

I bumped the door shut with my knee. "Romey never showed up," I said. "We even waited. We didn't leave till seven almost, but he never showed—I told him, too. I called him this afternoon, talked to his mom. She said he was coming."

Once more, her head came up from the paper. "He wasn't there?" she said.

"We waited a half hour—seemed like. People got mad because we kept waiting."

"Where was he?" she said.

"How am I supposed to know?" I said. "Everybody's asking me tonight—you know, about Romey. I don't know where he was. I haven't seen him for a while." It was actually a kind of joy to say that to my mother.

She pulled back from the table and swung around to face me. It was just past 9:30, a Thursday night, the beautiful pool water still clogging up my ears, and I was thinking about what kind of lunch I might have the next day, on what would turn out to be one of the last days of picking beans.

"Did *he* tell you he was coming along?" she said.

I was looking for a lunch to be sure she'd made it while I was gone. "Yeah—I called him. Hattie did. Hattie said he'd be there." I hunched my shoulders. "Romey says stuff that doesn't happen sometimes, Mom."

She turned away.

I found some sugar cookies in the cookie jar and poured a glass of milk. She closed the paper, a vacant look on her face, as if she were listening to a distant conversation.

I was tired, but the Braves were playing somewhere, and the idea of going to bed after such a great night—and the night before what could well be the last day of work—seemed wrong. Besides, going to bed without being told was something I'd done only in those first days after get-

History

ting caught stealing cigarettes. So I picked the sports section off the table in front of her, stuck it under my arm, and carried my cookies and milk into the living room, where I fooled with the dial on the new Magnavox. I laid out the paper on the floor and flopped down, taking most of the space in front of the couch, lying on my stomach, propped on my elbows, my cookies and milk beside me on the floor. "Dad gone somewhere?" I said, an afterthought.

She didn't answer. I hadn't heard her get up from her chair. But I wasn't thinking much about her silence because it had been a great night, the ball game was on, and tomorrow was one morning closer to the last day of picking beans.

When my father came in, he came through the living room door—which was odd, I thought, because usually only company used that door. He seemed surprised to see me lying there on the carpet, at least he didn't appear to know exactly how to look at me. He took off his hat, stood there with it awkwardly. "Had a good time at the pool?" he said. My father never made trite conversation with me.

I watched him take off his sport coat and hang it up in the living room vestibule, and I said it was a great time, swimming in the Brandon pool.

"Good," he said, in a voice that seemed almost angry. Then he looked at me again, a quick glance before he straightened the coat on the hanger. But that was a different look, not at all businesslike. It was quick, little more than a glance, almost furtive, but I read it immediately as something wrung from fear. His cheeks were red, flushed. With his fingers, he tried to straighten his hair. "Yeah," he said. "I'm glad you had a good time."

He went into the kitchen and barked something at my mother, something I didn't hear exactly—not a reprimand, nothing to make her angry. But he barked it, uncharacteristically. The tone wasn't meant for her or about her, because immediately she tried to comfort him—I could tell by her voice, even though their conversation was deliberately pitched to keep me from hearing. My father was very angry.

I swung myself around toward the dining room so I could hear them.

"On purpose, Fran," he said. "He did it on purpose. He had them all there—even the little girls. Can you imagine? There was the whole family, all dressed up as if we were coming for dinner." He coughed, as if he was really exasperated. "We figured we'd try to take him out of there—that was what we were going to do, but he had the whole family lined up, all dressed up."

"Pete—" she whispered.

"The man is crazy," my father said, raising his voice. "He's a maniac. He's dangerous and he's crazy. I don't know what we can do. It's like dealing with someone who's not even from this world, I swear."

I started to catch on.

"Romey was there too," my father said. "So I asked him, you know, in all innocence—I said to him that I thought he'd be swimming with the rest of the guys. And Cyril says, 'He ain't swimming in no company pool.' That's exactly what he said, Fran—his whole family is lined up almost as if some photographer is coming, and Cyril says, 'That place is full of my blood.' That's what he said exactly."

That's why Romey wasn't swimming. That's why Romey wasn't there when we were waiting for him, when we were having this great time in the Brandon pool, swimming in his father's blood.

"He was spoiling for a fight, Fran, from the moment we got there—and everybody was lined up, even the little girls. He said everything right in front of them."

Something about his having been there, something about Romey sitting there in a photographer's pose with the rest of his family when my father was over there doing something Cyril hated—what, I didn't know—something about that image made me mad. My first impulse was to get up to my room, to get out of there completely. I didn't want to have anything to do with it, with anything. I didn't want to answer questions. I didn't want to talk about the Guttners. I didn't want to talk about anything connected with Romey or Cyril.

But I couldn't leave. To get upstairs I'd have to walk past them, through the dining room and kitchen to get to the stairs, and I didn't want to do that, didn't want to be noticed, didn't want to be drawn in. I started thinking about going outside, but it was close to ten and I couldn't do anything just a room away without being heard.

"She looked beat, Fran," he said. "Hattie looked as if she was perfectly exhausted. I swear it. It hurt to have to see her like that. For a dime I'd have stolen her out of there, I swear it. The preacher said it too. 'The woman has to leave somehow,' he said on the way home."

Silence.

"I don't know how we're going to manage it," he said.

I didn't want to listen and I didn't want to give them a sense of my hearing any of it at all, so I rustled the pages of the paper in front of me as I turned them, as if oblivious, as if to make very clear that I wasn't hearing a thing.

"I've never met anyone like him," my father said. And then he lowered his voice and said something about evil.

"SSSShhhhh," my mother warned.

My father had gone to Guttner's to talk about something with Romey's dad—that much I knew. I didn't know what it was, but I wondered why it had to be my father who had to be over there. Maybe union stuff, I thought. Maybe they were still trying to pin all that mess at Zoot's place on Cyril. Maybe it was Zoot. Maybe they wanted to get the two of them together or something. I didn't know what it was, but I hated the idea that my father was at that place. I knew he was like a cop, a church cop.

He must have been standing at the table, and he was a room away, but I could hear almost everything, enough, at least, to make me realize how angry he was. He wasn't sitting down, and my mother was constantly trying to keep him quiet.

"You know what he said? 'There's nothing you can say about me that can't be blabbed right in front of my kids,' he says." He laughed sardonically, something I'd rarely heard from my father. "So what were we supposed to do, Fran? The whole time, he never looked at Hattie, acted as if she weren't there, weren't human—never looked at any of them, really. They were his shield—you understand? They were there so we couldn't do anything, couldn't say anything, but it didn't stop him. Oh, no—nothing would stop him."

My mother said nothing.

"So we told him," my father said. "Maybe we shouldn't have—I don't know. Maybe it wasn't smart, but how would it have looked if the two of us had just walked out of there without delivering what it was we came to bring?"

"How did you say it?"

"Delicately—we got it out but not with any force—"

"How can you say what you had to delicately?"

"It wasn't at all what we had planned, but we'd never figured on the whole family."

"What happened?" she said.

"He got mad—what else is new? The preacher tried to do it nicely, sort of beating around the bush because the kids were there. But we weren't going to let him bully us—and he did it well, too, I think, Reverend Kosters, I mean." Silence. An odd giggle. "We weren't going to let him have his way—that's what we told each other on the way over there. We weren't going to be buffaloed by him this time, so there he is with the whole family decked out. So what do you do? He makes things so terribly difficult. He's—I can't say, Fran," he told her. "I can't tell you what I think of him."

"What did you say?" my mother asked.

History

"I wasn't going to let that man call the shots—not anymore. He's done it too long. We've just let him go for way too long—seventy times seven, you know? There comes a time when something has to be done."

They'd gone to Guttner's to talk about something with Cyril, and Romey and the little girls had been there, and it was a mess, and when in my mind I saw Romey there at the Guttner's place watching my own father be righteous, I figured for sure Romey would never speak to me again.

"Honestly, I'm afraid of the guy," my father said. "That woman lives in fear. I know she does, and it's in me right now. I don't know what he'll do. That's the difference between him and us, Fran. I don't know what he's capable of—I really don't. With everybody else in church, I think I know their limits, but I don't know about Cyril—I just don't. He scares me because I don't know what he's capable of. I don't think he has any limits."

A thump of fists on the front door broke the stillness—the living room door, the door only guests came in, and I was closest, lying there on the floor with the radio on behind me. I put my hands beneath me and got to my feet. I honestly didn't know if they'd really assumed that I couldn't hear the entire conversation, but it made me uncomfortable to think that they had, so I yelled something about the score of the baseball game as I got to my feet. I snapped the outside light on when I got to the door. I saw Cyril standing there in his undershirt, his hands jammed in his pockets, his hair standing on end.

"Get your old man," Cyril said through the screen.

"You want to come in?" I asked.

"Get your old man here," Cyril repeated.

I opened the door, but he made no move to come in the house. I walked back into the living room, but my father knew who was there before I'd even said a word, and he was there behind me already.

I left, fast. When I came into the dining room, my mother's hands were up at her lips. Fear was in her eyes. "You go upstairs," she told me, pointing. "It's time for you to be in bed—work tomorrow." That's what she told me. She folded up the newspaper crossword puzzle and headed for the piano room at the other side of the house. She grabbed my arm and hugged me, as if it was a good-night kiss, something she'd not done much at all in the last year or so, something that had stopped after the stealing incident.

I climbed the stairs in silence, but I wanted to be out of there myself. It bugged me that Cyril had even seen me when I came to the door. I didn't want any part of this. It wasn't my fight. Romey and I were buddies, and it didn't make a bit of difference what our parents were like or who they were. I didn't have to be in the middle of this, because out in the field when we were hunting or along the river when we were trapping—even at ball games and just hanging out—it wasn't a matter of whose kids we were, not at all. We were just two guys. That's it. Maybe we were two guys who'd already got themselves in too much trouble that summer, but so did other kids—big deal. I didn't need any part of what was going on here. I hated it. The image of my father over there with the preacher, my father representing the church and acting like Jesus in front of Cyril and Romey and Hattie and everybody—it was sick, I thought. I didn't hate him for it, but I hated his being there in the cause of justice and righteousness and all of that. I hated it because I knew that's what it was.

In my bedroom, the sound of angry voices rose through the floor register. I sat on my bed and waited, my fingers tingly with some kind of hybrid fear, equal parts dread and anger. I didn't know what to do because I couldn't just forget about what was happening. I wanted to talk to Romey, to apologize for whatever it was my father was up to, coming over to their house that night and saying whatever it was he must have said right in front of him, right in front of the whole family, even his little sisters. It always had to be my old man who was straightening people out—that's what I thought. Who made him sheriff of the church? Who appointed him God?

What I wanted to do was head out to the river with Romey, get out there early as if it were just now winter and the dawn were coming up on the lakeshore to the east. I wanted to go check traps and maybe light up a cigarette, just the two of us, sit out there in the pale sky and wait for the sun. It was night, but I wanted more than anything to be out somewhere away from Easton, away from the strike, away from church steeples. We didn't need their wars—Romey and I didn't. He was just like Cyril, really, my father was. They were exact opposites, but without each other maybe they wouldn't have been. If my father hadn't been a saint, Romey's father wouldn't have been evil. It was that simple. If my father had kept his righteous nose out of Cyril's business, this whole mess wouldn't be going on.

Tightly sharpened voices rose and fell in emotion that moved in voluble gusts. What I heard didn't sound at all like my father's voice, but the words that came through the register weren't enough for me to put full sentences together—just bits and pieces. If I was going to know what had happened, if I was going to talk to Romey myself sometime, if I was going to make sense out of all of this, then as much as I hated knowing

History

anything, I knew I'd better try to figure something out. My old man thought this whole thing was his fight, but it wasn't—I knew Cyril Guttner too, maybe better than my old man did, far better, maybe, because I knew his son.

I flipped off my Keds and set them quietly on the floor at the side of my bed, then took two long steps to the doorway, bent over and put both hands on the hallway rug, and got down to my knees. If I were in my sister's room, I figured I could hear what they were saying.

I pushed myself out over the rug and crept forward through the hallway, past my parents' bedroom until my head stuck through the doorway of my sister's room. I turned on my side and wiggled under the bed until I could touch the heat register with my fingers. Only my legs stuck out from the bed frame. I knew that if I opened the register, I could hear every last word, so I reached up to the wall board and pulled gently, not wanting to make a sound.

"This doesn't have a thing to do with the union," my father said. Every word came clearly. "It's what you're doing to your family."

Cyril cussed, loud and hard, and then, "Who do you think you are telling me I'm a lousy father? I ain't going to let you get away with that kind of—"

"Don't use that language in my house—"

Cyril kept right on going. "Damned church people," he said. "You think you can run my life, don't you? Every one of you."

Cyril seemed almost calm compared to my father, whose voice was much sharper than I'd ever heard it, laced tight with anger.

"Fancy righteous people," Cyril said. "You all figure you can tell me what's right about how to do my life. You can go to Hell for all I care."

I'd never heard swearing in my own house before, never.

"The whole lot of you," he said, "the whole lot of you is holy fools. You figure you're perfect, don't you? People tell me long ago that I'd get myself in a snake's nest here in this town with all these religious people, but what do I know, right? I figure I'll leave them alone and they'll let me have my peace, but that ain't the way it works here, does it? You got to run other people's lives—the whole lot of you."

"We're not saying that," my father said.

"Fooling yourself if you think you aren't," he said.

I could feel my heart against the wood floor. Everything was out of control again, a rotten mess, just like the night of that home visit. It was my father down there talking to Cyril, but I knew what he felt too—a deep and fertile fear of Cyril Guttner. It seemed to me right then that if someone would take Cyril apart, piece by piece, if you'd look at every

History

last part of him—all his insides lined up and identified on a cold steel table somewhere—you'd probably still not find that black something in him, that shard of darkness, heavy as night, that made Cyril Guttner what he was. Would he even have a soul? I didn't know.

"It's your life I'm talking about—your family's," my father said. "I'm not accusing you of anything. I'm trying to help."

If you'd just let him be, maybe things would get better, I thought. That's what Hattie tried to do. But my father had tried to interfere. You have to just let Cyril go when he's around and hope he leaves—that's the way it was at Romey's place. That's what Romey said. You just have to stay out of his way. But my father couldn't leave well enough alone. I couldn't get that image out of my mind—my father and Reverend Kosters standing right in front of the whole family like two perfect saints. My Mr. Righteousness father.

"Only way people like you can help me is by parking yourself on the other side of town," Cyril said.

"Just think a minute, Cyril," my father said, trying to calm him. "Try to understand what we're—"

"Give me one good reason I should take you fussing around inside my life—give me one good reason any man should take that kind of messing around—"

"Nobody's trying to hurt you—"

"Road to Hell is paved with good intentions," Cyril said, "didn't I hear that once? That from the Bible? Ought to be if it isn't. You're in there too, you know—ain't just for me, the Bible ain't."

"Cyril, if we can't talk in peace—if you can't be civil here—"

"I can't be civil when you're parking yourself in the middle of my life—and my family's life—for no good reason except I'm union. That's the whole thing here. I'm the only man with guts enough to stand up for the truth over there, the only one in this town full of jerks, and I'm getting all the blame—"

I've never questioned the existence of God, always believed he's counted me as one of his. The Bible itself offered me reasons—Jacob the conniver, King David the adulterer, Peter, who stood in front of a host of people and told three bald-faced lies about his acquaintance with the disgraced Jesus of Nazareth. But I think I've always known myself a sinner, in need of grace, and for some reason, I've never felt all that comfortable with those who identify themselves, sometimes far too willingly, as the children of the light.

Despite the anger that came from him in words I won't repeat, I felt, at least in part, that I was on Cyril's side at that moment. Maybe because

History

I was Romey's friend. Maybe Freud would say my antagonism was born from much greater darkness than that, but something in my father I hated right then. When I think back on that moment, there was so much I never told him, so much going on in me.

My mother must have come up the stairs on tiptoes, looked for me in my room, then found me, spread-eagled beneath my sister's bed, listening to every word of a conversation unlike any I'd ever imagined could take place in our house. I never heard her, never knew she was behind me until she spoke. "Honey," she said, and I looked around quickly, as if the voice had come out of nowhere. "Lowell, come out of there, please," she said.

I pivoted and saw her house slippers at the doorway. I had no desire whatsoever to talk to her, but I had no choice—three-quarters of me was under the bed and I couldn't simply stay there. Awkwardly, I backed myself out while she stood at the door, waiting for me to emerge, the voices still climbing the heat shaft. I slipped my head out last, got to my knees, then sat on my legs, a thin coat of dust clinging to my thighs and chest.

Maybe it was the humiliation and guilt I felt in being caught the way I had, but when I came out from beneath that bed, I was definitely on Cyril's side of whatever it was that had gone on, and was still going on, downstairs. She sat in front of me on the bed and patted the bedspread beside her. "Come here," she said, but I stayed on the floor. "Please," she said.

I brushed at the dust on my clothes.

"I'm sorry," she said. "There's so much you don't understand."

I knew so much more than they did that it made me want to take a swipe at her. "What's there to talk about?" I said. "I know what happened. I'll never be able to hang out with Romey again. I'll never be able to go over there in my life again."

"You don't know what happened," she said. She reached for my arm, but I pulled away and got to my feet. "Please sit down," she said, her hand beside her on the bed.

No matter what I felt, I couldn't fight my parents. Too much had gone on—and not that long ago—right here, upstairs in our house. I couldn't just stand there beside her, either, so I sat down, not close, and when I did she put her hand up on the back of my neck and rubbed. "You were listening—weren't you?" she asked.

That was a stupid question. "How do you expect me to listen to a ball game?" I said. "There he is swearing his head off because of what Dad did. I couldn't help listening."

My mother was not like Monty's mom, who would shoo us off the yard the moment she thought we weren't being fair to her baby boy. She wasn't like Hattie, either—she didn't smoke or listen to the Everly Brothers or laugh herself into a riot of coughs. Neither was she at all like Mugsy's mom, who'd had two boys before Mugsy and really wasn't shocked by a whole lot. I knew it was hard for her to be straight with me, hard for her to talk to me as someone who was no longer only a child.

"Lowell," she said, "Cyril isn't like anybody else we know." She spoke very slowly, biting her lips between words. "He's your friend's dad and everything, but he's so hard to deal with—for everybody," she said. "Not just for Dad, either, for everybody." She was pained—she really had a hard time even looking at me. "I'm afraid you don't know the half of it, really."

That felt like a slap.

"He's very hard to live with," she said. "You must have seen that already—when you were over there? You must have seen him, the way he—"

"Romey doesn't complain," I told her. "Shoot, his old man takes him hunting."

She stopped, reached for my hand. I meant that as a shot at my own father and she knew it. "Dad's busy, isn't he?" she said. "Always busy—I'm sorry." She didn't take my hand, just laid hers on top of mine and patted it lightly. "It isn't as hard for Cyril maybe—he can get away more often," she said. She straightened her back, raised her chin, trying to get some momentum. "I don't know how to say this," she said. "I wish I could get it just perfect so you'd understand and you wouldn't have to be hurt, honey, but, well, some marriages just aren't very good. They don't work the best." She pulled her hand away and scratched nervously at the side of her face. "I don't know why, but the Lord doesn't bless some marriages."

She wasn't looking at me and I wasn't looking at her, but I knew exactly where she was going.

"It's not something you want to admit or anything, not to your kids, but it's true, and that's why I worry about Janine, you know, about her finding somebody right, because it can be such a big thing—of course, it *is* a big thing—marriage is." Once more she grabbed my hand, then turned slightly so that she looked at me. "You too someday, even though it's hard for me to think of it with you just now going into high school." She took a breath. "Everybody's in love when they get married, but sometimes things don't grow. It's like a plant, maybe. Sometimes they die, and you don't know why, exactly. They just do, and if you could figure it out, maybe you could save them, but sometimes it just doesn't work out."

She let all of that sit, not really expecting an answer, and turned her face away again. The voices from downstairs were still strident, and I think she was distracted by her own fear. "Cyril and Hattie should never have gotten married in the first place, maybe," she said.

I thought that was a stupid thing to say—that they shouldn't have been married. Romey was a kid *because* they got married. Romey was my friend because they got married. Without the two of them, there would be no Romey. That was stupid, I thought—what my mother said.

She looked up, as if hopeful, then tried to go on. "Your grandpa wouldn't marry them, Lowell," she said.

I didn't know what that meant. I had no idea. "Grandpa Prins?" I said.

"When he was the preacher here, years ago, they came to him and told him they wanted to get married." She brushed her hair back from her eyes, waited to hear something from downstairs, but suddenly there was silence. "They were really young, and nobody knew Cyril, and he'd never been to church at all—"

"I don't get it," I said.

"He wouldn't marry them. He wouldn't put the blessing of the church on their marriage, so they had to get married somewhere else."

"Why?" I said.

"Because that was his job—that was the way he saw it back then." She seemed unsure of herself now, and I thought what she was telling me was about the stupidest thing I'd ever heard. "People want to get married in church because they want the blessing of the church, of the Lord—and he wouldn't give them that blessing—"

"But why not?" It seemed preposterous to me.

"Because he was afraid, I guess—"

"What right does he have not to marry people who want to get hitched—"

"Every right," she said. "He has every right in the world to do that, because if he thinks that the marriage won't glorify the Lord, then he'd be wrong to bring those two people together."

"They're people, Mom," I told her. "They're just people."

"He wouldn't do it because he felt—"

"Because God told him not to?" I said. That was as sassy a comment as I'd ever given her. "Because the Lord said that he shouldn't?"

"After a fashion," she said. "He says in his Word that people shouldn't get married if they're of different faiths—"

History

"Different faiths?" I said. "Cyril is a Christian. Sometimes he goes to church—I mean, he's not an atheist or anything."

"It's just something that happened, honey," she told me. "What I'm saying is that there's a history here that you don't know anything about, a history that starts already with your grandfather."

I wasn't going to let her say things about Romey and Cyril and Hattie—after all, it was Hattie who hauled us out to the trapline on cold winter mornings, not my mother. Besides, Zoot was a jerk, and he went to church—all the time, he went to church. Monty too, and Monty was a jerk. "Church doesn't mean everything," I said.

She didn't buckle. "It means something," she said. "It means a great deal."

"Plenty of people who don't go to church aren't, like, criminals—"

"Nobody's perfect," she said. "I'm not saying that. But your grandpa thought it wouldn't be best—not the way things were going, Hattie and Cyril coming in in a rush, you know?" She looked up, "Your grandpa didn't think it was right."

I can't say I really knew my grandfather. He'd died when I was in first grade.

"He was asked to put the seal of the church—"

"What's the seal of the church?" I said.

She looked down into her hands. "The blessing, you might say—the blessing of the Lord," she told me.

"Everybody thinks they know the Lord here," I said. "Everybody in my family thinks they know exactly what the Lord wants to do all the time—like he calls you on the phone or something—"

"Your grandfather thought that marriage was going to be lots and lots of trouble—"

"Why?"

"Because of Cyril—he was so different."

"It's just because he's different, isn't it? That's the whole thing—he's not like everybody else in this town, so nobody likes him and he gets ornery and stuff—that's what's really going on here," I told her.

"I'm not so sure your grandpa was wrong," she said. "Honey, I don't know what you see over there, but life at Romey's isn't exactly like life here."

"I know that," I said.

"We just try to do what we can for them, you know. Even your grandpa tried to do that by not marrying them."

"Who gets to say who gives blessings?" I said. "What makes Dad always right about everything—you tell me that. How do we know who's a saint and who isn't?"

In the long pauses, there were no more voices from downstairs.

"It's just that Cyril is so different."

I knew what she was talking about. "Sometimes they go out in the woods and sight-in rifles," I told her. "And Romey says it's just great. He's just Romey's father."

"There's more," she said, putting her hand on me again. "You can't imagine how much I hate to have to tell you everything," she said, "but maybe it's got to be done and I'm the one who has to do it." She waited, as if listening for any sound downstairs, and then she just talked, almost as if I weren't there. "It seems like you spend half your life trying to keep your kids out of trouble, but you can't do it forever, I guess—not really. You want to keep them sheltered from what really goes on." She wasn't touching me then. She used her hands when she spoke. "You only get to be a kid once, you know?" She said it flatly, as if I weren't there. And then she looked at me again, squeezed my arm. "It's hard for you now—all you know about this is Romey—but there's history here, too, you know."

"That's not all I know," I said, sharply.

"I'm sure." She pulled her back straight. "But you don't know this stuff about your grandfather." She shook her head. "He didn't think of it as his decision at all—he thought of it as the blessing of God's own church." She took another breath and wrapped her housecoat around her legs. "They went and had it done somewhere else—by a judge," she said, "by the state. That's legal too." And then, "But I believe your grandfather did the right thing," she told me, "and so does your father. What I'm saying is that there have been big problems here for a long, long time. They shouldn't have been married in the first place."

I couldn't see my own grandfather in my mind, except in the old picture with the other former pastors of our church—a bald old man in a dark suit, little glasses perched on his nose, like Santa Claus, except not a Santa Claus, not a jolly guy but another Prins, somebody so perfect he wouldn't even marry two people who were in love. I could picture it, almost—Cyril and Hattie beneath the yellow outside lamp at the side door of the old church that used to stand downtown—standing there beside the white walls at the entrance to the basement, Cyril mad as a hornet, talking just like he had a few minutes before, not understanding anything the old preacher had said—my grandfather. Maybe it was the other way. Why should Cyril care? Maybe it was Hattie that was angry at the preacher, that my grandfather—I didn't have to be responsible for what he did—the preacher, had said no. *I won't marry you because the Lord Almighty won't have it, and I know exactly what the Lord wants.* If my grandpa had had his way, there would have been no marriage, no house just out front of the swamp, no Romey, no nothing. Even my grandfather was against Romey Guttner, and he never knew him.

"Honey, what do you know about Cyril?" my mother said, her face down. "I mean, really?"

There was so much I couldn't tell her—and wouldn't.

"You know that he drinks?" she asked.

"I never once saw him drinking." That wasn't a huge lie—maybe a beer sometimes on a hot day. My word, I thought, the whole world drinks beer on a hot day. "I've never seen him drunk, not once," I told her, but I hadn't seen anyone drunk, ever.

She pulled her hands into her lap. "There are things you don't see," she said. "There are things in everybody's life you don't see, I guess." She put her hands beneath her legs and shifted uncomfortably. "It's not been very good for her—for Hattie," she said. "I mean, this whole marriage—it's not been good at all for her."

I'd seen her laugh far more than my own mother ever did. I'd seen her smile.

And then both of us heard words from downstairs again, the snarling growing louder once again. But the words weren't clear, and they didn't seem as harsh.

My mother straightened her legs like a schoolgirl and leaned forward, bowed her head, then closed her eyes and folded her hands long before I'd even thought about the fact that she might be praying. She sat there for a long time—a long minute, maybe—in prayer. Then she raised her head quickly when, downstairs, the door slammed shut. She threw her head back, her eyes closed. "It's over," she said, and she grabbed my hand. "Thank the Lord, honey—it's over finally."

"It's not either over," I said.

"I'm sorry," she said. "We're both sorry for what this does to your friendship."

I looked down at my sister's bedspread and picked at the little cotton loops in the chenille.

"Sometimes I worry about something big happening with Cyril," she said. "Your father does too—something horrible, something I don't even want to imagine. But it could happen—bad things happen in life—and it could happen."

"What do you mean?" I said.

History

"If something really, really bad would happen over there, I'd have to say to your father—and he would too, he'd have to say it to me—that we should have known it was coming, that we all should have, and we should have done something to prevent it." She swallowed hard. "That's the truth." She laid her hand on the back of my neck for just a moment. "Maybe you're just too young."

"I'm not too young," I told her.

But she was crying. "I can't help it, honey," she said. "I'm like Grandpa Prins—I think maybe it shouldn't have happened in the first place. I think he was right." She shook her head, ashamed. "Just to have him gone—it's not right, really, but sometimes I wish he were gone altogether—Cyril. It's not just me, either."

"I've been in that house," I told her. "He's not so bad as you think. I've been there. You've never been there—neither has Dad. You've never been over there to eat or anything, and if Dad goes, it's just to cuss him out about something—"

"Don't say that," she said. "You don't know everything."

"I know lots more than you do," I said, because I'd been there and seen people laugh. And Romey told his mother everything, every last thing about what he felt when he was with a girl and things like that. What did my parents know anyway about what really happened over there? What did they really know about me?

"Cyril's right," I told her. "Dad hates him just 'cause he's union and Dad isn't—and neither are most of the other men around here." I stood up. "Cyril's union and he's tough, and he doesn't give a crap about church. That's the whole problem," I told her. "He's different than us, but Romey says what Linear does to its workers is plain wrong, Mom, you know that? That's something nobody thinks about around here—just because he's union doesn't make him all those things you said."

"Don't leave," she said.

"Romey likes his old man," I said. "I know he does. He says it all the time."

"Does he?"

"Yes," I said. "He loves his father." That was a lie. "He says it lots. You wouldn't believe it." He never did, of course, but neither did I. "His dad takes him places," I said. I pushed the knife farther in. "Sometimes they go to the union hall, too, and Romey says sometimes they eat there and sing songs, these union songs, and it's great, you know? That's what he says."

"Why do I hate to tell you this?" she said, shaking her head. "How come it hurts so much to have to tell you the truth?"

History

"I'm not a kid," I said. "I see stuff. But you don't understand. Shoot, he takes Romey out lots of times and goes shooting with him and does all kinds of stuff—they're always doing things together."

"Please," she said, "sit down."

"I hate it," I told her. "Why does he think he knows everything? Did he ever ask Romey? He ought to. He ought to ask Romey about it before he goes shooting his mouth off in front of the whole family."

She stood up and reached for me, then hugged me.

"You keep saying I don't get it," I told her, "but you're the one who doesn't know. Romey's my very best friend—I'm over there half the time." I tried to pull away, but she wouldn't let me go. "I never ever once saw Cyril drunk—never. I swear on a stack of Bibles."

She kept her arms around me. Downstairs, the refrigerator opened and closed. We both heard it.

"I've got to talk to your father," she said. "I have to go down, Lowell—you hear me?"

"He's wrong," I told her again. "He ought to go back there and apologize to the whole family. Cyril doesn't drink. I know he doesn't drink. I would have seen it. Don't you think I would have seen it, Mom, as much as I'm over there?"

I was already taller than she was, a good deal taller, so that when she pulled away and tried to look at me, she had to look up. I saw fear in her eyes, fear for her own son—not anger, like the night not that long before when Dad had told her to go downstairs—not anger at all, but something much worse—fear of losing me.

"You guys are doing this just because you don't want me over there," I said. "You guys do these things because you think I ought to be friends with other guys or something—you don't like Romey because you don't like his old man—"

And then there was anger. "Listen," she said, shaking me. "You listen to what I have to tell you because it's true—you know why your father went there tonight?"

"Because Grandpa was a preacher and he's got him in his blood. He's got to be snooping around in other people's lives—"

"Look at me," she said. "Your father went because Romey's mom *begged* him to come," she said.

"She did not—"

"Because of what Cyril was doing to her, to them—how he was wrecking their family." She dropped her hands. "Your father would have rather dug a sewer, Lowell—he would have rather done anything." She swung

History

away toward the door. "He doesn't think he's better than anybody—don't ever say that about your father—don't ever say that."

"You're lying," I said. "Hattie wouldn't say that—"

"Then you ask her yourself," she said, turning back to me. "If you think you're so smart, and you don't believe your mother and you hate your father so much, then go ask her yourself sometime." Her hands came up as if she wanted so badly to touch me again, but she didn't. "Go live there, Lowell. Just pick up your stuff and move over there." And then the big line. "You're the one who lied to us, Lowell—we never lied to you."

The moment she said it, she knew it was wrong. "I'm sorry," she said. "I'm so sorry." She pulled me back to her, held me against her. "I shouldn't have said that."

I stood still as stone, looking across the room at the vanity mirror on my sister's bureau, at the silly heart-shaped program taped up from last year's junior prom, a stupid valentine.

Her hands loosened, and she let my arms go, then slowly backed away from me. She reached up and took my shoulder, squeezed it, grabbed the back of my neck again just for a second. "I'm sorry," she said, "but I've got to talk to your father." Then she pulled away.

Not until I heard her descend the stairs did I feel the way my heart was racing. Outside, I was mad. Inside, I felt broken. I knew my parents wouldn't lie—I knew that very, very well. I also knew what Romey'd hinted at time and time again—how Cyril could go after him, after them. I honestly didn't doubt anything my mother said.

I went back to my bedroom, took off my clothes, and got into bed. I turned on the radio and lay there in the darkness waiting for my father to come up, the hall light shining through the slit in the door, just as it had no more than six weeks before, when so much had changed.

Cyril had a face I could see in my imagination, a voice I could hear. I could picture him right then, walking crookedly up the gravel driveway from the garage out back, where he parked his old truck. He slept in a bed like any other human being, had a shop in the garage where he patched Romey's flat bike tires. He hunted pheasants and ducks and walked down riverbanks on cold mornings and warm afternoons, just like Romey, just like me. He sat out on piers and fished for white bass until early dawn came up over Lake Winnebago. He pulled smelt out of Lake Michigan in seines. He kept his guns clean. Spotless. Sometimes he was even home nights. Sure, he swore a lot, but at least he was home, I thought—at least he cared about his boy.

History

Romey was sitting home madder than his old man, so mad he'd never talk to me again—that's what I thought. After what happened that night, that would be it for the two of us. How would Romey ever come over to our place after what had happened? It was my father who had ruined everything, my father and this thing he had about running other people's lives. It wasn't Cyril, I told myself. Cyril didn't go out of his way to get in other people's business. It was my father who'd broken the friendship because of God and Christ, because he was the big man in church and his father had been the preacher, the preacher who wouldn't marry the two of them in the first place, and I was just plain sick of being who I was. There'd be no Romey if it were up to my grandfather. There'd be no family, there'd be no trapping, no nothing. My mother was right—this thing had a history, all right. It was a long story, something that went way back and something that finally had to be broken.

When my father came upstairs, only a few minutes later, he stood at the edge of the bed, rubbing his hands nervously, never once sitting down. In June, he'd known his kid was smoking. He'd known his kid was stealing. His only son was not simply tinged with messy boyhood malfeasance, but hip deep in sins and misdemeanors I don't believe he ever really understood. That night, just weeks before, there was very little wiggle room for me. I was dead to rights.

But this time when he came upstairs, the positioning had changed. The moment he walked into my bedroom, we both knew he was coming in as someone duty-bound to ease me into a bigger tougher world than I'd ever known as a child, not to keep me out of it. He had to explain, not accuse. He had to humble himself, not humble me. But that night, he was no less a father than he'd been the night he'd come up toting the baggage of his boy's own sins. This time, even in weakness—in the full realization of his own complicity in threatening a friendship he probably was not all that keen on—he was no less powerful, no less a force than he was not much more than a month before. In fact, when I think of it now, I wouldn't doubt at all that in his weakness he was stronger, a better father.

I won't forget his first words. He didn't touch me. He stood over me, his hands at his sides. He waited for a moment, and then said, "Maybe you can help Romey yourself," he said. "I don't know what he goes through over there, but it can't be easy. I think it's good that you're his friend."

I understood what it took for my father to say what he did, how much strength he had to raise to squelch his anger at the whole situation, and at Cyril specifically, whose profanity still echoed through the downstairs passageways of our house, lingering in aftershocks around us. Romey was my buddy, somebody to goof around with, somebody to be yourself with, cigarettes or no cigarettes. And whether he liked it or not, he understood that.

"Why did you go over there?" I said. "You know Romey is my best friend."

He looked through the circular window on the south wall as if he were staring out at the lakeshore. "I didn't ask for the job," he said. "I'd rather pick beans."

"It's the preacher's job or something, isn't it?" I said. "Isn't that what we pay him for? Isn't that what he's supposed to do, make people be nice?"

My father locked his arms over his chest and stared out into the darkness. "Nobody *wants* to do it. I never for a minute *wanted* to do it—"

"Then why did you?"

He turned away from the window and looked at me, leaned over the bed, put his hands on the cool sheets, and stared into my eyes. "Because Romey's mom begged me," he said, and he stayed right there, right in front of me, as if he were putting everything in his heart on the line, begging me to believe him.

"When?" I said.

His shoulders fell and he stood again. "At work," he said. "She came in at work and talked to me, told me that somebody had to help her because—" he leaned back, took a breath, "because he hurts her sometimes—I hate to have to tell you this, but he does. He beats her."

"So?"

He let that question sit, turned away from me. But there was some irony in his voice when he asked me, "You tell me, Lowell—you think we ought to just let that go?"

"What?" I said.

"The way he treats her—you think we ought to look the other way?"

"How do you know?" I said.

"She says so. She tells me. You think she's lying?"

"Nobody knows," I said.

"Maybe you're right," he said. "Maybe I ought to just let it go until some night the ambulance flies into town and picks up her body—"

"Nobody knows," I said again.

He shrugged his shoulders. "You're right, I guess. Maybe I ought to believe Cyril."

I looked away.

And then, "I'm sorry for what this is doing to you and Romey."

I didn't say a thing.

"But listen—is it worth a human life?" He had his hands in his pockets, standing there at my bedside, remarkably calm. I see him yet, reasonable, thoughtful, persevering, fatherly, but persistent.

"He wouldn't do that," I said. "He wouldn't hurt Hattie. I don't think Cyril would do that in a hundred years."

"Maybe you're right," he said.

And then I said, "Even if he does, it's none of your business." Even though my father let that go, I knew I'd gone too far. But I kept going. "You know what Romey will think of me now?" I said. "He'll hate me. He really will. That's just what you want, too, isn't it?" I was a boy. I was a kid. "You don't *want* me to goof around with Romey because of Cyril, isn't that right?" I said. "Even Romey's not your favorite, is he? And it's all because he's not a Christian—I mean, Cyril isn't—like *you* are. That's the whole deal here—isn't it?"

He turned away his face, put his hands on his hips. "I didn't go there to spite you," he said. "I can't choose your friends, even though I might like to." He shook his head. "I didn't go to make you stop hanging around with Romey, Lowell. You're going to have to trust my word."

I did, but I wasn't about to let him know it.

"Cyril's been out of work since the beginning of the strike, and it's hard on a man, especially here—in this town." He turned around again and rubbed his forehead with the back of his hand. "Not too many people around here have sympathy for the strikers. Linear pays better than anybody in the county, so it's hard to be sympathetic, I guess." He sat down on the side of the bed. "You don't have to like it, Lowell—there's not much I can do about that, but I want you to understand." He put a hand on my leg. "I'm sorry it was Cyril's choice to have the whole family sitting there waiting for us. I hated it. The moment we walked in, I hated it, but you can't blame me for doing what I was begged to do—what the Lord wants us to do—to be our brother's keeper. That's what it's about. You understand?"

The truth was, I did.

And then he told me exactly what he knew about how Cyril often drank too much, how he sometimes hit Hattie, and about how she couldn't take it any longer. He went through every moment of the conversation he and Hattie had that afternoon. He told me things I couldn't believe, except that I was hearing them from my father.

"I'm sorry," he said again.

But I didn't say a thing.

153

History

Before he left, he hugged me for the first time I could remember in a very long while. And then he prayed, plain and simple, just a few words, for Romey and for Hattie—and for Cyril too. He spent more time on Cyril than anyone else.

The world was being pulled apart, and it was, I think, a measure of my respect for my father that made me very sure, when he left, that he was the one telling the whole truth, even though I didn't concede that fact to him right then and wouldn't have, for reasons it is difficult for me to explain other than saying that those reasons go to the very core of my humanity.

History

Baseball Practice

A day or two more of bean-picking, one and a half actually, and the work finally stopped that Saturday when Nick Van Dam ran out of fields and the beans left on the vine hung thick and hard as calloused fingers. It was late July, and even the cold waters of Lake Michigan were calm and warming up in the hot sun.

Once it was over, I went home and, in the few hours before baseball practice, got out some particleboard, sawed out goose decoys with a jigsaw, and painted them up—black necks, white chins—like Canadas, a job I'd planned on doing with Romey that summer. But I'd not seen him since the day he had walked home from the beanfields. I was reluctant to hang around with him again anyway, afraid of what he might say after what had happened at his place the night my dad and the preacher came.

Maybe Zoot was right, I thought. Maybe Romey was trouble and trouble wasn't always fun. That's what I was thinking. So I didn't go back to Romey's place right away, even though my parents asked me about him when we sat around the kitchen nook eating breakfast Cheerios—

whether I'd seen Romey, a question always asked innocently enough, but never meant in an innocent manner. They honestly didn't want to destroy our friendship, even though I'm sure they would have been happy to see it over.

It was baseball that drew us back together again, even though Romey never was much of a player. In later years he'd become one heckuva linebacker, I'm told—lean, tough, quick, smart, a kid who would throw his head into any fracas. In pure agility, in what sportswriters today call athleticism, he was not as blessed as a number of others, but he knew no fear. I was never the kind of football player Romey turned out to be.

The baseball team played in what was called the Pony League, for some reason no one knew or remembered. It was made up of high school wannabees—kids preparing to play high school ball. The whole structure was geared toward development, and we knew it. Even if we didn't like the coach or didn't care for the schedule, we knew that to be candidates for the high school baseball team the next summer, we'd have to stay with the program and take our licks.

Baseball practice is the most boring hour and a half in the year's entire schedule of sports. Batting practice is always first priority, and the only way to get that accomplished is to let each of the eighteen kids take dozens of cuts while the others shag whatever pitches the kid at the plate can get ahold of.

On our Pony League team the coach—a man nicknamed Beaner, for reasons that had nothing at all to do with beanfields or putting guys down with high hard pitches to the head—threw batting practice. He was thirty at least and had played semipro ball after graduating from college. He'd never made the pros because—and we knew the story— his speed was suspect and he'd never learned to hit a curve—at least that's the myth that grew up around him. So he'd returned to his father's dairy in Easton, where he had both the freedom and the clout to take time off the job to coach Pony League baseball—games and practice.

Baseball with Beaner wasn't fun for us, because he saw coaching as a calling. He'd pitch the whole batting practice himself, coming halfway up to the plate so that each of the hitters could stand back near the backstop and no one would have to chase balls back into the hayfield behind the screen. He hated to move off that spot where he'd deliver pitch after pitch, sometimes for an hour or more of batting practice. The infielders lived in mortal terror of missing his open glove when he'd call for more balls. He'd hold his glove up as a target; if you didn't hit it, he didn't move the glove. The ball would simply sail into the one of the dugouts

Baseball Practice

or over the screen. Whoever threw it had to run over to wherever it finally came to rest and, embarrassed, pick it up. He didn't glower at us, or curse or scream, he just made us wilt with his lack of movement, his stony perturbed silence. We lived in awe of his abilities.

Batting practice first, then maybe a half hour of situations—squeeze plays, rundowns, pickoffs at second, hit and runs. Practice was Saturday afternoon at four at the high school, and most of the guys were there, because Nick's beanfields were clean. A couple of days had passed since Cyril had showed up at our front door and filled the air with his angry blue language, but I didn't see Romey until that Saturday.

On a baseball field there is plenty of space to keep away from each other if you don't want to talk to someone, plenty of guys to warm up with or play fungo. Once batting practice started, you could while away your time in the outfield, suck clover or watch the starlings move like schools of fish out of the trees in town, and never have to talk to anyone, really, while a long succession of batters tried to nail curveballs.

I didn't say a word to Romey before practice started that day, or during the time when everybody got in their cuts. I was afraid—not *of* Romey, exactly, because even though he could be fierce and fearless, he'd never really threatened me. My fear had nothing to do with the possibility of Romey's getting physical. I was afraid of Romey in the same way I might say I was afraid of my own father—I didn't want to hurt him.

Beaner decided that the last half hour of practice would be spent going over this situation: runners on first and third, one out, and the guy from first is going to steal second if he can—in order to draw the throw, thereby allowing the run to score. In Pony League it was a given—the kid on first would take off to try to attract the throw, most catchers at that age not having an arm strong or accurate enough to throw out the runner with any consistency. Beaner thought we could do better than give up gifts, so he went over some options: throwing hard to the shortstop instead of all the way to second; throwing hard back to the pitcher, as if the catcher were going for the runner; faking a throw, the catcher wheeling as if he were about to deliver a bullet shot to second; or else the second baseman stepping in the way of the throw somewhere behind the mound and delivering the ball back home as quickly as he could. These were high school plays, but we were on track toward high school ball.

I had one of the finest arms on the team and had been a catcher since Little League. Most of the plays Beaner outlined I'd known already, but the coach wanted us to get the options down so he could call the play from the bench, the way he'd call a bunt or a hit and run—hold up a finger or yell some magic word so we'd all know exactly what was going on once the pitch was delivered. The whole thing involved no more than a few guys—me, behind the plate, and the infielders. Beaner tried to keep the rest of the guys gainfully employed while we ran through the possibilities, sending them either to first or third to run.

Eventually, Romey made it to the front of the line of runners on third, took a lead, and watched for Beaner's move to home. We were already keeping the plays secret, so he didn't know exactly what I was going to do with the ball. Once he saw the kid on first start to run and saw me pump my arm, he took off toward home, just as he was expected to, just as the opposing runner would do in that situation.

It was a play that Beaner called Colorado, for no known reason, and the idea was that I would pump fake, then twist and deliver the ball to third base with all the force I could muster, where, in theory, we were supposed to catch the runner already taken off for home—or at least leaning in that direction. Unquestionably, Romey was leaning. But then, Romey wasn't thinking about scoring runs.

At the very moment he was sprinting home from third, I was conscious of the fact that it was Romey bearing down on me and not any of the other guys. But I couldn't, after all, take my mind off the game, the ball presently zinging its way back to me from third at eighty miles an hour or so. I wanted to get the whole Colorado business right, both to please myself and Beaner, whose lack of grace in the face of his player's failures was something ballyhooed into myth. When it came to baseball, he was not a forgiving soul. "Take a third strike," he told us often enough, "and you'll walk home—I don't care if we're playing across the lake."

So while I knew it was Romey barreling down toward home, my mind was focused much more deliberately on the ball, on the play, on getting the whole scheme right. Jeff, playing third, a kid with a powerful arm himself, delivered a honey back to me, a strike so perfect that whoever would have been running the bases would be dead to rights. But whoever, this time, was Romey.

It's the most violent play in baseball, the tag at home. I knew it. I had taken hits before. I tucked the ball in my mitt and braced myself for the kind of hit Beaner had always told base runners is obligatory. "Take the catcher out in a situation like that—that's your job. Everybody knows it. Take the catcher out. He's got pads. You're not going to hurt him. Make him dump the ball."

This was practice, and there was no question about this runner being out—the play had worked that well. But the runner was Romey Guttner, and in that fraction of a second before the play was over, everything that had happened in the last two weeks flashed before my eyes. My mind slowed to a crawl and listed a dozen reasons why my old buddy would take this grand opportunity to deck me—legally, very much aboveboard.

I slid one foot quickly behind the other, by instinct, to broaden my center of gravity and lower it, my knees bending to bring me into a crouch. Nothing mattered, suddenly, but the two of us. Colorado was only a state, Beaner a bystander. That's what I knew as I waited for impact.

Just before he reached me, Romey slowed for the thinnest moment, as if maybe he was going to let it go or get himself caught in a rundown. I think I was the only kid on that diamond who knew why he hesitated, why for a just a flash he looked as if he might reconsider what was, in fact, an obligation and might even have been pure pleasure. I knew that for a fraction of a second Romey thought about not hitting me, simply taking the tag and walking back, like the others, to the line forming behind first.

That hesitation was there, but it was momentary. There were too many good reasons for him to lower his shoulder, just like Beaner would have wanted, so he did. I was heavier than Romey, but he'd been gathering all the speed he could as he hurtled down the base path, and he wasn't slow, never was. Romey left his feet, sailed into me with his shoulder pointed, and took me out like a blocking dummy, my feet coming out from beneath me. Both of us went down in a tangle of arms and legs. He had turned in the air deftly, like the linebacker he would become, then circled himself up behind that shoulder, rolled his head down, and pulled his body in tight so that, after impact, he actually rolled over in the dust and acrobatically came up with his feet beneath him. I wasn't so fortunate; I came down on the small of my back, my head whacking the hard ground behind home with such force that I swore I heard my skull crack. The impact sucked the air out of my lungs, and I lay there gasping, flat on my back, my entire breathing apparatus knocked out.

I don't know that that had ever happened to me before. It happened afterward—in football once in a while, even in basketball. One became accustomed to seeing teammates curled up in agony trying to get breath back from a body thrown temporarily into madness—lungs locked up tight, powerless, not even gasping. For a boy, it's not only awful physically, it's awful emotionally—you're absolutely powerless. You jerk almost spasmodically.

Baseball Practice

"You knocked the wind out of him," Beaner said. That was the first thing I heard clearly after impact, Beaner standing over me, grabbing me by the belt. "He'll be all right. He got his bell rung."

Bits and pieces of reality flashed across the screen of my consciousness—Romey coming at me, the two of us swimming, the beanfields, some remnant sketch of a bedroom dresser, my mother crying—all of it topsy-turvy, as if a cheap film were being shown on a ship in rough water. But once things began to focus, what registered with the most clarity was pure humiliation, eighteen guys standing around me because I'd been taken out of the play in a way all catchers are from time to time, despite their best positioning. Even though I found myself in what seemed a life and death battle for breath, even though my mind wasn't capable of focusing on what exactly had happened, what *was* functioning smoothly were my emotions, and humiliation arose meanly. In knocking the wind right out of me, Romey opened a gaping wound in my pride.

Beaner held me by my belt and pulled my whole body up at the waist, then dropped me slowly again, several times, trying to jump-start my lungs. The rigidity in my chest fell slowly away into emptiness, and my lungs began to fill with a series of deep breaths. Three Beaners standing above me focused finally into one as whatever mechanism that replays the film in the mind slowed the operation, then finally clicked off the delirium as I came back into what was going on around me.

"You dropped the ball," Romey said.

He was standing right above me, and I knew it was a taunt. I even saw the ball Romey held out in front of him like a trophy. I pushed my hands down beside me once Beaner let me loose, and I got to my knees, the playing field dipping and bowing as if we all were riding out some major California quake.

"You asked for it," Romey said.

Rancid humiliation turned my insides noxious and pushed me to cry, almost as if the process were a chemical reaction. Tear gas might well have been shot into my soul, stirring a reaction equal parts shame and anger. I actually cried, publicly. And the greatest humiliation was that I couldn't have stopped the tears anyway, even if I'd wanted to. I lost it— whatever the *it* is, the chemical balance making me a man—*it* was gone. I got to my feet like a boxer who'd just missed the count and went after Romey drunkenly, tried to grab him like some juice-lit cowboy cook, humiliation coming up into my throat like bile as I flailed away at his several images. Beaner let me be for a minute, let me stagger and fling my arms, knowing very well that nothing would come of it.

Baseball Practice

And nothing did, except more humiliation. Romey was quicker than I was even on a good day, even if I'd had all my wits about me and wasn't shackled by knee pads, a chest protector, and quadri-focaled vision. He could have merely avoided me, too—he could have done something more turn-the-other-cheek-ish than prancing and dancing in front of me like Cassius Clay.

I don't think anyone on the field that afternoon ever understood exactly how deep was the pain in me at that moment. To the guys who witnessed it, stood in the middle of it, the whole thing probably had the look of a drunken scramble, me trying as frantically to stay on my feet as I was to connect with Romey, Romey shadowboxing, bobbing and weaving in a way most of them probably thought considerate.

Beaner finally broke it up. He put a hammerlock on me, stood me straight up and held me. By that time my senses had come back somewhat, and I knew I was on the third base line. My coordination hadn't returned completely from wherever it had gone. I bucked and shook, tried to pull myself out of Beaner's hold, but it was futile. Finally, in a process that probably seemed to everybody standing there as inevitable as the death throes of some animal already shot, I stopped shaking, stopped yelling, stopped crying, and collapsed, in more tears, into Beaner's arms.

But he wouldn't let me fall or even sit down. He held me up and walked me around a little, finally shooing the other guys away, telling a kid named Andy to pull on the other set of catcher's equipment and another kid to pitch in order to pick up the drill where they'd left off, while he walked me over to the dugout and finally set me down on the bench. When the days got hot, he'd always bring along a big insulated jug of cold water and give us sips out of the metal cover halfway through practice. He tried to make me drink.

I'd stopped crying, but I don't think I'd ever hated anyone as much as I did Romey Guttner that moment. In fact, decades later, I don't remember ever feeling a murderer stirring so palpably in my own soul as I did right then. My breath was coming just as hard as it had when I had little of it to exhale. The dust on my cheeks, I'm sure, was tracked with the spiked lines of public tears.

"Drink some of this," Beaner said, lifting the lid.

I shook my head.

"Don't be stupid," he said. "There isn't a kid out here who doesn't know what you feel like."

Baseball Practice

Beaner put the lid down on the bench beside me when I still made no move for the lid. "You know," he said, "you only made one mistake there—you didn't tuck the ball away."

I nodded.

"You did everything else right, Lowell," Beaner told me. "I got no complaints. Next time, just don't drop the ball, hear?" He slapped my arm. "Got to hand it to Romey," he said. "He'll make a man of you yet."

Right then, I don't know that I had a grasp on where I was.

"Tell you what," Beaner said. "I got ten minutes at best here yet. Couple more things I want to go through." He picked up the clipboard from the bench beside him and rapped his knuckles on the plan he'd drawn up. "Romey did it right—you got to admit it. You did too. You stood there marking the spot, and he came in and leveled you. There ain't a kid who doesn't know that it happened just the way it was supposed to, except you dropped the ball—that's the only wrinkle." He slapped my shoulder with his glove. "Won't happen again, either, will it?"

With my hands in a ball, I rubbed the dirt out of my skin, and I shook my head because I'd have rather died than ever again drop a ball at home.

"Tell you what—you want to leave, go ahead. I won't hold it against you." He put a hand on my shoulder. "You're my starting catcher and you got every right to blow a gasket, see? I like that—means you got backbone." He laughed. "I maybe shouldn't have let you go after him like that, but I figured you needed a little of that too—the only thing is I thought maybe you'd catch him."

I swore at Romey, not loud, but loud enough for Beaner.

"He did it right," he said. "Say what you want, he did it just like I said. For a minute there, I thought he was going to let you live. I'da taken out his teeth if he had—you know that."

I reached a shoulder up to my cheek to get the tears out of sight.

"You want to go now—go on. It's no big deal." He hit me on the back three or four times. "You're no darn good to me right now anyway, mad as you are. Can't even think." Then he grabbed the back of my collar, like a mother cat. "You all right? He didn't hurt you, did he? No blood, no foul."

I shook my head.

"You'd never catch him anyway, with his speed," he laughed. "You're built too low to the ground, Lowell. You got yourself a good arm, and you're smart—that's what it takes to be a catcher," he said, slapping his hand in his mitt. "You're going to be a good one, y'hear?" Then he got

Baseball Practice

up and left the dugout. He got halfway back to the mound and turned around. "You sure you're all right?" he said.

When I looked up, my eyes somewhat cleared, my emotions settling, I saw Romey taking a lead off first base, trying to draw a throw. That was the thing about Romey—nothing ever mattered much. With me, things stuck—they had meaning. I held things in, snarled and quarreled inside. But with Romey, things bounced off and never really caught. The coach was right. If Romey hadn't hit me the way he did, Beaner would have screamed. Romey did the whole thing right. He did it by the book.

But that afternoon there wasn't anything I wanted to say to any of the guys, nothing I wanted to hear, either—no sympathy, no more questions about whether I was hurt. Of course I wasn't hurt. I unclipped the elastic from behind the shin guards, reached back and undid the chest protector, then lifted it quickly from behind and felt through my hair to see if there was any blood where my head had banged the ground. A bump was forming, and inside my head a sharp pain ran like a jigsaw through my brain, but there wasn't a thing wet back there except around my neck, where a line of sweat always formed. I looked around for the mitt and saw it still lying there in the grass behind home.

Practice was going on without me. Guys were yelling again, infielders shouting out code words. Nobody cared. Nobody was watching me anymore. Beaner wouldn't call on me if I stayed—he'd let me sit there for whatever time remained. I picked up a towel from the bench and wiped off my face. My head hurt. Sometimes, I told myself, I'd like to live without Romey. Maybe my grandpa was right about Cyril and Hattie. There never should have been a Romey.

I got to my feet, my knees rubbery and weak beneath me, and I tried to walk as powerfully as I could to the end of the dugout. Instead of going back on the field, I left through the door in the fence, without turning back to the guys on the diamond. I wanted to go home and die, I thought. I didn't want to go on another minute.

I was maybe fifty yards away from the backstop when I got on my bike and started riding up toward the school, over the grass, bumpy and uneven. I had to stand to pedal in order to keep up enough speed over the ground, and my head hurt and I felt wobbly and everything was messed up, like my compass was half a continent off. I never looked back, even though I didn't know where I was going, exactly, since I couldn't really tell my folks what had happened anyway—they wouldn't understand. I didn't feel like going home, but I didn't want to stay, either.

"Hey, Prins."

Baseball Practice

I pretended not to hear him.

"Lobo—"

I didn't want to talk. He had it all over on me now. Beaner was right about that. Romey did the whole thing by the book, and I was the one who dropped the ball.

"Hey," he yelled, called me a name he probably didn't mean as rough as it sounded, but I kept pedaling, trying to keep him behind me. "What's your stinking hurry?"

Even though I was the one on the bike, I knew Romey was going to catch me and it made me mad. It was tough going, riding on bumpy ground, and Romey was always quick. The guy was always there.

He caught me by the back of the seat, like some kindergartner's dad trying to control his kid's first trip on a bike. He held me there in the grass, kept me from spilling.

"Hey," Romey said, "no big deal, right?" That's all. Just that.

I put a foot down to keep my balance, but I never looked at him.

"Hey," Romey said again, "shake on it." He grabbed the back of my shirt and pulled me around. "I'm sorry, huh?"

I refused to look at him.

"Hey," he said, "he don't need an excuse to yell at me—Beaner, I mean. You know I'da got my butt chewed if I didn't take you out. You know that."

I deliberately swung a foot out at him when I got off the bicycle.

"Want to beat on me—go ahead," Romey said.

I pulled away, walking my bike now, left Romey standing there.

"Need a cigarette?" he said, mimicking Toad's whiny voice. "Got some Chesterfields in my sweatshirt."

I didn't stop. In a moment he was beside me again.

"Go ahead," he said, "be a twink, but I'm the one trying to be friends here, you got that?"

"Get out of my life," I said. "Just get the heck out, all right?"

Then he stopped.

I kept going, breaking into a faster walk, and then got back on the bike. We were already near the fence in left field, a long way from the infield behind us.

"I didn't want to do it," Romey said. "I'm not lying."

And I knew he wasn't. There was that moment of hesitation right before the impact, the reluctance I'd seen plain as day—even Beaner had seen it. He said so. I stopped, Romey not even the distance from home to first behind me.

Baseball Practice

"I'da got nailed if I wouldn'ta hit you, and you know it—you know Beaner," he said. "Shoot Matilda, I get nailed enough. I ain't going to play this silly game next year. You're going to be all right—everybody knows it. You're a good catcher, but this is it for me—this year. After this, I'm going to bale hay or something. I can't hit—"

"You hit me," I said.

"You know what I mean—I can't hit the *ball*." He kept trying to come closer.

He was right, of course. Romey's gargantuan swings were legendary, even hilarious. Three or four times a season he'd get lucky and wail on one, but most of the time he went down like a stickman with the velocity of his swings.

"I'm telling you I'm sorry, all right?" he said. "Is that a crime?"

I swung my leg off the bike again and kicked down the stand, but I didn't look at him, not once.

"We're still rooming together at camp, right?" he said. "Shoot, I ain't going if we're not. I didn't want to go in the first place, but my old lady keeps ragging on me all the time. She says it'll be good for me. Just what I need is something else that's good for me. You ever get dead tired of stuff that's good for you?"

"I don't want to go either," I said.

"That makes two of us, huh?" he said. "How about we take off—go to Vegas. My old man says it's a great place. Whatta'ya think?"

I couldn't help but laugh.

"What'cha doin' tomorrow?" he said.

"Tomorrow's Sunday."

"That's right—tomorrow's Sunday," he said. "What'cha doing Monday?"

I shrugged my shoulders.

"I'll be over," he said. He had to be thinking that, by then, my sore head would be a thing of the past.

Romey was always good at putting things behind him. I envied him that. There were so many things I couldn't put behind me, still can't. Romey had a penchant for forgetting. He did it all the time. I never really saw Romey play football, but I know he was good because I know Romey. I bet he drove the coaches nuts, though, because no matter what happened in a game, I'm sure he walked away whistling—win or lose. Somewhere inside him, big-time smoker and skirt chaser that he was, there was a kid with a mouth as perfectly foul as his father's and yet something closer to a Christian than I ever was back then.

He came over Monday morning, Romey being a man of his word in his own special way. I didn't see him in church. Hattie was there, and the little girls, but not Romey. I figured maybe he was out with his old man, sighting up the deer rifles somewhere in the dunes. But Monday morning, he came over, and when he did, there was nothing in his face or his demeanor to make me think he was carrying any kind of a grudge.

There were things to admire—really, to love—about Romey Guttner.

Baseball Practice

Bible Camp

Hattie had insisted that Romey go to Bible camp with me the first week of August, but then, as Romey himself understood, no one was more anxious for us to be friends than his mother. "I don't know what the big deal is," he told me at least once that summer, "but my old lady's tickled pink that you and me hang out. She thinks you teach me hymns. To her, your place is like Denver or something—a place you breathe clean."

Cyril thought Bible camp was a stupid idea, according to Romey. But Hattie got her way because, without her husband's knowledge or her son's, my father arranged for a retired farmer from church to pick up the cost, the Guttners having little money at all during the strike but what Cyril took home from the union hall. I didn't know that at the time. My father wouldn't have told me.

So Romey went to camp, like the rest of us, and missed the last of the baseball games. Some of us went to get out of work, some to horse around, some to get girls, and even a few, I figured, for spiritual enlightenment. All morning long on wooden folding chairs, we'd sit through Bible stories and sermonettes about counting on God being beside you in those times when you really need to fight off sin and the great horned beast— three hours of lectures and small groups in circles where the objective was to get us to give some form of testimony. Every morning, nine to noon, Romey stayed alive only because he could now and then sneak a glance out the windows at the way the breeze brushed sparkles over the lake, or else feast his eyes on the sun-bronzed legs of some girl on the other side of our prayer circle. And Romey wasn't the only one. The Bible stuff did get tedious, especially since every kid there knew the direction we were being herded. Bible camp's whole purpose was to get some spiritual high that would change our lives once we got back home. We had a great time at camp, but in some ways it wasn't all that different from getting a free weekend in the Ozarks on the condition that you sit still and listen to a good strong pitch from some flashy salespeople hawking time-share resort land.

Calvin Simmons, a college guy on his way to the ministry and a shortstop with the best range I'd ever seen, played counselor for us in the barracks where Romey and I were bunkmates. On cool nights Simmons would wear his maroon and gold college jacket when he patrolled the grounds, and he looked like just about everything I wanted to be—lean, athletic, sincere, and moral.

Every night, Cal read Bible passages he must have picked out carefully, one after another, for what they would bring to his late-night devotions. He was good, very good, and by the time the nightly bell sounded he always wore a shadowy beard we'd enviously watch him shave every morning.

I don't know about Romey—whether he looked at Simmons the same way I did—but I know Romey liked him. Put it this way, maybe—Romey didn't dislike him. Back then, it seemed to me Romey found him almost strange: he'd never really met anyone who could be so nice about things generally and who talked about Jesus with just as much enthusiasm as Romey could talk about shooting crows or deer hunting or grabbing a smoke somewhere behind the softball field. Some nights when the whole barracks would be together on the bunks late at night for devotions, Simmons would push Romey, try to get him to say something about who he was and what he was up to with his life—something serious, something spiritual. And Romey liked it, not because he felt himself coming closer and closer to the Lord, but because he liked the attention, not put-on attention, either, but the real concern of a great guy, this guy Calvin Simmons.

Bible Camp

Every night for evening devotions, Simmons would read from his Bible, ask one of the boys to comment, then pray, just before bedtime, eleven o'clock. And every night he'd manage a reminder about the campfire, Friday night's grand finale, when it was assumed we would all stand up before the whole world and explain what wonderful things had happened to us during the wonderful week of Bible camp. We'd make it a wonderful bonfire, and everybody would detail how they'd been led wonderfully by the Spirit, how they were going to go back home to be wonderful new kids for Jesus. That was the plan. Before the week started I could have sat down and made a list of the kids who, come Friday night, would get to their feet right away once the holy fires were burning. Girls would have topped the list mostly—and Monty, or kids like him.

Every night, Simmons told us how he'd be so pleased if just a couple of his guys gave testimonies. "I don't want to push anybody," he'd say. "That's not right. You got to do what you got to do, and I can't force you." He'd stand there in his T-shirt, that thick beard like a dark stocking over his face, a few chest hairs peeking above the neckline of his shirt, and he'd tell us we ought to all think about going public. That's what he called it. Testimony was a word he said he'd come to hate when he was a kid, so he called what was going to happen going public. "It doesn't mean you're all going to turn into saints just like that," he said, snapping his fingers, and he meant it. "But it's like anything else in life— it's commitment. It's a first step—going public is. It'll help you *be* something." We ought to at least think about it, he told us. He'd be proud. And the Lord's name would be blessed. That's what he told us after devotions, when mostly we were thinking about girls.

Then he'd leave, go out and start hunting up delinquent kids who were trying to sneak out to get what a lot of them were interested in—each other. With all those kids in all those barracks, a heavy hormonal mist rose from the lake down the hill and swept through the rickety sides of those old army barracks like a virus, infecting just about everyone.

The truth is, we nearly didn't make it through the week at Bible camp that summer, Cal or no Cal. We were almost sent home. Almost. Had we been, Romey likely would have walked, just like he did from the beanfields, even though the camp was 150 miles from Easton, at a little inland lake, one of many in the middle of the rolling glacial hills of Wisconsin.

On Thursday night a kid named Merrick let it be known that some girls he knew wanted a bunch of guys to come over to their place to play games after the mass meeting on Thursday. Play games, he said, but he said it with enough of a curl on his lips to let us all know what he meant. At camp, to be in the girls' barracks, even if it wasn't after curfew, was a sin punishable by death, and we all knew it. The only really unguarded time of any night was the two free hours after closing prayer at the evening meeting, the time when dozens of couples paraded around the campgrounds holding sweaty bottles of Orange Crush in one hand and with their arms around their dates. Romance was legitimate, even lauded, at Bible camp, as long as what went on between the couples stayed open and clean and under the lights. The real heavy breathing went on back in the woods, the area the counselors flooded, open eyed, flashing their foot-long Ever-Readies or Ray-o-Vacs constantly, as if someone had lost something really valuable. There was nothing sinful about courtship, of course, but there was something lustful about making out. That was the policy. We all knew the rules, even though the specifics wouldn't have been announced publicly.

This kid Merrick had it all figured out, he said, so that night seven of us headed over through the poplars to the female side of the camp, exactly where we weren't supposed to go. I figured there was safety in numbers. Besides, Merrick, a kid from a suburb of Milwaukee, was an operator. All week long I'd seen him buddy up to counselors; in ball games, canoe races, whatever kind of recreational activities we did, Merrick was always out there schmoozing. I figured Merrick would never get nailed for anything. He'd set out an agenda on his first day there to make sure every last authority was in his back pocket as quickly as he could stick them there.

Merrick held the flashlight that night, led us over to the girls' side as if we were an attack party of renegade Apaches. All week long he had talked as big as he was, a first baseman with very broad shoulders who testified, outside of Simmons' hearing, to a whole ton of memorable trysts with women, reviewing his sexual exploits the way other kids remembered great ball games.

He said he had it all arranged—a bunch of girls over there, hungry for attention—and he'd figured it all out with this fine girl he'd met. It'd be a game called Candle, even though we'd use a flashlight. We'd pair off and make out—that was the game—and the extra guy, the guy with the candle, would wander around seeking, like the devil, whom he might next devour. He had it perfectly arranged—one extra guy, he said. Once you settled on a candidate, you'd trade, he said, the flashlight for the lady. Mix and match, a sort of junior high key club. Merrick said he'd hired his little brother to stand guard, a sixth-grader. He said it was the

Bible Camp

way to get experience quickly. "It's something how different girls make out," he said. "This is how you learn."

For the most part, the participants were faceless once the screen door slapped shut and Merrick pulled the string on the lightbulb hanging from the ceiling. The girls were seated on the beds arranged around the single-room barracks. Romey started out with a bouncy girl whose name he never did get straight—Sandy or Candy or Mandy, a girl who obviously had a long record of prior engagements but was anxious to log more experience.

Not all of the girls were quite so willing, however, and I ended up with a girl named Dianne, a blonde with great legs, the only girl in that barracks from Easton, someone I'd rather quietly admired long before Bible camp. She parked her shoulder in close to mine and wrapped an arm around my waist almost lovingly—but that's all.

I was scared, I admit it. I didn't have much experience with girls. They were really something new to me, which is not to say I'd never felt that kind of hunger. We just didn't have time, or motivation. Sometimes Romey talked about girls, about being with them, about how great it was, but I'd really never pushed the issue much, even though I was growing up into maleness rather quickly, I think. So it was scary for me—going over there, risking being caught, and just being with a girl. But Romey never dragged his feet on such occasions, and whither Romey went, there I went also.

What actually happened when we paired up wasn't exactly what Merrick had explained. Dianne didn't jump into my arms the moment I got her alone, nor did we attack each other with our lips. Even there, in the electric darkness of the girls' barracks, whatever was going to happen was going to have to be earned. Some courtship was required. Dianne wanted to talk.

"He's really your friend, isn't he?" she asked me, the pleasant smell of Wrigley's Spearmint on her breath.

"I don't even know him that well," I said.

"You don't know him?" she said, "Romey Guttner?" and she pointed not far away to a place in the darkness where the bed creaked as if layered with insomniacs. "I hope I don't get him. Mandy's got him now," she said, jawing gum like a third baseman. "If he comes here, just tell him we're busy or something, okay?"

All week long, Merrick's stories had torqued my imagination, but Dianne was someone from Easton, someone I'd see again when camp was over. I figured I couldn't just push myself at her. "How come you don't like him?" I said. I remember the feeling in my chest, something not completely different from what I felt before big ball games, but a lot sweeter and more persistent. All around me, the game was going. "Romey's a great guy."

"I don't know," she said. "He scares me." She reached up and buttoned my collar like my mother might have. "Girls got a thing about some guys, you know, and I got it with him. It's like I'm afraid of him or something." She snuggled her hand into mine. "It's just perfect that Mandy's got him—you know what I mean? He ought to stay there."

The two of them sounded as if they were sucking juice out of the same orange.

"He burps," she said, and she was right. Romey was one of the finest burpers I'd ever known.

"You don't like him because he burps?" I said.

"I mean out loud. Ever hear him?"

"A million times," I said. "I mean, you just do it when you want to, when you feel like it—you suck in some air and you burp. It doesn't mean anything," I told her.

We weren't the only ones talking. In the darkness, you could sense places where the game was working according to Merrick's specs—and where it wasn't, little wisps of conversation coming up here and there like steam. Dianne had this great flowery swimsuit that I kept imagining as I was sitting there beside her. I was scared, but I was traumatized by the idea that the other guys would leave in a while and mock me for talking the whole night, when everybody else was doing what was supposed to be done. So I laid my hand fretfully over the back of her neck, tried to come up with something that would bring me down the road. "I don't feel like talking about Romey—he's not talking about us," I said. "I didn't think that was the idea anyway," I told her. "There's more to it, right—this little exercise we're up to here?"

She giggled. "Say that again—what you just said."

"What?" I said.

"What you just said—this little exercise or something. That's the way you said it." She put a hand on my chest. "You said that so neat. Romey wouldn't have said it that way—"

"You saying he's dumb?"

"Not dumb, but he wouldn't say things that way—the way you do, Lowell," she said. "He'd have said," she dropped her voice, "'Let's make out, honey.'"

Dianne wasn't wrong. "Look where it got him," I told her, and just like that she pulled herself close and turned her lips to mine.

Bible Camp

That was my first kiss, gentle as a morning song, almost passionless, really, but memorable nonetheless, maybe because she'd been the aggressor, delightfully so. She leaned her face into mine and we started. We may not have got to the goods in the manner Romey would have, but we got there, all right. Soon enough, we were hammering away at each other's lips in a fashion Merrick himself would have found entirely apropos. It was, as I remember, pure joy.

Through it all, outlines started to appear in the darkness, silhouettes emerged where before there had been only muffled whispers. Romey and this Mandy girl were pitching around like wrestlers. Mandy wasn't fat and she wasn't ugly, but she was what my mother would have called big boned. They were rumbling together, half wrestling, half smooching, creating, if nothing else, a whole lot of noise.

But then it would be hard to underestimate how hard Dianne Kampen and I pushed at each other in those few minutes we had together. I don't think I made the noise Romey did, but right then I'm sure I wasn't thinking about comparisons. The fact was, I'd seen Dianne throughout my whole grade school life, even admired her at times, had a crush on her in third or fifth grade. There we sat in the darkness of the girls' barracks, capitalizing on Merrick's idea of tag-team wrestling. Something that delightful just couldn't be all that sinful.

But it didn't last long. The way the lights came on in that barracks just a few minutes after our first kiss was the closest I'd ever come to imagining the shock of the trumpet's last sound. It wasn't the counselors who came in, either—Merrick's little brother, our watchdog, threw on the lights and claimed the entire staff was hiking up. There was no time to get out. Kids came up from those cots as if they were lying on red-hot flatirons. Wincing in the naked glare, we stumbled to the middle of the floor and sat in a circle as if we were just about to start in on a game of Uncle Wiggly. Nobody'd planned it, no one had even thought about it, but instinctively the whole bunch of us took a position of piety the moment we knew our goose was cooked.

We were a guilty lot, of course, and we didn't look at all as if we'd been sharing our favorite Bible verses. Merrick's hair was messed and his ears rouged. The whole bunch of us had lips as puffed and swollen as a French horn choir.

Getting caught brought out the worst in us. The girls cracked almost immediately when the counselor who rushed in, almost out of breath from sprinting through the trees, was Caroline, a willowy blonde they loved in the same way we respected Cal Simmons. The look on her face once she found us there—a whole circle of smeared boys' faces in the

Bible Camp

girls' barracks—seemed drawn more deeply from pain than outright anger. She didn't say a word, just stared at us, circled on the floor as we were, nothing at all in front of us—no cards, no nothing, just a circle of purple faces with no obvious alibi. Two or three other counselors came in behind her, but Caroline did all the talking. It was her barracks.

"I saw the lights go on," Caroline said, pulling hard breaths. "It was dark in this room. You can't lie to me. I wasn't that far away, and I saw the lights go on." She turned to each of the girls, as if the guys not only weren't her concern but were already gone halfway to perdition. "Look at you," she said.

She didn't mean us. She was adamant about flushing shame and guilt from her girls, who must have been warned countless times that any invitation to boys would result in the kind of horror she'd uncovered—necking, and sure enough, just down the road, illegitimate pregnancy. She was as pretty as Cal was handsome, and she stood before them straight and tall, her fingers pulling down the tails of her blouse as if she'd been manhandled herself. "I simply can't believe it. After everything we've talked about. After everything we've told each other, everything we've shared."

Romey looked at me and raised his eyebrows.

"I just can't believe it," she said again. "I trusted you guys." She meant girls. She was ready to cry, and if she would have just then, most of her girls would have followed lockstep.

"We better all go to the pavilion," she said, businesslike. "This is something I have to report to Reverend Stielstra." She waited, stood there without moving an inch, then took a deep breath, reached down to a table at the door as if to steady herself before she addressed the boys. "You guys know you aren't supposed to be in here," she said. "We told you that right from the start—it's almost the first thing we said."

I don't remember ever being so effectively reprimanded. She said it in an auspicious tone, this Caroline, whose last name I don't remember, but whose disdain I'll never forget. That night we were the serpents. We were exactly what Caroline's girls were warned about. We were not to be trusted. We weren't just vermin, we were original sin.

"I can't believe you'd try this," she said. "If there's any rule that you know, it's that this barracks is simply off limits—"

"Only after hours," Merrick said.

"Don't hand me that," she said. "You know what the rules are—"

"Only after hours," he said again.

It was gutsy of Merrick to take her on. What he was hoping was that she'd skip out on what she'd promised—hauling us all to Stielstra. But

I thought his talking back was stupid, too, because if she wouldn't alter her plans, talking back the way he was would only make matters worse.

Caroline was savvy enough to understand she didn't want to get in an argument with a streetwise kid like Merrick, so she did what Stielstra, the head man, had likely told them all to do should such a foul transgression occur: she pointed with her whole arm out the door, aimed the whole council of the ungodly back toward the middle of the camp, where we knew a tribunal would gather to deliberate our fate.

I wasn't surprised when Romey sat there chewing on his bottom lip, still eyeing Mandy, who seemed, at first, no more terrified than he was at having been caught in the act. I wasn't quaking myself, but then, the possibility of our getting booted really didn't occur to me until we met the man of booming voice, the Reverend Stielstra.

I looked at Dianne. It was obvious to me she'd forgotten completely what I couldn't so easily. I'd liked what we'd done, liked it a lot, but Dianne, wincing, her eyes puffy, looked to me like someone who'd gone through a radical change of character. There was no doubt in my mind that she loved Caroline far more than she loved me.

The huge stone fireplace in the pavilion was adorned with a tall crooked cross fashioned from pine limbs. The south wall was almost completely glass, offering a view of the trees on the slope leading to the lake below. Like most everything else at camp, those spacious windows were never really clean, clouded by dust or steam that climbed from the bottom up. But they were still windows, and that night, even though what happened in that room took place out of earshot of any of the other kids, the arraignment was definitely public spectacle.

Under the pressure of Caroline's disappointment, Dianne and a couple of others folded almost immediately. On the walk through the woods to the middle of camp, some of the girls were already holding each other up like survivors when they weren't wiping each other's tears.

But Stielstra had to be hunted up. At the counselor's command, we pulled as many chairs as we needed into a circle in the middle of the pavillion and sat down the way Caroline told us to. A hundred kids started wandering past the department store–sized windows almost right away. We were the big story that night—a dozen kids caught in the wrong place at the wrong time. Ours was immensely public sin.

When I think back to that time now, I'm surprised that I don't remember sheer terror. For whatever reason, I wasn't particularly scared, even though I knew that we'd committed what amounted to the unpardonable camp sin, messing around in the girls' barracks. They were our accomplices, of course; it wasn't as if we'd forced ourselves on them. And by the time the counselors got in the room, there had been no clear evidence—other than bleary eyes and smarmy lips—that we'd done anything more than sat in a circle and talked.

I was sitting next to Romey—that I remember, because he leaned my way when we were supposed to be quiet and sorrowful. "So?" he said.

I didn't have any idea what he was talking about, but I assumed it was his take on the trouble we were in—which made sense. Cyril would hardly think of what we'd done as assault and battery, after all. For that matter, neither would Hattie. She would have chuckled. She did, in fact.

"We're going to get read out," I said.

"That's not what I mean," he said. And then he pointed at Dianne. "How'd you do with the honey?"

It wasn't that I'd forgotten, but I wasn't about to go into a long monologue when contrition was the name of the game in the pavilion. I winked.

"Poof! You're human," he said, as if he had a magic wand.

Stielstra was a thirtyish pastor, no bully, but he was firm, square shouldered, with thick bushy hair streaked with silver like a TV star, the kind of boisterous half showman, half football coach most adults thought of as great with kids simply because he told good jokes and laughed hard enough to make others giggle. With some kids, he was good too, because he was powerful, authoritative, and—like Cal Simmons—handsome. And he was big into talking about faith.

"It was dumb," Merrick said when the big man stood there, hands on his hips. Merrick had tried to bully Caroline, but he was savvy enough not to take on Stielstra. "Mostly it was my idea, and I know it was stupid."

I wasn't surprised he would take the whole burden on himself—confess and throw himself at the mercy of the judge, get the whole mess over with fast, do a plea-bargain thing. Merrick likely became a politician.

"The rules are, you get caught in the girls' barracks, you go home," Stielstra said.

"What about the girls?" Romey said. "They live there."

I don't think Stielstra knew Romey, and he was stunned by that comment. He looked at Romey as if what he'd heard had come from a creature in whom no trace of the image of God could be found.

"It was a dumb idea," Merrick said again, covering for Romey, who he likely figured didn't have the chutzpa to deal with such ticklish situations.

Bible Camp

Stielstra stayed on his feet. "What you did is break the rules," he said again, almost as if starting over, and then he started something he never really quit all night—strutting back and forth like an admiral on deck, at first not addressing us with his eyes, keeping his face up and away, as if we were dirt and the words he was repeating were on some ceiling screen. "You knew it was against the rules the moment you snuck in there. Girls knew it too, didn't you? You aren't innocent here either."

Their assent came up in chorus. Three or four of them seemed already suffering the flames.

"It's not that you weren't warned," he said.

"Reverend Stielstra, nothing happened," Merrick insisted. "I can guarantee you that. We just got there. We no more than snuck in there and Caroline and all were right behind." His face was pinched with an earnestness I hadn't seen in him all week. "It was my fault," he insisted once again. "I put the whole thing together, and we just got there, and nothing happened—really. I'm sorry."

Stielstra inhaled one huge perturbed breath and let it out audibly. "Rules are rules," he said. "You know that."

Just about then, Cal showed up and looked at Romey and me right away, picked us out of the pack because we were his kids. But this wasn't Simmons' moment. Stielstra was very much in charge. He marched back and forth, arms across his chest. "So what were you doing in there with the lights out, anyway?" he said—didn't shout it, either, just said it plainly and squarely. "Playing checkers, I suppose?" He nodded as though he knew his way around every dark corner of the human character. "You got to have lights on to play checkers, don't you? I never heard of checkers in the dark. You got checkers that glow, Merrick? Is that it?"

I knew that approach wouldn't be the right way to take on Romey. Maybe it was the way he designed to humiliate Merrick, but sarcasm would only make Romey burn.

Almost all the girls were contrite because Caroline wasn't laughing at Stielstra's jokes, but she wasn't crying, either. These were her girls—they knew it and she knew it, and she'd taken the whole barracks thing very personally. So did they.

Stielstra stopped behind Merrick. "You want to explain that to me, Baker?" he said to Merrick. "You got all the answers here—you want to explain what it was you planned to do in the dark?"

Merrick made me nervous because anybody who talked so big-time about his exploits, I figured, had to be lying about just about everything. Say what you want about Romey, at least he never went on and on about things the way this city kid, Merrick, did.

"Lynn's got a transistor along and we wanted to listen to music," he told Stielstra, tossing his head slightly as if he were about to break out in tears. "Rock music," he said. "We wanted to listen to rock music."

That was a purposefully created red herring.

"With the lights out?" Stielstra said. One of the reasons he was head honcho was street smarts—he had 'em. "Do I have this down correctly now?" he said. "You wanted to listen to rock music with the lights out? What—it's something about the mood or what?" He looked around the circle. "That's the story you guys are building here—you were going to listen to music, is that it? Is that what you want us to believe?"

Merrick was starting to crumble. His best strategies against this guy went limp as wet tissue because all he really had in his arsenal was juvenile deviousness. Stielstra knew naughtiness; he banged through that as if it were whipped cream, and Merrick knew it. He started looking skittish, tangling and untangling his fingers in front of him.

"What about the rest of you guys here?" Stielstra said. "Anybody got a better story? You think the rest of us were born yesterday?" he said, pointing to the counselors. "I hate it when people think I'm stupid—don't you, Calvin? These guys think we don't know what happens between kids when they get in the dark." He was talking to the guys. The girls had broken long ago.

Cal would have worked on guilt in the same quiet way Caroline's tears pulled all kinds of contrition from her girls, broke them down in a minute. But Stielstra read the whole business as an arm wrestling match. He wanted to take on whatever alpha male stepped up to the plate.

"So who was with whom?" Stielstra said.

For the first time, Merrick said nothing. Neither did the rest of us.

"Who's going to sing here?" Part Nazi, part TV-show cop, Stielstra was hard core with us, and I was starting to get scared, basically because I read the man's frustration. He'd long ago dumped whatever religious armaments he might have brought to the fracas in favor of sheer wide-shouldered power. "Who's going to talk to me?" he said, parading around us. "Who's going to save themselves some grief here?"

Nobody said a thing. Dianne looked at me and even grudged a smile out of her weariness.

"So the carrottop's done," Stielstra said, pointing to Merrick, "and nobody else has anything to say, eh?" Tough guy.

In that silence, I remembered it wasn't that long ago I'd been caught smoking. I imagined what my parents would say if I came home early from camp. The preacher started scaring me, not because I felt shame or guilt or sorrow, but because I started to believe that there was no way to avoid capital punishment.

"What I want to know is—what went on in there in the dark? Who was with whom?" he said again.

"We were all together," Romey told him, something of a lie. "There was no pairs or nothing," he said. He shrugged his shoulders, pointed. "Wait, Lowell Prins there was with Dianne, but he likes her anyway, y'know." That was a gift I didn't know I wanted opened. "It's no big deal," he said. "I don't know what all the bother's about." He pointed at Dianne. "That one—she was with him," then he pointed at me.

Dianne was, among other things, the best pianist at camp. I figured Romey probably thought Dianne was the means by which to get out of this, someone Stielstra—and everybody else at camp—considered the next thing to heavenly. "Where's Dianne?" he'd say at every last hymn sing, "where's Dianne Kampen?" looking through the crowd for his pianist.

"You're telling me there wasn't any kind of monkeyshine?" Stielstra asked. "You had the lights out because the music sounds better in the dark? That's a good idea," he said sarcastically. "I have to try that sometime with my wife."

That made me nauseous.

"You know," the preacher said, "it'd be easier on everybody if you didn't compound this thing with a lie. I mean, if you guys weren't building a falsehood, I might start to think of letting you stay for another night—"

Romey picked up the challenge. "Nothing big-time happened, all right?" Romey said. He wasn't brokering a way out of a boot home. He was telling the truth, the gospel according to Romey Guttner. "What's the big deal? Nothing happened," he said, with a sharp enough edge to sound dangerously like sarcasm.

Stielstra stalked us silently, pacing behind the wooden chairs. He said nothing for a couple of minutes, prompting even more tears from kids who'd already turned their eyes up for repentance. Faces peered in through the glass.

"I'm sorry," Merrick said. "I told you once already, it was my fault, and I'm sorry. I knew going over there was against the rules, but we wanted to sit there and talk, you know—listen to music—"

"In the dark—"

"I don't know who put the lights out," Merrick said, not his first lie. "It wasn't my idea."

Bible Camp

"Then, who did?" Stielstra said. "If it wasn't you, Baker, then who was it? You were in charge, right?" He came up behind Merrick and grabbed his shoulders. "How come you didn't snap it back on then—all of this was your idea of a good time, right?"

Merrick was never at a loss for words. "I don't know who snapped it out—I wasn't looking right then, I guess," he said, pulling himself forward in overwrought repentance. "I thought about it, you know—I mean, I thought, 'Man alive, does this look bad'—that's what I thought, you know?" Face stark with horror. "But you don't want to be some old grandma either, Reverend Stielstra, you know what I mean?"

"You think I'm a grandma?" Stielstra snapped. "You think I don't want you kids to have fun here at camp? Is that what you think?"

"I think you're a grandma," Romey told him. "I sure do. We weren't doing nothing worth getting huffy about."

The whole room went pale.

"You again?" Stielstra said.

Only Romey would have said something like that.

Stielstra swung his ashen face around as if he'd been slapped by an open hand. "You think I'm a killjoy, do you? Who do you think I am, Adolf Hitler? Is that it?" He circled the chairs until he stood right behind Romey, his hands on the back of Romey's chair. "What's your name, son?"

"Romey Guttner."

"Romey Guttner," he repeated, as if it were a foreign language. "One of your boys, Calvin?" he said, and Simmons nodded.

I couldn't see Stielstra because he was directly behind us. "Romey Guttner," he said again, and then, "Son, it's a privilege to come to Bible camp, you know that?" His voice seemed controlled. "Do you understand that—that when you come here you've got to live by rules, and of course somebody's got to enforce those rules—you understand that, son? Somebody's got to watch over the mess or it will fall into a mess—you know what I mean?"

He was talking down to Romey, something he shouldn't have done. It looked to me as if he figured Romey was stupid. That was his first mistake, because Romey felt condescension in a heartbeat.

Romey turned all the way around as if he wasn't going to stand it for another second. "We didn't do nothing," Romey said, his shoulders twisted.

He shouldn't have tried to look directly at Stielstra—I knew that too. Instead of sitting forward on the chair with his face down like everyone else, Romey stared right back at the preacher, looked him flat in the eye,

Bible Camp

not a pinch of guilt on his face. He didn't owe anybody a thing here, had nothing to fear, and I understood that in a way nobody else in that room did.

"You didn't *have* to come here, you know," Stielstra said. "It's a privilege, and nobody twisted your arm up behind your back to make you go."

"My ma did," Romey said. "I wasn't big on it myself, but Ma made me come." He looked at me and shrugged his shoulders.

Everyone else was in the throes of penitence—some faking, some not. Even Mandy, who'd not shed a tear yet, was sitting forward on her chair, her elbows on her knees, not looking up. Only Romey was still untouched.

"You don't want to be here anyway—is that it, Mr. Guttner?" Stielstra said angrily, turning away.

Then Romey did something dramatic. He pulled his chair out of the circle so he could turn it all the way around, and then he got on backward, spreading his legs across the seat. He got sick of being talked to. He pulled a huge smile out of someplace inside no other kid in that circle had and announced, bluntly, "You think we got laid or what?"

I didn't have to see the look on Stielstra's face to know what happened. Romey had thrown one high and inside, a pitch aimed right at the head, but he wasn't finished. "From the way you're grilling us," he said, "you'd think it was something out of Playboy." And then he laughed, out loud. Not even Merrick would have laughed—only Romey. "What you want us to confess to anyway, Reverend? Why don't you tell us what it is you want us to say and have done with it?"

Stielstra said nothing. Only Romey could see him, but he didn't stop, probably because he figured it was the only way to be done with it, as he'd said.

"You'd think we robbed a bank," Romey said. "It didn't amount to nothing, what happened in that room. Merrick's right—it didn't amount to a thing. And you get on your holy horse and ride around this place as if we were all bound to Hell for doing a little kissy face."

Merrick looked like he'd just taken a poke from a live wire. The girls were bawling out their guilt, but Romey, in all innocence, looked up at Stielstra, not as if to challenge him, but to offer him little more than what was relevant here—the plain facts. If it came off arrogantly, it wasn't meant that way. I didn't believe for a minute he was trying to make himself a big shot. That was Merrick's way, but not Romey's. Romey was responding to the preacher in kind. To him, what had happened in the girls' barracks didn't amount to a hill of beans. That was the plain and simple truth, even if Stielstra wasn't man enough to take it. Every other kid overflowed with guilt, but not Romey. Romey would start the night all over again at the drop of a hat—take another run at Mandy, the wet kisser.

"You're not talking back to me, are you, Guttner?" Stielstra said. I honestly believed he really didn't know. "You're giving me lip, are you?" he said.

Romey balked for the first time, as if he didn't understand the question. From his angle, what he was doing was hardly talking back. He knew what he was up to, but it had less to do with some desire to put down Stielstra than it did with simply admitting the truth, and the gospel according to Romey was that nothing worth crowing about had happened in the girls' barracks. Okay, we'd broken a dumb law: we shouldn't have been there, but big deal. Maybe if we'd been there a while, it might have been better—that's probably what Romey thought.

"I'm not going to stand here and take back talk," Stielstra told him.

"I'm not lipping off," Romey said. "I'm telling the truth."

Stielstra came inside the ring of chairs. He circled in front of us and came at Romey the only way he could. "Then keep your mouth shut," he said, quietly. "Whyn't you let the others say what they think."

I knew what was happening. Stielstra was backing down.

"I'm telling you what happened," Romey said. He knew he had a leg up on the preacher, and he wasn't about to let it go.

"And I'm telling you to shut up, okay?"

Romey'd already won. I knew it.

"So who else is going to come up with a lie here?" Stielstra said, trying to take Romey out of the game. He walked away and paused, as if to win back something he'd lost. "Somebody else want to ante up with the truth here? Or do you want to keep lying? A lie is a bargain with the devil, you know—"

"I ain't bargaining with the devil—" Romey said.

"I told you to be quiet," Stielstra said.

The man was more dangerous than I'd thought at first, especially now that he'd lost to Romey. But I knew Romey didn't see that, didn't get it. The hotter Stielstra got, the more dangerous he became. Things could only go from bad to worse now. I knew Romey would keep it up, not only because he still hadn't understood the big deal here, but also because he'd already had the guy pinned. But Stielstra scared me. He was coming close to losing it, to dumping whatever grace he might have brought into this room full of windows. He was getting kicked, and he wasn't liking it at all.

Bible Camp

And I didn't want to go home. I didn't want to have to tell my folks we'd broken the rules. Neither did I want to sit here and wait for some conflagration. The steamy windows in that pavilion were still clear enough to make the whole thing a spectacle. Romey knew he was right, and he was going to hang on to Stielstra's shin like some mangy dog. This was going nowhere fast, and something had to be done. We were all no more than an inch away from Stielstra's picking up that telephone, and I didn't want to call my father.

"Romey doesn't mean to hurt you, sir," I said to Stielstra. "He's not talking back—"

"I'm not hurt," Stielstra shot back.

"What I mean is, he's telling the truth," I said. I looked over at Romey, who seemed shocked. "He's not lying when he says nothing happened," I said. "Nothing happened but a bunch of kids getting together to play a game and listen to the radio," I said. "I'm the one who turned the lights out." That was a lie. "It was stupid, but we didn't want to get caught— that's why we turned everything dark. We didn't want anybody to see us. Somebody running through the woods—they could have just looked in and seen us sitting there together on the floor."

It was a bald-faced lie, and I was now in much deeper than I'd been just a few minutes before. "I did it, and I'm sorry," I said, using Merrick's own ploy, hoping confession might pull us through this. What Stielstra wanted was contrition. "It wasn't in the planning," I said, nodding toward Merrick. "He's right—it was his idea, but I'm the one who turned off the lights." I even tried to look in Stielstra's eyes.

"Thanks, Lowell," Cal said.

I turned back to face the others. I figured I'd salvaged something here, but when I turned toward Romey, he arched his eyebrows as if what I'd said were plain falsehood.

But it worked, sort of. Stielstra breathed in deeply again, loud enough for me to know that something was over—like an amen, so let it be.

The man pulled up his pants and waded into the admonition. "You kids know that I really could throw the lot of you out, right?" he said, and then I knew for sure it was over. "I mean, you understand that when you break rules at a place like this, there's consequences." His pace had fallen off. "Not going into the barracks of the girls—or the guys—is the first rule here, and all these kids out here walking by this window," he pointed out at the faces, "all these kids staring in at you guys—they're all wondering what Stielstra's going to do, because they all know by this time that you guys got caught in the girls' barracks." We were supposed to feel a sense of shame. I'm not sure we did—I knew Romey didn't.

Bible Camp

"They all know that—all those kids. And every one of them is waiting to see if it really matters—the rules we make. That's what they're waiting for. You put me in an awful position."

He was begging our pity now, and I was feeling pretty good—given where we'd been. Stielstra was working on guilt, not judgment.

"You understand what kind of pinch you put me in: I got my word on one side—'Anybody caught in the barracks of the opposite sex gets sent home'—I got my word over there on that side, you understand? That's what I told you," he said, pointing to his uplifted left hand. "It's the very first rule, and you guys broke it. I ought to send the whole lot of you home because I'm breaking the rules." He was working himself up. He stayed on the inside of the circle and went back toward Romey, oddly enough, as if he hadn't had enough of that match. "How'd you like it if I called your father tonight yet and had him drive up here to pick you up?" he said without using Romey's name. "How'd you like that, son?"

That was entirely the wrong thing to ask.

Romey started laughing. "No way," he said. "Don't do that—"

"He'd be mad, wouldn't he?" Stielstra asserted.

"Dang right he'd be mad, and he wouldn't come, either," Romey said, as if it were the gospel truth. "You think my old man would drive way up here tonight yet? You got to be nuts. I'd walk home first."

Stielstra didn't get it. "That's right—he'd be that mad, wouldn't he? He expects you'll obey rules here. He expects that when you come to Bible camp you'll listen to what the rules are—"

"My old man don't care about your rules," Romey said. "My old man wouldn't come get me, because if he's sleeping, you don't want to wake him up for nothing—know what I mean?"

Things were going bad again. I had to do something.

"His old man's not a Christian," I said. I threw it in like yeast. "That's what he means to say, Reverend Stielstra—his old man wouldn't care if he was in the girls' barracks because his old man's not a Christian at all— he's not a believer. He's like a atheist or something."

The lines in the man's face fell as strain bled from his soul. He pulled himself out of the crouch he'd been prowling in, stood up straight, his hands suddenly clasped in front of him as if he might break into prayer. He'd had a revelation. I hadn't understood it when I'd said it, even though I knew it was a lie, a way of getting out of things. But Stielstra heard it and absolutely everything changed. Suddenly, a greater target loomed right there on the horizon—unbelief itself. All of this madness made sense to him. His forehead shone. This lippy kid he couldn't take—

Bible Camp

he was a child of an unbeliever. All that sass came from somewhere else, from skewed morals and ethics. This kid had to be reshaped, an exasperating kid who refused to hang his head. This kid needed grace.

"His ma's a member of our church," I said, "but not his dad. I mean, even Romey—" I pointed at him, then weighed my words, knowing that what I was about to say might not hit Romey right. But we were almost out of it, and if Romey did too much more talking, I was sure I'd have to call my parents. So I said it. "Even Romey's not a real Christian," I told Stielstra.

"I mean, not *really*," I said. "I mean, like with his old man—it's hard for him to be a Christian. You know what I mean." I figured Romey might buy that.

Just like that the barracks stuff dropped out of the picture completely. Stielstra was brimming with grace, not hellfire. He didn't fawn over Romey, didn't excuse the rest of us from the pavilion or let us off the hook right away, but his voice lowered into something soft as lake sand on a warm day. "I didn't know that, son," he said, his hand on Romey's shoulder, the very first time he'd touched any of us. "I never dreamed you didn't know the Lord."

Romey nodded. I figured he knew we had the guy.

"I had no idea—" Stielstra could hardly even talk. He didn't even know how to phrase it at first. "I never guessed your father might not know the Lord—and what about you?"

Even though Romey must have understood what was going on, he was not a kid who could lie all that well. "My old man knows who God is," he said, looking up at Stielstra. "That's not it." He was thinking now—you could tell by how slowly he spoke. "He just doesn't care much." He scratched at his nose. And then he said something that astounded me. "I got it bad at home, too," he said. "The old man—he beats on me all the time—it's really bad," he said.

"I want to talk to you personally, son," Stielstra said, swallowing something. "What's your name again?"

"Romey Guttner," he said, angrily—the first line he'd said really angrily, as if finally the whole ugly story was out in the light of day.

"After I'm finished here," Stielstra said, nodding, "you and me—I'd like to sit down with you, Romey, and have a chat." He smiled. "That okay with you?"

Romey looked at his watch.

"Doesn't matter about curfew tonight, does it, Cal?" Stielstra said, without looking up. "We'll just talk for a couple of minutes here."

For the most part, that was it. No calls home. No more passion. No more fire. We were saved.

Stielstra waded through a silence he hadn't planned on, and he didn't get back to the problem at hand for another couple of minutes, when finally he started into a testimony of God's enduring love throughout his own checkered past. He explained how he hadn't always loved the Lord himself when he was a kid, how he hadn't always done the right thing either, and how the Israelites hadn't always done the right thing, how they had to wander forty years in the desert because of it, but how God's love was forever, everlasting, never to be shut down or shut off or plugged up. It was a river of grace like a river of blood, cleansing blood, Jesus' blood, he said, his hands drawing flowing waters through the air.

It was that kind of sermon he delivered then, a sermon on love.

Romey brought out the best in the man.

Bible Camp

The Campfire

Even though Stielstra's anger had finally broken, the night wasn't over. The camp's head man offered us a homily on sex I assume was partly obligatory, a relatively graphic narration of the David and Bathsheba story, an explication of the horrendous effects of Solomon's thousand wives, and at least a half-dozen references to exotic biblical characters, some of whose names even I didn't recognize. The admonition came to a halt at the foot of Sinai, Moses descending with a tight grip on the seventh commandment, while Aaron and the people of Israel danced the night away around a silly calf made of gold. Even though he never hammered on us the way he'd started to, some of the girls kept crying—still afraid and riddled with guilt. Romey had turned his chair back around and sat beside me with his hands up behind his head, rocking on that folding chair in a way even Hattie wouldn't have allowed at home.

We weren't sent packing, and the reason was simple. Romey was the child of an unbeliever, a wandering sinner like few others at that year's camp. While the ninety and nine were safely laid in the shelter of the fold, one was still out on the hills away, far off from the gates of gold. He was the kid Stielstra bothered about, as well he should have, I guess.

But before the night was over, Stielstra sat down beside us and penned a letter right then and there, an explanation of our offenses to our parents. He told us every word as he wrote them down—"your daughter (son) was caught tonight with boys (girls) in direct violation of camp rules." It was long and torturous for all of us to have to sit and hear him narrate the whole epistle, and the process sent some of the girls to the tissue paper Caroline had graciously brought in from the toilets.

The night ended with prayer, as everything did back then—sentence prayers. Merrick did his part with a flowery offering that sounded like something old men from the church might have said, swelling with supplications and behooves and smittens. Dianne did her thing too, full of repentance and what I considered to be something of a show. Mandy didn't say much at all—when her turn came around, most everything had been said.

Even Romey prayed that night, which is not to say he was sad about whatever it was that was making everybody cry. He was last, so he said something about the lake, the temperature, and he asked the Lord if we could have a great time on the last day of Bible camp because it wasn't half as bad as he thought it was going to be and how glad he was he didn't have to tell his old man to pick him up. Amen.

Part of our punishment was having to go straight back to our barracks—there would be no more free time. So we did, Cal leading us, his arm around Merrick as we crossed the grounds, the rest of the kids gaping and staring at the dirty dozen. Romey, as requested, stayed behind with Stielstra.

But it wasn't long before he was back—maybe fifteen minutes. Cal had his own work to do, so he left us together, warning us that taking off now would be writing a ticket home.

"What'd he say?" I said when Romey sat beside me.

"Gave me the Jesus talk—" he said, "you know."

"Wasn't mad?"

"Shoot no."

"I thought we were dead meat," I said. "I could about see my old man getting up here—you know—after all that other junk this summer? We don't have any more fence to paint. But he mellowed out, didn't he?"

Romey pulled his feet beneath him and snapped the flaps of rubber on the toes of his sneakers. He didn't say anything for a while, and I wondered if the preacher had got to something in him I didn't even think existed.

"He scream and holler?" I said.

Romey shrugged his shoulders.

"What'd he do? Make you tell him the whole story—about your old man and stuff?"

He wasn't thinking about what I was saying.

"You with me here, Romey?" I said.

And then he turned to me slowly. "You think I'm not a Christian, Lobo?" he said.

I tried to wipe it away with a laugh. "I just *said* that," I told him. "I figured it would do something—get us somewhere. We were stalled, and you had him breathing fire."

"Diversion, right?" he said, laughing. "But you don't mean it?"

I didn't know what I meant, but what I meant wasn't the point. "I said that because of Stielstra," I told him. "I had to explain—I had to get us off the hook."

Romey stared. "Don't josh me," he said.

I had to find some way out. "You're just like me, you know—we aren't any different." I looked over at the other guys, who were sitting around Merrick on the other side of the room. Once Romey'd told them he didn't get a whipping or anything, they'd got out of our way.

But Romey wasn't buying equivocation. "That's a stupid thing to say," he told me. "We are too different—if we weren't, I wouldn't even be here. My old lady wouldn't have told me I had to—"

"Not in that way," I said. "I mean, not in whether or not we're Christians—we're not different that way."

"You a Christian?" he said.

I don't know whether anyone had ever asked me that before.

"I guess so," I said, but I didn't know myself where the line was between truth and falsehood. "I think there's a God—don't you?"

He looked at me. "Course," he said. "I never thought of not thinking there was a God—I'd be a terror without God, I think. I'd be more like my old man." He meant that as a joke.

We were sitting on the bottom bunk, the only two guys in our barracks from Easton. Merrick was holding forth on the other side of the room.

"What are you worried about, anyway?" I said. "We're off the hook. We just got our wings clipped, that's all."

"Too bad, too," he said. "I wouldn't mind getting some more licks in, but Mandy's history now."

"Dime a dozen," I told him.

189

"You can talk. You got Dianne—she'll be there when we get back."
He hunched his shoulders. "I'll never see this tootsie again, you know?
I don't even remember where she's from. I don't remember a word she
said, but she sure could kiss." He laid back and put both arms behind
him on the mattress, stared up at the springs. "You know, Lobo, I don't
think I'll ever be somebody like Stielstra—or Cal, or your old man." He
chuckled. "What does that make me, anyway?"

"Nobody's like anybody else exactly," I said.

"My old man—he says that everybody he knows around home,
they're all two-bit hypocrites anyway, spouting off about the Lord but
hating everybody who's not just like them." He let that appraisal sit.

So did I. "So?" I said.

"So, you think so? Or you think he's got his eyes crossed?"

I didn't know what to say because I didn't know what I thought. What
was already clear to me was that Romey wasn't altogether wrong—and
his father wasn't either. I figured guys like Merrick would be one of the
first guys to stand up at the campfire on Friday—that's just the way they
were.

"I think there's people who like to make everybody else think they're
Christians," I told him. "I don't know if they are or not."

"Who?" he said.

"I don't know," I told him. "It's not so easy to pick and choose about
things like that—"

"My old man says everybody."

"Not everybody—not every last person on earth."

"What about your old man—he a hypocrite?"

"My old man?" I said.

"Yeah."

"I don't think so."

"He lie?" Romey said.

"Never, that I know."

"Then he's not. Then he's a Christian."

I hadn't thought about it being that easy.

"You mean if you don't lie, you're a Christian?" I said.

"Something like that—there's more, you think?"

"I think there's more than that. It's not just lying—"

"What is it then?" he said. "How do you do it?"

"How do you do what?" I said.

"How do you be a Christian?"

"I don't know—"

"Big help you are," he said.

"How am I supposed to know everything?"

"You been brought up that way. If you don't know, who does?"

"Maybe I don't know any better than you do. There's lying, for one, I think—"

"And you got to go to church?"

"It doesn't save you or anything."

"Does me," he said. "I go to church and I feel like I got to straighten out."

"No kidding?" I said.

"What about us?" he asked, honestly.

"I don't know," I told him. "Sometimes I lie—so do you. About the women tonight—that was a lie—what you told the preacher."

"Only partly," he said.

"Lies aren't just partly lies—lies are lies," I said.

"So I'm not?" he asked.

"A Christian?"

"Yeah," he said. "So I'm not a Christian—and neither are you because you lied too, just like Merrick. We all lied, right? That part about me not being a Christian—that was a lie too."

He was right. I shrugged.

"So how do you know?" he said.

"Know what?"

"How do you know you're a Christian?"

I fell back on what I thought my father would say. "Do you believe in all that stuff about God and Jesus?"

"Sure," he said.

"Then you are, right?"

"Yeah, sure." He sat up quickly. "Then *we* are, aren't we? Both of us." He pointed up toward the fly-specked ceiling, looked around as if there were nothing but stars above our heads. "I think he's up there," he said. "I mean, sometimes maybe I don't act like I care if he is, but I flub up, you know?" He looked at me. "But that doesn't mean I don't think he's there, right? I mean, everybody forgets about him sometimes—maybe even most of the time."

He'd really thought about what I'd said. "I didn't mean it that way—I mean, like you were some kind of heathen or something," I told him. "I didn't mean it that way at all."

"Then how did you mean it?"

"I had to explain, you know?"

"Explain me?" he said.

"Yeah," I said.

Romey giggled, like a sheep might bleat. "Explain me—that's a good one. You figure that out and I'll put a blessing on you, all right." He reached up just for a moment and batted my shoulder with the back of his hand. "Like the guy in the Bible with the hairy arms," he said.

"Jacob," I said.

"Jacob or Esau or whatever, the one about the hunter, you know? I always liked him most, anyway. Who wants to sit around and eat soup when you can be out shootin' camels or whatever?" He looked at me.

"Esau," I said.

"Whatever."

"You know all those things, don't you?" He butted me again. "You know everybody's name that you read from the Bible—I mean, you know all those names and stuff."

I knew the difference between Esau and Jacob. I knew who it was God loved.

"Everybody around here knows that stuff," he said. "Sometimes I sit in one of those circle things in the morning, and I think I'm dumber than mud. Yesterday, it was Esther, some queen somewhere, a Jew."

"And Mordecai," I said.

"I don't know nothing," he said. "All I know is that she's beautiful, and I'm wondering why it is I don't know about this beautiful woman." He shook his head. "I don't know if I can be like you because I don't know much at all about any of that." He put his arms down on the bed. "Catch this, Lobo—Stielstra wants me to testify," he said. "He said with me it's different. He says it'd be real stuff—me saying something to-morrow night in front of everybody. 'Romey Guttner's testimony—'" He pursed his lips and blurted out a trumpet fanfare.

"Going to do it?"

"I promised."

"You did?"

"Otherwise he'd have made me stay all night," he said. "That guy gave me the heebie-jeebies for a minute."

"What do you mean?" I said.

"He wants my pelt." He swung his legs around and laid his calves over the end of the bed, then laid down behind me, his hands up around his head. "Any minute I thought he was going to put his arms around me and start the hugging thing, you know?" He shook his whole body. "I had to get out of there."

"You going to do it?"

He burped, hard and loud. "I can make something up," he said. "But I don't want to lie, either, you know?" His eyes were up on the springs

The Campfire

again, his jaw moving the way he always moved it when he made a little clicking sound with his tongue. "I don't know why you had to say that stuff, you know—about my old man."

"What do you mean?"

"We all broke the stupid rules."

"I saved your butt," I said. "And besides, it's true—he doesn't go to church."

"What's my old man got to do with the price of eggs? It's always my old man this, my old man that—you know?" He sat up quickly and spit like he always did, a little wad shot between the gaps in his front teeth.

"Sheesh," I said, pointing, "now somebody's got to step in that."

"Maybe it'll be Merrick," he said, hunching his shoulders. "I'll know there's really a God in Heaven if Merrick steps in it, barefoot." And then he laughed, like his mother might have, heartily and almost too loud.

Nine o'clock Friday night it was raining, so the whole event was moved inside to the cement floor of the pavilion, right where we'd sat the night before in a strikingly different mood. Kids put down sleeping bags in front of the roaring logs in the fireplace. Some of the girls prepped for the occasion, having brought along rolls of toilet paper, anticipating the tears many of them knew would accompany the litany of testimonies.

Caroline, who was dressed up as if this were a worship service, passed out candles in cardboard holders, one at a time. Cal wore a white shirt, the only time during the entire week, and both of them started lighting the candles during the second verse of a little lullaby Christian chant we all sang, meant not so much to be sung as whispered like a quiet prayer. Caroline lit Dianne's candle first, one of her girls; Dianne lit Mandy's, and so on until the pavilion lit up like Pentecost. The whole time, Stielstra stood up front, his rich baritone taking the lead for the heavenly choir he tried to call up. Soon enough, you couldn't see a thing out of the windows.

Mostly it was the girls who sang. Cal and the other guy counselors tried to inspire the boys, their heavy voices beneath the melody like a deep persuasive line. But more often than not they wandered off from the harmony into some wayward key.

Romey and I sat on the lining of my unzipped sleeping bag. I tried to get my candle to balance on the cardboard holder, while Romey had already removed his, dropped hot wax on the cardboard, and stood that little thing up so he didn't have to hold it in his fingers. He was sitting there cross-legged, elbows propped on his knees, his chin in his hand as he gazed into the diamond flame.

All day, we hadn't said much about what had happened the night before, Cal only tentatively referring to it when we got out of bed for breakfast. He didn't make a big deal out of it, either. Just asked something about how we slept, didn't make an announcement to the rest of the barracks. He said someday what happened would make us stronger, having seen and understood where we went wrong, his eyes on Romey specifically. And then, what followed on the last day of camp were contests and swimming and watermelon.

But that night, with the fire dying slowly behind him, Stielstra worked us over with the soft touch, the way somebody did every year—love and joy as the fruit of the Spirit. "We always get together the night before we leave just to sing and share," he said, "just to be together here and talk about all the fun we had this week and what it means to our lives."

It wasn't at all hard for me to read that shiny smile he wore as inauthentic. After all, I'd seen him about ready to burst with anger just the night before—same time, same station. But I also knew that the way he was acting wasn't manufactured from some diabolical will to mess us up. The man sincerely wanted commitment out of us, even if in order to get what he was after he had to pitch and wail like a salesman.

"Maybe some of you want to say tonight what Christ means to you," he told us. He was aboard a stool, a couple of heads taller than the campers sprawled over the floor in front of him, a carpet of lit candles all around.

Then he read some things—a little poem, some familiar Bible verses, a short meditation, nothing very loud, either, always gentle. He wouldn't have thought of making us sing something like "Onward Christian Soldiers," because it was time for testimony, not war.

A kid named Allan started the whole thing, the only boy who ever played the piano at camp meetings. He gave an ordinary speech in language that made it clear he was a brain: how so many times during the year he'd almost lost track of the Lord, almost forgotten about his grace completely, and how very good it was for him to come to camp and realize again how significant a place God had in his life. He was very thin and tall, so tall he used to catch some flack from the rest of the guys, who thought it a waste that this pianist with zero agility should be growing to a height where stuffing the basketball was a whole lot easier than an outside shot.

Then it was Mary Jane, whom everybody knew because she sang solos every year on request—her own. Then two or three more girls who were really more like counselors than campers long before they'd arrived. Romey might have called them collaborators.

The Campfire

There was a method to testimony, a liturgy of sorts, not unlike the great evangelistic crusades, where hundreds of specially designated prayer partners spring to their feet the moment the organ starts in to "Just As I Am." Stielstra did some orchestrating beforehand, and only the densest of the kids in the pavilion were unaware of the fact that the first to stand and testify were preordained to get the fires burning.

"Someone else?" Stielstra said after another little song. "Would anyone else like to say something tonight?" The lights were out, the silhouettes against the walls dancing and jittering in the shadows cast by a hundred kids holding burning candles.

It was Monty's first year at camp, and, while it had been weeks since the day of the home visit, neither Romey nor I had seen much of him since. At camp, he was staying in another barracks, staying clean, we figured, the source of sin in his life somewhere across the camp in another building altogether. It wasn't out of character for him to testify that night, even though he was a year younger than we were. He loved a crowd, in a way.

He stood up, the first of the first-year campers, and told the rest of the kids how he hadn't been so keen on coming to camp because he'd heard it was mostly boring stuff with a few good times at the lake. Some of his buddies laughed. But now that he'd been here, he said, he'd come to see what a great time camp really was—how much he'd learned. He'd go back home now, he said, and really look forward to coming again next year because camp—and his counselor especially, a guy named Matt—had led him closer to the Lord. He asked Matt to stand up, and I felt guilty immediately because I liked Cal too, but I wasn't about to make a big show of it.

Stielstra stood up in front throughout the litany of testimonies, smiling like a new father. Romey took his eyes off the candle and watched Monty for a minute, even though Monty was way up front.

"And I know this, too," Monty said. "I got plenty mad at some of my friends this summer already, plenty mad." He turned slightly as if maybe he'd actually name us, but behind him there was a sea of half-lit faces, most of them knowing nothing at all about what he was referring to. It would have taken forever for him to find us in the mob on the floor.

He kept going. "I want to ask the Lord's forgiveness for hating one guy especially," he said. "I'm sorry about that—and he knows who he is, and he's here in this room right now—"

Kids leaned forward in rapt attention.

"I'm not going to say his name, either," Monty said, "but he knows who he is, and I got reasons for hating him." He took a breath. "But I know it's wrong, and I'm going to try to be his friend. And I hope you'll all be praying for me."

Stielstra broke into prayer right then, even though Monty hadn't yet sat down. He brought that forgiveness in thanks before the Lord in the loudest voice he'd used since the night started. Monty was still standing when he finished. "I just had to pray," Stielstra told him. "If you've got more to say, son, go ahead. I'm sorry, I just had to pray—"

Monty thanked him.

"Did you ask for this boy's forgiveness too?" Stielstra said.

There couldn't have been more than a dozen kids in that room that knew the whole story.

"I want him to know that I'm going to try to like him," Monty said, and then something got crushed in him because he folded a little, almost lost it, not a rush really, but a hot breath of emotion that injected a tremor into his voice. "He's got it kind of tough at home—this kid," Monty admitted.

Stielstra wrapped his arms around him in a bear hug that had become standard fare by that time. No matter where you stood in the room, Stielstra would somehow get over to you and you got the hug if you gave up the fear of testimony. There the two of them stood, cutting a die for what would follow. I wondered if Stielstra had any idea Monty was talking about Romey—after all, they were both from Easton. He could have put two and two together. What he said next suggested he had some clue. "Maybe that kid would like to respond," he said, turning back to us. "If not now, then later," he said. "But the Lord would love to hear from him tonight, I'm sure."

Romey leaned over. "He hugs me and he's dead," he said.

That night, things couldn't have gone any better for Stielstra. Monty opened up the whole subject of violated friendships and snubbed acquaintances, sins against friends, snobbishness and pride, transgressions counted and never wholly forgotten. One of the girls brought up Romey, even though she didn't name names, and just like that the night's agenda was laid out so perfectly it seemed some director had staged the whole event.

For a while, there were confessions made that almost got to me, kids telling each other that they shouldn't have done things they did, shouldn't have said certain things, should have been better Christians. There were tears, and the glow in the pavilion got soft and warm and affecting.

Romey sat babying his candle. He picked it up and turned it in his fingers so the wax circled down toward the cardboard base. He kept star-

The Campfire

ing at the flame as if he might want to be hypnotized. Sometime along the line I knew he would contribute something, whether or not he wanted to. He'd told Stielstra he'd testify, and no matter how strange it got in the room, no matter how much he might not want to, he would because he said as much.

Once it all started in earnest, there were some surprises, as I remember. We both were stunned when Mandy got up, the hottest babe in camp. Most of what she said was unintelligible from our angle, even though we listened as closely as we could. She wasn't bawling, just as she hadn't bawled the night before, when she sat resolutely through the inquisition and never moved at all.

"I don't always do what's right," she said, her jaw a little shaky. "I know that much at least. When I do things I shouldn't, I know it too. But I . . . I don't know. I don't know how to say what it is I want to—" She stumbled, but most people did, at least the ones who found themselves dead serious, dead serious and scared. "I got to start being somebody better," she said. "And I'm going to."

"True?" Romey said quietly, to himself mostly. He leaned back and put his hands behind him for support. Just the night before, she'd laid a scar in his neck that would take another day to fade.

Cal was watching us the whole time. I didn't want him to see us talking.

"Sure hope it's no major change," Romey said.

"I didn't ever think I was one who would ever give a testimony," she said, and everybody giggled, like they always did at that line. "I *want* to say that Jesus Christ means everything to me," she told us, her eyes down. "I want to say that, because I know it's what everybody wants me to say, but I wish it was more true." She was standing up, but Dianne had a hand up on her waist as she spoke. "When I leave this camp, I want to start living for him. I'm going to be better," she said. "I'm going to try."

"She's off the list," I told him.

"I'm sorry to everybody, too, that I let them down," she said, looking for Caroline, finding her across the room. "You don't really know why you do things you do, you just do them—but that's going to change now. Pray for me."

When she sat down, Stielstra started reading from the Bible he had opened in his hands. "Create in me a clean heart, O God, and renew a steadfast spirit within me. Do not cast me from your presence or take your Holy Spirit from me." He stopped, waited, bit his bottom lip, looked at the floor, as if what was coming was going to take some coaxing. "I want you to understand this now, because it's very important." He stopped, raised his eyes to the ceiling. "This is the prayer David wrote after the whole dirty business with Bathsheba—and what an affair that was. It ended in murder." He seemed embarrassed to have to bring it up. "But what you hear in the psalm is that it's not Bathsheba's forgiveness he's after—although he should have been, that too, I mean," nodding assuredly. "It's the Lord's forgiveness he wants." He thumped the Bible against the heel of his hand. "I want you to keep your eyes on that fact tonight in what we say here—it's the Lord's forgiveness we want here. David is torn apart about himself," he said, looking straight at us, "but he knows that God can clean him up and make him into something good, his own vessel. He knows where to go for forgiveness. It's to him—this is David's note to God—even after what he's done to Bathsheba," he said, and then he pointed, book in hand, toward the cross of pine limbs behind him on the fireplace.

Dianne was already crying when she got to her feet. "I'm sorry for hurting Caroline too," she said. "Just like Mandy says—I really am." Still, it seemed something of a put-on to me, even though there were tears. "I want you to pray for me to be the kind of Christian I want to be," she said. "Would everybody pray for strength for all of us to stay away from wrong stuff?"

This time Caroline interrupted with prayer. She was standing at the opposite side of the room, but she covered Dianne's crying with a prayer aimed at both of them—at Dianne and Mandy. "Please, Lord," she said, "forgive these kids—they're good kids and they want badly to live for you." It went on from there, but not long. Once it was over, Caroline nodded through her tears and said she loved all the girls in her barracks, that she'd love them forever, that she'd continue to pray for them all through their lives, and they had to promise the same. Then she tiptoed through the kids on the floor until she got to the other side of the room and hugged them, each of them.

"Women," Romey said.

Stielstra started in on "Have Thine Own Way, Lord." He didn't need to pump his arms like he did when he tried to get us to sing at morning devotions. He didn't give us a beat with his hands. He simply started in, and even the boys joined, because everything was working, half a dozen girls standing there crying, making the whole thing move.

But other than Monty and maybe one or two other guys, it stayed a girls' thing, just like I'd guessed. I didn't get to my feet. I hadn't planned on it, even though there were times—especially when Dianne talked—that I felt something pinch at the top of my ribs. Besides, I wasn't about

The Campfire

to line myself up with Monty. I looked at Merrick, who had a glaze in his eyes, ready to go.

Romey slugged my leg. "I don't know if I can cry," he whispered. "Is that something you got to do?"

"There's no rules," I said, "as long as you sound sad."

"You think I'm supposed to cry—that's what he wants?"

"You mean, God?"

"No, Stielstra." He looked miffed. "Am I supposed to do that?"

It didn't surprise me that he was planning what he was going to say. "You don't have to—shoot, you'll never see the guy again after tomorrow."

"I told him I would."

"Cry?"

"No, stand up and talk," he said.

All around the room kids were whispering and talking—not out of order, really, but many of them still watching all the hugs. A bunch of seventh-grade girls were swaying back and forth in a circle singing their own song. Something was loose in the room, and I felt it too, even though I wasn't a part of it. Two huge hands seemed to be pulling me apart—like the saints who died when teams of wild horses bolted north and south.

Stielstra shoved his hands in the pockets of his shorts and swayed back and forth, heel to toe, smiling gentle like a lamb. He started into a soft kind of laughter. "Do you feel him with us now, guys?" he said, meaning boys. "You feel the Lord here, don't you?"

"All I got to do is tell him I'm sorry—right?" Romey whispered. "I don't have to make a speech like the women."

I wondered whether Romey would just start going off like he could, stand up and barge into all of this in some odd way, breaking it all up. "If you don't know what to say," I told him, "then don't do it." You never knew with Romey. You could never guess what he was going to say. That's why it was always dangerous to have him around—he could pull stupid things right out of nowhere. Once, he'd told my mother that he wanted to catch some frogs out at Piss Creek—piss, he said, as if it wasn't a bad word at all, even though that's exactly what we'd always called the little creek that ran through town. "We're going out to Piss Creek," he'd said right in front of my mother.

"Someone else?" Stielstra said. The room was buzzing. He raised his hands, opened them out in front of him. "Maybe someone else has something to say."

"I want to pray for my guys," Cal said, stepping out from the wall where he'd been leaning. "I got a burden for the guys in my barracks because I know they got things on their hearts they want to say, and I want to encourage them to say 'em—I want to encourage them to tell it to Jesus."

"We're saying all of this to Jesus?" Romey said.

I nodded.

"I hope none of them is afraid of speaking up, either," Cal said, "even though I know they all are—but I'm going to pray for them." A hush came over the place again. The candles were burning down, the place turning almost into night outside of the bundle of flame from the fireplace. All the way around the room kids shushed as Cal held up his folded hands.

Romey never dropped his eyes. I watched him stare.

"There's no sin you can't forgive, Lord," Cal said. He stood up straight, hands folded, face up to the ceiling, a bunch of guys at his feet—Merrick and his buddies. "There's nothing you won't wipe out of your memory. Forgive us for going into paths that we know won't lead us where we ought to be." A few sniffles from the campers, a couple of deep breaths. "Be with each of my guys, Lord, help them to know that I pray for them every night, each of them—because each of them have individual needs, Lord—each of them are special in your sight and mine."

Romey kept watching him—so did I. I was watching both of them.

"Give them the guts to speak out for you, to pledge themselves to your service, to love you forever."

Romey sat there and stared as if Cal might be the only one capable of teaching him how he was supposed to do this thing he'd promised Stielstra.

"I just know, Lord, that my guys are thinking that they really ought to, so give them what they stand in need of."

Cal was an okay guy. We all liked him. I'd seen him hit a low liner that ended up in the next county, even though it never got more than ten yards off the ground. Hearing him talk that way stopped me. When I looked over at Romey, he looked like a dog on point. There were twink counselors, but Cal Simmons wasn't one of them.

"Give them strength to stand up for you before all their friends," he said, "all these campers, and confess your name. Doesn't make no difference where they're from or who their parents are—you love 'em, Lord. Tell 'em that. Tell 'em that clearly."

Romey put his hands down to push himself up and started getting to his feet, even though Cal wasn't finished. I caught him on his way up, grabbed his shirt and kept him down, because I didn't want him breaking in like that, not when Cal was still talking. But just then Cal did quit, and just then there was a moment of silence, and then it was Stielstra's voice. "Romey Guttner, you have something to say?"

But I was the one standing. I'd used Romey to get to my feet, and I was the one in place, but I didn't want to let Romey talk just then—for reasons I'm not sure of, maybe because I was just plain afraid of how he might screw up. Stielstra called out my name once he saw Romey back down on the floor, and there I stood before all those kids with nothing to say, really, because I hadn't thought about what it was I wanted to say, only that I didn't think Romey should just barge in on Cal's prayer the way he was going to—and you never knew what Romey might say, either.

Kids were watching me, those candles like embers of an old fire slowly dying away. I looked down at a hundred faces, but didn't see any of them. Stielstra smiled hugely, made me freeze. Nobody moved. In the whole place, I was at center stage, speechless.

"Lowell," Cal said. "I'm proud of you."

"What do you want to say, son?" Stielstra said. "You're a Prins, aren't you? I knew your grandfather. He was fine man—he'd be proud of you." He nodded, begging. "I know your father, too."

Sitting there beside Romey, I felt those words like a body blow.

"Whatta'ya got to say, Lowell?" Cal said. "I know it wasn't easy to stand up."

For the thinnest moment I felt as if I couldn't open my mouth—not because I had nothing to say. I could have said a ton of things. I could have called on some reservoir of preacherly words and phrases that would have made the place sing. I could have leaned on my parentage, as many years as I could remember of strong prayers, three times a day at family meals. I knew the language, and I could have stunned them. I knew I could. But it would have been a lie. And this time at least, I didn't want to lie.

"Just pray then," Stielstra said. "Go ahead and pray. You don't have to say anything."

But I couldn't. I couldn't do anything. At that moment anything that would have come out of my mouth would have been untruthful—not that I would be trying to be a hypocrite, either. Were I to fold my hands and close my eyes, as was my custom, were I to stand in front of all those kids and whisper words of penitence to the Lord, it would only be another sin because I'd be doing it for the wrong reasons. I had the floor now; I was the one at the plate.

The Campfire

"What do you want to say, Lowell?" Cal said.

"I don't know how," I told him. I don't think I could have given a more vivid testimony. I was telling the whole world the gospel truth. I was born and reared in a hothouse of prayer, but right then, like a stubborn sinner, I didn't know how to pray.

Romey stood up. "This here's my friend," he said. "It ain't that he don't know what to say, either—he's been praying forever. Sometimes I go over to his place and his old man prays so long I wonder if he's ever going to quit."

He rammed my ribs with his elbow. "He knows what to say—that ain't it." He looked at me for just a second as if to straighten me out. "What he can't say is that we haven't always been the best kids in the world this summer, have we, Lobo?" He looked up at Stielstra. "That's what you want to hear, ain't it?" he said. "I mean, not that we're horrible or anything—we didn't kill nobody, but we do boy stuff, don't we?"

"What kind of stuff?" Stielstra said.

"Smoke," Romey said, the word coming out like something shot into the room. "Fact is, I could use one right now."

The place bubbled with muted laughter. Even Stielstra had to smile.

"And we're sorry about what happened last night," Romey said, zeroing in on what all the adults wanted said. "We knew it was against the rules and everything, but that only made it sweeter—know what I mean?" He was talking to Stielstra. He was actually talking to the preacher. "I didn't want to come here, you know. My old lady made me because she wants me to get all pretty like most Christians, you know? That's what she wants, all right—she wants me to be some Christian Boy Scout," Romey told them. "But I had a blast—other than all the Sunday school." Only Romey could get away with that. Kids roared. "Hey," Romey said, "my old lady says you go there and get religion—something like that. I don't remember how she put it and everything, but that's what she meant—that was the gist of it. Besides, beats picking beans."

Kids giggled.

"And I like Cal. We all do. Maybe someday when he gets to be a preacher, he'll come to Easton, 'cause he'll be a hotshot, the way he plays ball. Maybe he can get my old man to church—that'd be a miracle."

"I'm going to write down the address," Cal said.

People laughed again.

Romey wasn't finished. "Really," he said, "you think I'm making this up, you know—'oh, boy, Romey Guttner's going to testify—sure, and I'm Mickey Mantle.'" Then he pointed at Stielstra. "And I'll say this for him— I'd rather deal with him when he's hot than my old man, tell you that much—just don't be hugging me, see. Because nobody hugs me." And then he looked at Mandy. "Well, almost nobody. You can if you want," he said.

The spell was broken. What people would have largely acknowledged to be the Holy Spirit—that earnest misty-eyed fog—was gone. Kids were laughing.

"I don't really know either what I'm supposed to say, but I promised the big guy," he pointed at Stielstra, "that I'd say something for him." He looked at me. "Did I do it right?"

"I don't know," I told him.

"That's right—cat got your tongue, didn't he?" He looked around. "I feel like it's got to be more spiritual or something, am I right?"

"You're doing fine, Romey," Cal said from across the room.

"I got to be more like this guy," he said.

"I'm not saying nothing," I told him.

"C'mon, you say it," he said.

"Say what?"

"You say the spiritual stuff—you got training in that. I don't."

"Spiritual stuff?"

"Make 'em cry," Romey said. "Lookit here—there's nobody crying now. I can't make 'em cry."

"Nobody has to make anybody cry," Stielstra said.

"Then how come everybody tries?" Romey said.

"They don't try—"

"You mean it just comes natural?" Romey said. "You're pulling my leg. These little speeches, they just come right up from your middle all soft and full of tears and stuff?" He shrugged his shoulders. "I don't have a lick of that." And then he looked at me again. "You do it, Lobo," he said. "C'mon—you can do it."

"Can't either, Romey," I told him.

"Sorry," he said. Suddenly he looked as if he were really embarrassed to be standing there. "I've been going on and on and on here. Sorry, sorry."

I figured something had to be said. "Me and Romey were just talking—you know, last night, after we got caught and everything, and he says that a Christian is somebody who doesn't lie, so I'm not going to," I said. He was still standing there beside me. "I'm sorry—all right? I'm sorry that I got you disappointed in me—in us," I said, looking at Cal. "I'm sorry I let you down—that's the truth."

"It's okay," Cal said.

"Me too," Romey said.

"I don't want to say anything else right now," I said, because I could have. I knew all the right words.

"And you're sorry about what happened?" Stielstra said. "I mean about going over to the girls' barracks last night?"

Romey looked closely at him and nodded. "Sure," he said cleanly, no hesitation. "But I'm more sorry the stupid counselors had to break us up."

Suddenly, silence.

"Sheesh," he said, "can't anybody take a joke?"

The candles had just about gone out. Here and there flashlights left puddles of light on the floor where kids wanted them on, but the whole place was wrapped in semidarkness.

"That's my piece, I guess," Romey said, "and it's his too." He pointed at me.

I knew that I'd said almost nothing, that Romey'd saved me, that he'd stood and talked and helped me out, when I was the one who'd stood just to keep him from getting embarrassed.

"Romey's my friend," I said. "He's a great guy." I shrugged my shoulders as if it was self-evident. Stielstra kept prodding me. "And that's all I got to say." Then we sat down, both of us did. Cal came over from the place where he was standing, stood there in front of us, helped us to our feet, and hugged us—both of us, even Romey, who acted like he was going to get nauseous. Cal didn't say anything, just hugged us both for a minute or two and walked off.

We weren't the only show in town that night, and the whole testimony business went on for maybe another hour—more tears and prayers and people standing up to say things they might not otherwise say, kids with their own problems, their own burdens.

Romey waited until Stielstra was into something else before he whispered anything. "Really isn't that hard once you start rolling," he said, "but I don't know if I'd ever do it again." He pointed up at Stielstra. "I promised the big guy," he said, shrugging. "I gave him my word."

"We did all right," I told him.

"You think so?"

I thought we did.

And so did Cal. Later, back at the barracks, he said as much. But he didn't hug us again. That was only for the pavilion, I guess.

Later that night, Romey told me that with a little prodding he might be a preacher himself someday. Then he laughed.

The parental letter Stielstra sent from the camp didn't get back to Easton until Tuesday, and when it did my father read it aloud at the dining room table. But he didn't make much of the whole thing, really.

The Campfire

What had happened at camp seemed insignificant when compared with the news in the neighborhood. I'd seen it already the night I came home, when my sister Janine had told me about what had happened almost immediately, dragged me outside to witness it myself.

Even in the darkness the paint stains on Monty's place had turned the house into a nightmare. One of the paint bombs had hit about three feet above a front awning and skidded before bursting, the stain spreading sideways three or four feet into an odd scarlet shape. The paint widened sideways from the point of impact, then turned down so that the whole mess looked like the head of a hawk, its long glossy neck running over the awning's aluminum strips. It was as if whoever had thrown it might have been right on the front step instead of riding on the street in a truck or car.

Huge splotches of paint lay like banners over the red shingles and white siding. One of them had hit the front door perfectly, dried yellow paint forming a perfect half circle like an inverted moon over the screen and running down in swaths that slowly tightened into straight lines no thicker than braids. The house was a mess, a horror. It had happened Wednesday, but Zoot was so angry that he'd simply let the damage sit, a scarlike testimony to the town, a public indictment of Cyril Guttner.

Paint-bombings weren't uncommon that summer. Attacks on scabs happened all over the lakeshore region. I remembered my father driving by places just as horridly defaced, when we went out for hamburgers on a Friday night, remembered his silent horror, as if the picture were worth, in fact, a thousand sermons.

No one ever knew the identity of the perpetrators, of course, even though everybody knew who'd been responsible for it.

"People say Cyril Guttner did it," my sister told me. I didn't have to be told. But she said it as an admonition, as if I should know enough not to hang around with Cyril's kid anymore. "Couldn't have been anyone else."

"How do you know?" I said.

"Everybody knows."

"How?"

"Who else you know is that evil?" she said. "Quit trying to defend him, Lowell," she said. "Everybody knows."

And then she went over the story, how Zoot was incensed again, how Monty's mom was all broken up at our place that next morning, how the cops had come and stood out front with their hands on their hips, and how the street was full of cars for the rest of the week.

"I can't believe they didn't hit a window," she said. "Of course, a broken window would have been easier to fix than having to repaint the whole house."

I was so glad I was gone. I was so happy that I was at Bible camp, that we were at Bible camp.

"It's awful," Janine said again as we stood out there that night, "isn't it, Lowell? It's just horrible."

So when it came time for my father to read the letter and discuss the charges of his own son being caught in the girls' barracks, there was a whole lot more on his mind.

"What exactly did you get caught for?" he said. "You were really foolish enough to go in the girls' cabins?"

I nodded. We were sitting around the supper table, my mother already stacking the dishes.

"You apologized?" my father said.

"Sure," I told him. "We got a big sermon in the pavilion that night. Reverend Stielstra—"

"Stielstra," my father said, turning the letter over and looking at the back as if there might be more on the other side. "What'd he say?"

"It really wasn't such a big deal," I told him. "If it would have been bad, they would have called you up to come to get me. It wasn't that big of a deal."

My father folded the letter and stuck it back in the envelope. I knew the paint stains next door made some illegal trip to the girls' barracks little more than child's play. "I heard you testified, too—you *and* Romey," he said.

I nodded.

"Your mother and I are proud," he said. That was all.

I never told him how Romey had slayed the giant preacher, and I didn't tell him what exactly had happened in the pavilion on the night of the testimonies, what had been said. What my parents had heard was what kids from Easton remembered and brought home to their parents, that Romey Guttner and Lowell Prins gave testimonies too, and that it was really nice, almost unbelievable, to see Romey testify in front of all those people. They didn't remember much else, just that it was Romey.

My father nodded at me, his tightened lips in a half smile to tell me that I'd done the right thing. But I didn't tell him what I'd said or what I'd felt, didn't even tell them Romey's jokes, or about what Romey and I had talked about—about what it means to be a Christian. I didn't tell him any of that.

There was so much more going on at that time. Fear sat at the table with us at every meal late that summer, as the strike worsened. It muscled its way into our family's devotions. It stayed there in my father's serious silence, in the way he seemed always distracted, in the length of his prayers and the depth of his voice.

Games

For nearly two weeks after Bible camp, Dianne and I were an item. I'd pedal my bike over to her place in the early evening and sit outside in front of a huge garden her mother fastidiously kept, behind us the low August sun bringing a close to another summer day. Often enough, the night would end with sweet sunset kisses that were almost sinless. With Dianne, I was a gentleman, more so, obviously, than I ever was with Romey. And even though I never begged or pushed for a taste of more than what we silently assented to as being good, those nights kept me up for hours afterward, dreaming of what could be.

Romey didn't really have a girl, so what happened between Dianne and me in that short time affected our relationship in a way that he understood meant exile. Sometimes I'd get a ribbing. "Whyn't you just marry her and have it done with?" Romey'd say, loud enough for the whole town to hear. "Sheesh, you're over there all the time anyway."

But my love affair ended abruptly when Dianne decided a girl her age didn't need to be walked home by a boy on a bicycle, when for much the same price she could be riding in regal comfort in some guy's car, tuned in to Rock 92 on the radio. Dianne was a real honey, guys said, and since our eighth-grade class was on its way to high school, older guys spotted her and didn't hesitate for a moment if someone said she was Lowell Prins's girl. That was very junior high—bikes and messing around in the back yard. Dianne suddenly found herself in the big leagues, and she never looked back.

She started going out with a skinny kid named Squeak, a junior who worked at his brother's gas station and played second base on the high school baseball team, second string. I was left with the bicycle. Squeak had a '54 Chevy he'd painted gold, then upholstered with fuzzy white stuff—the steering wheel, the dash, the back window—and turned it into something really exotic by gluing lavender crepe paper into the dome light. What he'd done was take an ordinary car and transform it into the kind of chariot he thought he was destined to drive. When things got slow at the station, he'd lean over that Chevy and polish it so bright that at night beneath the streetlights it shone like a shiny ball of brass.

Dianne and I never formally ended what we'd jump-started one surreptitious night at Bible camp. But it became apparent that Squeak's Chevy stood out front of her place too often for me to be mistaken about why it was there—she'd obviously made a choice, even though she'd never consulted me. That rejection, like all rejections, was painful, and to my mind it was done very callously, without her even thinking of my feelings, even taking the time to talk to me. As far as I was concerned, nothing she'd ever said would have kept me from waltzing over to the garden some night and expecting a few innocent kisses.

Romey never suffered a conscience like I did, but he understood my pain. "Squeeeeak," Romey would say, mocking the kid. "Squeak, squeak, squeak," as if he were a trapped bat. "Squeak's a squirrel," he'd say. "You're crazy if you want a girl who likes him—he's a bug."

My sister made the pain very public one night at the dinner table. "Dianne Kampen's down at the drive-in just about every other night with Squeak," she announced. "I can't believe it. When I was her age, you wouldn't let me out of the house." She meant it for Mom and Dad, not for me.

"Dianne?" my mother said, incredulous.

"Yeah," Janine said, "Lowell's old sweetie."

I could have died right then and there. Had I been a year younger, I might have run off to my bedroom.

My mother put her elbows on the table, her fork poised over the meat loaf. "Lowell," she said, putting down her fork, "I didn't know that—I'm sorry."

My father was more practical. "Starting high school in a couple of weeks—you have a lot of life ahead of you. It's not the end of the world."

"Who said it was?" I asked.

"She's only going into ninth grade," Janine said. "You should see how close they sit. She'll be married by the time she's sixteen." She didn't mean to hurt me, but I was her brother, not a human being. It was our parents she was after. "You'd have never let me be with some guy when I was that young," she said.

"Jaa—nnneennn," my mom said—probably to protect me.

My sister pointed a knife. "Oh, he doesn't care," she said—meaning me. "Squeak is such a creep, Lowell. She's nuts if she wants him. Everybody says it—you don't want her anyway."

The fact was I did want her, more so, perhaps, because she didn't want me. But I bore my humiliation in angry silence. Without Dianne, there would be no girls during the last weeks of that summer, nothing but lawns to mow when the sun shone and long cool nights once the lakeshore breezes chased the heat farther west, inland. Hattie Guttner had thrown in the towel when it came to curfews, figuring that since Romey had made it out of grade school, he'd made it successfully out of kidhood. Cyril wasn't around often enough to care, and when he was, he didn't. He never had. All summer long I'd had to be home at 10:30, but by August my parents didn't watch closely, especially once they knew I wasn't with a girl.

Ernie, the beanfield Toad, drove his way back into our lives for a while just before high school. Maybe, on his part, what motivated his return was guilt—but probably not. Ernie had no high school friends. He'd dropped out; by consensus he was a loser, a kid who'd quit because school was a flat waste of time, he'd said.

For Ernie, Romey and I were the best he could get for buddies around Easton, minor leaguers far enough back in the farm system that it would be a while before we'd get to the big time. So Romey and Mugsy and I would mess around with Ernie on those nights we weren't playing baseball. Ernie was older, of course, but a whole lot dumber, and we used him. He had a car. He could buy smokes.

If you came into town from the east, Romey told us one Sunday, you could blow huge gas farts with a car. He claimed if you'd turn off the engine somewhere at the top of the hill, coast down through town with the transmission in gear, then turn the ignition back on, the car would blow a terrific Fourth of July blast—loud as an aerial rocket.

Easton was still church-ruled in the late fifties, nothing open on the Sabbath, when most people didn't go anywhere but to church anyway, most of them twice. Sunny Sundays became holidays—nobody working, everyone outside, the sidewalks full. The playgrounds were jammed, although kids from strict families, like mine, weren't supposed to be working up a sweat, no matter what the sport.

In the middle of all that Sabbath peace, Romey talked the Toad into sailing over the hill and into town in his big Dodge, the engine off, all of us except Ernie giggling in anticipation. Five or six blocks down Main we rolled along in reverent Sunday silence until Romey jammed Ernie with an elbow. "Now," he yelled. Toad hit the ignition and the engine blew cannon fire. A bony little Chihuahua on the sidewalk jumped high as a woman's shoulder, without even getting into a crouch. Straight up.

That afternoon we shot farts at girls and dogs and little kids and just about anything else capable of shock. It wasn't mean, really. We could have sent old folks into cardiac arrest, but we didn't think about that. It was scaring kids that gave us the kicks we wanted, turning girls inside out at the sound of the blast from the Toad's exhaust. That's what we were after.

But we grew bolder, finally. A half-dozen-block buildup grew into a half-mile coast as we tried to generate more and more explosive might, turning an M-80-sized crack into a blockbuster. We cruised down Main, engine off, until we got all the way downtown. "Now," Romey said that last time, and the explosion shook the cafe's front windows and blew a hole the size of a fist in Ernie's muffler, changing the Toad's purring glass packs into illegal straight pipes. At which time, Ernie let out a string of profanity that nearly drowned out the noise from beneath the car, anger in the shape of dollar signs in his eyes.

"I didn't do it," Romey said.

But we were all the Toad had, and no matter how much anger Romey could call up from the guy's insides, Ernie stayed with us for a while, happy to have somebody, anyway. Sometimes we'd pick up girls and take them down through the lake roads, where we'd follow old logging trails, shining for deer. Three miles northeast of town, the road to the lake ended at a spot of open beach, no cottages on either side for more than a half mile, a spot that generations of Easton kids had turned into a lovers' lane. Trees stood above the circle at the end of the road, but off to the right a swath of sand allowed enough space for six or seven cars, if you added the perfect spots out front, all of them close enough to the beach to see the moon over the lake, which was, of course, the purpose of parking down there in the moonlight.

Back from the beach, a little winding road twisted through the trees where there were no cottages, nothing but darkness, except for whatever flash you could create with headlights. Into the woods a third of a mile or so, the road angled sharply left around a huge pine with scarred bark where dozens of cars had scraped their bumpers. Then, a small barn appeared. All around stood huge pines shorn of their lower branches. Blacktop pavement ran beneath the pines like a wide parking lot between the house and the shed.

When you came up fast, the whole place materialized as if out of nowhere. A two-lane rut suddenly became blacktop, the woods turning into a castle—a big house, a mansion with a haunted turret, where no one ever seemed to live. Some chemical in the fallen pine needles turned the blacktop a dusky red when headlights washed over the yard. Red Road, we called it. Lots of people did. It was nothing more than a long lakeshore driveway.

The Toad loved nothing better than picking up girls, no matter how he could get them. He loved telling them the story about a guy, a hired man, who'd been hacked to death by his boss, a rich guy, right there on this spot. On the night of the murder, the victim's blood, he'd claim, had turned the road eternally red. It wasn't a story he'd made up, only retold. Easton kids had gone over all of that horror for years already.

Whenever we'd spot some young things walking along the sidewalk somewhere around town, Ernie would remember the Red Road. "Let's get those girls and haul them down there, then you tell the story, Romey," he'd say. "Let's do it."

No one knew the origin of the whole tale. My older sisters had probably heard it before I did, probably picked it up themselves when some guys dragged them to Red Road to raise the hair on the backs of their necks.

All the way out there Romey'd tell it, dressing it up with his own nightmarish details, changing it so the hired man was a Bulgarian or Romanian or some Laplander or something, usually someone with a voice like Dracula. Already on the highway, he'd start, sitting back with a cigarette he'd mooched from Ernie, and then building, slowly building. He thought of himself as Hitchcock.

What happened one Friday night at the end of my friendship with Romey Guttner, the night I'll never forget, began there, on Red Road, with a carful of kids—Mugsy, Romey, Ernie, me, and some girls I've long ago forgotten.

Games

The hired man, the story went, hated the rich guy who lived in the house, because the hired man was little more than a slave. But the rich guy had a lease on him, had bought him with free passage to America. That's the way the story went. The rich guy's wife made a play for the poor guy, the way Potiphar's wife put a move on Joseph. I had to tell Romey that Bible story after one of the first trips down to the lake—I told him the whole thing reminded me of Joseph, the lost brother in Egypt, who had this Egyptian princess hiking up her skirt for him. After that, Romey used that story every time because the Bible thing really helped in Easton, where everybody except him—he used to say—knew Bible stories.

This hired man didn't stay away from trouble as Joseph had. She chased him down and even promised him his freedom in return—that's the way it went.

"One night the rich guy came home and found them—you know what I mean," Romey said. "Found 'em doing the deed. He had 'em dead to rights, right there in the bedroom," Romey said to a carful of girls that night. "The guy was insane—that's how mad he was, and he had a gun."

The trick was to be near the end of the story when Ernie was turning into that short lake road. You had to get it just right, and Romey could do it, improvising details if necessary just to get the timing down. The whole thing was timing.

"His wife lied. She screamed at her old man that she got raped," he told them, "and the rich guy put a gun on his hired man and hauled him outside, really mad."

By that time we were creeping into the woods, Ernie's lights careening off the white birch, the girls sitting between us, almost in our laps, petrified. Ernie loved it. We all did.

"This was all years and years ago already," Romey said, "years and years ago, when there were no judges or nothing." He had to time the story's punch line to the exact moment we'd come out of the darkness, headlights flashing over what suddenly appeared as blood-red blacktop.

"What could the poor guy do?" Romey said. "He didn't have nothing—no justice. What on earth could he do, anyway—the rich guy right there and his wife screaming to kill him because she said he raped her? He had no chance. He was just a lousy working stiff, you know? The man didn't have no rights—there was no judge anyway. Curtains," he said, like always.

All around us, darkness. It was a theater, the bright lights in front of the car the only place to put your eyes, other than to close them, and nobody wanted to close them.

"Poor guy knew he was going to die," Romey said, his voice cracking with sympathy. "All his life he dreamed of freedom, and all it'd come to was this—at the hands of this evil woman." That was such an un-Romey-like phrase, but he used it every time: evil woman. He probably got it from a rock song.

The girls, like always, jammed their shoulders into our arms or reached for our hands. As if on cue, Ernie snapped off the radio.

And then Romey laid on the gore.

"So the rich guy takes him out to the big pine out front—you'll see it, it's right there by the walk out front—and he hacks this slave-type guy into pieces with a bayonet, pearl on the handle. And he doesn't just do him in, either, see? He lets him live as long as he can, hacks at his arms and legs because he wants to see the poor guy's blood. The guy's nutso, swearing as he hacks away, the slave guy's blood running down in long thick pools toward the middle of the driveway. You ever see blood in a pool, how thick it is?" he asked. "It's like goo. That's what it looked like, this big red puddle of hot steaming blood moving slow as a glacier." He let that picture sit in their minds for a minute, the silence mounting.

"He killed him right then and there, and he buried him out back of the barn. People say if you'd dig in the right place, you'd find the body of that guy."

At that moment, Ernie took us around the big pine, and suddenly, spread there before us was the barn and the house.

"And ever since that day, the road has been blood red—"

The blacktop rose from the darkness in lurid crimson.

Sometimes, there would be nothing but silence. Sometimes, nothing but screams. Whatever the reaction, the girls flew into our laps, even though they loved every minute of it as much as we did. Easton wasn't a big place, there weren't a lot of girls who'd get in the car with a dropout and three ex-eighth-graders—lots of them went more than once. Didn't matter to us, and didn't matter to them.

We'd even do encores. I'd get into it myself sometimes, point at that imaginary bloody body slouched there against the tree because Romey'd talked me into it. "There he is now," I'd say, and the girls would go nuts and Romey would just about die laughing.

For a while that night, what we were up to was pure and innocent. All the horror was little more than a show. But everything that happened that summer—the cigarettes, the beanfields, Bible camp, Blood-

Red Road—everything built to that one night, just before high school started, when everything changed.

The girls had to be home, they said, so we dropped them off in town. But we didn't want to quit. After all, it was almost the end of summer. School was coming, and Mugsy and I were going to sleep over at Romey's place anyway, in a tent on the golf course in the back yard. Who cared about time? Romey claimed he'd seen an old coffin out back of the sewage plant outside of town, an old pine box he said the village kept just in case some nameless bum fell over dead somewhere around the village.

Who knows why it was out there? But it was, an old pine box with sturdy square corners, something no one would use to bury a skunk, but it did resemble a coffin, and it was big enough, broad and wide enough, to hold a man's body.

Romey had this great idea to pick up some girls and have somebody stashed in that box, ready to jump out and scare the pants off them. One of us ought to stay behind and lay in the old thing, he said, and then spring up like some bloody horror show monster when he hears the rest of us outside—on a signal. "Be a perfect terror," he said. "Mugsy," he said, "you stay."

Mugsy coughed, hacked away for a while as if to establish a medical handicap. "Geez," he said, and it didn't take a genius to see that becoming a corpse all alone in the woods at the sewage plant wasn't his idea of fun—or mine.

"Hey," Romey said, "it ain't going to be long." The sewage plant was about a half mile from the north edge of town.

"Give me a flashlight or something," Mugsy said, swatting a bug on his face.

"You ain't got to be in there all the time," Romey told him. "Cripes sake, you'd go nuts—just when you see us come up the road. Then get in."

That made sense. "How long you going to be gone?" Mugsy said, looking around.

"Ten minutes, maybe," Romey said. "We just got to get some girls—it'll be the thrill of a lifetime."

It was a simple question of guts. Mugsy really couldn't back off, and Romey knew it.

Ernie was already giggling as he pulled out of the gravel road and headed back to town, Romey and I in the front seat beside him. It was exactly the kind of thing Ernie loved. We scoured the town, hit every last street in Easton, looking everywhere for girls—any kind, any num-

215

ber, any shape. But we didn't spot a thing, nothing old enough to be considered, anyway.

Then we found Monty. He was with one of his eighth-grade friends, balancing on the curb as they walked home from the town library. Romey and I had already pegged ourselves as high-schoolers, even though we hadn't once stepped into the hallways. Monty was a grade-schooler, but Romey didn't need more motivation than what he'd carried for a long, long time. "Let's get him," Romey said.

"Get serious." The Toad had some pride. All he wanted were girls.

"Come on," Romey told him. "We can do it again. Take a practice run on these twinks." He was on the passenger's side, where he always insisted on sitting. "Change places," he said. "He'll never get in this car if he sees me."

Quickly, we shifted places. "You talk to him, Lobo, and I'll keep myself hid."

"Hey, Monty," I yelled after Toad pulled over. It was dark, just after nine. "You wouldn't believe what we found. There's this old coffin out back of the village shed. I swear it. You ought to see it."

"So what?" Monty said.

"Want to see?" I asked. "You wouldn't believe it. It's really scary."

Monty's friend was a kid named Carl, whom Romey recognized only because he said the kid walked a poodle every night, his mother's.

"Come on," I said.

"What do I care about a coffin?" Monty said.

"You wouldn't believe it," I told him. "It's got junk written all over it, like in Egypt. Scary as heck."

Carl didn't dare even look at the car.

"Who's all in there?" Monty said. He leaned down to look inside.

"Ernie's driving," I said, my arm lying out over the side. "Come on, free ride."

"Who else?" he said.

"Romey," I told him. "We're not smoking, either. We gave that up."

"What's the big deal about a coffin?" he said.

He was likely more afraid of us than he was of the coffin. "You scared or what?" I said. That was a dare.

"I'm not scared," he said. Carl had his arms full of library books. The whole time we were talking, he never looked at us. "Want to, Carl?" Monty said.

"I got to get home," Carl said.

"Mommy's calling?" Romey said. "Mommy wants her little sweet peas home, I bet."

"I got to get home," Carl said again.

"Won't take ten minutes," I said. "We'll get you right back home. Take that long for you to walk home from here."

Carl shook his head.

"Bunch of bantam hens is what they are," Romey said, loud enough for them to hear. "Don't matter if they don't want to see it—that's their tough luck."

Ernie honked whenever some car drove past, somebody he thought should know him. He didn't want any part of grade school kids. He wanted girls.

"His ma won't let him," Romey said. "Just take off, Toad. Monty's old lady's got him scared to death." Which was partially true.

Monty stood there balancing on the curb beside us, sometimes taking a peek into the car to be sure there wasn't any more danger than he already felt. "We got to be back in fifteen minutes or I'll tell my old man," he told us. "Swear?"

"On a Bible," I said.

"It's already almost 9:30," Monty said.

"You turn into a pumpkin or what?" Romey said, and I elbowed him. I figured we were going to lose them both if Monty got really scared.

"I got to get back," Monty said, "but I'm not scared. You guys wouldn't do nothing."

He was wrong about that.

They got in, both of them. They sat in the back seat, and all the way out of town none of us said a word about the coffin, not until Ernie pulled into the lane and crept along toward the shed, a brick building with a solitary light out front but nothing behind. It wasn't like Red Road at all, this time, no buildup. But then, Red Road came alive only in the imagination.

Once he stopped the car, all you could hear was the swish from the nozzles spreading sewer water over the rocks in the big circular bins behind us. We jumped out of either side of the front seat, and I held the front seat up so Monty and Carl could crawl out.

"Back here," Ernie said, loud enough for Mugsy to hear. He was into it now—he had the smell of the hunt, even though from his point of view this wasn't top of the line quarry.

Monty said something about nobody having a flashlight.

The golden line of the horizon still glowed enough to cut outlines from the trees at the back of the lot, but the darkness was deep enough to make us steer our way through with our hands.

It was rich. I can't remember the whole story without smiling even now because I remember thinking about Mugsy buried in that casket the whole time—in the darkness. He didn't want to stay behind, but the whole idea was too rich to pass up. I was nervous as a wet hen myself, I remember. This was going to be good.

"Back here," Ernie said.

There was no need to create a mood for Monty. I walked behind him, watching the letters on his Pony League shirt jump with his shoulders in the darkness. An acre of woods surrounded the place, and out at the western edge, where the trees stopped, the village kept junk. We could have followed the fence line and stayed out of the darkness, but Romey led us all through the woods, in and out of the trees, zigzagging as if we were on some pirate's quest. It was all part of the act.

But Monty started smelling a rat. "This is a trick," he said. "You guys are fooling us."

"I lost the path for a minute there," Romey said. "I'm the only guy that ever saw this thing, but I got it back now. It's over here," and he pointed with two fingers. "You got to see this," he said.

For a moment I wondered whether Mugsy had stayed around in all the darkness and the smell. I don't know that I would have. Maybe he'd already hightailed it back to town.

"Here," Ernie said. "Look at this." He came up to the old casket and stood beside it as if it were a miracle. "We told you it was here. Geez, can you believe it? Isn't that awful? Shoot," he said, "I'm scared to death." Everything he said he turned up loud enough for Mugsy to hear.

Monty tried to act as if what was there in front of us were nothing at all. "Who said it was a casket?" he said. "It's nothing but a big box—big deal."

"Look up close," Romey told him. "This is what they put bums in— drunks—when they don't have money and they croak and the government's got to bury them. That's what it's for. Look—"

"Sure enough," Ernie said, everything up several decibels. "Here we are, all right. Yep. See it there? Get right up close now and take a look." He tried to push them closer.

Mugsy must have heard Romey say Monty's name and realized that there were no girls. At least, he didn't come up right away. I figured he was making the whole business worse—that's what he was doing.

"How do you know it's a coffin?" Carl said. "Maybe it's just a big toolbox."

"Kid don't know what a coffin is," Ernie said, laughing much louder than he had to.

"It's a coffin all right," I said. I couldn't believe Mugsy would wait that long.

"Naw it isn't," Monty said.

"If it ain't a coffin, what's it doing out here—right, Romey?" Ernie said, brimming with too many giggles. "Ain't that so, Romey? Tell him."

"Darn right," he said. "Look at this. Look here what it says." And he took Monty by the arm, walked up, and stood before the box like some magician. He searched through the darkness behind them, squinting, as if county cops were somewhere out there watching all of this, maybe looking for Mugsy. "You want to know a big secret, Monty Boy?" he said. I wished he hadn't said that. "Hold on to your butt, because here's something you ain't never going to forget."

Once more he stopped to look around. "There's a real body in here."

"Naw sir," Monty said.

"You think I'd lie? I was out here. I seen what's inside, but you guys are too little. You couldn't take it, see—that's why we aren't going to show you."

Romey grabbed the lid with his fingernails, pretended, just momentarily, that it was too heavy, then lifted it anyway, grunting like a TV wrestler. "Sure as heck," he said, then he let it back down. That's when I knew Mugsy was still inside. "Been hit by a train. They found him on the tracks out there. Nobody knows his name. What a bloody mess."

"You're lying," Monty said.

Ernie rushed up alongside Romey. He picked up the lid and stared into the box. "Ho man," he said, smiling again. "He's horrible. Lookit for yourself."

"He's got spiders in his eyeballs already," Romey said. "They nest in dead people—spiders do."

"Stinks awful," Ernie said. "Let's get out of here—stinks worse'n skunk."

Monty couldn't help himself. He was sure the whole thing was some kind of joke. It was a sheer test of principle, not just courage. When he got up alongside the coffin, Romey wouldn't let him look in. "This ain't for no weak tummy, my boy," he said. "Maybe the Toad ought to take you two back home."

"Let me see in there," Monty said.

When Mugsy blew out of that old box, the cover smashed back on his head so hard he winced. But Monty never noticed because he jumped like that Chihuahua on Main, turned in midair, and was gone like an apparition. Mugsy had wrapped his shoulders in burlap so he looked more like a mummy than a dead bum, and on his way out he made an unearthly sound, a moan, half falsetto, that cut through the trees like the wail of something brought back, steaming, from the netherworld.

But that wasn't enough for Mugsy—or for Romey. As soon as Mugsy was out of that coffin, he was after them, flying so close behind them—screaming constantly—that those two kids knew their only escape was to run all the way home. It never dawned on them to do anything else. They never even slowed when they passed Ernie's car. They took off through the trees, then up the gravel and out to the road, ran and ran and ran, Mugsy right on their tails, screaming out all kinds of vile threats—how he was going to get them, rip off their ears and poke out their eyes for disturbing the dead, the three of them running the full half-mile back to town before Mugsy finally threw in the towel. The whole time he ran, Romey was right behind him, just along for the ride.

I stood back at the car with the Toad, where we threw ourselves over the fenders, trying to breathe, laughing ourselves half to death.

"We got to do that again," Ernie said. "We got to get some women and do that number again. That's better than anything, Lobo." He pointed to the passenger side, and the two of us got into the car, then headed down the road and out onto the blacktop to pick up Mugsy and Romey. We found them leaning over, hands on their knees, trying to scoop enough breath to go on living, but laughing so hard it only made breathing more of a chore.

"He could have caught 'em," Romey said, pointing at Mugsy, "but it was more fun just to chase 'em."

There we stood in the street, Ernie's car parked in front of the slaughterhouse on the north edge of town, neither of them at all capable of moving, all of us wanting to replay every last second of that action.

"You talk about nightmares—" Romey said, "whatta'ya think the Monkey Boy is going to see all night long?"

"I can't believe how long you waited," I said to Mugsy. "I thought you weren't even there."

"Awful place," Mugsy said, spitting. "Next time it's one of you guys' turn."

All four of us got back in Ernie's car and rode around town searching for Monty and Carl, who must have cut between the houses on their way home.

"They ought to make a movie out of that," Romey said. "Something like that—that'd make a great movie."

"We got to get women," Ernie said. "We got to find some women."

"That little shrimp can run," Mugsy said.

"Scared the crap out of 'em, I bet," I said.

"Where can we find women?" Ernie said.

"Stunk in there something awful," Mugsy said, still wiping himself off. "What a smell. Do I got any on me?"

"Nothing worse than usual," Romey said. "Hey, Ern, how about we put Mugsy in the lake, clean him up a bit. You got garbage in your car here."

"Dang women," Ernie said. "Where are they, anyway?"

That night, the coffin was only the first of our games.

Water Torture

There was nobody worth picking up in town, so Ernie backed off his plans for wowing women and we decided to go out to the beach one more time. But first he dropped Romey and me off a block from my place, and the two of us delivered the books Monty and Carl were carrying home, set them down right on Monty's front step, where the red head of that paint bird from the last union attack was still visible.

Ernie picked us up again downtown, where we all stopped at the Wooden Shoe Restaurant, aching to tell somebody about our glory. But there wasn't a soul around, so we got root beer floats in tall paper cups, jumped back in Ernie's car, and headed east toward the lake.

It was a Friday night, and we really didn't have to mind the time since Mugsy and I were sleeping over in Romey's old army tent, a bottomless relic we'd dug out of the far corner of Guttner's spacious mess of a garage. We knew that ten o'clock was a little early to catch couples parking down at the lake roads, but we thought we'd head toward Red Road beach and hang out for a while, just in case somebody tried to hunt us down in town for the evil we'd just perpetrated on Monty and his buddy.

"I swear I heard that kid's voice change right in front of me," Mugsy said. "He wasn't so much yelling as blubbering. Matilda, was he scared." Then Romey let out a low-pitched moan.

"Like that, only worse," Mugsy said, "just like that, from way down deep in his guts."

"What the world was that thing, anyway?" I said, looking over my shoulder into the back seat, where Romey and Mugsy were sipping floats.

"A coffin," Romey said. "I'm telling the truth—it's a real live dang coffin."

"Naaaahh," Mugsy said.

"What—you don't believe me? It sure is. They dug it up when they put in that new road out by Landsmas, you know? An old guy had himself buried out there on his own land."

For the first time in an hour, no one laughed.

"You lie," I said.

"Geez," Romey said, "you guys'll believe anything."

When we came down the hill toward the lakeshore, a pair of red tail-lights snapped a reflection back at us from the end of the road, snake eyes in the darkness over the lake. Parkers.

"I can't stand it when somebody's making out and I'm not," Romey said. "Dang kids nowadays—all they want to do is neck." I turned down the radio.

Sometimes we'd yell at couples parking along the lakeshore—if Ernie didn't know who they were. We'd done it before, and we'd do it again. Sometimes we simply sat behind them with our lights up on bright until the goon got out of the car and Ernie burned rubber in reverse far up the lake road. That's what we were going to do, I thought. But once we recognized who it was down there at the end of the lake road, I knew whatever we'd do that night wouldn't be business as usual.

We were a hundred yards up the road when all of us recognized Squeak's brass Chev. I didn't want to acknowledge the truth, of course, even to myself. I had no desire to admit that my ex-sweetheart could be parked down at the beach making out with some other guy. But I didn't have to—the proof was standing right in front of all of us.

At first, nobody said anything, even though we all knew who it was. And nothing of what we did from then on was my idea. I didn't say a word the whole time. I had my pride, after all. To my mind, Squeak was only a step or two up from Ernie. All the guy had on me was a car, an old fur-lined '54, and a couple of years—and a driver's license. Big deal.

Somebody gave him that nickname for his mousy voice. He was a mosquito, really, but there he was with Dianne.

Ernie pulled up behind them and gave them the brights, like always. All we could see were the crowns of their heads against the seat and the outline of the finger little Squeak shot us once he was interrupted—which he shouldn't have done, either, because once he'd delivered that, I knew Romey wouldn't back off. Squeak was over to the middle to avoid having to wrestle the steering wheel, Dianne on the passenger's side—like a couple of pros, I thought, as if they'd been at the parking thing for years.

"Let's get 'em," Romey said. "Give 'em the big night they're looking for."

Ernie backed away, straight up the hill because he didn't want to turn around and get himself identified, not even by Squeak. When we came to the first cottage road, he backed in and stopped just out of sight of Squeak's car.

"What're we going to do?" Mugsy said.

Ernie didn't want any part of it. "Count me out," he said, once Romey'd run through his plans. "Squeak sure as anything knows my car, knows it already. I'm sure of it." He lit a cigarette in the glow of the lighter. "I'll stay up here," he said. "You guys just get out and do it—whatever."

Romey looked at me. "You in?" he said. "Or is this something I got to do for you?"

"I'm in," I told him. And then some bravado. "She don't mean nothing to me."

Romey banged me on the shoulder. "Terrible hot, ain't it?" he said. "Must be steaming in that car. Better cool 'em off for their own good. Too hot this summer. Everybody says it."

What could I say?

"Give me your cup, Ernie," Romey said.

"I'm not finished," he said.

"Tough," he said, "we need it."

The Toad inhaled the soft lumps of ice cream at the bottom and gave it up.

The moon seemed a white hole in the dark gap above the trees along the road, so we knew we couldn't simply walk down to Squeak's car without being seen in his rearview—if the lovers were looking, of course. Romey said we couldn't take that chance, so we hurdled the black water in the ditch on the south side of the road and followed the edge of the trees back to the beach, avoiding branches that could crack like gun-

Water Torture

shots in the stillness. Through the gap in the trees at the end of the road, the lake lay smoothly to the east, already bedded down for the night.

Squeak's car faced the water, standing off the road just past the edge of the pavement, to the right of the dead end sign. When we came up out of the woods, we were twenty yards from them, so close we could hear the bass line of whatever song was humming on the radio.

Romey pointed farther south, and the three of us cut around a stand of pines that stood alone at the edge of the beach, and then we headed for the lake, far enough down the beach from the car that we couldn't be seen unless the lovers got out to take a walk. When we took off for the water, Romey's heels kicked up sand behind him as if he were assaulting a beachhead. I felt sweat all over, on my neck and down the back of my pants. Maybe it was the heat that made Romey charge right into the water when he got there, shoes and all, as if he'd been dying of thirst and heat prostration. We followed suit.

The cool night made the water seem warm. We scooped our cups full and followed our tracks back through the soft sand, still out of sight of Squeak's car.

"Don't say a thing now," Romey said. "Stay low and sneak right up close so you can't miss—then let 'em have it and floor it back to the trees. He'll never find us." He looked straight at me. "We'll get 'em," he said. "He's a squirrel."

Mugsy just giggled.

"Hey, Lobo," Romey said, "you want to really get 'em?" He held the cup out in front of his zipper.

"I don't have to go," I said, but I told myself I would have done it if I had. Squeak had made my life that miserable. I told myself I'd have been as bad as Romey if I'd had to take a leak.

Nothing lay between us and Squeak's car but long sharp grass running up and down a sand hill hardly big enough to call a dune. We stopped and sat at the top, our Dixie cups full of cold lake water, then checked out the action down at the base of the road—Romeo and Juliet, thirty yards away.

"Look at that," Mugsy said. Something white glowed at the very pit of the dune. He jammed his cup in the sand, scrambled down the hill, and came back with a Styrofoam cooler with a chip out of it the size of a dog bite.

"The great flood," Romey said, pointing back at the beach. "Fill that thing up."

That much water might ruin Squeak's blessed interior fluff, I thought, but I wasn't about to hold back, at least not publicly. Mugsy ran down to the beach and filled the cooler, then lugged it back up, cradling it in his arms. He was breathless by the time he made it back, a couple of gallons sloshing around inside.

"You take it," Romey told me. "This is your war we're fighting here."

I couldn't turn down the offer even if I'd wanted to, not with the two of them looking at me as if I had a legal right to squash the jerk in the brass Chev like a basement cricket. Besides, I knew that Romey was doing the whole field general thing here just for me—that if it weren't Squeak in there, and Dianne, we'd all be back in town doing something else. This was a job that simply had to be done, the law of the jungle.

The old cooler was heavy—must have held almost two gallons.

We turned back to the Squeak's Chevy. "Seems to me she ain't fighting it," Romey said, looking at me. From where we sat, the moon's glow and Squeak's radio light were all we needed to get an outline of the action taking place inside.

All I'd ever done with Dianne was kiss, most often at her back door. Once or twice I'd gone over to where she was babysitting—once to the preacher's house—and we'd sat on the couch and pushed each other around with our lips, nothing but innocence. There I sat, suddenly understanding how, no more than a week before, I must have seemed like a chump to Dianne, some Monty type, a grade school kid demanding nothing more than kisses.

"Must tick you off, Lobo," Romey said. "All that teaching you did and now she's using it all on him."

All that teaching, sure.

"Let's do it," Mugsy said.

"You take her side," Romey said, as if it were some kind of blessing. "Me and Mugs'll go around and knock—they'll look at us." He smiled deeply. "Then it's your turn, buddy."

It was nasty, and I knew it. But Dianne deserved nastiness.

Three thick evergreens stood slightly behind the car, so we angled our assault, stopping behind those sweeping branches along the ridge of sand. Romey put his finger to his lips to remind us to shut up, and we crept along the edge, in a line—Romey first, then me, then Mugsy— duck-walking from the trees straight to the right rear fender, Romey and Mugsy waddling to the driver's side while I lugged the sloshing cooler around the trunk to the other side.

The window was open maybe three inches at most, not even wide enough to hang a drive-in tray, and there we sat, listening to every silly sound—much more than I cared to hear.

It's not wrong to assume that what I felt was jealousy, but that didn't mean I really wanted Dianne back, either. I sat there on my haunches beside the car, listening to the sound of bodies moving, rustling around beneath the music on the radio, and I wondered about always doing the right thing, something I thought I had been doing with Dianne, doing it okay, being nice. I felt like some kind of schmuck, a righteous little boy, when it was obvious she hadn't been thinking of me the way I had been thinking of her—as someone I needed to aspire to, someone heavenly I needed to earn.

Still, it was brutal to soak them the way they were going to get soaked. It wasn't nice—wasn't kind, wasn't loving, wasn't good. But I was going to do it anyway, because I'd always been nice with her, and all I got back was this—the sound of their heavy breathing over my head right now. I waited for the signal, but nothing came. I sat in a squat and balanced the cooler on my knee, listening, then felt something sting my ankle. Gravel cracked on the other side of the car. I put down the cooler and leaned over to peek beneath the frame. There was Romey, his Dixie cup at the side of his head, pulling a Hunchback of Notre Dame thing—everything scrunched as if he'd just gone daft, pulling a face meant to show he was ready to puke. Mugsy leaned over, doing everything he could to stanch his laughing, his cheeks ballooning, and Romey gave him a Three Stooges shove.

And then, "Mmmmmmmm," Squeak moaned. "You like that?"

I never would have said anything like that, never.

I felt another stone against my leg, so I ducked down and saw Romey pointing toward the back of the car, as if he wanted to talk. I crept back. There they were, both of them half crippled in laughter.

"You hear that?" Romey said. He scrunched his nose. "'You like that, baby?'" he said, mimicking Squeak. Then he grabbed my shirt, poked a thumb back toward what was happening inside the brass Chev. "We're going to get 'em, Lobo. Don't even think about it now—we're going to get 'em good."

"He kills me," Mugsy said, trying to grab for breath. "That mouse just kills me."

"What do you think he does to Lobo?" Romey said, pointing.

"Come on," I said, "let's do it," and I crawled back to the cooler and picked it up, then sat for a second to get my breath, my back against the front door.

"I just love this," Squeak said.

Romey and Mugsy had to have heard it too. I figured now they'd wait another half hour because who could guess what the heck Squeak would say next. I could just see Mugsy sitting on the other side of the car shaking, trying to hold in the giggles and still balance his precious water in the black cow Dixie cup.

"This is a great song," Dianne said. She loved Paul Anka—I knew that much. I heard her singing along, "Put your head on my shoulder . . ."

My arms had almost gone limp from holding the cooler. I reached for a stone and whipped it at Romey's feet, and when he saw me beneath the car, I jerked up my thumb to tell him to get the show on the road.

Then I watched Romey's legs straighten as he edged himself up to the driver's side. Just as slowly, I started sliding up the passenger's door, the cooler cradled in my arms. The very first thing I saw when I looked across the seat was Romey's googly eyes.

Beneath us lay a bundle, two outlines dimly lit by the light of the radio dial on the dash. "You're a good kisser," Squeak said. He was wrapped around her, his arm across her chest and on her opposite shoulder, his face in her neck, the look on his face an odd kind of shine, like a kid with a toy, I thought.

But Romey wasn't up to it yet. His face was gone again.

"I mean, considering," Squeak said as I ducked beneath the window.

"Considering what?" Dianne said.

"I mean considering you never kissed nobody before."

On that, Mugsy couldn't hold out. What boiled up from his belly emerged with the power of sheer nausea, but the rattling, full-throated belly laugh was pure joy. What came out was a purring blurt like crackling gas held far too long, and that's when Romey finally slapped the top of the car, chucked his cupful of water through Squeak's window, and yelled, "Good morning, breakfast lovers!"

I waited until Squeak had unfurled his skinny body from Dianne. He was already cussing, but he did exactly what Romey said he would: he went for the window. Dianne sat right there beneath me, leaning toward her sweetheart, staring in shock and outrage at her wet blouse, muttering a long succession of little ohs.

It wouldn't work to lean the cooler in and pour out the water. I had to slop it in, come what may. So I did—I leaned back and flung the whole coolerful at the partially opened window. Some got in—some splashed right back over me. But in that flash of a second, in that moment when Dianne lifted her face to the torrent coming in through the window, I was sure she recognized me.

I dropped the cooler in the ditch and took off across the road, following Mugsy and Romey, who were running up ahead, half in tears, I figured, from laughing. I hadn't planned on being spotted, never con-

Water Torture

sidered that she'd know it was me, but I knew that once the three of us took to the woods, Squeak wouldn't have a ghost of a chance of finding any of us.

Not that Squeak was a he-man. Romey could have taken him right then and there, single-handedly, even though Squeak was three years older—Mugsy might have too. The three of us could have hung him out to dry, stripped him cold and naked as ring bologna, right in front of his championship kisser. But part of the joy was the chase, so the three of us took off west as if we were about to lose our scalps.

A hundred yards up the road, Mugsy and Romey hit the ditch and sneaked in between the trees. We sat still for a minute because we didn't want to give away our position, then poked our heads out of the woods to check for movement at the beach where that brass Chevy shown in the light of the moon.

"I'm soaked," I said, because I was. That made Mugsy laugh even harder.

"Shut up and get down," Romey said.

"Did you hear the crap he was talking about?" Mugsy said. "I about died. Did you hear that? You supposed to talk that way? Girls *like* that?"

If Squeak had sat still, he might have heard us thrashing through the trees, but he didn't try to chase us on foot. He threw the Chevy in reverse and spit gravel against the frame, sand rising in clouds until his back tires caught the lip of the blacktop, then squealed and bounced down the pavement. He never turned the car around at all, just backed straight up the road, his engine whining like a big dog at a siren. In a flash he was past us, and we knew he'd never find us.

"She saw me," I told them. "I don't know, maybe she didn't, but I think she did."

"Big deal. You planted a big wet one on her," Romey said, "and she knows it."

"I didn't think she'd see me. It was stupid of me—"

"What? She going to call the FBI? What you scared of, Lo-man?"

"I didn't think she'd see me—"

"You heard him—he was talking like she never kissed anybody before," he said. "She must have told him that—what do you care?"

Ernie had parked a couple of hundred yards up the road, his lights doused at the end of a cottage road, far enough away that he couldn't have seen exactly what went on. But he must have known Squeak was mad when he saw the back-up lights flash, and he probably figured he was the one who'd suffer, so he hauled out of that gravel road, his rear end fishtailing over the pavement, and kept his foot to the metal all the way back up the hill, leaving Squeak way behind, his brass Chev still screaming in reverse.

"There goes our wheels," Mugsy said. "Now how we going to get home?"

"Swim," Romey told him.

"Take us an hour or two to walk from here," Mugsy told him.

"That's the price of glory, boys," Romey said, twisting a skinny branch off a birch.

We crept out from the trees to the ditch, jumped the ditch again, and laid up on the bank at the side of the road, watching Squeak get out of the car and slap his wet thighs, then run around to the trunk.

"Watch this," Romey said.

Squeak pulled a shotgun out of the trunk and ripped back the case. He jammed some shells in the clip. He had no idea where we were, absolutely no idea, so he pointed that shotgun down the road and blasted away, random blind shots that zinged past us, some of the BBs catching the dead end sign at the foot of the beach.

"He's nuts," Mugsy said.

"Squeeak, squeeak," Romey yelled, like a sick hog.

"Shut up," I said.

"Squeeeeeak," he yelled again.

I shoved him.

Mugsy was a ball of giggles.

Romey slapped me with the back of his hand. "No way he can touch us."

Squeak slammed more shells into the gun, jumped into the car, then rammed it into first and crawled back toward the beach, his headlights turning the road in front of him into broad daylight. The whole time, we stayed flat in the weeds against the bank of the road, watching the car come up.

The more I thought about it, her sitting in that car with her sweetie unloading shot after shot into the woods, the more I didn't care whether she had recognized me; in fact, I hoped she had. I almost hated her right then because she'd been kissing this twink who was flashing his bravado by ripping up the woods with his shotgun. Really, I didn't know what to think. There she was in the car right now, probably crying, Squeak blasting away. Maybe she wasn't crying. Maybe she was just like him. I couldn't help but feel sorry for her, either. But she must have told him she'd never kissed anyone before—that was a lie.

We hugged the weeds in the middle of the combat zone. When the Chevy was right beside us, Squeak blew another load into the trees. At

Water Torture

least he wasn't aiming at the side of the road, aiming to kill. But he had to be boiling over—here he was whispering all this smoochy stuff when the two of them got this cold bath of lake water. That he couldn't find us made him only more angry. Somewhere in all of the darkness, the perpetrators were watching the whole foolishness, laughing at him, mocking him.

"I love it," I said, as the brass Chev passed us on its way to the end of the beach, where of course they couldn't stay now; they knew that whoever they were that doused them were still hanging around.

Once he got to the end of the road, he stepped out, opened the trunk, shoved the shotgun back in the case, and jammed it in the back seat, flinging out a string of cuss words that sounded silly in the screechy voice that gave him his name.

"The boy's ticked," Mugsy said. "He's boiling. I don't know how she can go with him." He aimed that directly at me, as if I had some key to her character. "I don't know how anybody could go with him, but I never understood women anyway," Mugsy said.

Squeak turned the car around, laid what rubber he could, and went back up the road, the engine roaring, and just like that we found ourselves alone in the darkness, nothing but the surf, straight east, washing over the beach in a whisper.

"That was so great," Mugsy said. "We did it perfect."

"You get them, Lobo?" Romey said. "Get all that water inside?"

"Voooooosh," I said, like a tidal wave.

Down at the end of the road the cooler still lay like a dab of light on a dark canvas.

"I can't believe it," Mugsy said.

Romey sat up slowly. "If I were you, Lobo, I woulda killed him."

"He's dying right now," I said. "Think about it. He's lost for the night—all his glory is over."

"I don't understand how she can go with such a cluck," Mugsy said.

Romey got to his feet and looked around at the trees. "You guys don't understand women," he said. "The thing is, you don't *never* understand them—nobody does, except them. They're just different." He picked up a handful of stones from the shoulder. "It's no sense in trying, either."

"He's such a jerk," Mugsy said.

"'How you like this, baby?'" Romey said again in Squeak's voice.

"Makes me sick," I said. "Just shut up with all of that—she's a pig."

"What a cowboy." Romey raised both hands as if he were holding Squeak's shotgun. "Boom, boom, boom, boom," and then he swore the way Squeak had, his own voice coming back from the trees. "No kidding—what a cowboy."

It must have been about half-past ten. We had a long walk home.

We decided to walk the beach to Hurley's Drive-In at the end of the next lake road, a mile south of where we were, a restaurant where my sister Janine carhopped and where Romey could call Hattie for a ride home. A mile of beach was about the best we could do—better than a couple of miles up the hill west, at least, not to mention another couple south into town.

Along the shoreline, cottage lights burned in living rooms and over screened porches. Here and there campfires glowed in the darkness. We stayed at the edge of the water, chucking branches and logs into the shallow shoreline or skipping stones into the sprinkle of moonlight that fell like a speckled sheet of glass over the water.

"You know," Romey said, "one of these years we're going to be down there at the end of the road and some punks like us are going to come along and pull the same kind of crap."

"And you're going to get out of your car and fill the air with lead," I told him.

"Maybe," he said. "I'd have been ticked."

The beach was wide and ample that year, the cottages maybe fifty yards west from the wet sand where we were walking, barefoot, our prints gone with every wave. It didn't take all that long before we came up on a bonfire, just a quarter mile south of the end of the road. From the edge of the lake, we could see about a dozen faces glowing with the yellow light of the fire. On a night like this, you could walk along the water's edge, not more than twenty yards away from the warm circle of light, and not be seen or heard, the gentle rush of soft waves covering whatever sound might come up the beach, the intimacy of the fire holding all the attention inside. Most of the people who lived along the lake were unknown to us, even though they were practically our neighbors. They were vacationers from Milwaukee or Chicago, and most of them rich, far wealthier than any of the families from town. They were an exotic group to us, more worldly, more urbane, more sophisticated. Often enough, I was afraid of them—I'm not sure why.

For reasons he didn't announce, Romey walked right into the circle, coughed a little to make sure he wouldn't upset anyone by scaring them, and then said, "You hear them shots?"

We followed along. There were a mom and a dad—they looked younger than my folks, but they might have been the same age. You

232

couldn't always tell about lake people because they were so rich. But it was a mom and a dad, two boys—little—and four or five girls, not much less than our age, but then you couldn't always tell about girls either.

"We heard it," the man said. "What on earth was all of that?"

"Some guy had fireworks—big cherry bombs and M-80s, left over from the Fourth," Romey said. "It's nothing to get worried about, but I expect there'll be some cop down here in a while, checking." He looked at the girls. "We tried to tell 'em that those things were illegal, but they wouldn't hear it—just town guys," he said. "Bunch of 'em. Rowdies, you know?"

"Sure," the dad said.

"They gone now?" the mom asked.

"Hear 'em?" Romey winced. "I figure you could hear 'em take off—that's how much rubber they laid."

"I heard," one of the girls said.

"Figured you could," he told her. "Well, we were just going back home." He pointed up the beach as if the three of us owned one of the big cottages between Red Road and Hurley's Corner. "Just thought we'd tell you it's over and everything—wasn't anything to worry about or nothing. Just wild town kids is all."

The father actually got to his feet. "Thanks," he said. "You want a marshmallow?"

I didn't know what Romey would say. You never knew, really, with him. I wondered whether he was about to hit these folks up for a ride to the drive-in.

"Sounds good," he said, "but we got to get back." He looked down at his wrist, as if he had a watch, then turned to me. "Ricky," he said—he was doing some kind of game—"what time is it, anyway?"

"After ten," I said. I don't think I could have seen my watch in the darkness.

"We're late already," he said, then took a kind of bow, the way, I assume, he thought rich people might. "Sorry for interrupting," he said. "I thought maybe you'd be worried about all the noise."

"No problem," the woman said. "Thanks for telling us."

And then he walked away, and so did we.

"Never can tell when a good word might help out," he said.

"That was a lie," I said, laughing. "Remember what you said about lying—at camp? That was an out-and-out lie."

"Course it was," he said. "We supposed to live with everything we say at camp, Lobo?"

Water Torture

You have to be conscious of being heard when you walk on the lake. We were far enough down that I was quite sure that circle around the bonfire couldn't hear us. "How come you did that?" I said.

"You see those girls?" he said.

"Seventh grade," Mugsy said. "No more."

Romey shrugged his shoulders. "But they're city girls, and they're bored half the time," he said. "They don't have to work, you know. Shoot, we come by here tomorrow sometime, and we're heroes." He thumbed over his shoulder. "We're not just riffraff then, we're okay."

"Just in case," Mugsy said.

"We already got an in," Romey said.

"You going to marry some rich girl, you think, Romey?" I said.

We all had our shoes in our hands. Romey was closest to the water, actually kicking up surf with every step.

He started singing, "I want a girl, just like the girl—"

"Like Hattie?" I said.

"Long as she's great-looking," he said, "I don't care what's going on in her head."

"I'm not getting married," Mugsy said.

"You're going to burn," I told him.

"What do you mean?"

"Bible says, it's better to marry than to burn," I told them. I meant it as a joke.

"What does that mean?" Romey said.

"Means that if you don't get married, you'll be horny for all your life long," I told them. "You'll end up killing yourself or something. You'll end up burning."

"That's bull," Romey said. "Lots of people don't get married."

"You saying the Bible's bull?" I asked him.

"I ain't saying the Bible's bull," he said, "but I'm saying the way you read it is bull."

"No sir," I said. "It says it—somewhere in the New Testament."

"I don't want to get married," Mugsy said. "Really, I'm not kidding. I don't want to hang around here and work at Linear."

"You got to get married—at least I do," Romey said. "I need a woman who can control me—that's what I need."

"What do you mean?" I said.

"I need somebody who won't let me get out of hand—somebody like you, Lobo," he said.

"I'm not marrying you," I said.

"I didn't mean that—"

Water Torture

"What'd you mean?"

He didn't stop walking, none of us did. "My old lady's not wrong, you know. When I hang around you, I don't get way wild."

That made me angry.

"No, really," he said. "Like peeing in the float cups. I'da done it, you know? I'da done it, Lobo, but you're along, you know?"

"I'm like a preacher," I said, angrily.

"Maybe." He gave me a kick—not a mean one. "What you going to be, Lobo—you going to be a preacher, I bet, aren't you?"

"Me?" I said.

"No, the man in the moon," he said. "You grow up, you're gonna be a preacher just like your grandpa, I bet."

"I'm not good enough," I said.

"You don't have to be good to be a preacher," he said.

"Baloney," Mugsy said.

"No, really," he said. "Look at Stielstra. You wouldn't believe the stuff that guy told me—how he went after women when he was a kid, and smoked and everything, and then he says, 'There's things I'm not even going to tell you, too.' That's exactly what he said."

"But you got to hate it," Mugsy said. "If you do those things and you're going to be a preacher, you got to be like Monty—you got to hate it while you're doing it so that someday you can look back and talk about how much of a jerk you were."

It reminded me of the story of the apostle Paul, but I wasn't about to say it.

"You know," Romey said, "someday I'd like to have you for a preacher, Lobo, because you could never really pull any righteous junk on me, you know? Not with what I know."

"You got to forgive," I said.

"Nothing to forgive, really—you think God really cares about a couple packs of weeds? I mean, when he's got big stuff to worry about?"

"Then forget," I said. "You're supposed to forget."

"Forget what?"

"Forget bad stuff, you know?" I said. "I mean, like what we did to Squeak."

"You think that's sin?"

"You said it yourself, Romey—you said you'd probably get really hot if that happened to you—do unto others, you know—"

"That's not sin," he said. "Giving them a soaker or something—that's not sin. That's penny-ante."

"What's sin, then?" I said.

"Sin is bad stuff," he said. "I mean, sin is the kind of stuff that everybody knows is really ugly—not some trick like dumping on Squeak. My old lady, she'll laugh when I tell her."

"You going to tell her?" Mugsy said, astonished.

"Make her day," he said. "It'll make her day."

"What're you going to be, Romey?" I said.

"Air force—career," he said. "I'm going to fly those fighter jets, you know?"

"What if there's a war?" I said.

And then he said something that I've never forgotten. "There's always a war," he told me.

We were at the very threshold of our early manhood; it was 1959 and the Gulf of Tonken lay really not that far ahead of us or anyone else in the country. But we didn't think much about Southeast Asia or the advance of communism, starting out in Vietnam and Cuba like Hitler had begun in Poland and then tried taking over the world. Our concerns were adolescent, very much the here and now—what we saw ahead of us was not much more than what we could see in the darkness of the beach as we walked along the shoreline on our way to the drive-in.

Most of the other stuff Romey said that night I could have said myself. But I would have never answered my question that way. "There's always a war," he said, just the three of us coming back to town from a prank that would be only the beginning of a night I would never forget, and neither would he, I'm sure.

Water Torture

Scab

Hattie came out to pick us up that night, just as Romey said she would when he stuck a dime in the phone at Hurley's. Once she arrived, she wanted to know why we were out at the drive-in without a ride, and Romey told her everything, straight out, the whole story—about Dianne's telling Squeak she'd never been kissed before, about the bath, about Squeak's blasting away with the shotgun, and how he himself had wanted to pee in the cup but didn't because he knew that he shouldn't for my sake. He repeated every last word of Squeak's tirade, even added a little, and Hattie's wheezy laugh started in a tickling whirlwind somewhere deep inside her lungs, came up voiceless, like it always did, twisting in her throat to a fit of coughing. Mugsy and I sat in the back seat laughing, Romey up front with his mother.

"The old man around?" he said to her.

Hattie rolled up her window as if to cut down on the wind, but she didn't answer the question. She turned down the radio Romey'd cranked up. "Sounds to me as if you guys had enough of a night," she said, the hacking laugh gone. "Maybe you better just turn in."

"Sure, Ma," Romey said.

"I mean it," she told him.

"*You* go to bed," he told her. "What you don't know won't hurt you."

"I'm your mother," she said.

"And I'm your little boy," he said, "but not by my choice."

She didn't give in. "It's already eleven," she told him. "You guys aren't even—"

"Okay," he told her. "I got the picture." He reached down for the radio again to crank up the volume, but she swatted his hand away. He fought her, and he won, just as he usually did. "This is a good song," he told her, "Buddy Holly," and swung around to us. "Wonder what happened to the Toad?"

"Probably went nighty-night," Mugsy said.

"That's a good idea," Hattie said, both hands on the wheel.

Downtown, a circle of guys stood around the gas station, even though it had closed up hours before, older guys sitting and talking on the high cement bench in front, drinking Cokes from the machine, their legs stretched out and crossed in front of them.

"Whyn't you just drop us off, Ma?" Romey said. "We can walk home from here."

"No sir," she said, "that i'n't no good crowd for you to be hanging out with anyway."

She wasn't about to stop. We turned left at the bank corner, headed down the street past the telephone company, and looked for lights at Ernie's place.

"He ain't home," Mugsy said.

"Stop the car, Ma," Romey said. "We're getting out. Come on, Ma, don't be a jerk."

"You watch your language, Romey Guttner," she said. "I'm your mother."

"Oh, don't go gettin' holy roller on me—"

"I don't need your smart mouth," she said.

"This is all a big show," he said to us. "It's 'cause you guys are in the car, and she's got to act holy—isn't that so, Ma?"

"Listen to me," she said, "your father's at home, Roman—I can take these boys home right now, and I will."

"Get off it," he told her.

"I expect you guys to turn in," she told us. "Enough catting around for one night already, and with your father home, Romey, you may just

Scab

as well call it a night." She didn't stop until we got to the driveway. Then she turned to Romey. "You think I won't take them home, don't you? But I will—you hear me?" She got out quickly, slammed the door behind her, and walked up to the house, where the light was on over the kitchen sink and in the downstairs bedroom.

Romey didn't bark back this time. He watched her wiggle in through the screen door and could have said a whole lot more than he did. Other times he would have. But he kept it to himself, got out of the car, and walked to the backyard as if we weren't even around.

The tent was standing where we'd put it up earlier that afternoon, before all the fireworks. Mugsy was still caught up in the Squeak story, kept reviewing it the whole time we laid out our sleeping bags—how great it was when he shot off a couple of rounds, blind as a bat about where we were, how mad he was, how wet he must have been. We sat around in the light of Romey's gas lantern, laughing. I didn't want to leave again because I didn't want to hurt Hattie, didn't want there to be any kind of a battle, not with Cyril around. In the past I'd been around Romey's place for enough big arguments between Romey and Hattie to know they always made me feel awful. That night, I didn't want to go home.

"Where's the Toad when you really need him?" Romey lay himself out on the sleeping bag. "I'd give anything for a cigarette. We should have asked him to sleep over. He's always got butts."

"Don't you have any in the garage?" Mugsy said.

"Naah—I'm out."

"You want weeds, you get Toad in the bargain," I said.

"That's true." Romey took a deep breath, which I translated as an indication he was satisfied with the action we'd already had that night. "You can bet your butt I'm not going to end up like him," Romey said. "No way. All he's got is to hang around with punks like us—poor guy."

"You feel sorry for him?" I said.

He reached for a broom and slapped pine needles off the canvas. "He'll find some woman dumb as he is and have eleventy-seven kids. You watch."

"Who'd take him?" I said.

"Somebody will—you can bet on that," Romey said. He raised one arm and pointed at the top of the tent, letting his arm balance in the air. "Look at Hattie. Even my old man got a woman—there's hope for all of us, Lobo. You don't have to fall to pieces or nothing about your little sweetheart—all you lost is the world's greatest kisser."

Mugsy laughed. "Everybody gets somebody, finally," he said. "Everybody in the world's got somebody of the other sex who's just matched, lined up, waiting to go—that's the way it is."

"That's dumb," I said.

"No, really, even Squeak," Romey said, "but it ain't Dianne. You watch, she'll dump him once she's got something better. You watch, Lo-man. She will. She did it once—she'll do it again. Who knows, maybe you'll get her in the end."

"I don't want her," I said.

"Don't be saying what you want and what you don't want, either," he said. "People eat words like that all the time—"

"If you're meant for somebody, you'll get them," Mugsy said.

"You really think that?" I said. "You think someplace in some real house now, in some real bedroom, there's this girl whose like a perfect match for—"

"I can't stand it," Romey said. "Don't talk about bedrooms."

"You believe there's some woman somewhere, some girl who doesn't know any more about what's going to happen than you do—and that that girl is going to belong to you? Give me a break."

"It's true, i'n't it?" Mugsy said. "I mean, most likely all of us'll get hitched sometime, and when we do, it'll be to someone who's right now in some pajamas—"

"Will you cut it out?" Romey said.

"Whatever," Mugsy said, hitting the ground with the side of his hand. "There's somebody somewhere meant for you."

"*Here* meaning on the face of the earth?" I said.

"I'm not marrying anybody from this burg," Mugsy said. "Nobody here worth going after anyway—"

"My old man figured he'd never marry somebody from Easton," Romey said. "I'll tell you that much. But he knocked up Ma and that was that—"

"Your folks *had* to get married?" I said. My mother'd never said that.

"How on earth you think the two of them ever got together otherwise? Not by choice. Wasn't nobody else bringing them together, it was something else pure and simple," he said. "It was plain horniness—and my brother's the one that come out of it."

Romey's older brother, Dale, was out of the house long ago, working in Minnesota somewhere, I think. But I remembered what my mother had told me—how my own grandfather, the preacher, wouldn't marry them. "You think they wouldn't have married each other unless your brother came along?" I said.

Scab

"Who knows how to figure a crapshoot?" Romey said. He laughed hard, turned back toward Mugsy. "What you're saying is that someplace there's this girl just getting ready for me because someday me and her is going to be a thing, right? What's she look like?" he said.

Mugsy chuckled, but he played along. "Built—legs like Dianne maybe—really tan, you know."

"Hey, let her alone," I said. "She's got Squeak."

"Just legs is all I meant—I'm comparing," Mugsy said. "Don't be so touchy, Lobo."

"Wait a minute," Romey said. "Maybe it's Dianne fish face we're talking about here."

"You and her?" I said.

"You're right—I wouldn't have her after Squeak. No way. She's contaminated." He adjusted his head on his pillow. "Tell me more about this dream woman—"

"Listen," Mugsy said, "this makes sense. If God controls everything—"

"What's God got to do with it?" Romey said.

Mugsy started in. "If God controls everything, then someplace, right now, there's this girl and she's getting ready for bed—"

"Do the bed part again," Romey said.

"Someplace, right now, there's this girl—"

"You really think God controls everything?" Romey said.

"I think so," I said.

"Everything?" he said.

"Got to be," I told him. "If he doesn't control everything, then he's not God, right?"

"That's cute," Romey said. "I ought to go to Sunday school more often."

"Catechism," I said. "You don't learn much in Sunday school."

"I don't think he controls everything," Mugsy said.

"I don't either," Romey said. "We control some things."

"What?" I said.

"I don't know." He sat up on his elbows. "Okay, we're staying in the tent, right? The old lady, she says we ought to. But I still got a choice whether we stay or go, right? I mean—I make the decision."

"God does."

"Naah."

"He does too," I said. "He knows."

"What?" Romey said.

"He knows everything," I said.

"He knows I dream about women?" he said.

"Sure," I told him.

"He makes you dream about women—right, Lobo?" Mugsy said. "If God controls everything, then he puts that stuff in your head—even sex."

"That's decent of him," Romey said.

"All except bad stuff," I said. "I mean, we do the bad stuff."

"Give me a break," Romey said. "That's not fair."

"Tough," I said.

"Lobo," Mugsy said, "that's not what it says in the Bible."

"How come he stuck me with you guys when he could have stuck me with that girl I got coming someday? That's what I want to know," Romey said. He was laughing. "How come he stuck me with my old man, when he stuck you guys with dads that come out the other side of the factory? You know? You ever think of that, Lobo?"

The truth was, I had.

"How come there isn't a standard size or whatever for fathers, you know? And old ladies, too?" Romey said. "Why doesn't he just make one model and make it really good?" Then he looked at me. "I was reading someplace, you know, when men were dying in battle somewhere— I don't know, Second World War or something—when they were dying on the battlefield, often as not they called for their mothers. You believe that?"

"I don't know," I said.

"Their mothers?" Mugsy asked.

"Their mothers," Romey told us. "I read it somewhere. Some doctor who was out on the battlefield. He said when these guys were dying, they didn't ask for their girlfriends or their wives—they asked for their mothers."

"Not their fathers?" I said.

"No way," he told me. "I can't imagine being ready to go and wanting to talk to Hattie."

Neither could I. Neither could Mugsy, apparently, because neither of us said anything.

"If you knew you were going to die," Romey said, "who'd you want to talk to, Lobo?"

"Dianne, I bet," Mugsy said.

That wasn't even funny.

"I don't know," I said. "What a stupid thing to think about."

"Really—who'd you want to talk to? I mean, like your last words—"

"I'd want to talk to my old man," Mugsy said.

"Me too," I said.

"No sir," Romey said. "Most of the guys dying in the war—they wanted to talk to their mothers."

"You would, Romey?" I said.

"I'd want to talk to my old man, too," he said. "I suppose I would— my old man and then Hell or whatever, eh?"

At that, we laughed.

"You guys dream about Hell ever?" Romey said.

"I don't know what I dream about," I said. "I never remember what I dream about. Sometimes I wake up in the night and tell myself I had this great dream and I got to remember it and—poof! It's gone. No trace."

"I dream about women," Romey said.

"I thought you dreamed about swimming," I said. "You told me once about dreaming of being in the middle of Lake Michigan and swimming and swimming and not getting anywhere."

"That's nightmare stuff," he said. "I got other ones, too, like movies. In one of them I'm with this girl—"

"That's probably the one that's matched up for you," Mugsy said. "You know what she looks like?"

"Like Hollywood," he said.

From downtown, we could hear the buzz of cars passing and honking, kids still cruising through town. The wind was gone. Through the screens of the house, we could hear the sound of water running in the sink, Hattie cleaning up; and from next door, the garbled conversation of television.

"I'll say this," Mugsy said. "Who'sever for me is going to go without for a long time because I'm not getting married."

"Last of the wilderness men, right, Mugsy?" Romey said.

"'At's right," Mugsy said. "I'm going to Alaska or something."

"You got to have a woman up there to stay warm," Romey said.

"They got sleeping bags good for a hundred degrees below zero."

"You get cancer if you don't sleep with women," Romey said.

"Baloney."

"Lo-man, the truth?" Romey said.

"I don't know," I told them. "You read such stupid stuff, Romey."

"You got to keep your ears open," he said. "You know, like a cat; you never really sleep without your ears up."

In the silences that started to stretch a little longer between comments, I couldn't help thinking about Dianne, about how wrong it was somehow—not the dousing we gave them, but the whole business— how it was something like cheating for her to be in that car when she wasn't supposed to be. I'd given her my best self, something really nice

Scab

and good—not the Romey side, either. I'd done everything right, and she quit on me, tossed me out like some old rag, the me my parents would have been proud of.

"What a great night," Romey said.

"No kidding," Mugsy said.

"Sweet revenge, eh, Lobo?" Romey asked.

"Sweet revenge," I repeated.

"So if he's got everything figured out," Romey said, "why even pray about anything? Things fall like dominoes, right?"

No one said a thing. I'd never thought about it that way.

"Lobo," he said. "You're the preacher."

"I don't know," I said.

"You pray, Lobo?" he said.

"Sure," I said.

"Like now?" he said. "I mean, like now before we go to sleep?"

"Used to," I said.

"Here?"

"Probably not."

"How come?"

I hadn't thought of that either. "'Cause I'm not at home," I said.

"Does that make a difference?" he said. "You tell God, 'I'm not praying tonight because I'm at Romey's place'?"

"Sometimes."

"The Bible says pray without ceasing," Mugsy said.

"How'd you get any work done?" Romey said. "I don't think you can believe the Bible on everything—"

"C'mon," Mugsy said.

"Shouldn't have pulled that stuff? The whole coffin thing and drowning the love rats? Shouldn't have pulled any of that. Should have been praying instead. Is that right?" He pulled himself up. "Lobo, how come you don't say nothing? You're the one with the answers."

"I don't know anything," I said, irked.

"If your old man was here, we'd get someplace," he said.

I heard the car come up the street because there weren't that many going out of town past Romey's place at that hour. I heard it come but didn't think much about it until it wheeled violently into the driveway and stopped at the back, twenty feet at most from the back door. We peeled ourselves up from the sleeping bags and looked out, dust hanging in the air like a curtain through the blast of headlights. Mugsy pulled up the tent flap, but it was too dark to recognize the car.

244

Scab

"It's Toad," Mugsy said. "He knew we'd be back here. I told him we were sleeping over."

The driver pulled himself up and out quickly, then stomped to the back door, engine running, headlights still on. It was hard for us to distinguish anything. But I recognized the jacket. I'd seen it forever, and I was scared. "It's Zoot," I said. It was Monty's old man all right, and he was mad. The screen door shook as if it might break when he hammered it with his fist.

We'd drowned Squeak and Dianne, walked a mile on the beach, waited for Hattie to pick us up from Hurley's Drive-In, then laid there in the tent talking about things almost forever. Monty and Carl and the coffin out at the plant seemed light-years ago—Mugsy's screaming down the road after those two kids, Romey's chasing them halfway home.

Later, we'd hear the whole story—how Monty had run all the way home from the back of the sewage plant—maybe a mile, maybe farther, frantic with fear; how he'd come in and run directly to the bathroom, then thrown his supper all over the place, half of it making it into the stool, the other half splashing over the linoleum; how his body shook and quivered worse than anything Zoot or his wife had ever seen; how his mom nearly lost it herself to see her son in a heap on the bathroom floor, his arms up on the stool, trying to breathe between waves of nausea, as if his wind were forever gone; how Monty looked as if he were having an epileptic fit, gone into a seizure like a stroke or something; and how angry Zoot got, right away—even though it took a long time for them to get the whole story out of their boy.

Monty couldn't explain because he was that tired and that scared. His father had lifted him from the floor and wrapped him in a blanket, and his mother called emergency, and they put him in the car and rushed him to the closest hospital, which was on the other side of Sherburn, a drive of at least a half hour. The doctor had called it shock, once he'd had a look at him. By that time, Monty's shaking was only a strong nervous twitch that wouldn't settle.

The doctor had given him a shot to calm him down, and between the three of them they finally got the whole story, at least as much as Monty had sense to remember. And of course, one name stood out: Romey Guttner.

Once Monty was tucked into his bed, Zoot drove over to Carl's house. Carl hadn't run as far as Monty, hadn't pushed his body the way Monty had, and he hadn't been quite so scared. Carl's mother told Zoot that he'd come home sobbing and sweating, and she'd heard the story, knew who was responsible, and figured Monty, like Carl, was home safe. She was burned, but not hot like Zoot.

It hadn't been that long since Zoot's house was paint-bombed, and he hadn't forgotten the sound those smashing lightbulbs made up against his walls. Not long before that, he'd hosted a home visit by a bunch of union thugs Hell-bent on scaring him away from Linear. He knew who'd been behind all of that—everybody did, even my father—and he knew that no matter what Cyril did, he'd get away with it.

So he'd gone back home and listened to his wife bawl her eyes out. All the while, his rage burned straight through the asbestos wall of whatever better judgment might have remained in him concerning Cyril Guttner and his delinquent kid. Without saying a word to his wife, he'd convinced himself that what needed to be done had to be accomplished for the sake of the whole town—and the kid: someone had to act on behalf of the whole Christian community. Someone had to take on the most worthless father in town. The law was no good, but there was a higher law here, something God-ordained.

So he stayed with his son for a little while, watching the spasms of tortured fear slowly diminish, holding his boy's hand as the crying finally quieted into slow breaths. And all that time he was thinking of Cyril Guttner.

We didn't know any of that when he showed up. All we knew was he was violently angry.

"Where's your husband?" he screamed when Hattie finally came to the screen door. "Where's that kid of yours? I got to get some justice here, got to clear things up for once. Somebody has to be a father to that boy if his old man won't."

No more than a sixty-watt bulb hung out over the door, but even in the dim glow, the shadows drawn over Hattie's face showed the fear that rose in her, not from Zoot, either, but from a scene her imagination was already creating. We were lying little more than a hundred feet away, peeking out of a half-raised tent flap, but we could see it all and, in the silence, hear most every word.

"My kid almost had a heart attack," Zoot yelled. "He comes home and he heaves and heaves and heaves, and his eyes are rolling around in his head like he's nuts. He can't even talk, Hattie. My son—you hear what I'm saying? My wife's scared to pieces, and it's all your kid's fault. I'm not lying." He looked up at the house as if the place itself were an abomination. "I've put up with too much from this place. I've had it. You hear? Where's the kid?"

Romey pulled himself to his feet and slipped his tennis shoes on.

246

Hattie stood there speechless.

"You going out there?" Mugsy said, but like his mother, Romey didn't have any words just then. He laid the flap open quietly and stepped out into the darkness, then walked to a tree twenty feet away from the tent and got into a crouch, a long way from the back door.

"You shoulda seen him, Hattie," Zoot said. It seemed as if he was coming up quickly on tears. "If it'd been your boy, you'd know exactly how I feel—how I hurt."

Hattie was trembling. "Don't cause trouble, Zoot," she told him. "Nothing good is going to come of this now. Please? I'll call you in the morning. I'm sorry—I'm sorry. Just go home before things get worse. I'm sorry—I really am. You can't know how sorry."

"Sorry's nothing anymore. My boy's been to emergency," Zoot said. "We had to bring him in, for Pete's sake. Don't tell me you'll call me in the morning. I got to see that kid. Get him up or I'll come after him myself."

I knew Cyril was somewhere inside. Hattie'd said it.

She stood there in the door frame, too stunned to speak, the screen door swung half open, Romey still crouching behind the tree on the other side of the yard. I could hear Hattie take deep breaths from somewhere she'd rather not have gathered them, but I didn't have a clue as to what she might do. She could send Zoot out to the tent and he could beat on Romey, but Romey wouldn't take it, not the Romey I knew— he stood by the tree, as if waiting for Monty's old man to come get him. He would come out of the shadows like a cat if Zoot made a move.

Hattie stood there, shaking her head as if to deny that something inevitable was about to take place no matter what she did—something awful.

"Where is he?" Zoot screamed. "I'm not going home without taking care of your kid."

And then there was Cyril. He showed up behind her in his work pants and his undershirt, stepped right out the door and into the pool of light, slapping the door behind him, Hattie inside, as if to keep her away and in her place.

Zoot jammed his hands quickly in his pockets and stepped back off the slab of concrete at the back step. I don't think he'd ever planned on Cyril.

"I can't stand it when a man cusses out my wife right outside my bedroom window," Cyril said. "I'm a God-fearing man." Cyril was not tall, but when Monty's dad stepped back off the cement, he had to look up at Cyril, his arms crossed on his chest, looking hot, the kind of heat that's icy.

"Where's your boy?" Zoot said. Suddenly, he sounded a good deal less driven.

Cyril belched. Hattie stood behind the screen.

"He can come out and play in the morning, if you want to wait," Cyril said. "Or maybe you want to come back later." He slipped his hands into his back pockets. "Our kids got rules around this house. He can't come out after ten. He's just a boy, scab."

"Don't call me that," Zoot said. "Don't bring that word into this. This here's got nothing to do with Linear."

"Free country," Cyril said, shrugging his shoulders.

"Work's got nothing to do with this, Cyril. Don't be bringing it up or it'll just make everything a whole lot worse here—I'm trying to keep it out of my mind."

Cyril stood on the cement outside the back door and rocked on the soles of his feet, as if he were bored.

"All I want is your kid," Zoot said.

"I'n't it time for good Christian people to be home, Zoot?" he said, quietly. "I think I hear your mama calling."

"I'm not leaving till I see him."

"Geez," Mugsy said.

Romey was still crouching in the shadows in front of the elm at the edge of the gravel.

"I told you he can't play after ten."

"Get him out here!" Zoot said. The longer he stood out there with Cyril Guttner, the hotter his anger burned. "I got to ask the kid some questions."

"Whyn't you deal with me like the man you aren't?" Cyril said.

And then Zoot spun his wheels and went back into the story. "Your kid scared mine so bad I had to take him to emergency," he said. "I just now come back from sitting with him, and he's only now starting to stop shaking. He come in tonight and heaved all over the place, just heaved. Couldn't say nothing, either. Just sick like I never saw." He shook his head. "Cyr, you got kids—he was puking away and my wife sees—"

"You want to borrow a pail, I bet."

Zoot staggered in the grass as if he couldn't get his feet beneath him. He seemed almost punch drunk, even though Cyril hadn't laid a hand on him. There was no way of knowing how to figure Cyril Guttner. Zoot found it hard to talk, but he tried again. "If you'd think once of what I had to see—"

248

Scab

"Whyn't you just get off our property," Cyril said. "You make me sick, out all night at the back door of good people like us, telling your troubles. I don't see people wandering around your property bellyaching," he told him. "You want troubles—how 'bout scabs taking my job—how about that for trouble?"

Zoot raised the back of his arm up to his mouth as if he'd already taken a blow.

"Your little boy fills his pants and you want me to clean it up?" Cyril said. "What kind of father are you, anyway?"

The mix of emotion heaving around in Zoot's guts came out first in a kind of pity. The pitch of his voice dropped, and when he talked again, he was shaking his head almost sadly. "You aren't even human, Cyril," he told him, quietly. "People say you're a bad man, but you're worse than that. You aren't even human."

Cyril stood above him on the cement, as if words couldn't penetrate steel.

"You're an animal," Zoot said, not in anger, either. It seemed to tip out of his own shock and surprise. "You're worse than an animal, 'cause animals got feelings."

Cyril turned back to the screen door. "You hear what he said, Hattie?" Cyril told her. "You hear this good respectable Easton scab? You hear what he just said to me?"

"And you ain't a father, either," Zoot told him. "All the time you're gone and that kid of yours is way out of control. Shoot, Cyril, Hattie can't handle him. Somebody's got to be a father to that kid."

Cyril pulled his hands out of his pockets and hung them on his waist. "Don't tell me what I ought to be doing," he said. "You can call me what you want, but don't tell me how to live."

Hattie never moved from behind the screen door.

"You're worthless, Cyr," Zoot said. Anger rose once more in him. "Everybody knows it. Known it for years. You're trash."

"Cyr," Hattie said, "please?"

I'm sure Cyril never heard his wife's voice.

"Go home, Zoot," she said. "Please, just leave, okay?"

The space between the back door and the open flap of the tent seemed to glow. Things were out of control. I thought about calling the cops or something, because I knew this wasn't going anywhere I wanted it to go. But I didn't know where I'd have to go for a phone, and I wasn't about to walk past them, so I prayed. I kept my eyes wide open, but I prayed. "God," I said quietly, to myself, "keep this from happening—please, keep this from going on."

Zoot stood up straight just off the cement and tried to talk as if he were speaking to someone who just might understand good sense. "I have to talk to your boy about what he did," he said. "It's my Christian duty." He slowed down and tried to seal emotion out of the sound of his voice.

Cyril laughed.

"Where is he?" Zoot said. "Must I get him myself?"

"I'm over here," Romey yelled, and he walked toward the back door. "You got to talk to me, then talk," he said. "Don't talk to my old man. If you got something to say about me, then tell me, first off." He walked toward them slowly. "It ain't my problem your kid can't take a joke."

His old man was right there, and I knew Romey didn't want to disappoint him. He could have said he was sorry, but right then he wouldn't have, not in a million years. He may have said it if his old man weren't there—I don't know. There were times in Romey's life when he might have sidestepped the whole mess that was coming on us great guns, taken the whole business on himself. Without Cyril, I thought—or I wanted to think—Romey might have done it all different, maybe even taken some licks. But not with his old man already drawing lines in the wet grass.

"You know what you did?" Zoot said when he located the voice coming up out of the darkness. "You almost killed my boy—"

"Bull," Romey said.

I could have cried right then.

"He had to have a hypo—"

"What's wrong with your kid," Cyril said, "is he's a sissy, just like his old man."

Zoot let that go because he had Romey in his sights. "Whatever it was you pulled on him, Romey, whatever it was, it just about killed him," he said. "You never liked Monty anyway, did you? You did it on purpose. You went after my boy for that reason, didn't you? Just because you don't like him."

"Go home," Cyril said. "Get in that dump of yours and get out of here."

Romey got up on the concrete slab with his old man and stood there beside him, the same height. Something was grabbing my insides, clenching me in its fist way down somewhere deep.

Cyril crossed his arms over his chest. "Whyn't you go home and teach that kid of yours to be a man instead of a scab?" he said.

Zoot was trying to be rational, to hold himself together. "Somebody's got to be your father," he said, looking at Romey, "and I ain't leaving

Scab

until you catch what you deserve for what you did to my boy." He took a step toward him, but Romey just stood there beside Cyril.

"Come here," Zoot said, pointing at his feet. "Come down here."

Romey followed orders, came right down to him, daring him to swing. But what he pulled then was a trick right out of his old man's book. When he was a step away, he raised a kick that came from somewhere in the dark reaches of his soul, from a place I didn't really know, even though I was his best friend. He took a step, faked it almost, then aimed his foot at Zoot and let fly with a kick that would have crippled him if he hadn't twisted just enough to catch most of the blow off his thigh.

Just like that, the whole thing was rolling. Romey jumped from the back step and took off down the lawn, running just off the gravel. But he looked back—and he shouldn't have. When he did, he stumbled, went down in a scramble of arms and legs halfway to the tent.

In a second, Zoot was on him, whaling away with an open hand, like a father, slapping his butt whenever he could get in a good shot, with hands he considered righteous. It was only a licking Zoot was after, that's all. Nothing more. He just wanted to paddle Romey's butt, like he might have paddled Monty's, as if that would be enough to set the record straight and put Romey Guttner on some kind of straight and narrow.

But Cyril took off once he saw Zoot beating on his boy. He charged up from behind and hit Zoot in the square of his back with his shoulder, ripping him off Romey, and both of them flipped over in the grass, doubling up. Romey got to his knees and wiped his face with the back of his arm.

Zoot was bigger than Cyril—and he was younger, even quicker. He struggled to get his balance beneath Cyril's hold, the two of them growling and spitting anger, Cyril's arm in a crook around Zoot's throat, one of his legs up over Zoot's hips.

But Zoot turned in toward Cyril, barrel-rolled on his back away from the tent until he lay on top, then pinned Cyril with his back for a second, flat on the driveway. He squeezed an arm between Cyril's legs, locked his elbow, then drove hard with his legs, pushing him into the gravel. At the same time, he grabbed Cyril's arm, so Cyril was spread-eagled beneath Zoot's back. Then he pushed with his legs, powered both of them across the lawn until the two of them ran into a tree and Cyril screamed when the small of his back smashed up against the trunk.

Romey watched for just a second and then set himself like a sprinter.

Zoot tightened his arms around Cyril's arm and leg and pinned him there against that tree, his feet churning beneath him. Cyril spit out profanity with every breath he took, then reached up with his free hand

and ripped the front of Zoot's shirt, laying open his throat and chest. But Zoot kept bulldozing, even though Cyril tried slamming at his face from the only angle he could, swinging with the thumb end of his fist. Zoot turned his face to catch the blows on the side of his head.

For a minute, the whole thing seemed over. Cyril let up. "All right," he said. "All right—you're going to break my back."

Romey let it go, even though his old man was taking the worst of it.

Zoot planted his feet firmly and kept his weight braced against the tree, his butt actually coming up from the ground as he kept driving.

"I said all right," Cyril said again, yelling.

Then everything got quiet. Romey seemed frozen, maybe twenty feet away on his hands and knees. Zoot wouldn't let go, more afraid of dropping his guard now than he'd been at the moment he'd taken Cyril to the ground. He'd won something, he knew that, but he didn't know what it meant, so for a while, at least, he kept up the pressure, his face stretched tight. "You going to change?" he said.

There was something about it, just something about that question that even I understood, at that time, to be insanely stupid—You going to change? As if Cyril Guttner could, as if that would be all of it, as if being pinned against a tree was going to make Cyril a saint.

"Get off," Cyril said, cussing.

Zoot started letting up. "You heard me," he said. "You heard what I said." He unclenched his arms, one at a time. "No more crap," he said. "You hear me?"

"Sure, sure," Cyril said. "You got me, okay?"

Even Zoot knew it wasn't over. You could see it on his face. He didn't know what to do now that the physical stuff had shut down. Nowhere in his plans had he ever guessed it would turn out this way. He pushed his arms out and got his hands on the ground behind him, letting up on the pressure by peeling himself away from Cyril very slowly.

For a moment, lying against that tree, Cyril looked like a dying man in a doorway. Once Zoot was away, he turned over on his belly and hunched himself slowly to his knees, groaning as if he were injured. Then he sat there for a second before pulling his legs beneath him and pushing himself up with his arms. He twisted his back when he got to his feet, as if there were a kink where there hadn't been before.

Romey never moved.

But Zoot fell for the oldest trick in the book, just like we did. He fell for the one we used to use when we were wrestling, the one about your shoe being untied. He fell for it because he did the one thing no one I

Scab

knew, not even Romey, had ever really done fully and completely: he trusted Cyril Guttner.

The whole town—the whole church—really wanted to believe, like Zoot, that maybe someday Cyril would change at a moment only the Lord could fashion—maybe a vision, a bad accident, maybe even a death. Maybe if people were nice to him, invited him over for potluck, maybe if someone would talk to him like a man instead of an animal, maybe if someone would treat him with respect and dignity. Maybe if they'd let him usher in people at a church service, maybe if they'd serve him communion. Maybe if someone had him in a headlock and got him to promise that as of that moment, the man's whole heart was going to change into something soft and good and righteous. Hope springs eternal—maybe that was the difference between Cyril and Zoot, the real difference. Zoot still hoped.

"That your billfold?" Cyril said, and the moment Zoot took his eyes off him, Romey's old man kicked him in the small of the back so hard Zoot's knees buckled, and in a flash Cyril was behind him, grabbing his throat in both hands. It was a choke hold. I knew it immediately because we used to yell it when we were wrestling, when somebody's arm would get tangled around somebody else's throat. But Cyril wasn't about to stop for some kids' rule. He stood there over Zoot, all of his weight and strength poured into wrists locked around Zoot's throat. His back was to the tent, but I didn't have to see that hold clearly. I could hear what it was.

It was Romey who stopped Cyril. He came up behind his old man and wrestled his arms in under his father's shoulders, swinging his hands up behind Cyril's neck in one quick move and throwing him in a full nelson, all the time yelling at his mother to do something. She was still standing there at the back door, frozen. Once he had his hands tight behind Cyril's head, his old man couldn't do a thing but come up off Zoot.

But it didn't matter then who had Cyril pinned. What mattered to the guy was that he was pinned. He cussed like a brute, even though he was a dancing captive of his own kid, his arms flailing above his head.

"Ma!" Romey kept yelling as Zoot finally fell to the ground, holding his neck.

Cyril shook his shoulders as if he were fighting a harness. He stamped his feet, then tried to run with Romey behind him, pinning his shoulders. He pivoted round and round, trying to wrestle himself out, but all the time Romey held on, wouldn't give up, and kept yelling at his mother to do something. Hattie stood beneath the porch light, outside now, but still as silence.

Scab

Cyril went down on one knee, bent over like a man praying, then stooped forward quickly so Romey came flying over his shoulders when he stood up, lost his grip as he lost his balance, and came down in a sprawl in the grass.

"Lobo!" Romey screamed.

Cyril never bothered with his son. He went straight for Zoot again, but this time Zoot brought his arms and legs up high around his head to protect himself. So Cyril stopped short, then kicked him, like Romey had, kicked and kicked until Zoot couldn't help but open up.

"Mugsy—Lobo!" Romey yelled, and he got to his feet and once more went after his old man.

I was scared—too scared to move.

Romey spilled his dad in a flying tackle that sent them both falling over Zoot. Cyril came up first. When Romey got to his knees, he tried a whole different thing—he tried to plead. But Cyril let fly with the one solid punch thrown all night long, and Romey went down with a sound I'll never forget, because I felt it so deeply myself. I knew Romey wouldn't get up right away.

Cyril stood, and Zoot looked up from a half crouch. Cyril took another swing with his right foot and caught him in the jaw, spinning him backward like a rag dummy.

At that point, Zoot was finished, and so was Romey.

Cyril picked Zoot up by the shoulders and went back to his throat with both hands. From the tent, the two of them were clearly outlined against the back of the house, where Hattie stood straight as I'd ever seen her, pointing Cyril's rifle. That's when I first saw the gun.

I was barefoot, but I took off out of that tent with every bit of strength I had. I flew over the driveway, screaming, thinking only about Romey, and I swear I heard something crack when I hit Cyril, but I spun off and slammed my head into the gravel, then fell to the grass on the other side of the driveway. My balance was gone, and I turned back to watch, dizzily, as three or four Cyrils went back for Zoot in slow motion. Then Mugsy hit him and bounced off. Cyril swung a foot viciously and caught Mugsy in the flat of the belly and immediately went back for Zoot's throat. I was sure Zoot was going to die.

That's why I yelled what I did. That's why I looked up at Hattie Guttner as she aimed that rifle. She knew—just as all of us did—that Cyril was going to kill the man.

So I screamed the words that gave his wife permission. "Shoot him," I yelled, with strength gathered from fear and hate. "Hattie—shoot him, shoot him, shoot him."

Scab

Just for a second she looked at me in a way I'll never forget, in a way my memory has preserved and maybe even exaggerated over the years— but a way I later came to believe was something of the approval she didn't get from my grandfather, the warrant the old preacher wouldn't give her, even though the two of us—me and grandpa—finally and surely agreed at that moment on the state of Cyril's soul.

What I don't know is whether she would have shot her husband without it, but what I will always remember is that when I told her to do it, when I screamed at her to shoot the man murdering Zoot, she did. Maybe she needed the word of a Prins, as if it were the word of the Lord.

If she'd taken the .30-06, she'd have killed him. That flame of steel would have burned through him and taken along half his chest. But she'd taken the .22, and the shots she took stopped him, but did so slowly, so slowly I thought Cyril might still come after her.

It's likely he never heard the snap of the shots, but he felt them, because his arms dropped and he looked down at his chest as if something was suddenly missing. One hand came up and swabbed the blood that surged into a stain. Then he turned and looked at Hattie and raised his other hand to tend the wound.

Zoot lay on the gravel.

In disbelief, Cyril stood there in the driveway and looked around blindly, as if for the first time in his life he understood he really had nowhere to turn.

Romey came to. Mugsy lay in a ball at the door of the tent, crying. I was the one closest to Hattie. I got to my feet and staggered to the light at the back door and took the rifle out of her hands, took it in my own, and aimed it at Cyril Guttner. I'd have killed him right then if he'd gone for anyone else. I'd have shot him dead, and I wouldn't have thought anything of it. I know I would have. I was that scared, that sure of what it was I'd already done.

Cyril looked at his hands in the one and only gesture I ever saw him make that was even vaguely suggestive of contrition. Then he looked at his wife.

"I had to, Cyril," she said. And then she cried.

I was thirteen years old, and that night, I never doubted for a moment that she was right. "I had to, Cyril," she'd told him.

What I've struggled with for all these years is my part of it, my permission, my demands.

Ever since then, I've wondered whether she was right—and whether I was.

Scab

Prayer Meeting

Three days after the shooting, Romey came to stay at our place while Hattie continued to sit at her husband's bedside at the hospital. Monday night, the night she brought him over, I watched him through the dining room window as he stood at the front door. While Hattie knocked, he stood quietly, more dressed up than he almost ever was, a small suitcase in either hand and a shopping bag full of stuff—games and things—under his left arm. Silent and wary, he wore a Sunday shirt, leather shoes, and stiffly pressed pants and seemed to look more like Monty than Romey Guttner. His father was dying.

During that time, I found it hard to forget the way Cyril had stood there looking down at his chest, Hattie already a mess of tears, the rifle in her hands. I knew—even if no one else did—my part in the man's suffering. If he were to die, I would be a killer, even though it had been his own wife who'd shot the man.

Cyril had been rushed to the hospital, where the doctors treated the wounds. Most of what was going on I didn't understand until later, when my father told me what had happened—long after the funeral. Before his death, we waited with some optimism, actually, my parents praying nightly for his life, as I did.

What the bullets had done was perforate the bowel and tear the renal artery, at least one bullet remaining in his back muscles along the spinal column. The doctors repaired the perforations and the artery with a synthetic graft. Then, they put Cyril on antibiotics and hoped for the best.

Already on Saturday the graft had begun to leak and Cyril developed a clotting disorder, not uncommon with that type of wound. The doctors knew the situation was grave and attempted to treat him with anticoagulants, but his blood pressure dropped and they were unable to control the infection. The anticoagulants were necessary, but his condition was made worse by the fact that he'd been shot more than once, and after a process whose initial signs the doctors recognized rather quickly as terminal—and explained to Hattie as such—eventually, four days later, Cyril Guttner bled to death.

I was only thirteen, and while my parents heard the updates and understood the precariousness of his condition, the only measure by which I could read the gravity was in the soft tones they used whenever they talked about Cyril, and Hattie. Even though I didn't know what would happen, I think I knew—as did Romey—that Cyril wasn't going to live. No one ever said it, but we knew somehow what was going to happen. Maybe everyone did. Maybe no one ever said it as clearly as the doctors had said it to Hattie, but I believe we all knew that what had begun as a prank was going to end in the death of Cyril Guttner, a man who had more enemies in Easton than the rest of the town combined.

Even though I considered myself responsible, even though I couldn't forget what exactly had happened that night when Hattie stood with the rifle lifted, there were moments in those last days when, to me, Cyril's death seemed to promise no more or less than new life, for Romey especially, but for all of us too—for my parents, for me, for Hattie, for everyone. Guilt didn't shape my feelings that way, although I felt a deep sense of regret for having given my permission. But that night I never doubted for a moment that Cyril would have killed Zoot—even Romey, if Romey had continued to get in the way.

I didn't know a human being who seemed so eternally lost as Cyril Guttner. I remembered the sound of his cussing coming up through the heating vent as I lay beneath my sister's bed only a month or so before that night Hattie shot him. I'd never forget the way both Romey and Hattie seemed scared almost into madness the morning we had sneaked his rifle out of the basement—for reasons everybody would have considered righteous. And I remembered my own father's pain and his description of Hattie's. Not only was the shooting self-defense, now Romey was free—that's what I told myself. Hattie had shot the old man, who would have killed somebody that night, and now my buddy was free. The wicked witch was dead.

When Romey came Monday night, my mom hugged Hattie before she left her son to go back to the hospital. They stood at the front door, my mom holding Hattie but saying nothing, Hattie letting some silent tears fall that showed in the tracks they left down her cheeks. All the time they stood there together, Hattie kept one hand on the door.

"He ain't going to make it," Romey said when we were alone upstairs. He said it as if he'd known a dozen people with gunshot wounds. He turned his arm around to pick at the scab that had formed over the burn he took from the gravel. "Ma says it too. She said it looks like we're going to lose him." He looked at me strangely and shrugged. "That's what she said—I mean, it's the way she said it—'Looks like we're going to lose him,' she said." He shrugged again. "I didn't know he was ever ours to start with."

I hadn't been anxious for him to come over because I knew he'd have to talk, and I didn't know the words to say to a kid whose old man was dying of a gunshot wound his mother gave him, in part, because I said she should. I had slept through most of Saturday, because after the ambulance finally came and took Cyril away, after the police had questioned everybody and we'd all finally gone home, it was late—getting well on toward morning.

I had told the story to my parents, just the way it happened—everything, even the bit about Dianne and Squeak, every last minute of the fight, every move I could remember, everything except the swear words and the fact that I'd yelled at Hattie myself, told her—almost commanded her—to kill Cyril when she'd looked at me as if to ask permission. That I never said. I didn't know if anyone knew. No one ever brought it up. Not even Hattie.

I hadn't slept at all until midmorning, when everything around me and inside finally crashed. I was alone in my bedroom, my nerves as tight as they'd ever been, the whole scene replaying time and time again as if I couldn't find the switch for the projector. It was gruesome and awful to see and hear it again and again and again, and that was when it happened—when I was alone. I couldn't stop myself from crying, even though I wasn't sure exactly why. A man was dying, a man I knew—a man whose kid I knew—and those bloody stains on Cyril's shirt belonged in part to me. I kept telling myself he would have killed somebody. He would have. But it didn't help. The whole face of things around me had changed that night. Maybe that's what scared me more than anything else.

For a long time I couldn't stop crying. It had to do with everything that had happened, not just one thing, but this huge ache that was much bigger, much worse, than a sharp pain—it was all over me, inside and out, as if darkness reigned and there was no place the sun would shine.

I couldn't really believe that the Lord God Almighty, Maker of Heaven and Earth, would have twisted and turned certain knobs and gizmos and effected the death of Cyril Guttner the way it had happened. I'd done it. Romey had done it. Hattie had done it. Even Mugsy had done it. Zoot had done it. Everybody had played a part. Cyril had done it— more than anyone, he had.

The tears didn't stop for twenty minutes, maybe longer, which is not to say they came hard, or heavily. I was happy nobody was there to see me pull Kleenex, one after another, from the compartment above my bed.

And then I slept. That was Saturday.

Sunday passed—we went to church twice, like we always did. Cyril was holding on—it was announced before the long prayer.

Sundays were always quiet at our house, this one especially so. I spent most of the afternoon in my bedroom, despite the heat—it was August and the lakeshore gets heavy as a swamp with dank humidity. Once, my father came up to talk to me, and I pretended I was asleep. That night, after church, he came up again with a steel-winged fan, plugged it in the socket across the room, and set it on my dresser. It whirred in perfect silence.

"So," he said, "how you feeling?"

I had a magazine up in front of me. I looked at him, didn't say a thing.

He grabbed my leg. "The Bible says the world is full of pain and misery—a vale of tears," he said. "It's not wrong, either. It's just that learning that it is can be its own misery."

He looked at me as if he wanted me to talk, slapped my leg lightly. "The worst is behind you, maybe—that's one way to look at it." He shrugged as if what he'd said was worth considering. "Romey's going to have a new life now," he said. "It's changed—everything's changed." He grabbed his lips tightly between his teeth and raised his eyebrows. "Do you know who loves you?" he said.

I nodded because I knew what he was suggesting.

Prayer Meeting

"Then you can take whatever comes," he said. "You remember that game when you had two homers—against Plymouth, I think, wasn't it?" he said. "You know, last year, the first year you were in Ponies? That was great," he told me. "I could have sworn my heart came right out of my chest and beat out pride in front of the whole crowd." He smiled. "There'll be more good times," he told me.

"Tell me this," I said. "More bad times or good?"

"Nobody keeps records," he said. "In the war, you know, I used to type up records—records of people's names that went down on this ship or that one."

He never talked much about his war experience. I knew he'd been in the South Pacific, of course, and I knew he was never all that close to combat.

"I used to keep the records of who died, and every name I typed had somebody connected somewhere." He pulled his hands away and held them out in front of him as if they were perched over a keyboard. "They were keystrokes, but somewhere in Philadelphia or Seattle or someplace in Tennessee, real live human beings were going to bawl their eyes out when they learned what name I was typing out."

I saw my father as a young man, a guy in a T-shirt and fatigues, on some ship somewhere, his hands over a typewriter. When I remember it now, I wonder if our paths, just for a moment, didn't cross there— mine moving from childhood innocence into the experience of sin, his from a dutiful, even arrogant, parent to someone who would have to be much more of a trusting soul with a kid who was becoming, whether or not he liked it, less and less his responsibility.

"It makes you believe, you know—almost like you have to, or else life's nothing but a mess," he said.

"Is that why?" I asked. "Do you believe in God because otherwise everything is a mess?"

And then he smiled. "There aren't any easy answers, Lowell. If you're like me, it'll take the rest of your life to figure out things like that. When you find something out, let me know."

I don't think I'd ever presumed to guess that my father didn't know what he was supposed to, that he thought about things that didn't make sense, that sometimes they stayed a mystery. I didn't know that he was like me in some ways. I'd have to grow up to understand that.

It was supper time Monday when Romey came to our place. It had been too tough for Hattie to go back and forth to the hospital all the time and find places for the kids. Romey was going to stay at our place, my

Prayer Meeting

mother told me, because Hattie said that of all the places he could stay in town, he wanted to stay with us. The girls went elsewhere, with friends. "He always feels good with you," Hattie had said when she called, "and with you somehow it doesn't feel as if I'm imposing." My mother couldn't have said no. She wouldn't have, anyway.

That night, once Romey'd moved in, he sat on my bed as if he didn't feel like going downstairs with my folks. He sat down quickly and slapped the softness beneath him as if it were something he'd never felt before. "Going to be a lot easier without the old man around," he said. "He's been gone a lot anyway." He looked up at me. He wasn't just talking to himself. "He hasn't been around that much, but with my old man, it's like he's there even when he isn't." He reached over to some pins and medals my mom had tacked up on my wall, took off the longest one, which had little metal bars hanging from it, the one for Sunday school attendance. "What're these medals for, anyway?" he said.

"Sunday school," I said.

"How come I don't have 'em?"

I didn't want to tell him he didn't have those things because he didn't go. When I remember that night, I can't help but think about how infrequently Romey had been up in my room, how strange it was for him to be there, because even though we'd been together so much in the last year or so, the two of us, and Romey'd been in the house, downstairs in the kitchen when we were finishing supper and things like that, he'd really not been up in my room. Whenever he'd come over, my mom would ask him in and give him a cookie or a Rice Krispies bar. But Romey actually hadn't seen that Sunday school attendance pin before, even though it had been up in my room forever, right there beside the Milwaukee Braves team photos.

"Sometimes when he came home, you know, the stuff he said—he really didn't mean all of it, either," Romey said. "You had to take him the right way." He fiddled with the long bars of the pin, looking down at its sheen. "Ma knew it too. He had this plate in his head." He drew a finger over his forehead without looking up.

"A what?" I said.

"He had this plate in his head from an accident jumping off a train—you know, something like this, only bigger." He held up the bars of the pin, then dropped them and spread his finger an inch maybe. "Yaay big," he said, and he planted his fingers, still positioned on the right side of his forehead. "Ma used to say that sometimes that plate dug into his brain—threw him all out of whack." He looked up. "Shoot, Lobo, I told you that."

"I don't remember," I said.

"He had this stinkin' *plate* in his brain," he said, as if he were speaking to a child, as if he were angry. Once more, he reached up with his fingers and showed it, tapped at his skull. "Big stinkin' plate—I don't know, maybe to hold his brains together. That was the cause of it."

"It was?"

"Sure," he said, with the same authority his face wore when he'd name flowers in the woods—Dutchman's-breeches, trilliums, words I would have never heard if it hadn't been for Romey, who picked them all up from his old man. "You couldn't see the thing, but it was there. It was always there in his head. That was the cause of it."

"When'd he have this accident?" I said.

"Before I was born already. I never knew him without it."

"You couldn't see it or nothing?"

"Of course you couldn't see it. It was on the inside, pea brain." He pointed again. "He'd get headaches, too—that was the whole mess really." And yet he shrugged as if it made no difference finally. "When I took him down that night, you know—I had this picture in my head— I had it before too—I had this picture in my head of this plate like a bar of steel or something pushing into his brain." He pinned the Sunday school badge back into the wall.

"It's for Sunday school," I told him, pointing. "That's for Sunday school, for going."

"I can read," he said. "I didn't know you got awards." He held on to the successive bars. "If I'd start right now, this year, I'd be what—" he counted the bars, "twenty years old before I'd get something this big— twenty years old. They don't have Sunday school for people that old, do they?"

I shook my head.

"Even if I'd try, I can't make it anymore," he said.

My bed had no headboard. Built into the wall was a little compartment big enough to hold a reading light, my radio, and maybe ten books. Romey pulled his feet up on the bed, laid on his stomach, and riffled through the books, one after another. "She didn't have a choice," he said, "my ma didn't." He snapped a look at me. "Except she could have winged him."

"Your ma?"

"She didn't have to hit him where she did—I don't know," he said, pulling out a book, then letting it drop back into its place. "But what does she know about guns?"

I didn't know what to say.

"My old man's the guy who knew it all," he said. And then he looked at me. "There was good stuff too—at our place."

"I know," I said.

"There's this picture in a drawer in the dining room with all the others." He outlined a square with his fingers. "It's got him in it and my ma and some relatives, I don't remember who, and they're all laughing. They're down at the beach in these ugly swimming suits, and they're all laughing, my ma and my dad too." For just a moment he was lost in that picture. "Course they were young then," he said.

"Maybe just married," I said.

"Probably," he said. "Maybe not even." The thought tickled him and he laughed out loud. Then he looked at me. "You know, people pushed him around a lot," he said. "He was best at the union hall." He pulled himself up on his elbows. "*She* never came—the old lady, I mean. It was just me and him." He turned over on his back and looked up at the ceiling. "A bunch of guys in blue shirts and stuff, all of 'em sitting behind these tables and eating, the whole mess of 'em, eating soup and loving it, you know, because they had this thing they believed in, you know? And then everybody'd light up." He pretended to be smoking. His feet were at the bottom of the bed, his hands up behind his head. "You get my old man to the union hall and give him some of that soup, and those guys could sing, Lobo—all men, too. I mean, sing." He shook his head as if he couldn't believe it. "I told you that."

"Yeah," I said.

"I'm not pulling your leg."

"What songs?" I asked.

"Union songs mostly, and hymns."

"Hymns?"

"'Mine Eyes Have Seen the Glory'—that's a hymn, ain't it? It's all about God."

I couldn't remember ever singing it in church.

"And 'Amazing Grace' too. Sometimes at the end."

"No kidding?" I said.

"Shoulda taken you along," he said. "But my old man woulda had a kid." He laughed. "I think he always thought you guys were rich or something, I don't know." He shook his head. "I don't think you're really rich or you'd have a boat." He looked at me. "I don't know what it was, but there's lots of things he'd do didn't make much sense at all, really." He reached up to the wall and flicked the long row of bars strung from the Sunday school pin. They made a tinkling sound against the wall. "You think he'll be in Heaven, Lobo? I mean, it's a stupid question and all that, I know that much. But you think there's a chance for him to be there?"

If Cyril Guttner was going to Heaven, I thought, there was no Hell. "I don't call the shots," I told him.

"I like to think so, is that okay?" he said.

It was stupid, but I wasn't about to tell him so.

He pointed at the Sunday school pin. "I wasn't there enough, was I?" he said.

"It's something you get for perfect attendance," I said.

"Yeah," he said, "I'm sure."

Even though he'd never been to a prayer service before, Romey came along with the three of us Wednesday night. My sister was working.

"I don't have no sport coat," he told my mother when she came up that night and told him he should go with us.

"It's only a prayer service," she said. "It doesn't matter much how you're dressed." She said that especially for him. I'd be dressed—that much I knew. Then she reached down and gave him a little hug I recognized because it was like the ones she gave me when I was younger.

I knew better than to ask my parents if the two of us could stay home, but I was afraid of what might happen—I was afraid that somebody was going to stand up and pray for Cyril Guttner and say something about Romey's old man that wouldn't hit him right. Plus it was church, and something of an embarrassment—the whole business swirling around the whole town, a man shot right there in Easton, even if it was Cyril Guttner.

I knew Romey would think the whole meeting was weird—people standing up and begging God to do some miracle. He'd giggle, I thought. But my parents wouldn't have understood. They would have been disappointed in me for even thinking things like that—as if prayer wasn't exactly the remedy everybody needed right then, Cyril included, Cyril always included. I had heard Cyril prayed for in my house for as long as I'd been hanging around with Romey, even before. "May he come to see—" words like that, as if Cyril was somehow missing the big picture.

At best, the church was half full, people sitting in little clusters edging forward to six empty rows of pews at the front. We always attended. Zoot and his family went occasionally, but Cyril and Hattie, never. That night, Zoot wasn't there. I don't know why. Maybe he should have been.

What happened in prayer services was predictable, since the same people usually attended—the most faithful, requesting help for what,

Prayer Meeting

often enough, were the same problems. Maybe some different sick people, but almost always the predictable few standing up. The same songs were sung, a few fast ones at first, then lots of slow ones about praying. The prayers themselves were often similar, only the order changed from week to week. Some nights when the news was hot, people might race to get theirs in: Grandma's dying in Michigan, some kids in a car accident, a man scooted off to emergency for a sharp pain in his chest.

We walked into church together—first Mom, then Dad, then me, then Romey. I let him have the end of the bench. It was usually my spot, but it was my place to sit beside my father.

Reverend Kosters started singing the songs that weren't printed in the pew hymnbooks, peppier than the ones the church often sang at Sunday worship. After a couple of good choruses we all got on our feet, and he stood on his tiptoes, leaning over the pulpit into the mike, his voice on perfect pitch, even if it wasn't the voice of a great soloist.

Over the years there were likely more prayers raised in those weekly meetings for the Guttner family than any other single subject, even though the name wasn't always used. Sometimes you had to read between the lines, something God was good at, I'd figured long ago. That night, there wasn't a soul in church who didn't know what had happened at Romey's place, didn't know every detail of the shooting, and wasn't aware that right then a member of their church, Hattie Guttner, was sitting at the bedside of the man she'd married, sitting there praying for something none of us—not me, not even my mother and father—knew exactly, other than to say she wanted God's will for the whole mess. I'm sure lots of people felt the whole world would be better off without Cyril Guttner, Hattie at the top of the list, Romey just a step beneath. I had reason to fear that someone would bring it up, somebody who maybe hadn't seen Romey come in to the first prayer meeting he'd ever attended at the very moment his father was fighting for his life.

It felt very strange to have Romey beside me. As we stood and went through the songs, each of us holding a corner of the hymnal, I understood something I'd not thought about before, something that came to me so clearly I almost had to laugh: how much easier it is to pray for somebody who's not there. If Romey were with his mother, I knew it would be just another prayer meeting, but with him beside me, the whole service seemed cocked and ready, the whole church hair triggered.

I could tell by the way the hymnbook shook in my hands that I was nervous. Romey didn't say a word, not even between songs. I didn't have to talk to him—the prayer service offered us that kind of silence anyway. I had a feeling that I should explain what was going on, Romey never having been to one before, but I didn't say anything. We were in church, after all. Miles away in the hospital, Cyril Guttner lay dying from what he would have himself called a gutshot.

The organ started into "Sweet Hour," signaling the beginning of the praying part, when a number of short prayers were offered by people standing for a moment, then sitting again, having placed their requests before the Lord. Whether I liked it or not, I felt as if I were an inch beneath Romey's skin, feeling what he was feeling amid the chorus of supplications all around, my nerves jumping from the fear that at any minute somebody was going to say something stupid about his old man, a man nobody in that church knew as well as he did, even though Cyril had hardly been around enough to be anything at all to his son, and when he was, what was he, anyway?

I remembered a day the year before when I'd gone over to Romey's and found Cyril and some friends sitting out in the back frying bratwurst and drinking beer. Romey had picked up a new pair of mud flaps for his bike, and we were in the garage attaching them to the fenders. Five of Cyril's friends sat no more than twenty feet from me. They paid no attention to us—that's part of what scared me, too, I thought, the way Cyril could go on living as if his own boy weren't around, as if he weren't there at all, as if Romey didn't matter. I'd never known men like those burly beer drinkers, men who used language I hadn't begun to understand, the kind of language I knew Jesus wanted me never to use or even hear. To me, the way they held those bottles and gulped beer, the way they laughed almost viciously, meant there was something evil lurking in them. They were exactly what we'd always prayed about at home, men who were stains on God's ordered world, like the flat shadowy oil spots on their work shirts. I was afraid, deathly afraid, not because of what they might do to me physically—that wasn't it at all. They seemed not even to notice us. What scared me was what men like that could do to my soul. At Romey's place, people he didn't know spat in the grass and flipped empty beer bottles around so we could pick them up in the morning for two cents deposit. Romey had sat on the garage floor that day with a screwdriver in his hands, putting on new mud flaps, just as oblivious to the menace around us as those men were to him.

Maybe that Wednesday night prayer service was a first for both of us, because for the first time, I listened to the prayers. Even though, that night, my imagination spent a good deal of time wandering through the lake woods and Romey's own back yard, trying to pick up traces of what had happened and why, I listened to the prayers the people offered, and every last petition across the breadth of that sanctuary came home to me on a conscience as tender as an open wound, made that way by Romey's presence, as if we shared the same ears, the same mind, the same soul. Everything I listened to, I heard through him.

Margaret Alsum prayed for poor people who couldn't pay their bills. Perry Van Zee praised the Lord for his wife's new job.

I could hear Romey breathe.

There were more prayers—a grandma's cancer treatments, a new niece in Grand Rapids, a retreat for women, the strike—but only the strike.

Between petitions, people's eyes opened, and I'd glance over at Romey, who sat there without moving much more than his hands. He was working at his callouses.

"Not long and it'll be school," I whispered to break the numbness between us. "Two weeks."

But Romey shoved an annoyed look at me, as if that had nothing to do with anything. That was the only thing I said to him in church that night, and I said it only because I wanted to lug both of us away from the church that was anything but a sanctuary.

Sooner or later I began to understand why nobody was bringing up the Guttners—they were afraid; they'd all seen Romey come in. They knew he was there. But someone would have to do it—even I understood that. All the other prayers that night were so much filler.

So I wasn't surprised when my father rose, even though he stood a bit earlier than he might have otherwise. The moment he started in with the very first words, I had this strange feeling that Romey hadn't ever heard my father pray before. Maybe at supper at our place, but that was different—just the family around the table. Then there was no Cyril in the hospital. In church my father sometimes spoke a different language, words I knew and recognized, but not exactly the words anybody would use at home.

"Lord Jesus in Heaven," he said, "we ask thy blessing tonight upon Cyril Guttner, our suffering brother."

I shut my eyes.

"Be near unto him and bless him, give him what he stands in need of," my father said. "Shine your face upon him so he may see, now in the hour of his trial, that he needs your love and your grace. Help him to see forgiveness—"

I don't believe I would have guessed it would be my own father, but when it happened, somehow I wasn't surprised, either. My heart started to race. I should have told Romey ahead of time so he could at least know what was going on, all these holy people opening up for the soul of his old man, as if Cyril were actually there and they were all standing around the bedside like Hattie was, trying to wash him clean with God's hands.

But we weren't in the hospital. Only Hattie was. And as I listened to my father I realized he would have said it all in a different way if he were in with Hattie at Cyril's bedside. I knew he would have said that prayer differently.

"O Lord," my father said, "we know the waywardness in him. Please show him what your Word tells us all—how there is no one that is perfect, no not one—and that before your throne no one stands blameless, not one of us. Show him how we all stand in need of grace, each and every one of your children. Give him, Lord, in this time of his peril, the sustenance of your grace."

What he said wasn't wrong. Everybody had problems—that wasn't wrong. It wasn't just Cyril we had to pray for—that's what my father meant.

"Wash us, Lord, all of us—and this very night bring your saving power into our souls too, and his. Bring him peace in the hour of his trial so that he may know every good and perfect thing."

I knew what my father could have said, because I knew what he thought of Cyril. I remembered the time he got angry after Cyril had turned up at our front door. I remembered him saying that what was scary about Cyril was that you really didn't know what he might do—and wasn't that the truth? Wasn't that why I had screamed at Hattie to shoot him? Wasn't that why Romey himself had yelled at me and Mugsy to get into the fight? Wasn't that why Romey had flown into the strikers at the home visit—even though his old man wasn't there? You never really knew with Cyril Guttner. That's what was scary about him—not his politics or his union work, but that you never really guessed what he might do at any time. Even his wife knew that. Even she wanted my father to come over and do something—anything—to end whatever it was that was happening at Romey's place.

But when my father prayed, he'd not said any of that, and I was proud of him. He'd managed to do something I figured nobody would—pray for Cyril without a dime's worth of hate, even though dozens of people in that church hated him, even though most of them were scared silly of what he did and what he might do. My father could have said much

Prayer Meeting

worse. He could have gone on and on about sin and all that. He could have talked about Hell, but he didn't bring it up—and it wasn't as if it were Cyril who was the only sinner, either. He made that clear. He didn't talk that way at all.

I opened my eyes enough to see Romey chewing on a thumbnail and staring up as my father stood in the pew, his hands folded and resting on the bench in front of us. I had it figured that Romey couldn't hate Pete Prins now. He didn't say anything about the strike, about Cyril hitting Hattie or drinking or anything. He didn't say any of that.

"Lord Jesus, help his family too in this their hour of need. Be with Romey here and be with Hattie as she sits at Cyril's bedside right now, even as we pray, even as we ask you to intercede for his life."

He was praying for Cyril to live. He actually asked God to heal him. I was proud of him because it had been a strange few days, none of us really knowing whether to hope for the man's life.

"So often we've laid our burdens before you, and you've blessed us. You tell us in your Word to pray without ceasing, and we've prayed for him for so long, Lord. All of us have. Now show the family your lovingkindness, Lord—bless them, free them from all their burdens."

Romey grabbed the pew in front of him.

"Bring Cyril before the throne spotless, washed in your blood."

He pulled himself up to the edge of the bench.

"Now in the time of his trial, Lord, be near unto him and bless him. Take him into your fold so that someday he may sing with the heavenly choir—"

I wasn't so sure about the heavenly choir.

"Bring him to your bosom, Lord—"

That was wrong too somehow—Cyril to God's bosom.

Romey got to his feet and walked out quietly at just that moment, my father still praying. He made no noise, as if he were tracking deer in some lakeshore woods, but I saw him out of the corner of my eye.

I didn't turn to watch him leave. I looked up at my father, his hands folded and eyes pressed closed earnestly, and I knew he had absolutely no idea that Romey had left. He was going on with the prayer, bringing it to some conclusion, laying his petitions before the throne of God, but it was the prayer that did it. My father didn't see what was happening, didn't see what was going on. His eyes were closed, his hands folded.

"Deathbed," "sorrow," "guilt," "remove all of our sins," "cleanse us in your righteousness," "Hattie too," "burdens," "sorry for what happened." Everything after that moment came in chunks of words I could stick together in a picture puzzle I'd already finished a dozen times before.

"Hardened heart," my father said. "Unforgiving."

And that's when I left. I pulled myself up from the pew and took three steps to the row, then walked into the aisle toward the side door of the sanctuary.

"Our earnest prayer," "miracle," "water into wine," "life everlasting," "amen."

Even though Romey had been out for a little while already, I imagined the way he likely smashed through the double doors. I tried to guess where he might go. I walked as fast as I could up the aisle and into the fellowship hall, someone else's prayer coming through the speaker in the back of the church as if he were praying in a tin room.

The cool air outside stole my breath for a minute, as I stood just beyond the doors, the light from the sanctuary windows leaning in rectangles over grass already wet from thick dew in the lakeshore air.

He was gone. I tried to measure how much of a lead he might have, where he might go, what he might do. Then I jumped down the front steps and called out his name, at first fearfully, as if someone really might hear, then louder once I realized it was stupid to whisper, as if he might be hiding in the bushes. Romey wouldn't stay at church, no way.

I walked quickly out to the corner of the fellowship hall, away from the lights, where outlines emerged from the darkness down the block. There was no sign of him. Once I crossed the street and started home, I broke into a trot, still trying to spot some movement down the sidewalk between church and our place, somewhere Romey might be hanging around, taking his good-natured time. His bike was parked in front of our house, I remembered. If Romey wanted to go anywhere, that bike was in the grass beside the driveway.

"Romey," I yelled, as if maybe he were in the shadows somewhere and maybe he'd hear me.

There was no wind. I ran to the end of the block between our house and the church, then glanced back, hoping that maybe my father was following me. But no one moved through the shafts of light from the windows.

I passed Monty's house standing dark as night, the scars of the paint still there on the siding. Out front of our house, there was nothing to be seen, no one—and Romey's bike was gone. He wouldn't want to be at our place—why would he want to hang around there once he'd heard my father pray? And that's what sent him out, too—it had to be. Romey had got on his bike, and the only place for him now was home, even though no one was there.

Prayer Meeting

I pulled my own bike out of the garage, got on, and pedaled to the south side of town, remembering Romey was always faster than I was on a bike, his bike one of those with the new skinny wheels. I pedaled hard, avoiding even in the twilight's semidarkness bumps I knew were in the streets. I passed the big red church, where there was nothing going on, passed the downtown sidewalk and the bank corner, came up to the end of the street at the mill quickly, where I looked for traffic both ways, then veered left down the street to Romey's place.

It never occurred to me Romey might do something bad. What scared me was that Romey would hate me now. I turned and looked back, hoping maybe my old man would be following. I looked for lights coming up the street, but saw nothing. Maybe that was okay too—maybe my father would have been the wrong person just then.

Immediately, a thousand Sunday school lessons came to my mind—shoeless Moses in the desert, talking to a burning bush. "I don't know what to say," he said. Neither did I. The ninety and nine that safely lay. Jonah in a whale. Daniel in a lion's den.

In a minute I was at Romey's place, but the house, like so much else, was dark as night. I turned up the driveway toward the back. The gravel where the shooting had taken place glowed in the light of the yard light on the garage. I rode to the back door, thinking maybe Romey'd be in the basement or something, cleaning a gun, but I saw nothing—no sign of Romey, no bike.

I dropped my bicycle in the grass without kicking down the stand, and I ran to the back door, pounded it with my fists.

No answer.

Once more I whaled away at the screen door, then opened it and used the heel of my fist to bang on the closed storm.

No one came.

I opened it and went inside, feeling along the wall for a light switch. I yelled down to the basement. The outlines of the walls loomed in front of me toward a black hole at the bottom of the stairs, the musty smell of basement rising from the jackets hanging along the walls going down. Cyril was in the hospital, miles away—I knew that perfectly—but fear came into me like a virus when I looked down there, and I saw him coming up the stairs after me, that same stained shirt lit in the darkness.

"Romey," I yelled. "Dang it, you here?"

There was no response. Of course, if he'd wanted to stay here and hide in the darkness, he could, I thought—just the way we'd stayed hidden in the woods when Squeak was firing his shotgun. Nobody could do much about it. If he didn't want to have anybody bother him, he could just stay in the darkness and nobody would ever find him. But that wouldn't be Romey. Romey wouldn't hide, I thought. Romey was not the kind to go under a bushel basket. If he was mad at my father, he wouldn't go pout somewhere, he'd come up yelling and screaming, like his old man.

"Romey," I yelled again. "If you're here—" and then I didn't know what to say. "If you're here," I said, "then say something, dang it."

Nothing, no sound came up from the basement or down from the kitchen, where the door stood open to the first floor. There still was no light, so I walked up the steps and reached around the corner, where finally I found a switch.

"Romey," I said again. The kitchen was a mess, but then, most often it was. I looked down at the floor for some sign of someone having come in, but I found nothing, no blades of grass, no smudges. Then I looked at my shoes, wet from the grass. Romey would have wet feet too, but there was no sign that anybody had been there. I glanced at the clock above the sink. It wasn't even nine. It was the end of the summer, the days already shrinking. That's why it was so dark.

I slapped off the switch and headed out the door, looking down at the dew for any footprints other than my own. There was nothing there. I left my bike where it lay and headed for the garage, but in the light from beneath the eaves I found nothing to suggest Romey had been home.

Suddenly, I was angry at myself for not checking my own room. I hadn't even looked up at my window. Maybe if I'd gone up there—but that seemed wrong too. My place wasn't at all familiar to Romey Guttner. He had never even seen the Sunday school pins before, and they'd been hanging up on the wall forever. He'd stood there at the circular window, turning the crank round and round that night before we left for church, talking about how much he liked it, as if it were a window on a ship at sea. But Romey wouldn't hide in my room. It wasn't enough of a home for him.

He wouldn't have gone to our place, the bike was gone, and he wasn't home. Downtown there would be kids hanging around the gas station, but that wouldn't be it. They were too old. He wouldn't go to the Toad's, either—that's the last guy he'd want to see—and there weren't any girls right now. That wouldn't be like him either. Not a girl—not now.

The lake, I thought. It was just that easy, and I never really second-guessed myself. There wouldn't be anywhere else. I remembered the way he talked when we hiked back from giving Squeak and Dianne the bath. Hadn't he said it—how much he liked coming out there at night sometimes? The lake, I thought.

The faster I went east, it seemed, the wetter I got, dew collecting and falling like sweat when I took the road we always took, the one south of Romey's place—past the Spykmans, past the Damkats, past the old De Smith place, where the house was gone but the barn still stood full of hay this time of year.

My face was so wet I had to wipe my forehead with my shirt tails to keep the moisture out of my eyes, and that's when I realized I still had on my Sunday clothes. No tie, but I had on those long pants and the white shirt, my black shoes glistening in the moonlight as I pedaled that bike for all I was worth. Out in the country, out of the streetlights, it seemed brighter than it had been in town, the fence lines and the grasses at the edge of the road lit well enough to distinguish them clearly, the outline of the lake woods like a thick bar of darkness beneath the lake, where sparkles on the water drew a triangle out to a bright moon sitting like a silver coin in the sky.

It was a gamble, but there weren't any other possibilities. If he wasn't at home, and he wasn't at our place, he had no other place, I thought. All there was was the lake.

I pedaled so fast I could feel thick rooms of lake air, each of them a slightly different temperature—some so warm I felt my body unwind, some so cool my shoulders rose. The long roadside grasses stood still in the windless night. I stood on the bike and pedaled harder when I went up hills, the chill of the dew coming through my shirt as cold as a swim.

When I got close to the beach, the darkness of the woods leaned in toward me from both sides of the road. Once I came close to the opening at the end of the road, I saw the light of the moon on bike spokes, the outline of a dumped bike at the edge of the sand, and a glowing Mercury decal on the back fender. It was Romey's.

The fear I felt at church was gone in the heat of the hunt, the frantic pedaling to get to the lake, the whole chase itself. I forgot I didn't know what to say, because I'd concentrated every effort on finding him. As I coasted toward the beach, I looked back up the road, back toward town, hoping maybe a pair of headlights would be following, that my father might have cased the whole scene, might have guessed Romey would be at the lake once he'd seen that he wasn't at home. But I knew better. What did my father know of the lakeshore? That wasn't his place.

I was wet—soaked—when I got to the edge of the beach. My front wheel looped away from me in the dry sand and fell beneath me as I stepped off the bike without losing a second. I didn't want to yell. Anger stormed in me, something born from racing around trying to find the guy, the frustration of not knowing where he went. For a moment I'd almost forgotten my father's prayer, forgotten what I was doing. I stood there at the edge of the sand and waited for the silence to come up around me like the wash of the waves, and I listened, stood there, the trees like blinders. All I could see was naked beach—no sign of Romey.

I hesitated before walking out onto the sand because I knew the moment I did, Romey would see me. So I stood there hidden behind the trees at the edge of the beach, listening, even though I knew that if Romey were close he'd have heard the sounds of my chain guard rattling and the clink of metal when I'd let the bike fall from beneath me in the dry sand.

But I'd come this far, and if Romey didn't want to talk to me, if Romey didn't want to see me, then that would have to be his choice. I had to reach for breath because it was coming slow and hard from the race to the lakeshore. I dropped my hands from my sides and leaned over just for a second, then kicked my shoes back toward my bike, slipped off my socks and unbuttoned my shirt, rolled up the legs of my Sunday pants, and walked out, as if the beach were a stage where I'd come to play a part I still wasn't altogether sure of. I walked toward the water—slowly, without looking around, as if maybe Romey would think me just coming down to watch the moon or something. Then I stopped again and looked around for some sign of him. The beach was silver as far as I could see to the north, cottage lights like a long passenger train at the edge of the sand, here and there bonfires like nuggets of bright heat. I looked south, where the lake retreated from a long peninsula of steady lights. Up and down the beach, here and there, I could see people standing or sitting around bonfires, but I couldn't distinguish a single shape anywhere, someone who looked alone.

I started walking north because all the places we knew were north, all the places we'd ever hung out. Hurley's was that way up the beach. The spot where we'd really stuck it to Squeak was another mile up. If he was going anywhere, I thought, he'd go where we'd hung out, the woods we knew, the spots where we'd spent afternoons looking for arrowheads in the spring, when the frost annually turned over the sand.

A chunk of driftwood big as a tree rose from the sand thirty feet from the water's edge, easily distinguishable in front of me, and even though I couldn't see Romey, even though I couldn't pick out a figure, somehow I knew that he was there. I knew it because it was the last spot of open beach before a string of cottages, and he would have avoided people he didn't know, people on vacation or whatever. His father was dying.

Prayer Meeting

I slowed down and walked to the water's edge, where I followed the sharp angle of the heavy sand, lake water rushing over my feet, warmer, it seemed, than the air itself. The closer I got to the driftwood, the slower I walked, trying not to look at that bone-white skeleton in the sand.

Then I stopped.

"Get out of my life," he said.

Fear came back—fear of not knowing what to say.

"Get on your bike and go home to your daddy," Romey said. "You hear me? Who asked you to be my guardian angel, for cripes sake, Lobo—and your old man? Who asked you to look out for me—for us?"

I looked at the dead tree.

"None of this woulda happened if your old man hadn't stuck his fat nose into our business, you know that?" He was sitting just behind the driftwood, his elbows up on his knees. "None of this. That night he came to our place? My old man just plain lost it. We were minding our own business and everything, and here comes your old man about to tell my dad how to be." He threw down a handful of sand. "I get so sick of all this holy stuff. Don't you ever get sick of being holy-holy and trying to run everybody else's life?"

"I'm not trying to run your life," I said.

"You are too. What'cha doing here if you aren't? Answer me that, Mr. Big Shot Saint."

"I'm not," I said.

"Who told you to come?" Romey asked him. "Who told you to tail me, anyway?"

"I came on my own," I said.

"Bull." He threw a handful of dry sand into the air. "You can't even get out of the house this late. Your old man sent you, didn't he?"

"Far as I know, the prayer service is still going on," I said.

"Well, my old man was no friend of his, and that night he came to our place to scream at him—you don't know what it was like. You ain't ever going to know because now he's gone—or he's going to be." What came out, came in gusts. "He's going to be dead, Lobo. My old man's checking out, see? How many guys you know with dead dads?"

I walked to the edge of dry sand still warm from the afternoon sun. I was still grabbing breaths from lungs that didn't have much after the fast ride east. Sweat and dew ran from my cheeks.

"Your old man thinks he's such a hotshot," he said, "praying like that in front of all those people, talking about my old man like it's target practice. You don't understand—"

"Yeah I do," I said.

"Shut up," he said. "You got Saint Peter for an old man. You don't have a clue." Romey was angry, very angry. "He's perfect—that's what gets me."

What could I say?

"He's just like you. You don't know nothing—none of you. None of you know a fat thing. Your old man is such a pea brain," he said. "He stands up there like God and talks about everybody else's—"

"That's not true," I said. "You can say what you want about me—go ahead. I don't care." Something angry rose inside me. "My old man wasn't thinking about nothing but your dad."

"Well, la-de-dah," Romey said. "How do you think I feel? What do you think is going through my head with all that blasted moanin' about my old man?"

"He needs it," I said.

"How do you know?"

"Because we all do—"

"You too?" he said.

"Yeah, me too—and you, and everybody, and your old lady, all right—and mine too—and Zoot and Monty—that's what he was saying."

"Then how come he didn't pray for them special?"

"'Cause it's your old man who's dying," I said.

"That's right," he said. "And you don't know nothing."

I was mad. "I know why he came that night," I said.

"What night?"

"That night you were home—when you didn't come to the pool—"

"I wouldn't go to no Brandon pool if you paid me," he said.

"Your ma told him to come," I said.

"Who?"

"Your ma told my old man he had to do something about your father," I said.

"My ma didn't either."

You ought to be happy he's dying, I thought right then. You ought to be screaming with joy because the old man's on his way out—just one less huge headache that never goes away, even when he does himself.

"Your old lady begged my old man to come over because she was getting beat on," I told him. "He wasn't just going over to your place to get his jollies, Romey—he didn't even want to do it but for Hattie—"

"You think you're so good—your whole family."

"That's not true."

"I hate you," Romey said. "You hear me? I'm sick of you and I wish you'd never been born. I hate you."

Prayer Meeting

What pumped through every vein in my body was streaming from a heart full of poison. "I'm going home," I said. I stood no more than eight feet away from where Romey sat in the sand. "If you don't want to listen to reason—"

"I could wipe my butt with the likes of you, Prins," he said. "You know that?"

And then I said something I shouldn't have. It was dumb and it stung, and I said it with the same aim I would have taken with a fist. "You're starting to sound just like your old man," I told him. "You know that? You are."

He came up off the sand like the linebacker he would one day become. I didn't try to run. I stood there and took the hit full force, just as I had that day behind the plate. His shoulder pounded into my gut with such force my legs came up from beneath me, and he kept driving, his body low, until both of us were down in the shallow water.

At first I didn't try to fight back—I let it all go, let him push me under the water as if the only way to beat him was to let him think through what he was doing, come to some sense of what was going on here. He pinned me beneath the water, the ridges of sand rough as washboard against my back, the waves washing over my chest and my face. His knees were up on my shoulders, his hands fisted in the front of my shirt as he kept me under, the water no more than a foot deep.

I grabbed a breath when I could, figuring he was going to let up once I let him have his way, once he figured he was wrestling a rag doll—but he didn't stop. He stayed at me, kept me under so long my lungs started to tighten. Romey's weight, all of it, was on my chest, and the whole time, he kept screaming stuff I didn't hear well from underwater.

I couldn't scream, and I didn't try. I held on to the faith that Romey wasn't going to kill me, that it was all anger at me and my father and my parents and every last thing swirling around in his mind now, even anger at his father and certainly at his father's dying. It was something I'd have to take to stay friends—and we were, the two of us. All this anger was something I'd have to take, even though water filled my throat and threatened to choke me. I coughed deeply and hard.

Romey was always tougher than I was, and he was almost out of his mind. I went under again, my cheeks ballooned with air. And then, in that scramble for breath, something tripped, something huge, and what came up in me was pure rage. I didn't have to take this, I told myself. What my father had said wasn't meant as awful as he thought it was. I didn't have to take it. Something insane came out of my chest like nothing I'd felt before. I threw my back into a twist and spun beneath Romey's knees, getting up and out of the water in one motion, as if Romey weren't even there. I spun around and Romey's arms flew away.

He took off. I ran after him up to the edge of the water, tackled him around the ankles, caught him in a dive at his feet. And then I screamed exactly what I'd said just seconds before, but louder now, as if my voice were the battering ram that would take down Romey's walls. I climbed up over his chest the same way he had ridden me, our feet still in the water, our heads up on the edge of the sand. I grabbed him by the shirt. "You're no different than your old man," I said. I wouldn't let him up. "You're better off without him, you know that?" I screamed. "The whole world's better off without him—can't you understand that?" I held him down with my hands and my knees.

And then his limbs went limp. His chest kept lunging but there was no more real fight. His arms fell, and I knew I'd done something big. The truth had come out, even if Romey hadn't wanted to hear it. And I said it again. I was furious. "You're better off with him dead," I said. "That's the truth."

There was no fighting, but neither were there tears. I felt clear and purged because I'd told the whole truth. It was all out now, every bit of it. The truth shall set you free. I got off him.

He turned over on his stomach and hid his face in his hands. Lake water came up into his shirt, sand layered his pants legs, his shoes were sopping wet. He kept his hands over his eyes, his body shaking out breaths, until finally he pulled his elbows beneath him and turned over on his side. He sniffed hard, pulled a few shaky breaths together, and then he looked at me as if I were dirt. "I don't care what you say about my old man," he told me. "You can call him Satan or anything you want, Lobo, y'hear? I don't care what you say—maybe he deserved to get shot. Maybe my old lady was right—maybe she was getting beat up, I don't know." He kept digging for breath. "Maybe he would have killed Zoot— he probably woulda." He pulled his legs under him and threw his shoulders back and looked straight into my eyes. "I don't flat care what you or anybody else thinks, but you listen to me, Lowell Prins, little angel boy, because this is the truth—Cyril Guttner's my old man—okay?" He tried to wipe the water away from his eyes. "You can say what you want, but he ain't yours. He's mine. You understand that? I don't care what he is or what he was—he's my father."

In the range of beach that runs from the road we'd taken to the lakeshore, a mile north to the drive-in east of town, there may well have been two or three dozen people out along the water's edge that night, sitting around campfires, roasting marshmallows or drinking coffee or

Prayer Meeting

telling stories to their kids—ghost stories maybe. Another hundred probably sat in cottages just back in the trees, the lights on all down the line. But no one saw that fight or heard those words. And when it was over, nobody on that stretch of beach, no matter what kind of vacation they were having, no matter how great the night, had any inkling of what had happened.

I may well have had a hand in killing Romey Guttner's father, but that night, on that beach, at that time, Romey killed a part of me, too. Neither of us, I don't believe, were ever the same again.

We pulled ourselves into the dry warm sand away from the water and rested, just lay there for a long time, like we'd done often that summer when we'd hung out at the lake, just lay there beside each other as if the sky were full of rays to catch. For the longest time, we lay in the sand, soft waves rolling up at the shoreline maybe fifteen feet away, and no one said a word. To the east, the moon seemed high off the edge of the horizon, but it left a glimmering wake where the light fell in a path that grew wider and wider on the lake until it ushered itself right up to us on the shore. And there we lay, in silence.

"He's going to die," Romey said. "My ma says it—he's going to die. My father's going to die." Then he brought his hands up to his face.

Cyril Guttner died that night, late, sometime after three in the morning, six hours at least after the prayer meeting, just like Hattie said he would. He died without regaining much consciousness. No one will know here, in this vale of tears, whether any of my father's prayer was answered—whether Cyril looked up into the space beneath the ceiling of that hospital room and saw the face of Jesus.

Grace

Cyril Guttner's funeral was held in the parlor downtown because he'd always disliked the church, and Hattie said it just wouldn't feel right to have it there. No one objected. I went, and so did my parents, but we weren't the only ones there.

There weren't any smiles, because the place wasn't Oz—no one jumped and danced on a yellow brick road at the death of the wicked witch. People came, dozens and dozens of them, because they wanted to wish Hattie some of the happiness they knew she'd missed out on in her life. They wanted to console her, reassure her that she'd done the right thing that night in the back yard. The law said so, and so did the community. They wanted to be present for a woman who needed them very badly.

I didn't see much of Hattie Guttner in the days after Cyril died. I didn't see much of Romey either, for that matter. My parents visited her, and she had come over, but when she did, she would look at me wistfully before I'd leave for my bedroom.

A bunch of union guys showed up for the funeral, maybe thirty men and women who looked awfully tough amid all the Sunday-dressed Easton folks. They came in together and sat in back, and all of them went out to the cemetery on the hill overlooking the lake, when Hattie and Romey and his little sisters and his older brother put their father's body in the sandy earth. There's a tradition in Easton—after the committal, people go to the church for cake and coffee or punch in the fellowship hall. Most people did. But the union guys didn't. I suppose they didn't want that kind of fellowship.

At the church, Romey sat through the long line of well-wishers, one after another, old men and their wives who wanted to do what they could to make Hattie and the kids feel they were on their side, wanted to tell her they'd be around to help if she needed anything. I'm sure they were. Cyril's death made Romey's place a different place altogether.

Romey had on a white shirt, Sunday clothes. His hair was combed back. But he didn't smile much. When I think of him sitting beside his mother in that greeting line looking owly, I wonder whether some of those good folks couldn't help but guess at how much of the old man had seeped into Hattie's boy. Rarely did he look up when he shook hands with people. He was out of place in church, just as his father had been.

It was an hour, maybe, before the people left the fellowship hall. A few ladies washed dishes and forked the leftover pieces of cake into empty pans. I stayed because I figured it wasn't right for me to go home and say nothing to Romey. I hadn't gone through the greeting line. After what had happened the night of the prayer meeting, we hadn't talked to each other at all.

The night of the prayer meeting, he had left our place, taken his stuff from my room and gone home. On the bike ride back from the lake, he had told me he was leaving, even if he had to stay alone in the house. He'd had enough of my place, he said. "No hard feelings or nothing," he said. "I just want to be home. I ain't a kid."

Neither of my parents said much when we came in, still soaking wet, nor when, just a few minutes later, Romey left. I told them not to. When he was upstairs, I said they ought to let him be, let him do what he wanted. So they let him go that night, the night his father died, and so did I.

I didn't talk to him again until the afternoon of the funeral, when I saw him standing on the sidewalk just outside the north door of the church, the place where the three of us had come out that night Zoot made Cyril so mad in front of the preacher. He was alone.

"Got a butt, Lobo?" he said. "My kingdom for a butt."

"You don't have a kingdom," I told him, "but I don't have one anyway."

"Steal one off your dad," he said.

"My old man doesn't smoke."

"Course," he said.

He looked around. "My old man woulda hated something like this," he said. "I'm glad he missed it."

"He wouldn't have come anyway," I said.

"Isn't that right? My old man was so ornery he wouldn't come to his own funeral." He was fidgety, nervous. "Far too many church people for him," he said. He looked up at me, the only time, and then he shrugged and walked off toward his place. That was it, really. I saw him in the halls now and then during what he spent in Easton of his first year in high school, but for the most part, that was what he left me with, the end of our friendship, because once high school started, Romey and I didn't hang out much at all. He started football practice the week he buried his father, and the two-a-days took up most of his time and brought him into a different circle of friends. Football became his life. We didn't go out trapping that fall. He went hunting, but he didn't take me along. That first year, we went in different directions.

My mother wouldn't let me play football; it looked so dangerous to her that she thought it had to be sin. Had I wanted to play, had I been adamant, she would have given in. But I wasn't pushy about it, largely because I wasn't enamored with football myself. Her reluctance made a good excuse for me to explain why I didn't show up for practice. My mother wouldn't let me.

Cyril Guttner was gone. Life was easier in Easton. It was as if the community were a human body that had finally and even miraculously beaten cancer. What my grandfather had decided the church could never sanction, Hattie herself, in mortal fear and with the blessing of the preacher's own grandson, ended with her own hands.

But we were never friends again, Romey and I. Football separated us during that first year of high school, but by spring Hattie decided she was going to start over completely, follow the great American dream, and look west to new opportunity. She had a cousin in Tucson, Arizona, and that cousin told her that the best thing for her now was a new beginning in a brand new world. So she sold the house, took her family—Romey and the girls—and picked up and left Easton for the greener pastures of the desert.

Occasionally in the following years, Hattie would make the trip back to Wisconsin, but already that first summer, only his little sisters came along. And I don't know that I ever saw Romey Guttner again. If I did, it would have been fleetingly. He'd left my life one night when my father prayed for his, a stubborn, quarrelsome, violent man who was dying, and he never came back, never sent a card—but then, neither did I.

For many years my mother wrote Hattie faithfully, so I know what happened. He graduated from high school, where he'd been a football star, a mean and self-sacrificing linebacker. Those weren't his words or Hattie's or my mother's; they were the descriptions of sportswriters from Arizona newspapers in clippings that accompanied those letters. He went to a community college—I know that. But I don't know if he ever graduated. He went into air-conditioning and ran his own business finally, something he started in an Arizona town named Ajo, where he moved—and I'm speculating now—when he got tired of city life.

Romey married—twice—and he found the Lord, my mother told me. Maybe a decade ago already, my mother told me he'd become a respected businessman who, along with his second wife, homeschooled three kids. My mother never said as much, but I know people who homeschool, and most of them are fundamentalists. Somehow it's not that great a jump for me to think of Romey as a fundamentalist Christian. I'm not eschewing what my mother would call the work of the Holy Spirit, but somehow I can see Romey toting a Bible, weekly, to a small church where most people dress plainly but respectfully. I can see him sending those kids to Sunday school. I can see that, given the right wife. I remember what he said about needing a woman who could keep him straight. What he might never have done in Easton, I can see him accomplishing in a whole new world in the desert, I can see him doing it not only willingly but dutifully and even religiously in a town called Ajo, Arizona.

I'm a believer and always have been. I've really never struggled with God, though I've had more than my share of run-ins with his people. But I'm not a fundamentalist. I've become Orthodox in the last few years, the latest stop on a pilgrimage that has brought me into almost every fellowship of Protestantism. I'm Orthodox because there's something about the liturgy, the icons, the long and established tradition of the Orthodox church that seems to fit me now. To me, anyway, it seems less bothered with us, our joys and concerns, than it is driven by the divine. I'm not foolish enough to say this is where I'll stay. I can never be comfortable, I guess, in my faith. I think that's a legacy of my childhood, as so many things are.

But what does it mean to be a believer? It was a question Romey asked, and a question I've never answered completely, for him or for me. I speak to the Lord every day. I pray. I talk to him, not in the language my father did, but I talk to him, not only because I know all too well how dark the world can be without him, but because I know he is there. I can't fight that assurance, and my guess is that sure knowledge comes, at least in part, from my own parents.

Grace

So it's Sunday, the day after my father and I cleaned out his closets, the day after the early season snowstorm, the day after we'd stumbled across what wasn't there—that old bayonet I'd flung in the river after having heisted it from the very closet we were cleaning. It was Sunday, and all night long I'd wrestled with how, exactly, to tell my father so much of what I never told him, about Romey, about the death of Cyril, about what really happened that last night Romey was my friend, about how prayer did it—my own father's public prayer.

But you should understand that, armed with righteousness, I haven't spent my entire adulthood blaming my father for chasing off my friend. There always were differences between Romey and me. He spent hours working on his bike; I didn't. I'll bet anything he never stopped hunting; I never picked up a gun again. Romey grew up in a place where strife and anger were heard almost daily; I grew up in a place where gospel music rang from whatever windows were open to the street. Romey puts in air-conditioning units; I keep a museum.

Romey Guttner left my life because we were inescapably different, I think. And once he left for Arizona, he never looked back.

And I have not been harboring bitterness toward my father for his prayer that night at Wednesday meeting years and years ago. I don't know whether I would have thought of all of this at all had he and I not swept out those closets and discovered what wasn't there. It was my coming home to Easton, alone, without my family, and the memory of that booty bayonet as I lay in a bedroom with a circular window against the south wall—that's what made this whole story come back so richly.

But that Sunday morning, I was determined to tell him because there was so much I'd never said about what had happened, so much I wished I would have been able to tell him then, when so much was going on in my life, so much that seemed to me then to be a species of sin my father never knew and would not have recognized in himself.

Saturday night we were up late trying to save my father's trees. When we finally got back to bed—a cup of hot chocolate and a cookie or two later—I couldn't sleep, and it all came back. And when it did, I told myself that I wanted to talk through that whole story and tell him everything that had happened at Romey's place that summer so long ago. I wanted to talk to my father in a way that I had felt I never could.

We both slept late. He woke me like he would have years ago, speaking quietly so as not to shock me awake. "It's too early for morning, Lowell," he said. "But it's here anyway." He didn't say I had to get up for church. There are some things that don't need to be said.

We gobbled down some toast and I had a shower, and then it was time. But I was determined to tell him—probably at lunch, when we'd sit together at the family table where he'd once diffused Zoot's anger, right across from Hattie. I'd bring it up somehow, I told myself—by mentioning the strike maybe, or bean-picking. I'd find a way to nudge the whole story into the conversation, and then I'd tell him how his public prayer for Romey and for Cyril and Hattie, his standing up in our church and praying that way, had finally done what he and my mother had hoped for, maybe even prayed for—ended my friendship with Romey Guttner. He'd prayed to keep Cyril alive, but Cyril died, and so did whatever it was that kept Romey and me together. That's what I wanted to tell him—his heartfelt concern and love, his goodness, had severed a friendship.

The church in Easton hasn't changed all that much. The building still looks modern, even if it's not new, as it was when I was a boy. Worship proceeds differently today; what was solemn, dignified, and traditional has become more flexible and accommodating, more people-oriented. The church in which I grew up, like so many others in this new time, is moving into a new age with a modified mission that emphasizes growth and evangelism, rather than the edification of those already safely in the fold, if any of us really is.

My father is uncomfortable with those changes. Preaching has changed to meet the needs of people who don't read the Bible as often or as closely as he thinks they did years ago, or should today. Even though he and my mother rarely sang the old psalms at the piano in our house, even though they almost always opted for gospel songs of joy and praise, he tells me that he thinks the new music, like the new preaching, is more than a little flimsy, often cheap. But he grudgingly admits his age, his prejudices, and the fact that he's arrived at a time in his life when change is humanly difficult.

Not so with Monty. He was there with his family, his hands raised in praise during a chorus of happy songs. His mother and father sat in the same pew as his own family—his wife and three girls; but Zoot didn't seem to be in the same kind of spiritual reverie.

Dianne left town long ago, as did Mugsy. And Mugsy's parents, like my mother, are already singing in some place where there's very little oppressive lake humidity and the pianos don't go out of key.

But my father wouldn't miss a Sunday service, morning or night, no matter that his sensitivities aren't beguiled by the frothy atmosphere nowadays in the Easton church. To him today, as in the past, worship is something one doesn't really choose to do. It's as natural, as instinctive, as drawing breath.

So I sat beside him this morning, both of us hardly refreshed after our short night of sleep, and together we sang the hymns and spiritual songs listed on the gothic plaques at the front of the church, a medley of choruses I didn't know, and then some old favorites.

We were using separate hymnals—by my choice, I'm sure, not his. But when we got to "Blessed Assurance," I didn't sing at all. I listened, both to the words and to my father's deep bass voice, as audible today as it was when I was a kid.

> Blessed assurance, Jesus is mine.
> O what a foretaste of glory divine.

There I was, in my fifties, still stumbling over identity, something my father appears never to have questioned about himself. I couldn't sing because I was listening, but soon enough I was listening because I couldn't sing, because it came to me there, in the church, in the sweet light of those lyrics. From my father I learned about righteousness, about faith and its sources within. He gave me a conscience that has been forever with me, sometimes a bother, but then again sometimes a powerful check on my human limitations. I'm not an alcoholic. I don't spend a dime on the dozens of gambling operations that have grown like weeds all over the Midwest. I've never hit my children or been unfaithful to my wife. I've worked hard at my job, and I'm relatively successful. My aversion to public and even private forms of iniquity, I owe, I believe, to him and to my mother. People who know me, I'd guess, would say I am, as he is, a good man.

> This is my story, this is my song,
> Praising my Savior all the day long.

I was watching my father from the corner of my eye, just as I did that Wednesday night—in a bench not far from where we now sat—when my father prayed with all his heart and mind and soul for the Guttner family, every one of them. I was listening with my memory of thousands of hours of my parents' songs carrying through the hallways of our house, the house he's leaving now. My mother was there beside him, really—not in body, but in spirit. I could see them together there in the church where they'd poured so much of their whole lives.

> Perfect submission, all is at rest;
> I in my Savior am happy and blest;
> Watching and waiting, looking above,
> Filled with his goodness, kept in his love.

What struck me dumb was what those lyrics said of my father, whose testimony was lifted right then and there from the page of the hymnal and brought, in his own way, to the altar of the Lord, a sacrifice and a pledge. That old hymn is his soul's tribute. He is filled with God's goodness. He's been kept in his love. He is happy and blessed in the loving arms of his Savior. His perfect submission has given him peace. And now, in these last years of his life and painfully alone, he is even closer to God than he was years ago, when I was a boy and he was out pressing the concerns of godliness at the Guttner's and elsewhere.

So I said to myself, Why should I trouble him now? That's what I asked myself as the Easton church sang through the final chorus of "Blessed Assurance." What right do I have to afflict this man's peace with some long remembered offense from my past? Why should I bring up how his righteousness had so fouled Romey's aching sensibilities, that night in that very church, that he had to leave? Why, really, do I need to tell my father all about that night? Why do I want so badly to tell him that in a moment in which he was eternally confident that bringing Romey's burdens to the Lord was the right thing to do, it probably wasn't—not at all? Why do I want to teach my father a lesson?

And how do I really know I'm right, anyway? What basis do I have to believe that my father's prayer that night was answered in horror, not in love? Isn't it arrogant for me to believe that God's ways are mine? Or that my sense of my father's error—his sin, really, in praying aloud and in public—is God's own judgment? How do I know? After all, today Romey may well be a more earnest believer than I am. Maybe my father's prayer worked to perfection.

My father put down the hymnal, looked at me, and smiled, unaware of the battle going on in my head.

I told myself he didn't have to know the whole story, he didn't have to hear it, didn't have to spend what little time the Lord tarries in his life wondering whether he did it all right. Because he would. I know my father, and I know this: he is at peace. Why should I shoulder this old burden into his life?

I didn't tell him. He didn't need to know. Maybe I needed to say it, but that's for me and not for him. He didn't need to hear about his prayer. Hattie was right—sometimes what we don't know doesn't hurt us.

My father is an heir of salvation; he's been purchased by the blood of Jesus, and he knows it—he always has. He's an old man. He's lost his wife, his companion, his love. When he put the hymnal back in the pew, I knew I wouldn't tell him, wouldn't bring up the bayonet again.

Grace

Romey was my friend for a couple of years at most. He brought me into adolescence. Today, when I sit all alone on a lake in Minnesota, my electric motor trolling softly through the dark green underworld of bass and walleye, when I hear the cry of a loon or watch seagulls hang-glide on breezes that barely ruffle the leaves of the trees on the shore, I recognize one of the gifts he gave me, the sense of joy and awe in nature. I don't hunt anymore, but sometimes, just to be outside, I'll take a camera and shoot things that never look quite as good on film as they did in the woods. I love sunsets. I love the hidden wildness of prairie rivers cutting through tall sandbanks and making hairpin turns around giant cottonwoods, all of that secluded, like an odd joke, in the middle of miles and miles of open farmland. On great days, I find it difficult to stay inside the house. That's Romey in me.

But he gave me much, much more. That night on Lake Michigan, when we wrestled in the warm waters of the shoreline, when by sheer anger I eventually I got the upper hand and beat on him, that night he taught me something I never forgot in just one line: "He's my father," he said.

No matter what Cyril had done to him, to Zoot, to Hattie; no matter that he wasn't home half the time or that when he was, he was tough as nails; no matter who his friends were or what he thought of Linear; no matter what might happen to him that very night in the hospital bed; no matter how he cussed and swore; no matter about anything, Romey loved his father. At the moment our friendship ended, Romey gave me the greatest gift he could have in those years we were buddies.

Just as he was for so many others, my father—bless his soul—was forever a peacemaker. Throughout my life, in a hundred varied ways, my father showed me the paths of truly selfless righteousness. Even now, in his last years, I still thank God for offering me a model of what is pure, what is holy, and what is true.

But now that I've walked through those years again, now that I've gone back as deeply as I can into a story that ended in Cyril's death, I've come to believe that Romey's place in my life has become more consequential in the decades that have passed than that place may have seemed at the time. What my own foolish soul has come to understand is that while my father taught me goodness, it was Romey who taught me grace.

And that's why I don't need to tell my aging father the long story I couldn't bring myself to tell him years ago. There's no need to explain what role he played the night I lost a friend, no need to remind him of what, for years, I might have called his sin. All I need to say is that no matter what, he is my father. That's what Romey taught me.

Grace